Nick and Stefanie knew the cardinal was expecting a rescue team. With somber faces, heads slightly bent, they walked toward Raisa Seminary.

"We turn here," Stefanie whispered.

They knocked lightly at a side door and a woman admitted them, her eyes wary, questioning.

"We are friends of the cardinal come to ask his blessing," Stefanie said, as instructed.

"Come with me."

They walked into a small, simple study. A man in clerical garb stood at the window, his back to the young couple.

"Cardinal Raisa," Stefanie said softly, "we're here to take you out of Poland."

"I'm not sure I should go. As long as I can be useful here—" His gaze settled on Nick and he frowned oddly.

All at once Nick's throat went tight. His mouth was dry.

"Forgive me for staring," Casimar said. His eyes moved to a table against the wall. There Nick saw the huge cluster of framed family portraits. "I know it's absurd—" all at once the cardinal's voice was trembling—"but you resemble someone very close to me."

"Yes, Uncle Casimar." Nick's voice was uneven as his eyes met those of the aging man. "I'm Nick."

"God has been better to me than I deserve," Casimar said humbly. He rose to his feet as Nick moved to him. "Nicholas. Johanna's son. . . ."

JOHANNA

by

JULIE ELLIS

This title first published in Great Britain in 1992 by
Severn House Publishers Ltd.

This edition licensed by Severn House Publishers Ltd,
produced by Magpie Book Ltd, and published by Parragon
Book Service Ltd in 1994.
Formerly published in paperback format only in the
USA under the titles *The Poles* with the pseudonym
Susan Richard.

A copy of the British Library CIP data is available
from the British Library.

ISBN 0 75250 003 1

Printed and bound in Great Britain.

For Harry, 'Tasha and Tobin

BOOK ONE

Chapter 1

Warsaw was already hot and sluggish. The lime trees were parched, the lilacs' sparse blossoms drooped, discouraged by summer heat on the heels of May. The streets were dusty, for Warsaw was the driest spot in the country in 1889.

At the Café Okocim in the old quarters of the city a handful of patrons slumped over their tables. They swigged large quantities of beer and they mopped their foreheads at steady intervals.

Johanna Boguski, the youngest and prettiest of the waitresses, brought bowls of *barszez* to the four Russian officers sitting at a table at one side of the café. Barszez was much like their own borscht, served with mounds of sour cream and cucumbers. It was Johanna's unpleasant task always to serve the hated Russians; she spoke their language as though Russian-born, and her blond Slavic beauty always drew sighs of approval from the soldiers stationed so far from their homes.

Though small of stature, Johanna carried her slender,

curvaceous figure in a fashion that made her seem inches taller. She had a habit of tossing her long fair hair and putting up her chin when dealing with the Russians. Like young Poles everywhere, she harbored deep hostility for the Russian conquerors. She managed to avoid a slap on the rump as she moved among the officers.

Only those who knew Johanna well realized that when her luminous grey eyes seemed deep sea blue, she was both angry and alarmed. She'd only this moment overheard a scrap of extremely indiscreet conversation. She must rush from the café and travel as fast as a droshky would carry her to the flat near Stare Miasto Square, where she had lived with the Raisa family since she was twelve and her entire family was exiled to Siberia.

The beet soup served, Johanna returned to the kitchen and whispered an excuse to Vladislav, who owned and operated the café. The bearlike former wrestler understood why it was so important that loyal, Russian-speaking Johanna Boguski work for him.

She fled from the kitchen through the rear door. Her mind raced as she sought a droshky to take her to the flat where the three Raisa brothers would be gathering after their day's work. After supper they were to meet with a group of young Poles who were plotting a civil protest against the Russians.

The Russian officers knew about the plot and were to arrest everyone involved. Even before her parents disappeared to Siberia, Johanna, like most Polish children, lived in dread of the czar, the police and fear of exile to Siberia.

In 1762 Poland was dismembered and apportioned to the Russians, the Germans and the Austrians. The country had been fragmented ever since. The Russians were determined to wipe out the Polish nation and language, and the Poles were dedicated to survival. The children were taught publicly in Russian and secretly in Polish. The deepest humiliation was to have to say one's prayers in Russian. No one ever got used to living under the Russians.

Although only sixteen, Johanna had been assigned by Leon Raisa, the intense and eloquent leader of the young partisans, to work at the Café Okocim, much favored by Russian officers. Vladislav was delighted to have her; she was a good worker and the Russians liked her and her excellent Russian. Of course her real work was to pick up important tidbits of information from the Russian officers, some of whom were shockingly loose-tongued with or without Vladislav's good vodka for lubrication.

Her long fair hair flew behind her as she left the droshky and hurried up the stairs to the Raisa flat. Tonight Johanna and the three Raisa brothers must alert the others.

A secret collaborationist was to meet within the hour with the high-placed Russian officers who were dining at the café. He would hand over a list of conspirators; they must all flee to the countryside.

"Casimar," she said, her sweet light voice breathless with anxiety, "there's trouble!"

Even in a moment like this she was aware of her love for Casimar. He was the ugly duckling by contrast to his handsome brothers—brownish hair and eyes, big nose, clown ears—but he had helped her through the loss of her family. Though he never allowed himself to say so, his eyes often told her that her only rival was the church. They had cared silently like this since the day she realized her loss and wept in his arms when she was twelve.

"The Russians?" he asked, putting down his glass. Johanna nodded. "Michal," he called, "Leon."

His brothers crowded through the kitchen doorway. Looking troubled, Mama Raisa hovered behind them. Tall and stocky, she was the bastion of the family. She had worked hard for forty-odd years and looked it, but her wrinkles, grey hair and laborer's hands meant nothing beside the iron will, good humor and sheer animal vitality that shone from her. Now, though distressed, she was far from daunted.

"The officers were talking again in the café. This time it's serious. A collaborator has betrayed us. He's on his way to the Okocim now with all our names." Johanna danced and wrung her hands with urgency. "We have to tell the others."

"We'll each take six," Leon said authoritatively. He was the oldest of the brothers and the smallest, a bantam rooster with a huge dark handlebar mustache. Quick, lithe, aggressive, he was shrewd but not particularly intelligent; it was his courage and energy that gave him leadership. "Now I can be glad there are so few of us—only eighteen to reach."

"I can help," Johanna insisted. "I'll go to Stanislas and Manya and Jozef—"

"That's enough," Michal interrupted, his bright blue eyes warm and tender. He was the tallest, broad and strong, brown of hair and skin, much like Casimar but more vivid, more graceful, and without such exaggerated features. Leon was full of excitement; Casimar was romantic and kind; Michal made a person feel perfectly safe. It unnerved Johanna that Michal, who was like a brother to her, lavished on her all the love that Casimar begrudged her.

"Johanna should stay here with Mama," Leon said impatiently. "This is work for men." Only because of Mama, Johanna knew, did Leon resist his urge to throw her into his bed. Handsome, swaggering Leon thought he was irresistible to everything female.

"I'm in this as deep as any of you," Johanna cried. "My name is on that list too." She dared not let herself consider the consequences of being caught fomenting rebellion against Czar Alexander III. Direst consequences had befallen those who only two years before, in 1887, plotted to assassinate the Russian tyrant.

"Johanna is right," Mama said calmly. "There is no time to be lost. Go quickly, all of you, and when everybody has been warned, go to Father Gregorie at the church. He'll hide you."

"Mama, what about you?" Casimar was anguished. "The Russians are brutes when they want information."

Mama shrugged. "I'm only an old woman. The Russian soldiers come here, they'll find me setting the supper table. I'm really very stupid, you know." Her eyes twinkled. Mama was full of pride that her three youngest, her three handsome sons, fought for Polish freedom. Her two daughters were married and living in the country.

Johanna and the three young men hastened out into the early evening to warn the other conspirators. They would be the only ones to go to Father Gregorie's, the best hidey-hole they had. The Raisa brothers were the leaders of the rebellion. They would be in most need of sanctuary; and the officers would quickly realize that the pretty little waitress who spoke perfect Russian not only had suddenly disappeared, but was on their list to boot. They would want her as much as the Raisas—maybe more.

The streets had never seemed so dangerous before, even when there was hunger in the land. It made Johanna feel alive, though, to know the dangers—a bullet, or Siberia. Which was worse? A knock on the door, a few whispered words, and she moved on to the next desperate destination.

At dusk Johanna arrived, breathless and fearful but full of passionate patriotism, at the forbidding gothic church that overlooked the Vistula. Almost stumbling, she hurried up the narrow twisting red stone path that led to a side entrance.

Father Gregorie opened the narrow door as she

approached and drew her inside. "Is Casimar here yet?" she asked anxiously. "And Michal and Leon?"

"No." He spoke with reassuring calm. "Come with me and tell me what has happened."

While she reported on the disaster, Johanna heard sharp knocks at the door within minutes of each other. After each knock a Raisa brother appeared. Very soon Casimar—with whom Father Gregorie had a special closeness—Michal, and Leon were closeted in the office with Johanna and the priest.

"We know who betrayed us," Michal reported. "It was the schoolteacher who boards with the Sklodovskas. Mrs. Sklodovska knows he was having supper at the Okocim, though he has never before missed a meal at her house on any other occasion. She thinks he was currying favor in hopes of a university teaching post," he added scornfully.

"You'll all stay here," Father Gregorie said. "When things are quiet, you'll move into the countryside. We have a series of safe houses. You must not set foot in Warsaw while this regime lasts." He looked from one to the other of the four somber faces before him. "You understand? You must not come back to Warsaw." He was very old, parchment-skinned, but he looked out of hawk eyes over a hawk nose and even Leon did not argue.

"But our mother," Casimar said desperately, "how can we know what will happen to her?"

"Your mother is more than a match for the Russians," Father Gregorie assured him. "They will find she knows nothing, speak harshly and move on."

"How will she survive without us?" Michal put in.

"Like other Polish mothers before her." Father Gregorie maintained his air of tranquility, and they remembered other times that the church and he had provided succor for desperate fugitive Poles. "She will take in roomers to support herself. I know a few who'll be grateful for a home with her."

He rose behind the desk. "We have two small rooms where you will be comfortable enough until it's time to move on. You will not set foot outside them. Food will be brought to you. Tomorrow I'll go out and find out what I can."

Three days and nights passed without news. Johanna remembered other attempted rebellions. A hundred uninvolved Poles had been slaughtered in the backlash against an attempt by a few radicals to assassinate Czar Alexander III. Johanna and the Raisas had plotted only a protest against the government, not an assassination.

The Russians once suspected her father had written some revolutionary poetry in circulation around Warsaw, so they gathered her whole family and shipped them off to Siberia. Father Gregorie eventually managed to learn that all of them, even her fourteen-year-old brother Nicholas, had starved or been shot. Johanna escaped only because she was at the house of a neighbor when the soldiers arrived.

On the fourth night Leon insisted that Father Gregorie was being overcautious. "We can't stay in hiding forever." Twirling his mustache, he paced in quick, impatient steps. As the eldest of the three sons at twenty-three, Leon had always been the one to make decisions. "We'll leave tonight at dark."

"I don't know," Casimar objected. "I think we should wait until Father Gregorie says it's saf~."

"What does a priest know?" Leon scoffed. "He knows to pray."

"He's harbored a stream of fugitives like us through the years," Michal argued. "I agree with Casimar."

"Funny, I thought I was in charge here," Leon sneered.

"Lost your nerve? Tell you what. You and Casimar can stay here with Johanna." Leon's eyes settled on Johanna with sardonic amusement. "Unless you wish to come with me, my beautiful little sister." He did not look, act or feel brotherly, as they all knew.

"I'm staying." She had to remind herself of Mama Raisa before she could speak mildly. "If you're smart you'll do the same."

"I'm leaving." His face was etched with determination. "I won't stay here hiding behind a priest."

"Where will you go?" Casimar asked. "Leon, why can't you have a little patience?"

"Warsaw is a big city and the Russians are stupid. By morning I'll be in the country. What Pole will turn me out?"

An hour after moonset Leon opened the door and headed down the long hall out of the church. Everyone else had long been asleep. Nor would it have been of any use, Johanna thought in the morning, if Father Gregorie had been awake. Leon had the mind of a bull—stupid and stubborn.

"Doesn't Leon know what will happen if he's caught?" Michal paced and muttered. "Is he so anxious to see Siberia?"

"God will watch over him," Casimar said. "We must all pray for Leon."

Not until late morning did Father Gregorie discover that Leon had taken off. Johanna was instantly aware of his consternation. His aged hands shook with agitation and his nostrils flared with anger.

"I'll go into town to learn what is happening," he said with a show of confidence belied by his eyes. He had never in a long acquaintance been so angry with the young wastrel.

"Leon has gone to Mama," Michal guessed. "He'd figure the Russians have been there already. They won't waste time coming back again. He'll expect Mama to hide him until he decides where he wants to go." Michal frowned. "He won't once think about the danger to her."

"I'll go into town immediately," Father Gregorie said again. He too was worried about Mama Raisa's welfare, Johanna guessed. "Enjoy your breakfast." He had brought a tray laden with bread, butter, kielbasa and a pot of tea. They settled down to eat but with little appetite, each anxious about Leon and Mama Raisa.

"Leon never thinks about anybody but himself," Michal said impatiently. "Sometimes he thinks about Poland," he admitted after a moment.

Johanna was aware of Casimar's furtive glances in her direction when he believed himself to be unobserved. Casimar was the youngest Raisa, only two years older than she. She knew he loved her as she loved him. When would he abandon his thoughts of becoming a priest and say so?

Michal settled down to read the newspapers that Father Gregorie had left for them. Johanna knew that Casimar, sitting tiredly with his eyes closed, was praying for Leon and Mama Raisa. Why must Leon always be so willful? He never could sit still, even in church.

Each minute that Father Gregorie was away seemed an hour to them, Johanna thought as the sun became intense and uncomfortable, even within the walls of the church. If Leon was caught, could he keep quiet? Could anyone?

"Father Gregorie has returned," she guessed at the sound of a cart clattering along the path that led to the church.

"It could be a delivery cart," Michal said gently.

"No." Casimar was on his feet and peering through a high window. "It's Father Gregorie."

Within minutes the door to their two rooms, used often before for similar purposes, was opened. Johanna involuntarily gasped at the sight of Father Gregorie's face. Like Casimar and Michal, she knew at once that Leon had been captured.

"Mama?" Casimar asked, his voice uneven.

"Your mother is safe," Father Gregorie told them. "Leon was caught crossing Stare Miasto Square. He never reached home." He sighed heavily. "He is to be shot as a traitor. Fortunately, they are in too much of a hurry to put him to the question. They plan to make an example of him. We can only pray for his soul. And then," he said slowly, "we must spirit you three out of the country. You are going to America."

Chapter 2

All three prayed with Father Gregorie for Leon's soul. The Russians would not say when Leon was to be shot, but the Raisas suspected it would be at dawn of the following morning. Johanna was suffused with grief. Not only was a young Polish patriot to die, but she knew the anguish Leon's death would bring to his mother, who had claimed her for her own the day the Russians came for the Boguskis.

In the area where they must remain in hiding until travel arrangements were made, Johanna and the two young brothers prayed throughout the day. Father Gregorie had gone to be with Mama Raisa, who was surrounded by sympathetic friends.

"She's proud of her son," Father Gregorie consoled them when he at last returned to the church. "Who among the young of Poland doesn't yearn to die for his country?"

"Why didn't he listen to us?" Michal had never had any patience with Leon's impatience. "I should have made him stay."

"Michal, no one could ever make Leon do anything

13

he didn't want to do. It was his wish to leave, and we could not stop him," Casimar said with fatalistic calm. "It was God's will."

Johanna knew that Leon secretly dreamed of being part of an assassination plot. Once he confided to her that he wished to throw a bomb at the carriage of the czar when he was next in Poland—or at least at the carriage of the governor. Casimar was leaning more toward the new movement among the intelligentsia, who considered that independence through revolution was impossible at this time. These new positivists had arrived at the conclusion that they could best serve Poland by working to educate the poor and to spread knowledge among the masses, whom the Russians deliberately kept in ignorance.

Johanna had been studying English in the floating university which held clandestine classes in first one home and then another, always moving lest the authorities catch up. Michal and Casimar had been studying engineering and chemistry respectively for two years now. Casimar, of course, was always against violence; he had joined the just-aborted protest plot only to keep an eye on his brothers.

Johanna and Leon's brothers did not sleep that night. They waited with Father Gregorie for the dawn. With bowed heads they listened to the mass to entrust Leon's soul to God. With the first pink shafts of dawn spilling into the room from the discreetly small and highly placed window, Father Gregorie began to urge his fugitives on their way.

"Father, I must speak to you," Casimar said with sudden agitation. "Please, it's important."

"Alone?" Father Gregorie asked.

"I can speak before Michal and Johanna. I've made my decision. I must serve God. Is it too late to be enrolled in the Academy of Catholic Theology?"

Father Gregorie squinted in thought.

"There are ways," he acknowledged quietly. "It will take some doing, but to bring a young man like you into the priesthood is worth every effort." Father Gregorie's eyes glowed. "I've watched this struggle within you, my son. Your decision makes me very happy."

Johanna was stricken with pain. Casimar, whom she yearned to call her husband, was marrying the church. Why, why must it be this way? Casimar loved her. He didn't have to say so; she knew. Every time their eyes met, every time their hands touched, she felt his love.

"There's much to be done," Father Gregorie said briskly, "both to arrange for your studies"—his eyes rested on Casimar—"and to provide safe transport for you two to Gdansk, where you'll board a ship for America. It must be soon before even the church becomes suspect."

Not until Father Gregorie had left them did Casimar confide his thoughts for the future of Johanna and Michal. "You'll have a long and arduous journey ahead of you," he pointed out. "It would be improper for you to travel together without the sanction of God."

"As brother and sister," Johanna stammered, color flooding her high cheekbones. "I am only sixteen, Casimar."

"As husband and wife." Casimar was firm. "You'll need a husband to protect you."

"No!" Johanna cried.

"I'm willing," Michal said, his bright eyes soft as they rested on Johanna, "and you will be safer, my dear."

"There would have to be an understanding," Johanna whispered. How could she marry Michal when she loved Casimar? Michal was a cherished brother. "We—we mustn't have a family for years yet." Maybe someday she could come to accept Michal as her husband. "If we escape from Poland, then I want to dedicate my life to helping our country win its independence—even if it must be from

America." This was the secret dream of every young Pole. "I will make a home for you, Michal," she agreed, "but I'm not ready to give you children."

"I'll wait. What's important is to get safely out of Poland and to begin a new life in America. I'll always care for you, Johanna."

"Then it's settled." Casimar was palpably relieved. "Father Gregorie will marry you before you leave for America."

That same evening, with the windows covered against intruding eyes, Father Gregorie married Johanna and Michal. She felt the trembling of Michal's hands as he drew her to him to kiss her gently when Father Gregorie had pronounced them man and wife. Her heart pounded; now there could be no reprieve. She was Michal's wife and Casimar was destined for the priesthood. For a poignant few moments she had prayed that Casimar would have a change of heart.

"At dawn we leave," Father Gregorie told them.

Involuntarily Johanna's eyes, blue with desolation, moved to Casimar. She might never see him again. Despite his determination to become a man of God, Casimar felt the pangs of loss that tormented her, Johanna told herself. Still, she knew a dream was dead.

"I'm taking a cart laden with clothing to a poor parish an hour's distance from Warsaw," the clergyman continued. "You will lie in the cart beneath the clothing. Holes have been drilled in the bottom of the cart. You will lie face down so that you can breathe. With God's help you'll be on your way to America."

"How do we manage this escape, Father?" Michal's eyes were troubled. "We have no passports, no money—"

"I've been busy all day." Father Gregorie smiled wickedly. "How many priests know a master forger? Passports are being readied and will very shortly be in hand.

You will sail from Gdansk. Tickets to America are also being provided, though not by the forger; those are real.''

He fished in a pocket. ''Michal, here is a pair of plain-glass spectacles. Never take them off. There is a reason I never brought you that razor; you are not to shave until you are safe in England. You are a farmer; this black dirt is for your hands. Dig your fingers into it. Good. Rub it in several times a day and it will stay with you until you are safe.'' Shaking his head and laughing, Michal did as he was told.

The priest turned to his other young friend. ''Johanna, braid your hair in a matron's coronet. I have brought you a pair of wooden clogs; they will make you walk like a countrywoman. Remember, you cannot read, cannot speak anything but Polish, want only to get home and see to your garden.''

Next he pulled something small from an inside pocket. ''I have a wedding ring for you at last. You will notice that it is not quite new; it is the gift of a patriotic pawnbroker.'' He blessed the ring. ''Michal, the wedding was of course quite binding without the ring, but it would be suitable for you to put it on your wife's finger.''

''Now that my hands are dirty?'' But he did so and took his opportunity for a second wedding kiss. Johanna blushed furiously.

The priest cleared his throat. ''You will travel as Johanna and Michal Zamoyski.'' Michal bridled. ''In America you can be Raisa again,'' he promised. ''Your chances are quite good, you know. They will be looking for two brothers and a sister, not a young married couple.'' His face saddened. ''But we must assume they are looking.''

Johanna lay face down at the bottom of the cart, as instructed by Father Gregorie. Her hand was lost in Michal's huge one. Warm and strong as always, his touch gave her strength and courage. The cart, piled high with old clothes from affluent families—some who were in the favor of the Russians religiously attended Father Gregorie's church—rattled through the dawn-empty streets. Only when they arrived at the edge of the city, where Russian soldiers inspected all traffic, did Johanna begin to tremble.

"You're traveling early, Father," a soldier remarked. Michal's hand pressed hers as the cart came to a halt.

"Before the heat of the day," Father Gregorie said easily. "In Russia you didn't feel heat like this," he guessed.

Johanna stiffened in terror as the pitchfork of a soldier performing a rudimentary search pushed into the pile of clothing, missing her by no more than half an inch.

"In Petrograd it's never like this," the soldier said wistfully. "The winters are sometimes cold, yes—but never a summer like this."

"I hope to get back before the sun is broiling," Father Gregorie said. The cart began to move again and they were past the checkpoint.

It seemed to Johanna that they would never get out of the cart. Under the weight of the clothing and the intense sun Johanna felt herself soaked with perspiration. Breathing was uncomfortable despite the holes.

Only now did Johanna realize what had befallen her. Married to Michal, and they were leaving not only Warsaw but Europe. Michal and she were going to America—if they were not caught by the Russians.

At last the horses came to a halt. Johanna heard voices close by, two women and a man. The clothing was hurriedly removed from the cart and hands reached to help them out. They were at an isolated farmhouse. The two women pushed them indoors before a passing traveler might see them.

"I'll give you bread and tea," the older woman said

calmly. "Then you must hide in the eaves. Tonight the moon rises at midnight. Between full dark and then Walter will take you to the next house."

Father Gregorie came inside to say farewell and to bless them.

"Father," Johanna asked with fresh trepidation, "are you sure Casimar will be safe? The Russians know he was one of us."

"They'll not challenge me when I deny it. A priest still has some standing. Casimar has been studying with me and that's that. The church does not foster revolutionaries." But Johanna saw the rebellion in Father Gregorie's eyes. Like the rest of them, he yearned for an independent and united Poland.

Again at night they were secretly taken north. It would be at least another four nights, they understood, before they were in Gdansk, in the German sector. Once, before the partitioning of Poland began, Gdansk had been the most populous city in eastern Europe and a mighty port. Now it was only the chief town of the province of West Prussia. The Germans called it Danzig.

Their passports were masterpieces; Father Gregorie was a wizard. Summer was no time to grow a beard, Michal complained, but Johanna thought it very handsome. Her mane of flaxen hair was scraped back and sedately contained in coronet braids. Their tickets would take them from Gdansk to Malmo, Sweden; from Malmo to Copenhagen; and thence to Liverpool. From Liverpool they would cross the Atlantic to New York City.

In the ancient city of Gdansk, situated at the mouth of the Vistula River, Johanna and Michal were delivered into the hands of the operator of a two-story frame boarding house. Close to the docks, amidst factories and warehouses, Johanna and Michal were at last alone in a furnished room until two mornings hence, when their ship left for Malmo.

"Johanna, don't look so frightened," Michal pleaded after the landlady closed the door. The small room contained only a bed, two chairs and a chest. "We're in German territory. The Russians can't touch us anymore."

"What will it be like in America?" Johanna's clear eyes were deep blue with distress. "Michal, we hardly speak the language."

Unexpectedly Michal chuckled. "You speak a fair amount, I none at all. You must begin to teach me."

Johanna tried to brush aside her fears and doubts. "Could we leave this house and go to church?"

"I don't think it's a good idea," Michal told her, his eyes disconcertingly passionate.

"I want to go to church," she said stubbornly, unnerved by what she saw in his eyes. He sighed and agreed.

Though Johanna understood only a few words of German, Michal was fluent in it. After he made a polite inquiry for directions they were able to make their way to St. Catherine's Church, one of the oldest in the city, built in the first half of the thirteenth century.

They prayed together. It made Johanna feel close to her new husband. Leaving the church, she felt fresh courage. The sun poured upon the city. Within two weeks, Michal told her, they would be in America. They were young and strong. All at once the new life in America seemed a challenge. For the first time Johanna considered accepting her fate.

At last they returned to their room at the shabby boarding house. Night had descended on the city. Johanna was conscious of an odd expectancy in Michal. Up till now they had been caught up in the urgency to put Russian territory behind them. They had slept in fits and starts, in attics and under eaves, glad just to lie down and close their eyes. But now they had time on their hands.

"Michal," she said unsteadily while he locked the

door to their room, "we should be wearing black. Mourning for Leon." They traveled with sparse wardrobes, picked out of the bundles in their escape vehicle.

"We do mourn for Leon." Michal turned to face her. "For a long time we'll mourn for him."

"I'm tired." How could she get in bed with Michal? How could she avoid it?

"You don't look tired. You look beautiful." His eyes caressed her. "Let down your hair, Johannusya. Please."

"All right." She reached for the pins and pulled them free. Her hair fell into golden splendor about her shoulders, breasts and back. It reached past her waist. The soft glow of the petroleum lamp lent warmth to her features.

"My wife," Michal whispered. "You can't guess how long I have wished for that to come about." He reached to pull her close.

"Michal—" She fought against panic. "You remember what we said."

"We won't have a child, not until you are ready. I know what to do."

He drew her against his hard lean length. She had forgotten he was so tall. With one hand he lifted her face to his and brought his mouth down to hers. At first he kissed her gently, his hands content to move about her back. She was aware of the rising mass between his thighs; it elicited disconcerting excitement in her. His breath was hot as he released her mouth.

"You can't guess how many nights I have lain in my bed and imagined being alone with you like this." He reached for the buttons at her bodice and opened them slowly until the creamy white velvet of her breasts was visible above her low-cut chemise. "I knew you'd be like this." He lowered his mouth to deposit an avenue of kisses along her throat and into the valley between her high full breasts. His soft, curly beard felt like feathers brushing her skin.

She closed her eyes and gave him next to no help with her clothes, merely shifting her weight a little when it was necessary. She was shameful, she told herself, for loving Casimar and yet feeling so strangely excited with Michal. She had always considered him her brother, and he was making love to her.

"I hated having you work at the café," he confessed when she stood before him wrapped only in lamplight. "I hated every man who dared to look at you."

"Michal, you agreed I should work there," she reminded him. He stripped to skin before her and she tried to avert her eyes from the sight of his passion, aware of emotions normally kept locked away within her.

"It was important that we know what was happening." He reached for her again. "Above everything else we must think of Poland."

Brave words, but here in this strange little room in Gdansk they were in another world. No man had ever kissed her before tonight, and now she was a wife.

Mama Raisa had taken it upon herself only last year to tell Johanna what a man expected of a woman in bed. With Zosia and Hela, her closest girlfriends, she had whispered about making love. There was no forgetting pious Zosia's stern admonition. "You do it only to have children."

Michal's mouth closed over hers again and his hands moved on her breasts. His tongue drove between her teeth and found her own. She felt the heat of him prodding against her small flat belly. Without relinquishing her mouth he moved a hand to her curvaceous rump and urged her across the room. She felt the hard edge of the bed against the back of her knees.

"I'll turn off the lamp," Michal said thickly. She waited for him to return to her.

Michal lifted her onto the bed. She felt wanton to allow Michal to take her this way when they both knew they must not have children. What would she say to the priest when she next went to confession?

"Johannusya," Michal whispered, separating her trembling thighs with one leg, "I will be a good husband to you. We'll have a good life."

She started at the thrust within her; a hand fondled her breast. It hurt but she did not care. Everything forgotten but the newness of desire, she cried out faintly and he paused.

"Johannusya?" he hesitated.

"I'm all right," she managed, her hands tightening about his shoulders.

The stab of unimportant pain became a frenzy to receive him. They moved together as one, caught up in soaring passion.

All at once Johanna abandoned motion, her mind in control again. "Michal," she gasped, "Michal, be careful!"

With a low oath Michal pulled himself away from her and swung over onto his stomach. With one fist he beat into the huge feather bolster that extended from one side of the bed to the other. The sheet rather than his wife received his seed, and he swore again in frustration.

Johanna lay sleepless long after Michal was oblivious to the world. Michal understood when she married him that this was the way their life must be for now: no family. She was only sixteen and they were going to a strange life.

Her mind raced back to Warsaw. Casimar would stay with Father Gregorie and continue his studies. Mama Raisa would be proud of her son the priest. How could she, Johanna Boguski—no, Johanna Raisa now—love Casimar as she did and yet respond to Michal this way? Was she a wanton, like one of those girls in certain houses on the square?

Tonight—her whole existence now—seemed unreal. She would never see Warsaw again. She would never see Casimar again. Tears filled her eyes and spilled over. If Casimar had not persuaded himself to go into the priesthood, he would be her husband. Tonight she would be lying in bed with Casimar.

She turned on her side, away from Michal, clinging to the edge of the bed.

Chapter 3

Their meager luggage beside them on the dock, Johanna and Michal waited to board the ship that would take them across the Baltic Sea to Malmo. Russian, Polish and German blended with the sounds of the harbor in the crisp young morning. The sea air considerably diminished the heat of the summer.

"Michal, we'll have no trouble." Johanna's eyes were huge and blue, but she put up her chin and sneered at fear.

"No one will stop us," Michal agreed confidently. "We have the papers we need, and money." Nonetheless, Johanna knew he was worried about their arrival in Liverpool. Frightening stories had circulated in Warsaw about the poor souls the ship attendants at Liverpool rejected for travel to America. The shipping companies made a policy of turning away any whom the U.S. Immigration Service would consider undesirable, as rejects who got as far as New York would sail back and pay nothing.

From Malmo they crossed by ferry to Copenhagen,

...here they boarded a ship for Liverpool. On this ship Michal met a young Polish peasant, Jan Dluski, en route to America.

"I was sad to leave Marya, who is to be my wife, but I mean to make a better life for us. I don't want to live forever like a peasant, in a hut without windows and only earth for a floor. I saw once in Warsaw how people live, with glass windows and a separate place for sleeping. In America Marya and I will live like that." Jan was even bigger than Michal. He had curly black hair cut in clumps, for he hated any length on it and would never dream of paying for a haircut. He just hacked it away when it annoyed him. His farm-healthy face glowed in anticipation. "I'll find work in a factory in Massachusetts, where my oldest brother already works. He has a house with windows and floors and three rooms besides the kitchen for himself, his wife and his two children," Jan continued with pride. "Soon Marya will come and cut my hair again. You go also to family?"

"No," Michal admitted. "Johanna and I know no one in America."

"Come with me to Massachusetts," Jan urged. Johanna knew he was impressed by their learning, which went far beyond his own; Jan could neither read nor write. "My brother will help you find a job and a place to live."

"Where is this Massachusetts?" Michal hedged.

Johanna was a little irritated at his hesitation. With Jan they would not be alone. He would help them. "Is it far from New York?"

"It will cost only a few American dollars to get to Fall River," Jan said. "You'll find a job there. The women work too, until the children come."

"My wife will take care of the house," Michal said firmly.

"Michal, I'm strong. I can work," Johanna insisted. "We'll save more money that way."

"Already my brother talks about buying a house," Jan boasted. "He earns on his job two American dollars every week."

"Michal, let's go with Jan to Fall River," Johanna urged. There would be a piece of home, other Poles like themselves.

"We'll think about it on the ship," Michal decreed.

In Liverpool they had to wait two days for a ship to America. New fears assaulted Johanna. They were about to put a formidable distance between themselves and Warsaw to go far from all Johanna had ever known.

With their new friend Jan they presented themselves to the Liverpool shipping officials for examination and at last were settled on the great transatlantic liner. The three of them were awed by the size and grandeur of the steamship. Jan was to travel steerage. Johanna knew that Michal and she had tickets for the second cabin, but she was uncertain what these accommodations would provide.

Tense and excited, they sought out their accommodations, Johanna and Michal assuring Jan they would seek him out later. The second cabin, Johanna swiftly realized, was only a slight improvement on steerage. These between-deck facilities were stuffy, cramped and always rocking. Still, Johanna was grateful for the privacy they afforded, denied those in steerage.

Settled in their cabin, Johanna and Michal hung away their two changes of clothing and went in search of Jan. They found him belowdecks in steerage, a vast, low-ceilinged room crammed with poor families. Here the motion of the ship was more violent even than in their own quarters. Johanna prayed she wouldn't be seasick.

Because steerage was so uncomfortable in the summer heat its passengers were herded on deck. Johanna and Michal joined Jan at the railing, all three conscious of the splendor of the upper decks, which catered to the wealthy.

"I've heard," Jan said, eyes wide with awe, "that in first class there are bathtubs of white marble and a room for eating that is like that of a palace."

"Someday," Michal declared, his eyes glistening with fervor, "when Poland is free again, we'll go back to Poland on the top deck of a ship like this."

With what Johanna thought was miraculous speed—only eight days—the ship was within view of Castle Garden, their entry to America, steerage and second cabin passage almost behind them.

Since their night in the Gdansk boarding house Michal had not made love to her. Johanna wondered why as she packed to leave. Was it the cardboard-thin walls and squeaky bed? The heat and motion? She dared not hope it would last.

With their small knapsacks in hand Johanna and Michal left their accommodations for the last time to join Jan on the steerage deck, all of them conscious that one last hurdle lay ahead. Not everyone who arrived at Castle Garden was allowed to enter America.

Castle Garden, a Polish-American crew member told Johanna and Michal, was at the tip of Manhattan. A huge building in New York harbor, it had earlier been an army post. In this reception center each immigrant must pass the final examination for admittance.

Jan, who had only once before been out of his village, was astonished at the sight of New York City.

"It is not like this in Fall River," he said with relief, "though my brother says the cotton mill where he works is four stories high. That is high enough for me," he grinned.

The passengers, especially steerage class, were as excited as the Raisas. With tags bearing their name and manifest numbers, clutching their bundles, they hurried down the gangplank to be channeled into lines by shouting, sometimes impatient uniformed guards.

They were submitted to a series of tests, beginning with a medical examination. This was no threat to Johanna, Michal or Jan, but devastating to some. Occasional loud wails proclaimed their despair.

The medical receptionist gave them all numbers and sent them to stand in yet another line. "You've got the money?" Michal asked Johanna. Each arriving immigrant must show twenty-five American dollars or the equivalent.

"I have it," Johanna assured him, her heart pounding with the excitement of arrival. They proved they were not penniless and this time found themselves in a waiting room with benches. They all sank down sighing.

After several hours of interrogation the three of them, adjudged suitable, were allowed to leave Castle Garden. Jan, who had specific instructions about how to find the way to the train, was suddenly in panic when faced with a huge foreign city.

"Johanna, you speak English," Jan clutched at her arms, his eyes pleading. "Ask how we get this cable car to—to—" he looked again at the much-folded sheet of paper in his trembling hand—"Forty-second Street. From there we take a horsecar across to Grand Central Depot."

Pleased that her covert studies at the floating university in Warsaw were to be useful, Johanna made the necessary inquiries, acutely aware that Michal was self-conscious and frustrated at his own lack of knowledge. The three climbed aboard a northbound cable car jammed with passengers. Leaving the cable car at the direction of a friendly ten-year-old New Yorker, they hurried to board a horsecar traveling across town to the train station.

They left the horsecar to stand with awe before a huge triple-towered structure on the north side of the street. A line of hansoms and horse-drawn jitneys sat before Grand Central Depot. Etched in the stone front of the central tower they saw the legend *New York and Harlem Railroad*. The tower on the right bore the name of the New York and New Haven Railroad.

At street level a row of shops irresistibly drew the eye, notably one where wine, spirits and cigars were dispensed to gentlemen in bowler hats. For a moment Johanna viewed the Park Avenue Oyster House with interest, but obviously it was not for the likes of poor immigrants. Its clients looked very elegant indeed.

Inside the station, breathless with anticipation because they were only hours away from their destination, Johanna bought three tickets to Fall River via Boston.

Resolutely ignoring their hunger, they avidly watched the scenery on the trip north. This was America. The realization lent rich satisfaction; they could not see enough of the legendary land of freedom. Here no one would deny their right to speak Polish, to get an education. Here were no tyrants, no Siberia.

They lingered only briefly in the great city of Boston. Soon the train that was to take them fifty miles southwest to Fall River arrived. Johanna said a silent prayer as she settled herself on the fine seat of the train for the hour and fifteen minute ride. Her heart pounded when they left the train.

Jan supplied her with the information she needed to inquire about the house of his brother. Smiling deferentially, she asked directions from a well-dressed rotund man who was obviously meeting relatives. With a rather surprising air of arrogance he told her where they were to go.

"Thank you," she said politely in her accented English and turned away, stricken by the attitude of the first new neighbor they had met. She shrugged and smiled at Michal and Jan. "We go down this street."

"More damn Polacks come to work in the mill," the man said to his companion. Color flooded her face. At least Michal and Jan did not understand. She had not expected bigotry in America.

Clutching their belongings, the three made their way to the modest houses adjacent to the Riverside Cotton Mill, where Jan's brother worked. The mill was in operation; even here they could hear the racket. Henryk Dluski would not yet be home.

"Henryk said to ask for him from anybody in the first six rows of houses," Jan said, his face aglow with pride. "They are all Poles and Henryk is popular. Everybody knows him. For four years he has worked here."

Michal approached a door and knocked with confidence; here Polish would be spoken. The houses were little more than shacks, but each was neatly maintained and had its own patch of well-tended garden.

A door opened and a young blonde woman with a baby on her hip appeared. Before Michal could ask directions to Henryk's house, the pale-eyed, buxom housewife stared past him and burst into a brilliant smile.

"Hela?" Jan asked tentatively.

"Jan," she cried joyfully, "you're here at last. Somebody from home!"

"Hela, I have friends with me." All at once he was nervous. "I tell them to come with me and they'll find a place to live and work."

"Come inside," she ordered. She patted them all with dozens of tiny pats, urging them kitchenward. "You must be hungry. You'll eat while you tell me about home."

Hela had come to America a year after Henryk. "Jan, my mama, she is well?"

Jan gave his sister-in-law Hela news of her family and of his own while she bustled about the immaculate kitchen. At one end was a gleaming black cookstove, table and chairs, and at the other, a small bed where her toddler son played with his toys and shyly watched the new arrivals. Beside the bed was a cradle where Hela deposited the baby.

Hela piled a plate high with *mysliwska* and ham and sliced a loaf of bread just out of the oven. She went to the stove to heat up a pot of sorrel soup, all the while talking animatedly to Jan and their guests.

"Jan, is there room here for Johanna and me?" Michal asked softly when Hela left the room for a moment.

"When does a Pole not have room for friends?" Jan sniffed. "Tonight we will sleep on the floor and in the morning Henryk will take us to talk with the boss at the mill. We will find jobs and houses as well," he said confidently.

Johanna knew that Michal was disappointed by the extreme modesty of the house. To Jan and his family this was a real improvement on the usual hovels of Polish peasants, but to the Raisas, who had considered themselves poor in Warsaw, it was a shock—not at all what they had expected to find in America. Hela had made a home from nothing, Johanna thought admiringly, and she must do the same.

"When will Henryk be home?" Jan asked.

"He works from six to six," Hela told him. "Soon the whistle will blow." Her eyes moved from one to the other of the new arrivals. She seemed to sense Michal's discomfort, Johanna thought. "It is good here. Soon Henryk will have money to send for his sister to come to us.

Sometimes I don't like the noise, the factory whistles, but already we have a garden. I keep chickens. Henryk works—most of the time he works." She lifted her head proudly.

"Nobody goes to bed hungry. One day, if we work hard and save, we'll buy a house and a piece of land of our own." All at once her face was alight with pleasure. "We have a priest of our own at last—a Polish priest, not the Irish one who has no time for us except an occasional mass. I ask you, what good is mass without confession?"

All at once Johanna was assaulted by anguish. She was here in America, Michal's wife, and in Warsaw Casimar was to study for the priesthood.

"Jan," a jubilant voice obtruded from the doorway, "my little brother!" Henryk, approximately two thirds Jan's size, swept Jan into his arms.

"Henryk, I have brought two friends from Warsaw with me," Jan said. "Permit me to introduce Michal and Johanna Raisa. They also wish to work in the mill."

Johanna saw Henryk's suspicion as he looked from Michal to her. Polish peasants preferred to avoid intellectuals. Henryk knew at once that they were of the young Warsaw intelligentsia.

"You wish to work in the cotton mill?" he asked dubiously.

"We're young and strong," Michal said, determined to dispel suspicion of their motives. "We must work to live."

"Tomorrow I take you to my boss," Henryk agreed. "Two dollars a week he'll pay you. For a man who speaks only Polish that is very good."

"Michal is learning English very fast," Johanna said quickly. "I studied it in Warsaw and I'm teaching him." She hesitated. "I too wish to work." She ignored Michal's reproachful glare. With both of them working they could save more, better themselves faster. "Jan told me that women work in the mill."

"I take you too," Henryk said. "Now let's eat, let's drink. Hela, bring out the vodka. My baby brother is here."

Chapter 4

Johanna and Michal listened intently while Henryk and Hela talked about their lives in America. Henryk spoke scathingly of the mill owners and of the townspeople who looked upon the Polish—and other foreigners as well—with contempt.

Hela reproached him gently. "But Henryk, here we have a house with three rooms. Remember what Walter, who came here from the mines, told us? With his wife and seven children he lived in one room. The bosses did not always pay. The Irish beat up on Walter and a lot of other Polish miners because they were afraid to ask for better wages."

"We came here to make money and to go back home," Henryk admitted; it was the goal of many immigrants. "But what can a man save out of two dollars a week when he has a wife and children to support?"

"You'll make more," Hela said soothingly. "Didn't the boss promise you that soon he makes you a foreman? Then we'll save."

Henryk turned to Johanna. "It's good that you speak English. In the stores they cheat us because we don't understand. They laugh at us because we have not yet learned to talk like them." He poured a shot of vodka and drank it. "But a day will come when there will be for the workers in the mill a union."

He banged his glass down on the table and refilled it. "Anyone else? No? Too bad." He drank again.

"Please, Henryk, don't talk to us about unions." Hela crossed herself with trembling hands. "Last January the miners in a place called Shenandoah Valley went out on strike when their wages were cut. Already their wages were low—how could they live on less? The police beat them. Within two months twelve were shot down. A law was passed that kept the Poles out of the pits. They had to speak English to dig for coal. That is why Walter works at the looms now."

"The day will come when we have a union," Henryk insisted. "We won't be 'them damn Polacks' anymore. We'll belong here and earn a fair wage."

"Henryk, we have two children and more to come. The children will be our riches," Hela said firmly. "They'll work in the mill beside you and we'll save. We'll own land here in America." It was clear that Hela did not expect to return to the old country.

Henryk stifled a broad yawn. "The mill whistle blows early. It's time already to go to sleep."

Tonight Michal and Johanna slept in the tiny bedroom that just managed to hold a double bed and a chair. It would be Jan's bedroom when they were in a house of their own. The larger bedroom, where Hela proudly displayed a pine chest in addition to the bed, was Hela and Henryk's. Soon the little boy must give his bed to his growing sister. A new baby, Hela blushingly admitted, would sleep in the cradle, and Jan must share his bed with his nephew.

Johanna lay very still under the patchwork quilt lest she disturb Michal, but it was difficult to sleep with so much of the evening's conversation on her mind. She was disturbed that Hela and Henryk expected their children to work in the mills by the time they were ten or twelve. In Poland education was denied the children of the peasants, but surely in America their children could go to school. Did they want their children to live like this? At last Johanna fell asleep. At five-thirty the shrill whistle from the cotton mill warned the workers that they had half an hour to get to work. She remembered with quickening pulse that she was to go with Michal to ask about work.

After a quick breakfast of bread, eggs, ham and coffee, which must sustain them until noonday, the three men and Johanna left the house for the Riverside Cotton Mill. Like most of the mills in Fall River, this one sat on a granite ledge rising steeply from the river.

As they walked, Henryk explained with some rancor that the houses were divided by nationality. The first six rows were Polish, the next few Irish. Then came the houses of the Welsh and the Germans. The further from the mill, the higher the status.

"All the others look down on us," Henryk said bitterly, "because we come here last. But we give the boss a day's work, and that's what matters."

The mill was four stories high, built of red brick and granite. The windows were huge iron frameworks full of four-inch by six-inch frosted panes. Henryk laughed at Johanna's careful scrutiny of the windows. "Don't bother your head to count the panes. There are a hundred and seventy-six of 'em. The chimney is three hundred and twelve feet high."

The noise beat on them as they moved closer to the

mill. She recoiled from the prospect of spending a dozen hours a day with that clamor. Would she be able to sit at the machines? Still, Henryk said the work was not hard.

Their host opened the door and they were assaulted by the hot moist air required for spinning and weaving. With a proprietorial air he took them to the superintendent, who did the hiring.

From months working at the café in Warsaw Johanna had become accustomed to appraising male stares, which she soon learned to ignore. She also learned how to spot and fend off amorous customers, and she suspected that the superintendent would have to be discouraged.

The first thing he said was, "Do they speak English?"

Henryk was surprised to see Johanna firmly shake her head, but he was obedient. "No sir, not yet."

With Henryk acting as interpreter the three of them were questioned by the superintendent. Within five minutes all had been hired to work at the looms. A low-rent company house would be assigned to Johanna and Michal as a married couple.

"Tell her not to be startin' a family right away," the superintendent said to Henryk. His hot bold eyes rested on her breasts. "I don't like trainin' a worker and havin' her walk out six months later."

Johanna blushed furiously at such talk from strange men, but it would give her an argument against Michal's advances.

"You got jobs," Henryk told them. "I'll take you to the foreman."

By the end of each day Johanna was exhausted. The damp hot air was enervating, and she must stand in place before a machine for twelve hours a day, less half an hour for lunch. The incessant noise made it impossible even to talk. Nevertheless, at the end of the week Michal and she each had two American dollars as their wages. That made it all worthwhile.

Michal worked beside her to help make their little house livable. This was very unusual; normally a Polish wife must take charge of the house even if she worked full time. A woman might in a pinch do man's work, but a man could never be expected to lower himself to reciprocate. But the gardening especially soothed Michal, who found the mill work distasteful.

He tried to conceal his dissatisfaction, but he had never expected to do pure manual labor. Unlike Michal, the other Polish workers at the mill, mainly peasant farmers back home, had raised themselves in America. There they had been glad enough for bread, potatoes and cabbage, with an occasional bottle of vodka to lift their spirits. This business of earning a wage and having money was entirely new to them.

On Sundays Michal and she went to church with the Dluski family. Hela was big in pregnancy, and sometimes Johanna saw Michal glance hungrily at her belly. He desperately wanted his own wife out of that factory, pregnant and at home.

In the starkly simple church to which their Polish priest came regularly from a neighboring community, Johanna felt close to home, close to Casimar. She waited eagerly for letters that came regularly from Casimar and from Mama Raisa.

Most nights Michal and she were content to eat their supper, talk a little and go to bed. Most nights Michal was too tired to reach for her in the darkness. When he did embrace her she steeled herself to be submissive but not to respond as her body demanded. Michal must remember—no children yet.

Each Sunday night after a day's rest from the looms Michal exercised his marital rights. Each time he left her at the crucial moment lest she conceive. He could not conceal his frustration, though he tried valiantly. Johanna was torn; she longed to keep him within her, to respond, but she struggled agant her feelings because the holy fathers told them regularly that what they did was a sin against God.

At the mill she was nervous because of the attentions of the superintendent. The women around her were aware of it and gave her one unanimous piece of advice: "Don't tell your husband."

Five months after she started working at the mill the superintendent contrived to corner her in the storeroom at one end of the floor. In the dark grey shadows of early winter he towered before her, palm against the wall, blocking her way.

"Why do you keep runnin' away from me?" he asked reproachfully. "I can show you a hell of a good time." His eyes were fastened on her breasts.

"I'm a respectable married woman," she cried. Perhaps one of the other women would come in and rescue her. They must know what he was up to; he had bothered the rest of them too.

"You're enough for both of us," he grinned, then reached to fondle her breasts.

"Take your hands off me!" She twisted away, her eyes blue with rage.

"You don't mean that, little one." His smile was triumphant. "You want your job here. All you Polacks need your jobs." He pressed his hips against her.

"Get away from me," she shrilled.

"Be quiet," he snarled, sliding a hand down the front of her dress, open because of the heat.

"Get your hands off me!" She kicked him hard in the shin.

"Damn little Polack spitfire, you're fired! You and your man both. Go to the timekeeper and pick up your pay."

Not until they got home did Michal understand why he had been fired. Quietly, only her blue eyes showing her rage, Johanna told him what had happened.

He jumped to his feet and towered over her, beating his fists on the low ceiling. "I'll kill him! How dare he touch my wife!" His eyes popped, his face blazed, his teeth were bared, the veins stood out on his temples, neck, arms and clenched fists.

"No." Johanna laid a restraining hand on his arm. "He'll say I led him on. Besides, we should be glad to be away from there. We'll find another job. There are lots of mills in Fall River."

"The bastard only gave us till morning to leave the house," Michal fumed. "I'd like to wring his neck." He turned to her, suddenly anxious. "You don't think he can blackball us at the other factories, do you?"

"Surely they know about him all over town. I'm not the first; he does this all the time. Michal, the really awful thing is that all those women have to say about it is, 'Don't tell your husband. He'll either beat you up or pick a fight with the super or both. Best to keep quiet and have patience.' Patience! Give in, they mean." She snorted. We'll find other jobs. Henryk says the mills are always hungry for workers. So why do they put up with him? They act as if it's his right."

"Workers are pouring into Fall River," Michal reminded her. "There's not much shortage now."

"We'll find jobs."

That night they ate with little taste, though the meal was very good. Johanna reheated the *bigos*, a combination of sauerkraut and several kinds of sausage, and served yesterday's leftover *kolduny*—dumplings in broth. Excellent leftovers, but she wished she had planned a fresh meal; it would have been good for morale.

"I'm going to ask for a job as foreman," Michal said with sudden resolve. "I'm learning English fast." He grinned. "You're a fine teacher, Johanna. I think I can talk enough English to be a foreman even for the Irish, German and Welsh workers."

"Ask," Johanna urged him. Already she toyed with the idea of trying for a job in the office. She could speak, read and write English and was good in mathematics. Why not try to better herself even in a mill?

Michal fueled the stove against the sharp shrill wind that blew against the poorly insulated house while Johanna did the dishes. They must vacate the house by tomorrow at noon. No difficulty there, she acknowledged. Michal and she had few possessions. The house came sparsely furnished, so they had bought nothing, but hoarded every cent they could, as they had been brought up to do.

Even with the wood burning in the stove and the door to the bedroom wide open to let the heat in, Johanna got chilled as she changed into a flannel nightgown in the darkness. Despite the cold winter Michal slept nude. He was already huddled beneath the heavy feather comforter Hela had given them as a housewarming present.

"It's cold," she said. She joined him beneath the comforter and curled up tight against him, shivering hard.

"I'll make you warm in a few minutes," Michal promised.

The heat of his body was a blessing in the dank cold of the night. For a few moments he was content to hold her close, but then she noticed his rising passion. She tried to steel herself to be the quiet, compliant wife. A husband did not expect his wife to respond, she exhorted herself.

The whores in the brothels on the square pretended to respond.

Hela and she talked sometimes about what happened under the comforters with a husband. To Hela making love was to make children. If it satisfied her husband, then that was a bonus. A woman was not supposed to enjoy.

So why did Johanna tremble this way when Michal touched her everywhere? Why did she want to hold him within her? She had never dared tell the priest that she was so wanton. Nor that they contrived not to have children.

"Johanna, I wanted to kill that superintendent for laying a hand on you," he whispered. "To touch my wife like this." His hand moved gently on her breast.

He rolled her onto her back and lifted himself above her, too impatient to delay. Her nightgown already high above her thighs, she opened her legs and he thrust into her. She tried to stifle the faint cry of pleasure that escaped her. Tonight her hands tightened at his shoulders and she moved with him.

"Michal—" She stiffened in sudden alarm. "Michal, no!" But he was seized with new frenzy, filling her with exhilaration. Suddenly they gasped and stiffened as they reached the crest together. Then he lay limp and exhausted upon her. She felt him soften within her and knew he had remained too long.

"Michal, you promised," she said. "We must both be more careful—and more chaste."

"Johanna, I'm a man. Lying with you—with my wife—it's not wrong."

"I didn't say it was wrong," Johanna stammered. But was it? It was Casimar she loved. With Michal it was that other thing that good Catholic women avoided. "I just don't want to start a family when we're both out of work."

"Johanna, there are ways," he said after a minute. "It is possible to make love and not have children—"

"No!" Johanna exclaimed. She too had heard of such things. "It's a sin, Michal. The priests all say so."

"I'm sorry," Michal said tiredly, "but there are times when the priests and I do not see eye to eye."

They found jobs within a week, though neither Michal nor she had ventured to try for a promotion in the new mill that hired them. Though they were no more than a twenty-minute walk from Hela and Henryk, she was sorry to leave their first friends in America.

Again she labored along with Michal to turn a hovel into a home. This one had a great advantage over the other: a beautiful view of the river. Michal loved to stand at their door and look out upon the water. Ever since their ocean crossing he had been intrigued by boats and ships. She was pleased that he had this small pleasure. It made up a little for the lowly mill work, for having his wife work, for no children yet, for constant frustration in the bedroom.

On a bitingly cold night ten days after they moved into their new house Johanna stood at the stove reheating the *flaki*. She had made it on Sunday in preparation for suppers during the week and stored it in the cold cellar Michal had dug. As she set the table she noticed a small insidious pain low in her back. Her face lighted with relief. In the morning her monthly flow would begin. She was not pregnant.

Chapter 5

It seemed to Johanna that the winter in Fall River was far more severe than any she had ever known in Warsaw. Michal pointed out that the mill houses were too flimsy to withstand the wind and cold. It was particularly harsh after long hours in the overheated mill. When she arrived at home after her working day, by law restricted to ten hours, she piled wood into the stove. Doing the housework would warm her up, but Michal would need the heat when he got home and sat down. Thank God they could afford plenty of fuel.

Every Sunday after church Johanna and Michal went to Hela and Henryk's house for dinner. Johanna always took a pot of food. She occasionally invited the Dluskis to her house instead, but Hela insisted it was easier to keep her three children at home.

In spring of 1890 Hela announced she was pregnant with her fourth. "Our riches, Johanna," she said with satisfaction.

At ten a child, girl or boy, could become a doffer in

the mill. When Johanna protested that this was too young despite Federal law, Hela shook her head in denial.

"A doffer works maybe fifteen minutes each hour. All he does is take off the full bobbins and put on empty ones."

Johanna could not make Hela understand that standing in one place ten hours a day six days a week was too much for a ten-year-old. No child of hers would be a doffer at that age, she told herself. That was one major reason why she still denied her husband. She intended to rear her family in prosperity. This was the time to work and save.

She knew Michal was not happy. In the mill he stood all day at a machine doing the same thing over and over, drowned in heat, humidity and noise. At home he craved books, comforts, children—and Johanna. On Sunday nights he came to her, but she always kept her head and made him pull out without the full satisfaction he craved.

Each week they went to the fine two-story granite Fall River Savings Bank at Main and Bank and added another dollar to their account. This gave Michal much pleasure, as it did her. Then they strolled to the spacious public library, which took up the entire lower floor of City Hall. This was their greatest pleasure, though it made their coworkers suspicious and kept them from making friends in the mill.

With the arrival of spring Johanna and Michal began to take long walks on Sunday afternoons after leaving Hela and Henryk's house.

Henryk thought Jan was drinking too much, like many mill workers. It was mainly discouragement. Jan was taking longer than he had anticipated to save Marya's travel money.

Johanna and Michal particularly liked to walk along the river. At the library Michal sought out every book on ships, and in the harbor he would point out various vessels and explain them to Johanna. He was cheerful about it, but she was always aware of his restlessness.

Since childhood Michal had yearned to see Poland free. He ranted when Casimar wrote that the Polish nationalists were against protests and open rebellion, that those who loved Poland fought to improve both its economic situation and its national consciousness. Casimar was convinced that within a dozen years Poland would be strong and in a position to make demands.

"Casimar dreams," Michal said impatiently, "while the Russians stamp out our language, our culture. And what do I do? I stand at a loom all day to keep a roof over my head."

"Michal, you did what you could. That's why we had to leave Poland."

"Yesterday at the mill," Michal said slowly, "a loom broke down. I went to the overseer and told him I could fix it. I was afraid to speak out, but he was pleased with me."

"Michal, that's wonderful. Tell the superintendent how you studied engineering at the university. Perhaps you will not stand at the loom too much longer, eh?"

"But my English—I speak poorly still."

"You speak well," she insisted. Her duty as Michal's wife was to encourage him. Though Casimar ruled her heart, she felt much sisterly warmth for Michal—and sometimes more. Sometimes lying with him on Sunday night she wished they could forget the priests, pregnancy, everything but pleasure. Her body ached to draw him deep within her—and that was wicked.

"Michal, talk to the superintendent tomorrow."

Michal waited three days before he spoke up. That night he came charging into the house with a new air of satisfaction. He picked Johanna up and swung her around.

"Johanna, I did it. Another loom broke down and I showed the super why they always do that. He asked me some questions and I forgot myself and told him how he could make room for several more looms. I'm a foreman now, and I make two seventy-five a week."

"Oh, Michal," Johanna said, "you see? In America you have to speak up. No one will send you to Siberia because you talk."

"I wouldn't have had the courage except for you." Johanna saw the glow in his bright blue eyes and trembled. Was she to spend the rest of her life afraid to go to confession because of this indecent passion of hers? Even from Michal she must conceal it.

"My beautiful little wife—" His voice sank to a tender whisper.

"Michal," she said tremulously as he pulled her hard against him, "the soup is ready to go on the table." He buried his face in her long blond hair.

"Let it wait." He swept her off her feet and carried her into the bedroom. This was her first time in daylight. Now, seeing his warm skin, his powerful frame, his passion, she forgot herself again. Their lovemaking was fiercely satisfying to both of them.

Once more Johanna did not conceive.

Michal was jubilant about his new position at the mill, though now both Johanna and he were aware of a wall rising between them and their friends. Henryk had worked at his job for five years now without so much as a raise in pay. Michal had worked at the mill for only a year and had a raise and a promotion.

Michal further antagonized the Dluskis by talking about labor unrest in other mills. Henryk and Jan wanted to hear nothing about strikes and unions. They needed every penny they earned. Who could afford to strike?

Johanna, emboldened by Michal's success, started thinking about working in the office. When she discovered one of the clerks was pregnant, she tidied herself up and went to the superintendent.

"I can read and write both English and Polish," she said. "I studied mathematics at university in Warsaw."

"So you're educated. Can you typewrite?" the superintendent drawled. Johanna saw the twinkle in his eye. "I make no promises," he cautioned, "but next week you come to the office and we'll see how good you are."

Johanna prepared a special supper to celebrate. Next week! Only two more days at the loom. Bless Amy O'Reilly and her unborn baby. Saturday was to be her last day.

She was at the door of the house with supper on the stove when Michal strode down the road toward her. The air was soft with the scent of flowers. The small garden was in riotous bloom despite a dry, hot summer that made children fret and sent the men to the saloons.

Michal was smiling when he handed her his lunch pail.

"You know what I did today?" His eyes crinkled in satisfaction.

"I saw it. You amazed the whole floor by fixing a machine that everybody was sure could never be made to work again. Know what I did today? I got a job in the office. I think it pays more, but I forgot to ask. Michal, I start Monday. Only two days more on the loom!"

More money would go in the bank for their future. Johanna was reading about generals Kosciuszko and Pulaski, who were heroes of the American War for Independence, and Haym Salomon, the Polish Jew who helped finance the American Revolution. She had finished a book about Dr. Maria Zakrzewska, who had not only become a doctor but started a hospital in New York and another in Boston, just for women and children. Many Polish men and women had helped build this country and Johanna wanted to be one of them. Michal thought constantly of Poland, but Johanna felt at home in the United States as she never had in Poland. "We'll send Mama a new coat for Christmas," she decided extravagantly. "It's not too late for it to get there."

"Johanna—" All at once Michal was serious. "Isn't it time you stayed home? I know we're young, but isn't it time we started a family? Every letter from Mama she asks when. Casimar belongs to the church and poor Leon is gone. Only I remain to carry on the Raisa line. Johanna, we can manage without you working." His eyes implored her to agree.

All at once she was cold and trembling. "Michal, not yet," she whispered. "Please, not yet. I thought you'd be pleased about my news. I want to make money too, Michal, to make sure our children never even think about being doffers. If we start a family now we'll be stuck here forever."

Michal's shoulders drooped. Johanna cringed before his desolation, but she was right. She must never be like Hela, who each year presented her husband with another child to work in the mill beside him.

"Michal, we won't stay long here at the mill. When we have enough in the bank, we'll go to New York. It's bigger even than Warsaw. There you'll find a job working on the ships." She saw the sudden excitement that took hold of him. "We're young. We have far to go. We'll work together and someday we'll be able to send money to Poland." She saw the crusading glow in his eyes again. "In New York we'll meet other Poles more like ourselves."

"I don't understand Henryk and his friends," Michal confessed. "They think only about how soon they can take the children out of school and put them to work in the mills. That's not the way we thought in Warsaw."

"Michal, we must make them understand that to rise in the world their children must be educated. They don't even know enough to think about it. But why don't the children mind?"

"The Polish children have a hard time in school," Michal admitted reluctantly. "The American children make fun of them."

"Then we need our own school," Johanna said fervently. "They did it in Chicago. I read about it in the Polish newspaper in the library. I'll go back and find out how." Johanna and Michal between them read every newspaper that came into the public library, especially the Polish-language one that a sympathetic librarian ordered from Chicago.

In their fresh determination to try to help their fellow immigrants from Poland Johanna and Michal were bound more closely together. They encountered painful frustration. The Polish workers at the cotton mills were not educated. Ancient custom was to mistrust learning and follow in one's father's footsteps.

Johanna and Michal began to talk openly about the need for a Polish school. The Polish in America must band together to protect their heritage, they said. More and more they were disconcerted by the suspicion they encountered from their peasant countrymen.

One night they came home early from a meeting in the church. "Michal, what is it?" Johanna wailed in frustration. "Don't they understand we want to help?"

"Johanna, you're talking to people who for centuries were downtrodden by the so-called intellectuals," Michal pointed out. "They've been used, stepped on, lied to. They don't dare trust anyone but themselves."

"Then let's teach them to read so they can learn," Johanna said impetuously. "Father Wieczorek will help us get started. Let's teach them pride in themselves and in being Polish.''

They could never have done it without Father Wieczorek. No one distrusted the priest who along with the Polish mill workers had built the one-room wooden church on a vacant lot donated by the city. He visited every family, told them it was their duty to provide their children with opportunity if they could. The Poles were a great people and they must not bar their children from their heritage.

Within a year, with the help of sympathetic mill owners, Johanna, Michal and the good father had organized a one-room school, though some parents continued to snatch their children from the classroom at the legal age of ten. The first time it happened Johanna wept and railed.

"Hush, my daughter," Father Wieczorek said. "They have always been poor and ignorant. To them money is far more important than learning. You cannot change that overnight.''

Just three weeks before Christmas of 1891 the owners announced that the mill would close at the end of the week for an unlimited period. Johanna had known that troubles were ahead because orders had dropped off shockingly. The southern mills and their cheap labor had become stiff competitors.

She walked to the house in the cold grey dusk and tried to analyze what the closing meant to Michal and her. They had savings to tide them over, yet the prospect of not adding each week to their bank account but to take instead unnerved her. She thought about the families that lived from pay envelope to pay envelope. She thought about the schoolteacher, who could no longer be paid. Well, at least no one was to be evicted—yet.

The house was warm and cozy, full of the aromas of

dinner when Michal walked inside with sagging shoulders and somber face.

"You were afraid the mill would close and you were right. I never thought it could happen."

"In the South the workers earn far less than in Massachusetts," Johanna reminded him. "Their mills can sell cheaper."

"But for fine goods the northern mills can't be beat," he argued. "Our machinery far surpasses theirs."

"I heard in the office that the mills close for a while every year or two." She tried to be consoling even while she was afraid herself. Without the mill they had nearly nothing.

"It'll be harder on the others than on us," he admitted. "We'd best sit down tonight and talk with Father Wieczorek about what lies ahead."

Christmas was a bleak holiday. Three weeks without pay envelopes had already taken a painful toll. No more did the men chip in to have a pail of beer brought in from the saloon. The women, always the backbone of the family, looked about for ways to keep food on the table. Some went out to work cleaning, cooking or sewing. Some took in boarders at fifteen cents a week.

Jan's Marya arrived at last. Her passage was an early Christmas present, sent before the closing. A frightened Jan had searched frenziedly for another job since the closing of the mill but found nothing. Yet Marya did not mention the bad times when Johanna, as the local *pisennik*, wrote home for her.

Johanna was touched by Jan's delight in his bride. After church services on the first Sunday of the new year she persuaded them to come home with Michal and her for dinner. She knew they were down to bread and cabbage and tea, like most mill families.

"Only a Polish girl would I marry," Jan said, an arm about his tall dark love. "American girls are lazy. They want to do nothing. American bosses think Polish women are stronger than all others."

"Is there any word about the mill reopening?" Michal asked gravely. Jan's face fell. Every mill along the river was closed.

"They say in a few weeks." Jan shrugged. "Who's to know?"

"How are Henryk and Hela and the children?" Johanna asked. For the first time since she could remember they had not been at church for Sunday mass. Hela was poor but proud; if there was no money for shoes for the children, then she would stay home with them.

"Broni is sick," Marya said. "All the time he runs a fever. He coughs much and sweats at night."

Johanna's eyes sought Michal's. "Has Hela taken Broni to a doctor?" Broni was her firstborn, her only son. Hela would lay down her life for Broni.

"Who has money?" Jan shrugged. "Doctors are for rich people. You can't put a doctor on credit at the company store."

"Hela's baby must have a doctor." Johanna leapt to her feet. Henryk and Hela had of late looked upon them as stuck up because of their efforts to improve life in their community, but for her baby Hela would forget that. "Michal, you go get him."

"Of course. I'm on my way. We'll meet you at Hela's."

At the house they discovered that Hela was keeping Broni in her own bedroom, away from the other children. Hela obviously knew that little Broni suffered from the bad sickness. Tuberculosis hit young and old, rich and poor. Johanna's heart ached for the Dluskis.

"I could not come to church," Hela said defensively.

Johanna hardly heard; she stared with shock at Hela's belly. Pregnant again! Didn't Henryk understand he was making an old woman of his wife? Hela was not yet thirty.

"Broni has a cold. All winter he has a cold." Hela lowered her eyes. It was far worse than a cold and she knew it.

"Michal has gone for a doctor." Johanna turned to Marya. "Put the kettle on. We'll have a cup of tea while we wait for them."

Within an hour the doctor had come to the house and left. He gave Hela medicine for Broni and ordered her to keep him away from the other children. He told Henryk that his son was dying. It was too late to do more for frail little Broni than ease his pain.

Two days after the mills reopened Broni died. Johanna and Michal stood with his family when the tiny pine box was lowered into the still-hard earth. Hela sobbed in Johanna's arms. What could be so painful as losing a child? Father Wieczorek reminded her that she carried another, perhaps a son, in her womb. What does a priest know of a mother's feelings? Johanna silently demanded.

She lay sleepless that night, her mind beset by many questions. She saw no good future in Fall River for Michal and her. Both of them hated the mill. The city offered them only few small pleasures: beautiful walks on its outskirts, the library that was their sole diversion. Workers at the mill could not afford tickets to the symphony or trips to Boston. The other Poles distrusted them and everybody else looked down on them. They could make little money and few friends.

It was not enough.

Chapter 6

As soon as the mills reopened Johanna and Michal recommenced their weekly trips to the Fall River Savings Bank, determined to put back what they had taken from the bank when the mills were idle. Johanna lived with a sense of waiting, knowing that this life was a temporary one, not able to discuss it with Michal.

In the early autumn, Johanna's favorite time of year, a letter arrived from Casimar to give them good news and sad. He had been ordained as a priest. He thanked God their mother had lived to see the ceremony. Two weeks later her heart gave out and three days after that their grandfather died of a stroke.

"I should have been with her," Michal wept. "She always hoped to die with all her children around her." He hugged himself and rocked in his chair.

Johanna put her arms around him. "You couldn't be in Warsaw. Mama knew that. She wanted what was safe for you.

"Michal, let's leave Fall River and go to New York.

We have money enough to live on for months—until we find jobs again. And not in a cotton mill, either.''

At that Michal wiped his eyes and began to pull himself together. "We'll go to New York." He sighed heavily. "But what Mama would have thought—you must promise me you will stay at home and be a wife—and mother.''

Johanna sighed too. Michal was right; Mama would not approve of her working—or of their married life. Besides, Casimar was a priest. All thoughts of him must be erased from her mind now, even though she had no control over her heart.

"In another six months," Michal continued, "when we have put more money into the bank. But no more jobs for you. I want children, Johanna.''

"I know, Michal. I'll stay at home," she promised. "In six months we'll go to New York.''

It was six months to the day when Michal and she boarded the steamer to New York. They would travel overnight and wake up in the city of their dreams.

The day of their departure from Fall River was warm and sunny, a harbinger of what lay ahead, Johanna told herself romantically. Michal and she walked around the deck as the ship sailed south and watched the skyline of mammoth mills and church spires disappear from view.

They left Fall River with relief. They had expected to find a piece of home there, but the Raisas' way of life was far too different from their Polish neighbors' ways.

"We stop first at Newport and then New London. After that we go straight to New York," Michal told her with relish, enjoying being aboard ship. The sea spray on their faces, they leaned on the railing and smiled at each other. Michal took her hand and his blue eyes grew tender.

All at once Johanna was anxious. "You have the

name and address where we are to have a room?'' New York was a huge city, over a million and a half people. To know where they were to sleep was important.

"I have it,'' Michal assured her, "but it won't be long before we find a place of our own. And in New York I'll find better work.''

Johanna reflected on their first arrival in New York, when she had been so grateful that Jan provided them with a definite destination. How things had changed since then. Michal spoke English almost as fluently as she, though with more accent. They drew confidence from having enough money to see them through for four months.

They were almost the first down the gangplank. Ahead of the crowd, they easily found a horsecar and went to the address on East Seventh Street and the cousin of a Polish family in Fall River.

Their landlady, Mrs. Zabriskie, was a warm, friendly widow, an excellent cook and housekeeper. They liked each other at once. The Raisas took a room with her for a week and then moved to an apartment next door. Mrs. Zabriskie, still their landlady, had plenty of advice about where to buy a bed, which neighbor had a table and chairs for the kitchen.

Michal and Johanna scrubbed and cleaned and painted for another week. Then their white-haired, roly-poly landlady was invited in for tea and pastry.

Johanna enjoyed their Polish neighbors but was glad for a chance to meet others too, which had been very difficult in Fall River. She was beginning to feel more like an American; nevertheless, she hesitated to express her hopes that Michal and she would become United States citizens. It would not be disloyal to Poland, she told herself, to make the most of life in their new home. Still, instinct told her to wait before she spoke.

Each day Michal went off in search of work; Mrs. Zabriskie offered plenty of suggestions from her many years in the city. Johanna took long walks to explore and discovered Washington Square, where Stanford White's Washington Arch was one of the sights of New York. She loved to walk past the elegant old red brick mansions on the north side of the square and to imagine living there someday.

On sunlit afternoons when the flat was scrupulously clean and supper ready to go on the stove when Michal came home, Johanna liked to sit on a bench in Washington Square and listen to the birds singing in the trees. Then she would take a roundabout route home via charming Fifth Avenue and its stately mansions and then across Eighth Street to window-shop. She found herself lingering at toy stores and children's shops. Perhaps it was time at last.

Michal found work exactly where he had hoped to: on the docks. He was young and strong and willing. While his heart was in Poland, he must make this his home. Ambition took root in him as he looked about the great city and envisioned his opportunities.

He hurried home through the late afternoon hordes who had pushed their way off the Third Avenue El, the cable cars and the old horsecars that still traveled on the crosstown streets. He would work alongside the great ocean liners that fascinated him. He would learn all about shipping and someday he would sit at a desk in a white shirt and never again do manual labor.

On impulse he stopped at a street corner and bought a bunch of daffodils. Today was a landmark in their lives. He would earn on the docks five times what he had in Fall River. He felt like a man at last. Now was the time to start their family.

He rounded the corner of Second Avenue and was in

front of their freshly painted building and its window boxes, lush with red geraniums. He took the steps up the stoop two at a time in his impatience to impart his news to Johanna. He was glad they had lived awhile in Fall River. Now he felt prepared for a big city like New York.

"Johanna, I have a job." He grinned at her and held out the flowers.

"Michal, I knew it wouldn't take long." She pushed back a lock of wavy fair hair. Her eyes widened. "Oh, they're beautiful," she cried and reached for the daffodils.

"Like my wife," he agreed, aware of a stirring in his loins. He dropped the nosegay on the table and kissed her hungrily.

"I made *kisiel* for supper," she said almost shyly, "after we have the meat dumplings. Now tell me about your job."

"I'm starving," he laughed. "I'll wash my hands and we'll sit down to eat. Then I'll talk."

He knew how Johanna felt when they stood up before Father Gregorie in the small chapel in Warsaw. Leon, rest his soul, always said Johanna couldn't see anybody except Casimar.

Now, however, Michal believed his wife loved him. She didn't merely submit to him, but was sometimes as passionate as he, though he was sure she was ashamed of it. Tonight, he told himself, he would show his wife how much he loved her.

He dried his hands and returned to the kitchen. His eyes were gentle as they followed Johanna's movements about the kitchen. He had loved her almost since the day she came to live with them. He had never spoken of his feelings to Johanna, though. He was sure she was aware of them, but he dreaded to hear Casimar's name on her lips. His own brother, and a priest. Tonight he would take her away from Casimar for good.

While they ate he told her about his job as a stevedore. It was good, he said, to be so big and strong. The money was enough to care for a family with modest needs. Looking at Johanna, he realized his needs would not remain modest. He wished to shower his wife with riches. For his children he wanted only the best. As a rich man he could help Casimar in Warsaw and his sisters and their families in the German section of Poland. He could obey his father's deathbed instructions to work tirelessly for an independent Poland.

"You are excited about this job," Johanna said with a certain wistfulness. It got lonely at home sometimes.

"Yes," he confided, "I believe it's the beginning of our life, Johanna." It was difficult to sit here at the table without touching her. He wanted her in his arms in their bed. He was conscious of the throbbing between his thighs.

"I wish we could see Casimar now," Johanna said softly. "At least Mama lived to see him a priest."

Damn Casimar, Michal thought savagely. Before he went into the priesthood many girls in Warsaw looked at Casimar with lust, but Michal's saintly brother had nothing to offer them; it was all for God. Could Johanna never learn that?

"Someday we'll see Casimar," he promised rashly. "Someday we'll go back to Poland and see what we left behind."

He made a great pretense of sleepiness; as soon as Johanna had done the dishes they went to bed. In the bedroom, just large enough for their bed and a chest, he waited in the dark for her to put on her nightgown. Tonight he would take it right back off. He loved his wife with a passion that sometimes startled him.

Johanna fell into a new, restless pattern of living. Up at dawn to pack Michal's lunch and to make a substantial breakfast; Michal worked long hours at hard physical labor. Once she had cleaned the house and shopped for food, she had idle hours on her hands. She would not be idle, she thought guiltily, if she had any children. She sought comfort in books.

She was conscious of Michal's zest for living, which had been missing in Fall River. In spite of his fatigue they made love every night and she knew he waited eagerly to hear that she had conceived. As spring turned into hot city summer, Johanna began to worry about being barren. Michal's disappointment was harder and harder to bear, though she reveled in his unremitting passion.

She told herself that she had put Casimar out of her heart. She must devote herself to her husband. Yet at odd moments she thought about her childhood sweetheart. Michal was dear to her and there were moments in the darkness of their bed when she welcomed him with abandon that frightened her and delighted him. But still there was Casimar, forever unattainable.

Johanna discovered Cooper Union, Peter Cooper's free night school for the working class. Twice a week Michal and she attended lectures. Michal was delighted and began to talk about going to evening classes at one of the city colleges. They would start a tuition fund next payday.

Here in New York was stimulation beyond anything they could find in Fall River. They were thrilled to discover a Polish theater on the Lower East Side; they walked in awe through the galleries of the Metropolitan Museum. In early autumn Michal decreed that they would treat themselves to family circle seats at the Metropolitan Opera to hear *Tannhäuser*.

For three days Johanna stayed in and sewed to finish a new dress for the opera. She had never owned such a frock as the fine lilac-grey silk. It was cut in the popular Empire style, close-fitting with a high waist that emphasized the perfection of her bosom. Tonight she would be glad she was not pregnant, but slim and lovely in a silk dress among the elegant crowd.

From their seats far up in the family circle Johanna leaned forward eagerly to see what she could see. Two tiers of elegant boxes dominated the auditorium. The lower tier, a neighbor commented, was called the diamond horse-shoe and the upper was becoming known as the golden horseshoe. Even at this distance she tried to study the dress of the fashionable ladies in the boxes and their jewelry. She was amazed at how many obviously expensive outfits she just didn't like. How could a woman be rich and still not dress well?

Michal, who understood a fair amount of German, told her the story of the opera. When the final curtain rang down Johanna glowed with exhilaration. She had never heard such music.

After the performance Michal and she decided to walk home in the balmy autumn air. Tired but pleased by the evening's diversion and mindful that tomorrow was a working day, Johanna climbed the two flights to their flat with light steps. Michal and she must take advantage of all the pleasures the city offered. Many were free; and if some—like the opera and the theater—were not, what of it? Was she not a frugal housewife and her man a good provider?

"We'll have tea and cake before we go to bed," Michal decided. "It's been a fine evening."

"It has, Michal, but shouldn't you go to sleep? You have to get up early and it's past midnight."

"I'll sleep another night." He was in high spirits. "How many times have we been to the opera in America?"

"Tonight only," she admitted, her face softening. "I'll put the kettle on."

The water was just beginning to boil when they heard a sharp knock on the door. Johanna stiffened in alarm and turned to Michal. "Who is that at this hour?" she whispered.

"Not the Russian soldiers," he teased her. Michal went through the tiny parlor to the door. Johanna heard him cry out a moment later.

"Dear God, I'm seeing a ghost." He lapsed into Polish. "It's you! Johanna, it's Leon."

Johanna dashed to the parlor door and stopped short. Leon was pallid and thin and he looked forty. His magnificent mustache was gone, shaved off and just beginning to straggle back.

"Leon, they told us you had been shot." Michal grabbed his brother in a bear hug. "Because you were a traitor, they said, we could not even have your body for burial." He pounded Leon's back.

"Where were you all evening?" Leon said reproachfully. "For two hours I have been coming by and knocking every twenty minutes. All those stupid stairs."

"Johanna and I went to the opera and afterward we walked home." His eyes devoured his brother and he could not stop smiling.

"Ah, to the opera," Leon said. "I go to Siberia and do hard labor and my brother goes to America and gets rich."

"Siberia! How on earth did you escape? Johanna, bring tea—though tonight we should have vodka."

Too bold as always, Leon's eyes settled on Johanna. "All this time you have been living with Johanna? Our little sister?"

"My wife now, Leon. But how did you escape?" He was still shaken.

"I killed a soldier, stole his uniform and rode away

on the back of a garbage wagon." Leon dragged his eyes away from Johanna's breasts long enough to sit down. "Don't ask me to speak of life in a labor camp in Siberia. Eighteen months ago I saw a chance to escape and took it. Another man was not so lucky. He was killed at the border." Leon sighed heavily.

"How did you know where to find us?" Johanna asked. After all this time Leon still made her uncomfortable, but surely even he would not push himself upon his brother's wife.

"For almost a year I lived in England. Casimar wrote that you had left Fall River to move to New York. He gave me your address. Tonight I finally get here—and you are gone. Americans already," he teased.

"Poles first," Michal shot back. "Always we remember Poland." It seemed to Johanna that he could not bear to move his gaze from Leon for a moment; he still needed reassurance that his older brother was indeed alive. "Casimar writes that nobody fights back anymore. Everything is quiet. No longer do young men think it is wonderful to die for Poland."

Leon uttered a low oath. "They humiliate themselves to keep the peace. They talk about the need to wait and build a stronger country. How can this happen when every day the Russians step on us?"

Johanna moved about the kitchen, bringing them fresh tea, more cake, feeling painfully homesick as Michal and Leon talked. If Casimar were only here with them it would seem that she was home again.

Tonight Leon would sleep on the parlor floor and tomorrow they would buy a bed. When Michal reached for her under the covers a little later Johanna was uncomfortably aware that Leon was just a few feet away—and always would be.

*　　　*　　　*

Michal was overjoyed to have Leon. To him it was natural that his older brother should live with them.

When Leon had been with them for five weeks Johanna suggested to Michal that he help his brother find work. She was completely unprepared for Michal's shock.

"Johanna, for over two years Leon worked in the labor camp in Siberia. He needs to build up his strength, put on weight. He's in no shape to do dockwork."

"It's not good for a man to lie around all day the way he does," Johanna argued. Michal didn't know how Leon followed her with his eyes every minute they were alone.

"When Leon is ready, he will find a job." And Michal dismissed the subject.

She knew Leon teased him because they had been married four years and there was no child. Leon boasted about the children he had left behind in Warsaw, children who would never bear his name. Already he swaggered about with one girl after another here in the neighborhood. Two years in a labor camp had not been enough to break down his health, and he was gaining weight rapidly and getting his looks back. Wherever Leon Raisa walked among women, there were some eager to fall into his bed.

When American Thanksgiving arrived Johanna insisted they celebrate it as their own. She chose that day to plead with Michal to apply for American citizenship. That didn't mean they loved Poland less, she argued.

On Thanksgiving Day Michal and Leon both slept late while Johanna started dinner. First she must prepare the bird. Yams would go into the oven along with the turkey later. Last night she had baked her first pumpkin pie from a recipe carefully copied out in the library.

Leon awoke at noon. Johanna looked up from the pot of cranberries to see him lounging in the kitchen doorway, naked from the waist up, stroking his flamboyant mustache. Leon was like a tomcat, she thought, small but dangerous.

"I forgot to tell you last night," he drawled, "I'm bringing a friend to dinner, Patty Murphy. She boards with Mrs. Zabriskie. I told her you'd be glad to have company for your first American Thanksgiving." Somehow he made it a challenge.

"There's plenty," she said shortly.

"You grew up since Warsaw." His eyes trailed over her small curvaceous body. "Too bad you didn't wait for me, little sister," he drawled. "I'd give you plenty of babies."

Johanna's eyes flashed. "Mind your own business, Leon."

He ignored her. "I was surprised you married Michal," he said. "I thought you were always dying to get into Casimar's pants."

"Leon, I don't care if you are Michal's brother. I don't care how long you spent in a labor camp. I don't want you talking to me like that." She went into the bedroom with a cup of tea for Michal. It was high time her husband got up.

"I think I like this American Thanksgiving," Michal said appreciatively, reaching for the tea. "What a feast." He gazed around the kitchen and sniffed deeply.

"We'll have dinner in two hours," Johanna announced. "Leon's bringing some girl who boards with Mrs. Zabriskie."

"Leon has a girl?" Michal's face brightened.

"I doubt that he's thinking about marrying her," Johanna said drily, "though I wouldn't mind if he did." Then he would move out and leave Michal and her to privacy again.

They were ready to sit down to dinner when Leon's Patty appeared. Johanna decided she had not been a girl for at least ten years. Leon couldn't keep his hands off her. His arm about her waist and one hand reaching for her heavy breast, he stared at his sister-in-law, enjoying her discomfort.

After dinner Leon and Patty left the house. They returned hours later, slightly the worse for beer. Patty's color was high, her smile provocative. Her hair was disarranged and her shirtwaist rumpled. Leon cornered Michal in the kitchen and whispered in his ear. Soon Michal yawned elaborately and reached for Johanna's arm.

"Tomorrow's a work day." Michal tried to be casual. "Johanna and I go to bed early."

"You go ahead," Patty giggled, clinging to Leon, pressing her hips against his. Leon and she couldn't wait to get them out of the room, Johanna thought furiously.

Lying in bed with Michal, Johanna struggled to shut out the sounds that came from the parlor. Michal, bless him, fell asleep moments after he pulled the covers over them. Johanna buried her face in the pillow while the sounds of passion from the parlor came to her as clearly as though the four of them shared a bed.

She detested Leon's vulgarity, his boasting about his prowess with women. Her face flamed as she recalled what Leon had said to her this morning. "I thought you were always dying to get into Casimar's pants." She loved Casimar. It wasn't like Leon and his girls.

In the morning she stalled as long as possible before going out to the kitchen, recoiling from the prospect of finding Leon and Patty in bed together. Her eyes averted, she headed for the kitchen. Leon slept on his back, the covers drawn up to his waist, his hairy chest on display. Looking the worse for wear, Patty was struggling into her clothes.

"I have to be at work in twenty minutes," she told Johanna. "It's too late to go home and change." Her eyes were appraising for a moment. "If your man's anywhere as good as Leon, you should be happy."

"Would you like a cup of tea and some bread?" Johanna asked, fighting against an odd feeling of sickness.

"No time. Thanks for that Thanksgiving dinner," she said with unexpected politeness. "My old lady back in Dublin would never believe anybody would serve all that meat at one time."

Patty tiptoed out, closing the door to the hall with exaggerated care. In the kitchen Johanna stood at the sink and grappled with nausea again at the sight of food. This was the third morning in a row she had felt sick when she made lunch for Michal. Her period was over a week late, she suddenly realized.

A flurry of excitement replaced her queasiness. She stood still, transfixed by knowledge. Hela would say that it was too early to know for sure, but she was sure. She placed her slender hands across her still-flat belly in a gesture of maternal tenderness.

Hearing Michal stirring in the bedroom, Johanna poured a cup of tea to take to him before he emerged from beneath the warmth of the comforters. She would wait until Sunday when they were dressing to go to mass to tell her husband, Johanna decided. By then she would be sure.

Michal and she had breakfast while Leon snored in the parlor. Michal had not read the books on shipping that she had brought him from the library.

"I should have read yesterday instead of lying around doing nothing," he chastised himself.

"You have to rest sometimes," she told him, feeling a new closeness to her husband. He would be so happy when she told him about the baby.

Michal left the flat. She moved quietly about the kitchen and then the bedroom, doing her daily cleaning, knowing Leon would not wake. He slept every day until noon. When would he go out and get a job? When would he move out of their flat? She was outraged that he dared to bring his sluts into her home.

"I'm hungry." Leon's voice spun her around. She had not heard him come into the bedroom.

"I'll make your breakfast." She tried to remember this was Casimar and Michal's brother, Mama Raisa's son. But when he looked at her like this she wanted to slap his face.

"It can wait a few minutes, little sister." He reached to pull her against him with startling suddenness. One hand moved to her breast.

"Take your hands off me!" Her voice was like a whip. "Even Michal will throw you out if his pregnant wife asks him to."

Leon froze for an instant, then chuckled as he released her. "Michal doesn't know," he guessed.

"I'm hardly sure myself." Her voice was unsteady. "I meant to wait until Sunday to tell him." Her eyes stung with tears of rage. Why had she allowed herself to tell Leon before Michal?

"Wait till Sunday. I won't say anything. I can't wait to see you all puffed out." There was disconcerting passion in his eyes. "Little sister popping out with a baby."

She stalked away from him. He made her feel dirty.

Chapter 7

Michal's tenderness toward her when he learned about the baby filled her with warmth. She felt cherished and protected. And in the darkness of the night they made love with fresh abandon.

Only Leon's continued presence in the flat irritated her. She kept expecting him to come home and say he had found a job, that he was moving into an apartment of his own. Michal kept introducing him to pretty Polish girls, all of them smitten by his charismatic maleness. Michal was eager to see Leon married, but Johanna doubted that Leon would ever take on the responsibility of a wife.

She hated the way Leon's eyes followed her. She knew he would not touch her again, but it seemed obscene to her that he was so fascinated by her pregnancy. She heard him ask Michal if they still made love and her face flamed.

At Mrs. Zabriskie's insistence she went to the New York Infirmary for Women, founded by the Polish doctor

Maria Zakrzewksa. The doctors there taught her how she could best care for herself to insure a healthy baby.

Only now did Michal agree that Johanna and he become American citizens, since their child—who Michal was convinced would be a boy—would be one anyway. "But he will be also a Pole," Michal insisted.

At last Michal was encouraging Leon to come to work with him on the docks. Together they would save their money until they had enough to buy a small boat and go into business for themselves.

"Leon, we can make real money in shipping," Michal said earnestly. "This is a country full of opportunities."

"All right," Leon said indulgently on Michal's dozenth try. "I'll see this man you talk about at the docks. If he offers a decent wage I'll take the job."

"Leon, be pleasant to him," Michal cautioned. "Don't make him think you're doing him a favor. With immigrants coming into the country by the thousands every month he can find all the workers he needs."

"Michal, I'll get the job." He dismissed Michal's misgivings. "We'll save money and soon we'll have our shipping company."

He said nothing about moving to a place of his own. Nor did Michal expect him to, Johanna realized. The baby would sleep in their room and Leon would continue to occupy the bed in the parlor.

On a hot August midnight after much travail Johanna gave birth to a son, named Bernhard after Michal's father. Tears filled her eyes as she saw Michal's happiness.

"I'll work hard for him," Michal said humbly as he held his son in his arms. "He'll want for nothing. Nor shall you." His eyes were bright with love.

"Let me have the baby," the doctor said with sudden urgency.

"What's happening?" Michal's face reflected his own

anguish as they saw their newborn son all at once losing color. "Dr. Abramowiez, what's happening?"

"Quiet, man," the doctor ordered brusquely, snatching the infant from Michal's arms. "I have a life to save. You can pray," he added, working with the tiny limp form. Moments ago it had been a normal flailing newborn.

For three hours Dr. Abramowiez worked over tiny Bernhard, his face tense and anxious. "Should we send for the priest?" Michal asked once.

Johanna cried out in reproach. "He'll live," she vowed. "God will listen to our prayers. We'll never sin again as we have in the past," she told her husband. Her eyes bound Michal to a silent pact; he must never come to his wife again unwilling to make a child.

Together they watched for some sign that the baby would live. Already Dr. Abramowiez had told them that Johanna must not conceive again too soon. This birth had been difficult. She was small, the baby large. Not for at least two years should they risk another pregnancy.

Dawn was already pink in the sky when Dr. Abramowiez brought Bernhard to Johanna again. "Take your son to your breast," he said gently.

"He's all right?" Her face was incandescent as she reached for her son.

"In three days we'll know for sure, but I think your prayers have been answered."

With Bernhard tugging at a nipple Johanna lay back, still exhausted from the difficult delivery but caught up in the miracle of her firstborn.

Three weeks before Bernhard's birth Michal and Leon bought a cargo boat to ply the Hudson River. When he was scarcely a month old—and thriving—they already had acquired a respectable list of accounts. To Johanna's astonishment Leon relished selling and had a gift for it. He left to Michal all the details of planning and administration for their partnership. It was very successful; Leon's salesmanship was backed by Michal's excellent scheduling and service. Word was soon out that the Raisas delivered cargo on time and in good condition.

The first year of Bernie's life was one of the best in his father's. Michal had a wife, a son, a brother, a business—the day was finally here when he wore a white shirt and worked at a desk.

Prosperity arrived almost overnight. Within six months the profits were such that Michal talked about a second boat. Leon was a little reluctant, as it would mean less salary for a while, but he eventually conceded to Michal's judgment.

Before little Bernhard took his first steps, Michal and Leon owned two riverboats and employed half a dozen Polish immigrant workers. Michal read everything he could find about the shipping business. He loved the great ocean liners that steamed daily into New York Harbor and he absorbed every bit of gossip and news about the competition among the Cunard Line, the White Star and Inman.

Flush with cash, Leon spent his evenings enjoying Manhattan night life. In the 1890's the city was wide open, and nobody relished it more than Leon. He was a steady patron at the Haymarket, a combination of restaurant, variety show and dance hall, where willing females were in abundance.

On an uncommonly warm late September eve Johanna tried to soothe little year-old Bernie, who was struggling with a rash of new teeth in addition to the humidity. Michal was waiting for Leon to come home from his Saturday night socializing. Though Leon admittedly found no real need to seek out professionals, tonight he had decided to visit a house of prostitution reputedly favored by millionaires and politicians.

Michal longed to share with Leon, as he had earlier with Johanna, an intriguing tidbit that had come to his attention. His quick mind saw how to make a fortune, but what if he couldn't raise enough cash to do it? The project would require financing far beyond their means. How long before some other enterprising businessman saw it and moved ahead? He slammed a fist against his thigh in frustration. This was a shortcut to a gold mine if only he could raise the money.

He glanced up as the door opened and Leon sauntered into the flat. "At last! Leon, we have to talk."

"At last? Brother, I'm early tonight. I found out something," he said with an air of profundity, but his grin was rakish. "In a whorehouse in New York the women work by the clock. You want to stay a whole night and sample special treats it can cost as much as fifty or a hundred dollars. That kind of money I don't waste on any woman."

"Leon, I know how we could be rich in six months," Michal said quietly. "I mean really rich."

"How rich?" Leon dropped onto his bed and leaned toward Michal.

"Enough to buy a brownstone house on the East Side and to invest in the railroads."

"How do we do it?"

Michal sighed. "We need a man who is willing to invest a fortune to make an even bigger one."

"So we find this rich man." Leon was totally serious now. "What do we do with his money?"

"We buy an ocean liner." Michal waited while Leon whistled at the scope of the idea. Then he continued, "The Fortuna Line fleet is up for sale. Those ships carry mail subsidies from the British Exchequer. It means," Michal explained, "that we carry the mail and get paid so well to do it that the British government is subsidizing us."

"Why is the fleet on the block?" Leon asked.

"Because the owner died and his heirs aren't interested. It's right there in *The New York Times*. Someone else will figure it out, and we need to buy before the price is bid up. On one page I read that the ships were for sale. Two pages later I saw a few lines about the mail subsidy. Other people read the papers too. Leon, we could make a fortune with a liner and a mail subsidy. We could build our own ships—luxury liners for the tourist trade. You know how people are flocking to Europe from America. We'd build a ship finer than anything else on the seas." Michal's face lit up as he imagined the future for the Raisa brothers—the three of them, he thought. Some of the money would go to Casimar for the church in Poland.

"Where on earth do you expect me to find somebody with that kind of money?" Leon blustered, but Michal knew his brother's mind was racing, greedy for what Michal visualized.

"You know all kinds of people," Michal said mildly. "You go to places I never go—like that fancy whorehouse and the casinos." He knew that Leon—young, handsome, brash—was popular, always the center of a group. "Haven't you met anyone there?"

"Let me talk to some men I've seen at the casino." Leon grinned. "I don't gamble much. How can I on what you let me spend? But tomorrow night I'll visit Frank Farrell's place." Michal looked blank and Leon chuckled. "Michal, you work in this city without knowing what goes on. In New York there are three places where the rich go to gamble. Daly's is a big fancy house on Twenty-ninth Street near Fifth. Frank Farrell's place is near the Waldorf Hotel on Thirty-third Street. The third one is Frank Canfield's. I don't think I could get inside there. That's where the Vanderbilts and the Whitneys go to throw away their money. I can bluff my way into Farrell's, where the sporting crowd goes, even Diamond Jim Brady."

"Leon, we have to move fast," Michal said urgently. "Those ships will be priced to sell—and sell they will."

"Tomorrow night," Leon repeated, enjoying the importance of his role in this scheme. "I'll need some expense money. Lots of expense money. Think of it as an investment."

The next evening Michal and Johanna sat in the kitchen drinking tea way past their normal bedtime. They were waiting for Leon.

"Michal, you should go to sleep," Johanna said. "You have to be up at five."

"This is important," Michal reminded her. He tried to be calm.

"Do you think that important men with a lot of money will listen to Leon?"

"They'll listen. I remember Papa talking about Leon when he was no more than eleven. He said Leon could charm a man out of his last *groszy*, and I believe it."

They both started at a sound at the door. His derby set at a jaunty angle, Leon sauntered into the flat. Michal was already on his feet and moving into the parlor.

"Damn cold tonight for the first of October," Leon complained. "Get some beer to warm me up," he called to Johanna, stalling in order to enjoy their air of expectancy.

"You have any luck?" Michal demanded, in no mood tonight for Leon's games.

"I saw them," Leon acknowledged. "We talked."

"What did they say? Leon, have a heart. Are they interested?"

"I said I didn't want to bother them with business after hours. I said my brother has a good idea and needs backing. I asked for an appointment tomorrow. I told them we could make a fortune fast, before somebody else grabbed it.''

"Why didn't you tell them?" Michal demanded.

"Because you can do that part better than me," Leon said frankly. "You tell me and I understand—but for me to make them understand—" Leon spread his hands in a gesture of futility. "Still, they're interested. They got money. They're big men with connections to Tammany." Michal frowned. He had only distaste for the graft and corruption that enveloped the city. "They want to talk to you tomorrow," Leon wound up triumphantly.

Michal sat still, trying to assimilate the news. This time tomorrow he might be on his way to wealth at last. "How can I persuade them? Rich Americans will never listen to me," he groaned.

"Explain it to them the way you did to me." Johanna spoke with quiet confidence that warmed him. "If I know what you're talking about, surely these rich important businessmen will understand."

Michal fought off panic. Leon and he were young— Leon twenty-nine and he three years younger. Worse, they were immigrants whose speech still carried the accents of their native country. And he, Michal Raisa, wanted a fortune to buy an ocean liner. "What time should we be there?"

Michal remembered how much was at stake when he walked into the elegant gambling casino with Leon. He listened with a fixed smile when Leon told him that a famous architect named Stanford White had recently remodeled the casino at a cost of half a million dollars. He must learn not to flinch at the mention of so much money. Who in Poland except a titled landowner ever had so much money?

They walked through a massive Italian Renaissance bronze door at the rear of the entrance hall into the quiet refinement of the casino. Waiters circulated with trays of wines and liquors. At midnight, Leon told Michal—though they would be long gone before then—a fancy buffet supper would be served.

"Last night a man won two hundred thousand dollars at the roulette table," Leon remarked. "Money flows like water here."

"Leon," an expansive voice called out, "we've been waiting for you."

Leon smiled and held out his hand. "Mr. Alsop, Mr. Grady, Mr. Sudbury. Good evening."

Michal turned to see a trio of expensively garbed men—diamond stickpin, ruby ring, gold cuff links. All in their early fifties, all exuded an aura of money.

Michal politely acknowledged the introductions, noting that indeed his brother had ingratiated himself with their prospective business associates. At Alsop's word to an attendant they were ushered into a private room, supplied with the finest of cigars and left to their discussion.

Immediately Michal realized that while they liked Leon, they were not convinced that the Raisa brothers had a deal worthy of their attention. Michal sensed that it would be wise to present their proposition in a simple and concise fashion. He had anticipated their questions and was prepared with answers. His enthusiasm grew as he felt their interest soaring.

"It's a matter of time before some other group realizes the value of the ships and the subsidy. It requires fast action."

"What line is putting up these ships for sale?" Sudbury asked with studied casualness.

"That is something I can't say unless you're sure you

want to do business," Michal said politely. His audience chuckled.

"Young man, we're already in business," Alsop said after a fleeting eye consultation with his companions. "Have your lawyer call on me tomorrow. We can't afford to waste time."

Michal couldn't wait to get home and tell Johanna their good news. He remembered that the son of the Polish butcher on Second Avenue was a lawyer from Columbia. He would represent them.

Leon insisted on stopping at a neighborhood saloon for a beer. "Michal, we gotta celebrate." He slapped Michal on the shoulder. "I knew you'd make them come up with the money." His eyes narrowed in reluctant admiration. "Mama always said you were the smart one in the family. I didn't like it," he admitted, "but I knew she was right."

The business was successful almost from the start. Before the year was out Michal insisted they move from the flat on East Seventh to Central Park West. "We need to entertain, Johanna, to build a social life, and we can't do it here. It will help the business—and a person needs a few friends anyway." He told her to hire servants and go shopping—clothes, furnishings, a carriage—so they could live up to their new address.

The yellow-brick Dakota with its gables, dormers, balconies and turrets looked to Johanna like a European castle. Johanna began to understand the extent to which their finances had expanded. Michal was so quiet and earnest that she was inclined to underestimate the success of the company of which he was now the head.

Michal announced on the seventh anniversary of their wedding that he was transferring a startlingly large sum to a bank in Warsaw to be dispensed as Casimar saw fit.

Johanna realized that Michal considered his younger brother a partner in the business, to share with Leon and himself.

She had been glad to move into the large apartment overlooking Central Park; it seemed palatial in comparison to the flat on East Seventh. It was a relief, too, that now Leon had an apartment of his own, though she would have been more pleased if he had not moved into their building.

Leon's womanizing upset her, though Michal regarded him with indulgence. She knew that Leon enjoyed flaunting his women before her. He was constantly in pursuit of showgirls and actresses. He talked amorously about Lillian Russell, who was seen bicycling in Central Park in a white serge costume with leg-of-mutton sleeves. Her bicycle, Leon reported with relish, was entirely gold-plated and had mother-of-pearl handlebars monogrammed in diamonds and emeralds.

Michal spent long hours at his office, though he always made time to play with Bernie. He encouraged Johanna to have parties. It was Leon who made her understand that this was useful to the business. Restless now that servants cared for the apartment, Johanna was pleased to spend her efforts on entertaining.

Much shopping and a few mistakes had taught her how to dress—with good advice from saleswomen and assiduous attention to the fashion press. She had had the apartment redecorated by Elsie De Wolfe, secretly shocked at the cost, though Michal insisted they could afford it. Johanna began to give weekly dinner parties. They were a lot of work, but the pace kept her from thinking about Warsaw and Casimar.

Michal seemed obsessed by the need to enlarge the business. He was talking now about building a ship, though his partners had earlier rejected the notion. He envisioned a passenger liner that would surpass anything crossing the Atlantic, that would attract every prospective traveler to

Europe. He never spoke of Poland. Johanna realized with a shock that her husband was becoming a stranger to her.

Leon had a disconcerting habit of dropping in for dinner once or twice a week, ostensibly to play with his nephew, but Johanna knew he had his eye on her. Despite the stream of women through his apartment, Leon wanted his brother's wife.

As much as ever Johanna clung to the church. It seemed a link to Poland and to Casimar. Occasionally she went downtown to visit with Mrs. Zabriskie. Despite Bernie, the church and her heavy schedule of entertaining Johanna was lonely.

Michal and Leon were emotionally drawn into the fighting in Cuba. Here were the Cuban insurgents struggling for independence, as they wished Poland would struggle for its independence from Russia. They read every news story, contributed to every relief fund. When the American battleship *Maine* was blown up, Leon declared he would fight on the side of the rebels.

Troubles in the company suddenly demanded the attention of both Michal and Leon. Johanna was startled when he came home on a late spring afternoon hours before he was expected. He looked tired and drained of energy.

"Michal, something's happened—"

He forced a smile. "You look beautiful, Johanna. Go on to whatever party you were bound for." Michal was proud that she was always dressed beautifully.

"I was only going shopping." She dropped into a chair. "I can go tomorrow."

"Where's Bernie?" He sat across from her.

"Nurse took him to the park. They'll be home in an hour. Michal, would you like a glass of wine?" It disturbed her to see him looking so dejected—so beaten, she thought involuntarily.

"Vodka," he said with an unexpected smile. Vodka was a drink from home, though not fashionable in their new circle.

"I'll get it for you." She poured a drink. "Michal, what's happened? I have a right to know."

"We're in serious trouble. The British government is taking away our subsidy."

"Can they do that?"

"They are doing it," Michal said grimly. "I've called an emergency meeting of the board for tonight, here at the apartment. Without that subsidy we operate at a loss."

"Michal, why are they doing that?"

"Because we're building a new ship that will be a challenge to everything the British have on the waters. Word has spread about the *Johanna*."

"Michal, you didn't tell me it was to be named for me." Her voice dropped to a whisper. Of late she sometimes felt that Michal forgot that he had a wife. He usually came home from the office distracted by business problems or so exhausted he fell asleep in his chair after dinner. He never reached for her in bed, though the two years Dr. Abramowiez had stipulated were long past. Sometimes she asked herself if Michal no longer loved her.

"Who else would I name my ship for," he asked gently, "but for my wife? But now I'm not sure we'll be able to finish it. Johanna—" His voice dropped to an agitated whisper. "How can I tell you this? We may lose everything."

Chapter 8

In the kitchen Johanna prepared coffee for the dreary group in Michal's study. The servants had retired for the night. She was oddly pleased to be needed, even for so minor a task.

She poured coffee into the delicate white and gold Haviland china cups that had so delighted her when she bought them last month. Now she shuddered at her extravagance. Michal talked about their losing everything. Not true; they had each other and they had Bernie. They were young; they would manage.

Bracing the heavy silver tray in her hands, she went into the room where the Raisa Line investors slumped. Leon sprawled on his spine, feet extended before him, eyes half-shut and focused on Michal. The men had been closeted in this room for three hours.

"It was not a mistake to take on building a ship," Michal said stubbornly. "The world is entering a new era of travel. We were preparing to accept the challenge. The mistake was in not realizing that we could not operate

84

under the American flag." Michal sighed. "I should have checked. No ship not built in an American shipyard can fly the American flag."

"Hell, Michal, you couldn't know everything," Bill Grady, one of their earliest investors, said calmly, "but we can't compete with the other British lines without that mail subsidy. We've got two ships—almost two ships," he conceded with a smile. The second, a fast and costly vessel, was within two months of completion. "We've got to find a way to use them."

"We need to be able to fly the American flag," Michal said tautly. "I've studied this from every angle. We have to register our ships or we can't sail them."

"Why don't you go to Washington?" Johanna asked. Suddenly she felt herself the focus of every pair of eyes in the room. "This is a democracy. Michal, you've told me how this country has fallen behind in shipping. Surely the American government wishes to see the country's prestige on the high seas restored. You gentlemen can help do that." Her eyes moved about the room.

"Hear, hear," Grady called out.

"Just exactly what are you proposing, Mrs. Raisa?" Alsop asked with an indulgent smile.

"I'm proposing that a committee from the company go to Washington and talk to members of Congress." Color filled her face. "This is a democracy. Laws are often changed when it proves necessary. It's not in anyone's interest to put us out of business. We can try, anyway."

All at once every man in the room—except for Leon, who watched and listened with amusement—seemed to have something to say. The argument continued with increasing heat. Johanna went out for more coffee and a cup for herself. When she returned, she met a sea of smiles.

"We're taking your advice, Mrs. Raisa," Grady said warmly. "We're asking you and Michal to go to Washington together. With your charm and wit I'm sure Congress can't refuse you.''

Three days later Johanna, Michal, Bernie and his nurse were en route to Washington. Johanna delighted in Bernie's excitement about traveling on a train, his flow of questions. She was also conscious of Michal's pride in the admiring glances she garnered from male passengers. Now she was aware of how little she had seen of Michal in private in the past two years.

Finally they arrived in Washington.

With one of Bernie's small hands in hers while Melissa, his nurse, held the other, Johanna walked with a sense of adventure behind Michal and the porters coping with their luggage. She found the huge colonnaded waiting room of the white granite Union Station much more elegant than Grand Central.

With their luggage stowed away atop the hansom cab they traveled toward the fashionable Willard Hotel, where Michal had reserved a suite for himself and Johanna and another for Bernie and Melissa. Always organized, Michal had already arranged appointments for Johanna and himself with important congressmen.

While they dressed for their dinner engagement with a senator from New York, Michal confessed to the doubts that plagued at him.

''Michal, you'll make them see that it's important to the country to have the ships registered here. Think of the taxes we pay,'' she said confidently. ''Congress can change the law or put through a special bill. You've told me yourself it often happens.''

Soon Michal and she would be citizens of the United States. Bernie was a citizen by birth.

''It would have been wiser to send Leon,'' Michal said, full of the misgivings she had sensed in him ever since they agreed to make the trip. ''Leon is so—so glib.''

"Leon would have been a bad choice," Johanna insisted. "People trust you, Michal. You're smarter, too. The board was right to send you."

"Send us," Michal said, his eyes warm and admiring as they swept over her new Worth gown. "If we succeed you'll be equally responsible. You're quite a woman, Mrs. Raisa."

"I try to keep up with my husband," she laughed, relishing the compliment.

The next four days were hectic with meetings, luncheons, dinners, though Johanna contrived intervals of sightseeing with Bernie. Johanna was intrigued by this inside glimpse of the workings of the nation. She sat in the gallery of the House of Representatives listening to the debate on the floor. Tears stung her eyes; when Michal next wrote Casimar, he must tell him about this visit. Someday Poland would be a democracy, when it was governed by Poles.

As prearranged, Johanna sat in on all the meetings. Michal encouraged her to join the discussions. Tonight at their final meeting in the representative's elegant townhouse she listened carefully as the conversation continued well past midnight, sipping at the Dom Perignon lavishly supplied by their host.

Now she intervened on instinct to back up the senator from New York when he insisted that the company make some tax concessions if Congress adjusted this rule on its behalf.

"Michal, surely the board will go along with a reasonable assessment," Johanna said crisply, in no way giving away her conviction that at this point Michal and the board would accept any compromise that brought the ships under American registry.

The senator further asked that the new ship be readied for refitting as a troop ship before it was launched, as at this point the United States was mentally gearing itself to a long war with Spain over Cuba. He further suggested that any shipbuilding in the United States would be encouraged.

"To change the specs at this late date would be a tremendous expense." Michal appeared quite shocked at this stipulation.

"Michal, the board will go along if you agree," she said urgently, knowing how Michal longed to see the company set up its own shipyard. If he rescued the company in this crisis, he could demand it. "Settle the terms right now. Senator Cartwright's committee—" she turned to drown him in a dazzling smile—"can go ahead to put through the rule and then bring it up in the House."

Back in their suite at the Willard Michal was jubilant. He ordered that a bottle of champagne be brought up to them immediately.

"Johanna, I couldn't have done it without you." His face glowed with success. "You knew what building a shipyard means to me."

"The board can't turn you down now." She too felt stimulated by success. Michal had pointed out that with the shipbuilding the company would expand greatly. There would be even more money to send to Warsaw—and this had become a compulsion with Michal, as though to assuage his unhappiness that he was not there to help Poland physically. Michal considered that it would help Casimar's rise in the church to be responsible for bringing in so much money. Someday he might even be a cardinal.

"It's important to go into shipbuilding." Michal took off his jacket and draped it across the back of a chair. "With all the new technological advances coming through the owners will soon be at the mercy of the shipbuilders. That's why we must be in a position to build exactly what we want."

"It's been a long day." All at once Johanna was

startled by the ardor she saw in Michal's eyes. She had not seen that look for a long time. The champagne, she told herself. "I think I'll prepare for bed." She faked a yawn.

"Before our champagne arrives?" he said reproachfully.

"I'm tired and I want to be up early tomorrow morning to have breakfast with Bernie. It's almost one."

"We'll both have breakfast with Bernie," Michal decided, but Johanna had already moved into the bedroom.

With cold hands, too conscious of his look of ardor, she changed into one of the severely plain white silk nightgowns made by the nuns of an upstate convent. As a private penance she never showed herself to Michal in their bedroom except in the most modest attire.

Settling herself under the covers, Johanna heard Michal in conversation with the waiter. She had never known Michal to go past one or two drinks. Tonight he had drunk champagne like mineral water.

That was why he had looked at her that way. It was the champagne. She had thought that once Bernie was two, Michal would come back to her arms, but he would lie beside her without reaching a hand out in the night.

She lay immobile, eyes closed, as her husband came into the room. The lamplight from the parlor lent a sliver of illumination to the bedroom.

"Johanna?" His voice was low and husky. "Johanna—" He sat on the bed and dropped a hand on her shoulder.

"Hmm?" She forced an apparently sleepy response.

"Have a glass of champagne with me to celebrate our victory."

"Haven't you had enough tonight?" She opened her eyes reluctantly and saw the two glasses on the bedside table.

"I can go to confession in good conscience," he said

with an effort at humor. "I'm not drunk." He brought her hand to his mouth. "At least not yet."

"If I have a glass of champagne, will you go to bed then?" She was aroused just because Michal sat at the edge of her bed and gazed down at her with desire.

"I promise." She sat up and he gave her a glass. "To my beautiful wife," he murmured, "who charmed the Congress blind." His eyes lingered hotly on her. "Who dazzles her husband as well."

Acutely conscious of Michal's nearness, Johanna sipped at the champagne, longing to be in his arms. So many nights she had felt this way, though normally she refused to acknowledge it.

"You don't want that champagne." He took the glass from her, put it down and started undressing. Johanna clung to the edge of the bed. It had been so long since Michal came to her. Heat washed over her. How had she waited so long?

Michal got up and put out the light before he finished undressing. In the darkness she heard one shoe drop to the floor, then the other. A moment later he slid beneath the covers and touched her cold foot with one of his.

"You're cold," he said.

"A little." He was completely naked.

"I was very proud of you at all these meetings," he murmured, moving against her. He thrust one leg across her thigh and reached under the covers to fondle her breasts.

"Michal, do you want another child?"

"I want my wife," he said impatiently. "You're the only woman I've ever wanted in my life."

"We made a promise when Bernie hovered between life and death."

"Johanna, don't talk to me as though I were a baby-making machine. I want to make love to my wife."

"You're drunk." Michal had never talked to her this way.

"No, my love, passionate. It's not wrong to want my wife. No priest can convince me of that." His mouth was impatient on hers, his tongue prodding its way between her teeth.

She lay immobile while his hands thrust the white silk nightgown high above her hips and remained to caress the velvet softness of her. She felt his passion rising between her thighs.

"Johanna—" His voice was uneven. "I know you're a passionate woman. Don't close me out tonight."

"You are drunk."

"No, a man who's drunk is only half a man." He reached for her hand and brought it to him. "Am I half a man?"

"No—"

He found the hooks at the throat of her nightgown and released them. With involuntary help from her he pulled the nightgown over her head and thrust it beside them. His mouth sought one taut nipple while a hand burrowed between her thighs.

It was almost as though she had never been with him, almost as though she had never borne a child. But then he was within her and they moved together with frightening and exhilarating abandon. Their climax shook her to the core.

They lay motionless now, Michal's perspiring face against her own, his body seemingly limp and spent. Then she felt a faint stirring within her again.

"No," she said, although already her own body was responding again, "I'm not some woman you've bought in a brothel!"

She felt him tense in shock. Then he pulled away

from her. "I'm sorry," he said tersely. "I won't bother you again. I won't ever bother *my wife* again."

She lay with her eyes shut, hearing him move out into the parlor and close the door between the rooms. Her face was hot, but beneath the covers her body was cold. Had she really driven him away for good? She wanted another baby. Besides, tonight Michal had aroused her as never before.

Unable to sleep, she tried to comprehend her feelings for her husband. She felt a traitor to her church. Still, she remembered that living on East Seventh Street she had heard other wives talk about desiring their husbands. Young American wives often said there were things the priests can't be expected to understand. They went to confession and told what they believed the priest should hear, reserving what they thought was not for his ears.

When they were back in New York she would go downtown and visit with Mrs. Zabriskie, who had her own special understanding about the church. Could it be that Michal was right and she was wrong? It was a disturbing question and it kept her awake until dawn.

She knew that Michal too was restless. Through the closed door between bedroom and parlor she could hear him tossing about on the sofa in the night stillness.

When Johanna awoke in the morning, Michal had dressed and left their suite. It was well past the time she had planned to arise and she rushed into her clothes.

Knocking on the door of the next suite, where Bernie was staying with Melissa, she heard Michal's voice and Bernie laughing. Michal had remembered to have breakfast with their son.

She walked into the parlor, where a breakfast table had been set. The nurse was in the small bedroom packing for the return to New York.

"You slept late, Mama." Bernie held out his arms to her.

"Coffee, Johanna?" Michal asked. A cup and saucer sat at one side of the table. His eyes managed to avoid hers.

"Please." She kissed Bernie and sat in the chair that Michal pulled up to the table for her.

"I've already spoken to Senator Cartwright this morning," he reported. He pretended to have forgotten last night's bitter scene. "He's had an early breakfast meeting with his committee. He's confident we'll have no trouble."

"The board will be so pleased." She spoke to Michal but focused her attention on Bernie.

Remembering last night, she grappled with feelings that belonged in the bedroom. After all these years of marriage—after having borne a child—she at last felt totally a woman. Never had she been so aroused. She loved Michal and passion with love could not be wrong. Still, the priest had always told them that a man and woman came together in marriage solely for the sake of children.

Chapter 9

Johanna tried to conceal her dismay when Michal moved into a guest room in their apartment overlooking Central Park. Pride kept her from reproaching him, but she wished she could recall the ugly words she had thrown at him that final night in their bedroom at the Willard Hotel.

She took long walks through the park, which was growing lovely with the approach of summer. Fighting to come to terms with her religion, she went downtown to East Seventh Street to visit with Mrs. Zabriskie, but could not bring herself to discuss such intimate matters. All at once it seemed inconceivable that it was wrong to share such ecstasy with her husband. She found that she wished to share it again and again.

Michal was deeply involved in business; he visited Bernie early each morning and left the house until late in the evening. He was polite, solicitous and withdrawn with Johanna in private. On Sundays, when he accompanied Bernie and her to church, and when they had dinner guests or attended dinner parties at the homes of his associates, he played the warm and loving husband.

There was no morning sickness to alert Johanna to a new pregnancy. A consultation with the calendar on another matter startled her; she was three weeks late. The realization filled her with joy; she longed for a second child, a sister for Bernie. Surely Michal would be pleased. Johanna sat and stared at the June page. It must be true. Her fingers trembled when they touched her cheeks. It *must* be true.

Since the memorable night in Washington he had made no effort to come to her. Night after night she lay alone, yearning for him. Surely this news would bring about a reconciliation.

It would be hours before Michal came home. Johanna roamed restlessly about the apartment. At last she decided to go shopping downtown. That would help pass the hours. There was no way of knowing when Michal would come home tonight.

At Lord & Taylor she bought a tea gown with Watteau pleats in Michal's favorite shade of blue. Then in a fit of recklessness she picked out half a dozen lacy hand-sewn nightgowns and negligees in delicate silk. Surely Michal could not resist these. She returned to the apartment in a hansom cab and a mood of warm expectancy. Michal would be so happy that he was to be a father once more—they would both be much happier now.

Emerging from the hansom cab, she spied Leon crossing the sidewalk to their building. The woman on his arm was beautiful and flamboyant—another of Leon's actress friends, Johanna guessed. How outrageous of him to bring these women into his apartment in broad daylight.

"Johanna," he called out buoyantly as he spied her. "Buying out the shops again, I see."

"Hardly," she said coolly, though her smile for his

companion—whom he made no effort to introduce—was pleasant. Leon irritated her with his raillery; he seemed intent on making her feel an idle young society matron.

Leon and his companion got off the elevator at the fourth floor and Johanna continued alone to the top floor. Her face lit up when she heard Bernie's voice inside the apartment. Good—Melissa had brought him back from the park early. Johanna could play with him a little longer than usual before Melissa gave him his supper and put him to bed.

Tonight, as they were not entertaining and Michal would not be home for dinner, she dined at a small table by a parlor window with a view of the park, conscious of her loneliness. Soon she would be busy preparing for this new baby—a little girl, she promised herself.

After dinner she retired to her bedroom to change into a set of her new nightclothes. Soon Melissa and Molly, the cook, would head for their own rooms and the other servants would go home. Then she would go out to the parlor and read until Michal came home.

Pleased but self-conscious in her delicate lace-trimmed negligee, Johanna curled up in a blue velvet Queen Anne wing chair and tried to concentrate on the short stories of Stephen Crane, which everybody was talking about. She read with one ear trained on the door to hear when Michal came home.

He was not home at ten. Johanna went out to the kitchen to make a pot of coffee. She moved quietly so as not to disturb Molly, who slept behind the kitchen. Molly considered her presence there something of an affront, and would insist on making the coffee herself.

Johanna was already stifling yawns when she heard a key in the door. Noticing the lights in the parlor, Michal peeked into the room.

"I have coffee on the stove." She smiled tentatively. "Would you like something to eat with it?"

"I had dinner with Bill. We had to go over cost estimates again," he said tiredly and sank into a chair.

"I'll bring the coffee."

Johanna placed the coffee tray on a small table convenient for Michal, who loathed balancing a cup and saucer on his knee. Then she returned to her chair and waited for him to take a sip, sensing Michal's curiosity. He plainly wondered why she was up and in the parlor at this hour of the night.

"I was reading Stephan Crane." She held up the slim volume. "He writes wonderful short stories."

Michal smiled wryly. "I don't have much time for reading these days." Nor for his family, Johanna thought.

"Michal, I have news." All at once she was stammering, remembering the night responsible for what she was about to tell him. "I'm pregnant."

She was appalled by the dismay that swept over his face. "You want this baby?" he asked urgently.

"Of course I want it. Don't you?"

"Johanna, of course." The words were wrenched from him. "But you must take good care of yourself. We'll cut out those blasted dinner parties, and you must see a good doctor immediately."

"I'll call Dr. Abramowiez in a few weeks," she said. "We'll just have the dinner at the end of the month; the invitations are already out."

"Call him right away," Michal insisted. "And cancel the dinner party at the end of the month too."

"Michal, I'm only in my second month. I can keep a full schedule for ages." In truth she enjoyed their dinner parties. The wives of Michal's partners were her only women friends since she left East Seventh Street.

"You must rest," he said. "It's important that you don't get overtired."

"Michal, having a baby is a normal process, and it's not my first. With a second a woman is always more relaxed. Tell me what's happening with the shipyard," she urged. "You tell me so little these days."

Finally Michal got up and approached Johanna's chair. Here he comes, she thought exultantly. Then her heart sank; he stooped and kissed her brow. "Good night, my dear. Sleep well."

Johanna threw caution to the winds. She put her arms around Michal's neck and when he stood up he had to take her with him. She did not let go; she kissed him, thrusting her tongue forth, rubbing her loins on his, her hands on his neck and in his hair.

"Johannusya—"

"Michal, Michal, I'm so tired of sleeping alone. Come to bed now. Come on, my dear." She took his earlobe in her teeth.

He pulled his head away. "I said never again, you know. Do you think I'm not a man of my word?"

"Michal, I apologize for my behavior and I release you from your vow. I have been sorry I said it from the moment the words were out. I am even sorrier that I didn't say so at once. Now, will you please come to bed?" She tugged at his belt and slid her hands into his waistband.

"Don't do that, woman, my pants will fall down." Since she persisted, he had to pick her up and kiss her to get her to stop. It seemed then that the only sensible thing to do was carry her up to bed. Later, tugging at a peach silk strap, he murmured, "I wondered if I was in for a seduction when I saw this. Very fetching, my love, and thank you for a wonderful evening."

* * *

Michal found sleep elusive. He had never forgotten Johanna's long and difficult first labor and his terror when Ladislas Abramowiez said he must not make his wife pregnant for at least two years. How could he go on living without Johanna? He groaned and punched his pillow.

Even after two years he was afraid. Only in Washington, full of champagne, had he dared to make love. Afterward he'd told himself one night was hardly likely to make her pregnant. He thrashed under the blankets when he remembered how long they had tried before she conceived Bernie.

Though the night was pleasantly cool, Michal was perspiring as he gazed into the darkness. What would he do if anything happened to Johanna?

He winced at the thought of the night when this second child had been conceived. Johanna thought he was drunk, that he was taking her like some slut in a brothel. Didn't she know he had loved her since she was twelve? He had been staying away from his wife because he was afraid of losing her.

In the ensuing weeks Michal clearly demonstrated that he was eager for a second child. He phoned her at least twice a day and he made a point of not missing dinner more than one or two nights a week.

Michal slept in her bed now, but he did not approach her as often as she would have liked, and he was curiously restrained, even tentative. She loved the new gentleness he showed her, but sometimes she yearned for the bull-like thrusting passion he used to show.

Johanna was deeply involved in Polish-American activities. With Michal's ardent approval she contributed to the building fund of a social club for immigrants, helped establish a school. In Warsaw the Raisa brothers and she had had to struggle for education; now it was her duty to ease that struggle for other young Poles.

She talked with Mrs. Zabriskie, the priest and the immigrant women she knew, concerned about the life of her countrywomen in America. Peasant women sewed in the sweatshops of the Lower East Side; they scrubbed the floors of offices and restaurants, washed dishes—and then came home to shoulder all the work there too.

By thirty they were old women, and their daughters could expect little better. They had been brought up to see in themselves the image of the Mother of God, tireless and uncomplaining, and they strove all their lives to achieve the ideal. They were the backbone of the community, and if Johanna could not fight for Poland, then she would help these tough, stolid women improve their lives.

She had to battle Michal over her habit of spending hours each day with Polish fund-raising committees or donating services such as English lessons and neighborhood tours.

"Think of the baby when you run around the city in this cold weather," he reproached her as winter descended on New York. "Suppose you fell on the ice? You could lose the baby."

"After this month I'll stop the tours and make them come here for lessons," she promised, wistful at the prospect. She liked getting out, and she gloried in Casimar's letters, which praised the work to the skies.

"When the baby is born we'll talk about building a house on Fifth Avenue," Michal said. Business was better all the time and the board of directors had given Michal carte blanche for building the shipyard.

"Michal, that's wonderful," she smiled. Leon would not always be underfoot—these days she saw more of Leon than of Michal, as Leon had developed a habit of dropping in unannounced for dinner. Molly adored him; she never complained at this unexpected guest.

"Start thinking about your dream house," he told her. He looked at her with such concern that she ached to take him in her arms and soothe him. Michal was increasingly frightened of her approaching delivery. "Anything you like," he said, "no matter what it costs."

Six weeks before the baby was due Michal came home to announce unhappily that it was necessary for him to go to London on business. "I'll be back in New York in less than three weeks," he said contritely. "Leon will stay here so there's a man in the house."

"It's not necessary," Johanna said, trying to conceal her distaste, "Melissa and Molly sleep in. Besides, nothing will happen before you get home."

"I'm writing Casimar," Michal told her. "With any luck at all he'll be able to come to London for a day or two. I don't dare go to Warsaw, even after all these years."

"Do you suppose he will?" Her heart began to pound. Casimar never seemed totally removed from their lives.

Michal grinned unexpectedly. "If the point of the trip is to accept a hefty donation for the church, I think he can arrange it. Even to be with Casimar for a day or two would seem like a miracle."

"I suppose you could never persuade him to come to America," Johanna said. She felt her face grow hot. How was it that after all these years she had the old feelings for Casimar? She was Michal's wife for ten years, a mother and pregnant again.

"No, Casimar will live and die in Poland." The look in his eyes told Johanna that he was remembering the days when the four of them fought for Poland. "But Leon must stay with you. I'll rest better that way."

Three days later Michal was bound for Liverpool on one of the company's own ships. She knew the pride he felt in this return trip and tried to conceal her irritation about Leon's visit. It was only for three weeks, though, and he would be at the office all day and with his women in the evening.

Leon made a point of coming for dinner every night, talking to her about the play he was seeing that evening or the racy supper parties attended by such celebrities as Diamond Jim Brady and Stanford White. The talk was casual, but his eyes dwelt too often on her breasts.

A few nights before Michal was to return she awoke with a start to realize her bedroom door was open. "Who's there?" she cried, alarmed.

"It's all right," Leon replied. "I just came home from a supper party and I thought I heard a sound in here. I was worried about you."

"I'm all right, Leon," she said brusquely. "Good night."

"What's the matter, little sister?" he drawled. She realized he'd been drinking. "You miss Michal in your bed?"

"Leon, you're drunk. Go away." She stiffened under the covers, trying awkwardly to pull herself higher against the pillows. This late in pregnancy it was difficult to find a comfortable position.

"I'll go in a minute," he promised. He sauntered over to stand beside the bed. "How's the little fella doing?" He dropped a hand on the vast bulge of her belly.

"Leon—" She strained for patience. "Please leave me alone."

"I'm the little fella's uncle," he reminded her, his hand moving from her belly to her swollen breasts.

"Leon, get out of here," she shrilled.

"Even when you're pushing out like that you make

me hot." He hiccuped. "All the Raisa boys were hot for you."

"I told you never to talk to me like that." All at once she froze and clutched at her abdomen. Oh, no, not now. Not when Michal was still on the ship bound for home. Not alone with Leon.

"What's the matter?" Leon seemed both alarmed and oddly excited.

"Go wake Melissa," she said after a moment, when the contraction subsided. Now she knew what woke her up—her water breaking. The bed was soaked. "Call her right now."

"The baby's coming?" Leon stared fascinated at her.

"Yes, it's coming. Now go call Melissa."

"It'll be a long time yet—" He took her hand.

"Not this one," she gasped. The pains were coming one on top of another. "Call Melissa. She knows how to reach Dr. Abramowiez."

Sobered by the emergency, Leon hurried off to call Melissa, who stepped into the bedroom to confer with Johanna. Then she hurried off to phone the doctor, blessing Alexander Graham Bell for having invented such a wonderful contraption. Leon hovered in the doorway.

"What about Molly?" he asked. "Oughtn't we wake her?"

"What for? Nothing she can do." She clenched her teeth. She didn't want to waken Bernie.

"Dr. Abramowiez will be here soon," Melissa said breathlessly. "He said you weren't to worry. The baby won't be here for hours."

"This time he's wrong." Johanna braced herself for the next contraction. "This one is in a hurry."

"What can I do?" Leon paced and paced, fingering his mustache. He no longer waxed it into handlebars, but it grew down luxuriantly from the corners of his mouth nearly to his jawline.

"Stay with Miss Johanna," Melissa ordered. "I'll go put on the kettle and get some sheets."

"I remember when Casimar was born," Leon said, coming to stand beside the bed. "I was no more than five. Nobody even realized I was there in the room. Four children before him and she carried on like it was her first."

"It doesn't necessarily get easier," Johanna retorted, writhing with another contraction. When would Dr. Abramowiez get here?

"I'll get you a belt of Scotch," Leon offered.

"No." She shook her head. "Oh God, I mustn't scare Bernie—" She thrust a corner of her pillow into her mouth. The pains were no more than a minute apart.

"Miss Johanna, which sheets should I put out for the doctor?" Melissa was clearly frightened.

"Any sheets, woman," Leon snapped. "Don't bother her at a time like this."

Her face contorted with pain, Johanna opened her mouth to scream, but suddenly Leon's mouth was on hers, stifling the shriek. His hand held hers in reassurance.

For a few moments her body relaxed. She lifted her eyes to Leon's face as he reached to switch on the lamp beside her bed. Only Leon would kiss a woman in labor to quiet her screams.

"Oh, no—" She closed her eyes as she fought with this anxious baby within her. "No . . ." The thin wail that threatened to become a scream was lost as Leon's mouth covered hers again.

"Where the hell is that doctor?" Leon demanded. He saw Melissa in the doorway. "Call him again," he ordered.

"That baby's coming," Johanna moaned. "Melissa, help me."

"Melissa, go bring a towel or something for the

baby." Leon swept the covers off Johanna. "Damnit, do what I say!"

"Leon, you shouldn't be here," Johanna protested. He leaned over and peered between her legs.

"You want to do it all by yourself? This one's got a head of black hair," Leon said. "Come on, Johanna, push." His face glistened with perspiration, as though he were in labor too. "Push that little fella out into the world."

"It's a girl," she argued.

"Push a little harder and we'll know," Leon urged. "Come on, Johanna, you can do it."

"She's so big— Oh, dear God!"

Melissa, scared but determined, appeared at the other side of the bed with a huge white towel in her hands. "Come on and finish, Miss Johanna."

With one last desperate effort she pushed and could feel the shoulders leave her.

"It is a little girl," Leon said triumphantly. "Damnit, you were right."

The doorbell rang insistently.

"Take the baby, Melissa," Leon ordered. "That's Dr. Abramowiez now." He wiped the sweat off his face and tidied his full dark mustache.

Chapter 10

Three days later Johanna leaned against a mound of pillows as Helen sucked greedily at her breast. Michal chose this moment to get home. Melissa had taken Bernie out to play in the early January snow and the parlormaid got to tell him about the birth of his daughter.

"Johanna—" White-faced and anxious, he rushed into the bedroom.

"We're both fine," Johanna assured him. "Come and meet your daughter."

"I should have been here," he said. "I never should have gone to London."

"It's over and we have our daughter, so take it easy. Did you see Casimar?"

"You would be proud of him," Michal said happily. "Already he's moving up in the church." His smile was wry. "Part of that is encouraged by the Russians. They know Casimar is opposed to armed rebellion."

"And his brother's support helps," Johanna added.

"Casimar sends love and blessings for Bernie and the new one."

Tears filled her eyes. Could it be ten years since he stood up with Michal and her at their wedding?

"Mama Raisa would have been proud of him."

"Before I went to London, I spoke to a real estate agency about a house. I don't want to wait to build. We'll buy a house. When you're ready you can start looking for our home for the rest of our lives. Whatever you wish, Johanna, it will be yours." He reached for her hand. "Forgive me for not being here with you when she was born."

Helen had relinquished the nipple and slept against Johanna's breast. With infinite tenderness he took his daughter into his arms.

"She's beautiful, like her mother," he said after a moment. "Someday Casimar will see our children and they'll see Poland."

Early in February Johanna began househunting. It was harder than she thought to find one; they tended to be long on grandeur and short on comfort. Eventually, however, she was satisfied.

Johanna knew when she saw the red brick and grey stone chateau in the low Sixties that this was to be their home. It was large and suitable for entertaining, but the private quarters were surprisingly cosy. Johanna called the decorators in for a complete refurbishing and then began to interview applicants for the staff, which must be considerably enlarged. She would hire only Polish immigrants. It was three months before they moved in, but the wait was worth it.

Johanna was embarrassed and infuriated by Leon's oft-repeated account of his part in Helen's birth. It was useless to try to silence his dramatic story of her anguish and his assistance. In some strange fashion it excited

Leon. He never told about the kissing, though. It made Johanna uneasy to think of it as a secret, though she would have been mortified if anyone had found out.

Worse, something—Leon's boasting?—was keeping Michal away again. He moved back to the spare room when Helen was born, saying two in a room was enough from anyone's point of view, and quietly stayed away when his daughter went to the nursery at six weeks of age.

Johanna longed to approach him again, but how often was she to fling herself at him? She had been taught that such behavior was shameful in a decent woman. Besides, she had made her point. If Michal did not come to her now, he must not want to.

So she poured herself into the house, the children, the immigrant Polish population. They would be her life.

Bernie was fascinated by his baby sister and Michal, although absorbed by the business, always found time to spend with his children. But in their spectacular Fifth Avenue mansion Johanna lay alone through endless nights, haunted by the passion that pride decreed she hide from her husband.

Two years after they moved into the Fifth Avenue mansion Michal commissioned a twenty-six-room "cottage" to be built in fashionable Newport. It was ready for occupancy in the summer of 1902, only months after the assassination of President McKinley.

This event had especially distressed Michal and Johanna because it brought back memories of violence in Poland, although Michal was of the opinion that President Roosevelt would be a good leader, concerned for the citizens. His "mornings on horseback" made him accessible to people who had never before dreamed of approaching the President.

Late in June of 1902 Johanna prepared to move the Fifth Avenue household to Newport. Michal was to stay with the family until late July. It was the first real vacation he had ever allowed himself. In addition to some of the staff of the New York house Johanna had hired several local domestics. She hoped to be able to spend a lot of time with Michal.

Johanna and Michal were filled with nostalgia on the trip by boat, via the Fall River Line, to Newport. They had last seen Newport from this same boat when they left Fall River, poor but ambitious, to take up residence in New York City. Bernie, soon to be eight, and Helen, some months past her third birthday, were wide-eyed with excitement at sleeping overnight on a ship.

They arrived in Newport during the awesome coaching parade. Every afternoon of the week from three on Bellevue Avenue was a spectacular scene. Meticulously groomed horses pulled barouches, landaus, victorias, tandems—every kind of turnout—with uniformed coachmen on the boxes.

"The Vanderbilt coachmen wear maroon," Michal whispered, "and the Astors wear blue."

"They look as though they belonged in a Broadway musical," Johanna giggled. "The black boots, the white breeches, all those gold buttons."

"Pretty," Helen said from her perch on her father's shoulder, staring round-eyed at an exquisitely gowned young girl in a T-cart.

Johanna was enthralled by her first view of the cottage, which sat on a cliff high above the Atlantic. She had inspected the endless parade of marble mansions along Bellevue Avenue with detached interest, but this elegantly simple house was far superior to the medieval castles, the Florentine palazzos, the ersatz Grand Trianons. She had seen the architect's sketches and drawings, but the house itself surpassed her expectations.

"Do you like it?" Michal asked with pride.

"It's beautiful," Johanna said. Michal reached up to help her down from the carriage.

"Bill Grady and his wife will come up next month for a week," Michal reported. "I'll come along with them. His father-in-law and his wife will be up for the weekend."

"His father-in-law is retired, isn't he?" Johanna asked.

"That's right, but his assets are tremendous. Bill is trying to persuade him to invest in the shipyard so we can expand further. The old lady has a great deal of influence with him and Bill counts on your charming her."

"I'll try, of course," Johanna promised. Everything in their lives, she thought rebelliously, revolved around the business.

There were moments during this first week at Newport that Johanna felt Michal growing closer to her again. They were both in love with the sea. For hours each day they strolled along the cliff walk, talking little, enjoying the scent of the ocean, the soothing roll of the waves. Sometimes Michal had long, heated telephone conversations with his business associates, but for the first time in years there was plenty of time for his family.

Then Michal went back to New York. He would return in two weeks for a long weekend.

"Arrange a dinner party," he suggested. "We have to introduce ourselves to our new neighbors. Invite about fifty people. Hire more help if you need it. Spare no expense, Johanna. Let Newport know that Johanna and Michal Raisa are summer residents."

Johanna understood Michal's thinking. He wasn't taking a vacation; he was opening an unofficial branch of his business in Newport. All at once the summer in the Newport house seemed less intriguing. She would have been content with long walks along the Atlantic, quiet dinners with Michal and his friends who came up to visit, lazy days with Bernie and Helen.

Still, Johanna knew her duty. She threw all her efforts into planning a lavish dinner. She ordered the invitations— regrets only—from a local printer and hired additional help for the night of the party, though Molly refused to have strangers in her kitchen. In a burst of inspiration Johanna contacted a theatrical agent and arranged for a concert pianist and a coloratura soprano from the Metropolitan Opera to perform after dinner.

Michal arrived from New York on the night before the party. No one had sent regrets. Johanna filled him with all the details. She had ordered a dinner dress by M. Felix. The florist would arrive early in the morning to decorate the ground floor. At last Michal and she would meet some of their Newport neighbors.

Bernie and Helen got permission to stay up and watch the guests arrive from a vantage point at the head of the stairs. Both children were delighted with their mother's appearance when she emerged from her dressing room in a mauve silk gown embroidered at the hem and at the tight-fitting bodice.

"Mama, you look beautiful," Bernie said reverently.

"Mama, you look beautiful," Helen parroted with a dazzling smile.

Michal came out of his bedroom to swoop his daughter up in his arms while he inspected his wife.

"Is my dress too fancy?" Johanna asked anxiously.

"It's perfect," he assured her. "You'll be the most beautiful lady at dinner."

Melissa appeared to watch the children as the host and hostess descended the staircase to stand under the crystal chandelier and await their guests. The footmen were in position before the house. The dining room table was resplendent, covered in white damask and lace, set with Sheffield silver, Waterford glassware and the newly purchased Sevres china. A butler waited to open the door and announce the guests. The maids in their crisp uniforms and dainty aprons stood by to serve.

The pianist and the coloratura soprano, a recently married couple, arrived and were settled in the small sitting room. Here they would be served dinner privately, since it was incorrect for the entertainers, no matter how illustrious, to join the guests. Later they would appear in the grand salon to perform.

Finally the knocker sounded. Johanna and Michal looked at each other and smiled. It was starting.

The butler flung open the door. There stood no wealthy couple but a footman with an envelope. He bowed and handed it over. "The Denvers regret . . ."

Fifty regrets came back in the next twenty minutes. After the fourth time the knocker sounded, Johanna spoke.

"Michal, no one is coming." Johanna's voice trembled with rage despite her efforts to appear calm. "We're being snubbed."

"To the Vanderbilts and the Astors and the Belmonts we're those upstart Polacks," Michal said. "Their families came to this country too, and ripped out fortunes for themselves. Does it matter that they were here fifty or a hundred years ahead of us? Come on, let's go into the drawing room and have a cocktail." They left the poor butler alone to preserve his wooden face and take in those hateful envelopes. Thank goodness he was one of their faithful city staff and not some local, laughing up his sleeve.

"We don't need them." Johanna's face set stubbornly. She had heard much about the humiliations of the Polish in America—from Mrs. Zabriskie and others. For a while

Michal and she had managed to escape that. "Let's sit down to dinner."

"Tell you what. We'll get the musicians to join us, since we're none of us good enough for our neighbors." Those persons, though confused by so much democracy, turned out to be excellent company.

"Welcome to our table," Johanna said with forced tranquility. She knew she would remember this slight for the rest of her years. "Eat up, there's plenty of everything."

They all sat together at one end of the table and ignored the maids removing forty-eight places. The soprano was beautiful and well traveled and the pianist was a rather elegant man in his fifties. They made light conversation as the staff circulated about the table, serving one course after another. When they had eaten, they retired to the salon to hear the musicale. Their worldly guests slid gracefully from the role of guests to performers and gave a superb entertainment.

When they had left and the extra help departed, Johanna and Michal retired to the sitting room for coffee before going upstairs to their rooms.

"We'll put the house on the market at the end of the season," Michal decided. "Next summer you'll take the children and tour Europe." But not Poland, they both knew. The Russians had long memories.

"Michal," Johanna said with sudden vivacity, "I'd like to bring up house guests from New York."

"Of course, but who?" He gazed at her inquiringly.

"Fifty young Polish children," she decided, "for two weeks by the sea. Let's fill this town with Polacks," she laughed. "I'll go see Mrs. Zabriskie and invite her to come help look after the children."

"It's miserable on East Seventh Street in the summer, and the children will enjoy being out of the city. Johanna, we needed to be reminded who we are." He smiled grimly. "We won't forget again."

Johanna was relieved when it was time to return to New York. For all her bravado she could not quite ignore the memory of the dinner table set for fifty-two and graced by only two guests. However, Michal was well pleased; business was satisfactorily transacted with the guests he brought up from New York, and he considered the summer a success.

Back in New York Johanna threw herself into education projects and support services for immigrant families. She found them jobs, housing and medical care. And she bullied even the grandmothers until they learned English. "You must speak it," she would insist, "or you will always be a stranger."

With Leon's encouragement and with Newport fresh in her mind Johanna began to welcome theatrical and musical celebrities to her parties; she sought out Polish luminaries of business and politics as well. She entertained with flair that was attracting attention, though not from the Four Hundred, which still snubbed performers and immigrants.

Three weeks before she was to sail for London, Johanna received an anonymous note in the mail. It said that her husband was having an affair with Betsy Connelly, the hottest young singing star on Broadway.

Johanna sat with the note in her hands and tried to tell herself that the writer was vicious or mistaken. It must be Leon who was having the affair; he was always involved with some actress or another. Michal was always pleading with him to settle down and marry. After all, in two years he would be forty.

Leon still continued to drop in at odd times for dinner.

Michal often was away until late in the evening on business—at least she had always believed it was on business. No, she rebuked herself, she mustn't believe a vicious anonymous letter. Leon was having an affair with Betsy Connelly, not Michal. When Leon next came over for dinner, she would ask him about it.

Two nights later he arrived in his usual boisterous manner, bearing gifts for the children and announcing that he couldn't survive another day without Molly's cooking. Since Helen's birth, when he stood in for Dr. Abramowiez, Leon had displayed a special attachment to his niece. Sometimes, remembering that night, Johanna was overcome by embarrassment, though Leon had finally stopped talking about it.

"That's enough, Leon," Johanna laughed when he had romped with the children for half an hour. "It's time for Bernie and Helen to go to sleep. Tomorrow's a school day."

"It's wicked to send the little princess to school," Leon objected. "She's no more than a baby."

"They don't sit at desks and do lessons. She goes to play with several other little girls for three hours each morning." Johanna was ever aware of the indignities suffered by the children of newly arrived Polish immigrants, who continued to pour into America. Luckily, her children were spared this by virtue of Michal's financial success. "Leon," she said, feigning amusement, "is Betsy Connelly as beautiful as people are saying?"

Leon shrugged and kissed Helen a vigorous good night.

"I've never even seen Betsy Connelly," he said while the children scampered upstairs. "From what I've heard she's not my type." He grinned. "You know me, Johanna. I like big women, excepting present company."

"Behave yourself, Leon," she said automatically.

"Let's go in to dinner." She stood up and shook out her skirts.

Johanna was poor company that evening. Leon didn't know Betsy Connelly. Was it true that Michal was having an affair with her? It wasn't like him, but how did she know what Michal was like these days? They saw so little of each other.

Michal was impatient for the board meeting to be over. He had been tied up at the office four nights in a row. He was tired and tense. He needed to relax. Why did Grady keep droning on? He was fond of Bill, but all this carrying on because of something they couldn't change was stupid. Steel prices fluctuated like mad between here and England, what with the cartels in Britain and the price controls here at home.

Michal finally interrupted his partner. "Bill, we're still operating in the black. We're showing a decent profit and improving the fleet."

The other board members, also anxious to wind up the meeting, rushed to agree with him—even Bill's father-in-law. In another twenty minutes he could be out of here. This was Betsy's night off from the theater. She'd be waiting at the apartment for him, and she didn't like to wait long.

He took a hansom cab from the office downtown to Betsy's, only a block above their old Central Park apartment. Leaning back in the cab as the driver hurried the horses through the cool summer evening, he considered his situation. When he first began to see Betsy four months ago, he grappled with guilt; not because of Johanna, but because of his strict upbringing. However, his physical needs overruled the church, and he was determined that Johanna would risk no more pregnancies.

Betsy came to the door as soon as he rang. She knew

that the sight of her in a filmy black negligee was enough to make him passionate.

"You're late." She pretended to pout. Small, curvaceous and beautiful, except for her coloring she was much like Johanna, he realized. "It'll take awhile for supper to heat up." These evenings were all the same. She cooked for him, they made love and he presented her with some costly little trinket.

"Let's wait for supper." He reached to draw her to him.

"I was hoping you'd say that," she murmured, allowing the negligee to part and display lush breasts. "I've been sitting here all day thinking about us." She toyed with the buttons of his shirt.

"I've been thinking, too," he breathed in her ear, fingers tweaking a nipple.

Betsy never suspected his passionate love for his wife. She never dreamed there could be love without sex. That was one of Betsy's strongest attractions: her candid pleasure in making love.

"Mike, let's go into the bedroom," she murmured after a few moments. "I want you so bad, honey."

Johanna reread the anonymous note one final time. Then she burned it in a wastebasket. She could confront Michal with it, but what good would come of that? If he wanted to run around, he would, and she might as well keep the peace.

In her heart she knew that Michal was having an affair with the new young Broadway star. Did he think she was beautiful? Was he in love with her? And who had sent the note? A man in Michal's position accumulated enemies along the way.

She would say nothing to Michal. She would pretend she knew nothing. She remembered what Mrs. Zabriskie had said on a night when they had talked long and intensely about marriage and the church.

"Johanna, a woman has to decide what to tell the priest when she goes to confession. She's not married to the priest. She's married to a man. What happens in bed between the wife and the husband isn't really any of the priest's business."

Chapter 11

On a steamy June afternoon Michal accompanied Johanna, the children and their nursemaid to the Cunard dock, where they were to board the sumptuous new liner the *Caronia*. The sun bathed the black hull, the huge funnel, the whole white vessel in gold as their small party stood on the dock before boarding.

"Remember, Johanna," Michal repeated, "I want to know every detail about the *Caronia*—its appointments, its service, its special touches. Overlook nothing—particularly any complaints you have or hear."

"I'll keep notes," she promised once more. At first she had been disappointed that they were not sailing on one of their own ships, but now she relished the opportunity to be useful. "Both going over and returning."

"Cable me when you arrive in Liverpool," he instructed.

It seemed to Johanna that his farewell kiss was more impassioned than was suitable before strangers. She was trembling when he released her to kiss the children. But she remembered that he would rush from the dock to the arms of Betsy Connelly. She hated the new young Broadway star with a fury that startled her.

Their suite, compact but not cramped, consisted of a salon, a stateroom for Melissa and the children and another for Johanna. It was a comfortable, elegant apartment with a particularly fancy bathroom in black and white marble. The tub was nearly the biggest single item in the suite. Six feet long, it had huge brass lion's feet resting on balls. Massive brass fixtures carried out the theme: a lion's maned head spewed hot and cold water out of the two sides of its mouth and the faucets were shaped like paws. Bathing at sea, of course, was done in salt water, but one could draw a curtain around the tub and rinse in fresh water from the overhead sprinkler.

It was a quiet crossing. Johanna and the children ate most of their meals in their suite and Melissa kept her charges busy the rest of the time with the entertainment facilities and with the few other children on board. Johanna, with time on her hands for the first time in months, caught up with some of her reading, including a remarkable first novel, *The House of Mirth* by Edith Wharton.

At Liverpool Johanna cabled Michal of their safe arrival before taking the train to London. Michal's secretary had made all the arrangements for their tour of Europe, even including a private viewing of the Crown Jewels. She wished Michal were with them, though she realized he could hardly take a month off from business. Nor would he wish to take himself so far from Betsy Connelly, she glumly supposed.

They stayed at the glittering Savoy Hotel, by far the most fashionable for the American tourists who thronged London each summer season. Johanna took the children to the zoo and to look at Buckingham Palace, but they were too young for much sightseeing. Melissa took them to

Hyde Park while Johanna toured the Tower of London, Westminster Abbey, The British Museum, the Tate Gallery and the famous churches.

All the while Johanna followed the tourist paths she was aware that no ocean lay between Poland and her. From Paris, their next stop, it would be simple to take a train to Warsaw. Johanna longed to visit her homeland, but she dared not. Even after all these years she might be apprehended and imprisoned.

In Paris they stayed at the famed Hotel Crillon in a suite with a balcony that overlooked the Place de la Concorde. Johanna fell in love with the city at sight. It seemed that she was living apart from reality. She wandered alone about the charming streets; often she found herself tired and lost and had to take a cab back. Once it was a half-hour drive; Johanna had walked ten miles in what seemed to her like ten minutes.

On their fourth morning in Paris, dressed and ready to leave for a day of sightseeing, Johanna answered a knock, thinking perhaps there was a cable from Michal. She opened the door and froze in disbelief. The years had added maturity to his face and a streak of grey to his hair, but there stood Casimar, big ears, bony nose and all. He was wearing glasses, but he took them off and put them in his pocket.

"Casimar—" Johanna flung her arms around him. "Casimar, how wonderful to see you." The years evaporated and she felt like sixteen again.

"Michal knew I was coming. He wanted it to be a surprise," he explained, holding her back so his eyes could devour her. "Officially I'm here to pick up funds at a Paris bank. Michal is building a chapel in memory of our mother."

"How lovely." Johanna laughed and took off her

coat. Bernie and Helen were standing by wide-eyed. They knew, of course, about their uncle who was a priest in Warsaw. "Casimar, my children." She reached to pull them toward her and all at once they turned shy.

Casimar bowed gravely. "How do you do? Helen, Bernie, I'm delighted to meet you. I am your father's brother Casimar from Warsaw." He smiled. "I am a priest, but you had better call me uncle, not father." He turned to Johanna. "I wish Mama could have lived to see them."

"How long will you be in Paris?"

"My train goes late this evening," he told her. "May I spend the day with you?" He winked at the children, who were fast recovering their aplomb.

"There is nothing we'd like better. Melissa, we won't need you until dinnertime. We'll take the children with us. Do enjoy yourself."

Bernie shyly remarked on the strong resemblance between his father and his newfound uncle. Helen demanded to hold Casimar's hand. With Casimar, who knew Paris well, they strolled through the Bois de Boulogne, lunched at an outdoor café on the Champs-Elysées, marveled at the Eiffel Tower, which rose to a height of nine hundred eighty-four feet. They waited briefly in the bank while Casimar conducted his business, then resumed their tour.

When Helen began to yawn, Casimar picked her up and they returned to the hotel for dinner.

"When I grow up I'll marry you, Uncle Casimar," Helen announced over Melissa's shoulder as her nurse carried her off to bed.

"Bernie, it's your bedtime too," Melissa said firmly. "Kiss Mama and your uncle good night."

Bernie reluctantly followed Melissa and Johanna and Casimar were at last alone. Johanna found herself growing nervous and glanced at him. His eyes blazed with such love that she gasped and swayed. How on earth had he ever chosen the church? "Casimar—"

"Tell me about your life in New York—with Michal," Casimar said gently. "Are you happy there? I want to hear about your work for our arriving countrymen, too."

Haltingly she told Casimar about her work in the Polish community, her hopes for Poland's independence. She surprised Casimar with her comprehension of the problems in America between the Polish Catholics and the Irish Catholics. He listened to her with deep respect when she spoke of the Polish priests, who strove to preserve their native language and customs. The Polish people with their fierce national pride sought to keep in America the forms of their old religious life, and for this the Irish Catholics, always eager to be assimilated, showed only contempt.

"I think," Johanna concluded, "that the Pole is more loyal to Poland than the Irish to Ireland. For the Irish the church comes first."

"Michal told me that the Irish think our Polish-Americans cling too much to the old ways," Casimar said. "He tells me in his letters that Polish priests have little stature in the Roman Catholic Church in America. But that will change.

"This new trouble between the Russians and the Japanese may well prove helpful to Poland," he went on. "In Warsaw we watch with hopes that it will weaken the Russians and bring some measure of reform for us."

All too soon Casimar spoke reluctantly. "I must leave or I will miss my train." He half raised his hand as if to touch Johanna, then let it fall.

"Have a glass of wine with me before you leave," she suggested, maneuvering to prolong this meeting.

"One glass of wine," he agreed, his eyes warm and admiring.

They sipped at their wine and chatted a little, each

quietly reveling in the other's company. Then at last Casimar rose to leave. He bent down to kiss her good-bye, and impulsively Johanna lifted her mouth to his. For a heated moment their mouths clung, Casimar's hands at her shoulders.

Even as she felt the answering passion in him, Casimar withdrew his mouth and his hands. Still, for a moment the priest had been a man.

"Bless you, Johanna, and bless the children. I'll treasure these hours we've spent together." He kissed her quickly on the forehead and crossed to the door. He let himself out without looking back at her.

Lying in her bed, Johanna wrestled with tumultuous emotions. She had felt tonight for Casimar what she felt for him at sixteen. However, she could not deny that for years she had wanted a full, intimate marriage with strong, steady, reliable Michal. Was she responding to Casimar because of the wall that had risen between her and her husband? Would she have felt this way if Michal were in her bed every night? Which of them did she really love?

Back in New York the day with Casimar seemed a dream. She fought to keep herself busy lest she hurt too much because her husband had turned away from her. Night after night she lay sleepless in her bed yearning to be in Michal's arms. Casimar belonged to her girlhood, far behind her.

Bernie talked earnestly about following his uncle's footsteps and becoming a priest one day. Johanna suspected it was a fleeting ambition. Bernie was intense, like his father; he had been drawn to Casimar and that intensity led him to emulate his uncle.

Months passed and Bernie held steadfast to his intention to become a priest. He went to church with new fervor and displayed dedication that was reminiscent of Casimar, Johanna at last agreed.

On a Sunday evening fourteen months after the Paris visit Michal sprawled in a comfortable chair in the family sitting room and confessed his unease about Bernie's attraction to the church. While Johanna would be happy to give a son to God, she knew that Michal wanted him to carry on the family name and to join him in the business.

"Damnit, Johanna, it's not that I don't appreciate what it means to be a priest," he said in exasperation, "but we have only one son. Leon will never marry and for Casimar it is out of the question. Who else but my son can carry on our line?"

"I know how you feel," Johanna said gently, her mind racing. There was one way to bring Michal back to her. "We don't have the right to deny Bernie what he wishes to do with his life. I think we should have another baby and pray for a boy. She was trembling, feeling herself in bed with Michal, filled with him. "Please, Michal."

Michal gazed at her with disconcerting intensity. "You want to go through that again?"

"For us, Michal, If you wish it." She lowered her eyes in sudden confusion.

Michal embraced her and kissed her passionately. "I can't wait to get started. Let's go to bed right now."

Johanna laughed and blushed. "Oh, Michal!" But she allowed herself to be drawn upstairs.

Night after night Michal came to her bed, and Johanna returned passion with passion. She asked herself if Michal thought this was only so that she might conceive. Surely he must understand that her chief desire was for her husband.

*　　*　　*

The war between Russia and Japan was followed avidly by Polish-Americans. Russia's defeat with the loss of almost a million lives brought about a revolt in St. Petersburg that in turn rekindled Polish desires for liberty. Polish deputies now had seats in the Russian Parliament and their language was restored in the government. The schools, too, were allowed new freedom to set curricula.

For all this Johanna thanked God, but many months rolled by without her becoming pregnant and she feared again that she was barren. She knew how anxious Michal was for her to conceive again. He had broken off with his mistress and she didn't want him ever to seek another woman again.

Freed at last of religious scruples, Johanna worked hard to make herself attractive to Michal. She went to a Paris parfumier on Fifth Avenue; she bought scandalous nightgowns and delectable robes; she kept brandy in her boudoir and learned to rub the aches out of Michal's back.

She even told him he could smoke in her bedroom, but he, courtly as ever, would not dream of doing such a thing. They were very happy indeed.

They would go upstairs soon after dinner and get undressed. Michal would pour a little brandy for each of them—Johanna never drank hers—and talk over their day and their plans. Soon Johanna would start to brush her long blond hair. When she was done they would go straight to bed.

One night Michal took away her brush. "Let me do that," he said gruffly. He brushed her hair very carefully and thoroughly, and when he was done they were both on fire. They never went to sleep that night.

A few days before Christmas she realized she was pregnant. This Christmas Michal would receive the greatest present of all. She was convinced the baby was a boy.

On Christmas Eve, when the tree had been decorated and the children sent off to their rooms, she told Michal that somewhere around Bernie's twelfth birthday she would give birth to their third child.

"Johanna, you are a wonderful wife," he said gently. "You must take care of yourself. This time I'll call Ladislas Abramowiez. You'd put it off too long."

"Michal, don't start already. Your mother never had a doctor, nor mine either, and they had nine children between them."

Michal ignored this. "You must rest. No more of this constantly running around after help for the immigrants. And this child will be born in a hospital. We take no chances."

"This child will be born at home, where he should. And Dr. Abramowiez will be with me even if we have to insist he move into the house when my time comes near," she laughed. "Leon won't be here to stand in."

"No trips to Europe this time," Michal vowed. "I'll be with you." He continued to fuss and fret and at last Johanna realized what the trouble was.

"Michal, don't look so fearful. I'm not the first pregnant woman of thirty-three. Your mother was forty when Casimar was born."

"Yes, and she had a hard time of it. You'll take it easy?" he pleaded. "You'll get plenty of rest?"

"Oh, bother resting." But she was secretly pleased and took care not to alarm him.

The next months were the happiest Johanna could remember. Michal hovered about her with constant solicitude. He abandoned his own bedroom to stay with her each night. Even when they didn't make love, she slept in his arms.

At first Bernie was disconcerted by his mother's pregnancy and avoided looking at her increasing girth, but Helen was excited about the new baby from the start. She was delighted to put her hand on her mother's belly and feel the baby kick.

And then early in her seventh month Johanna's happiness gave way to fear. An hour after the children left for school in the fine new Cadillac Michal had bought for the family use, she doubled over with a violent contraction. The baby was coming early.

She called for Melissa, who had been with her when Helen was born. With both children in school Melissa had begun to act as Johanna's personal maid, though Johanna would not have thought of such a thing on her own.

"We'll get you right to bed," Melissa soothed her, but her eyes were frightened. "I'll send Molly to help you while I call Dr. Abramowiez."

Molly helped her into a nightgown and held her hand as one contraction after another made a hard knot of her abdomen.

"Into bed now, Mrs. Raisa," Molly urged, half-lifting her into the bed.

She gave herself up to waves of pain, conscious of the noise as first Dr. Abramowiez and then Michal arrived. But she could deal only with the pain that ripped at her.

"I shouldn't have allowed her to do this again," Michal groaned. "My fault." He continued to castigate himself until his old friend lost patience.

"It takes two to make a baby Michal," Abramowiez snapped. "And what the devil are you doing here at a time like this?"

"I belong with my wife." Johanna heard Michal's voice as from a distance. "Where else should I be?"

"Johanna, you have to help," the doctor urged.

Johanna heard herself scream. A long time passed, hours and hours. The pain was unremitting. Her throat was raw with shrieking.

"Ladislas, do something for her," Michal pleaded.

"The baby's breech, Michal," he said seriously. "We don't want to lose it if I can help it."

"Johanna comes first," Michal said tautly. "For God's sake, how much more of this can she take?"

Semiconscious, Johanna finally felt the doctor taking the baby from her. She wanted to ask if it was a boy, but there was no strength left in her to speak.

"She'll sleep now," Ladislas murmured. "I'm sorry, Michal. There was nothing else I could do."

For two days Johanna was never fully awake. When at last she roused, she saw Michal's haggard face leaning toward her.

"Michal—"

"You're going to be all right." He took her hand. "Thank God for that. For the first twenty hours we were afraid."

"The baby?" she whispered.

"We lost him, Johanna. But we have Bernie and Helen. God gave us riches with those two." He tried to smile at her, but she turned her face away from him.

"I wanted to give you another son, Michal. I prayed all through those months. I'm sorry."

"Sssh," he urged. "It's not your fault. I blame myself, for that matter. Now hush up and rest."

"I disappointed you." Her voice broke. "Oh Michal, I wanted him so badly." He gathered his love into his arms and held her while she cried and cried. Then they both slept.

Ladislas Abramowiez was pleased with the speed of Johanna's physical recovery but less happy about her depression at losing the baby.

"Never again, Ladislas," Michal swore. "I'll never let her go through that again."

"She's not an old woman, Michal," the doctor argued. "She can have another baby. Just wait a year or so until she's completely over losing this one."

"No more children," Michal insted, his face taut. "I couldn't go through this again myself."

He must never go to Johanna's bed again. Contraception was out of the question and he was determined never to put her at risk again. That part of their life was forever over.

Chapter 12

Johanna understood why Michal refrained from coming to her bed. However, understanding did not ease her loneliness or frustration. She only wished Michal were less afraid—or contraception less of a sin.

The children would have to be her life, she told herself. For Michal's sake she was relieved when Bernie, growing tall and handsome, gradually forgot his thoughts of the priesthood. When at seventeen he was accepted at Columbia College, she realized this was possible largely because of his family's wealth. Less-rich Polish-Americans, however gifted, faced stultifying prejudices.

It saddened both Johanna and Michal that so few of the children were going to high school or college. It seemed to immigrant parents far more urgent that their children start earning money as soon as possible rather than go to school. A dollar or two a week for sure seemed far more sensible than sitting in school hoping to get rich.

Still, Johanna knew of a few mothers who understood what education could do. These devoted women went out to scrub office floors at night, worked in factories, took in laundry so that their sons could stay in school. It was always the boys, of course. Girls were thought to need little education.

Johanna would point out as an example of opportunity seized their countryman Ignace Paderewski, who first toured the United States in 1891. A few years later every family in America who could scrape together the money had a piano in the parlor. She often spoke of Helene Modjeska, the reigning Shakespearean actress on the American stage, and of Marie Curie, born Marie Sklodovska in Warsaw. With her French husband Curie discovered radium and shared a Nobel prize for physics in 1903.

Late in 1913, bored with the shipping business, Leon sold out his shares and took a train to a small California town called Hollywood. The business of making moving pictures intrigued him, though both his brother and his sister-in-law warned him that he could lose even his considerable fortune.

In New York's Grand Central Station, full of confidence, Leon boarded the luxurious Twentieth Century Limited. This was the greatest train in America. It carried two sleepers, a dining car, a buffet with a library, a bath and an observation car.

Four hours out of New York in the elegant dining car Leon encountered the beauteous and ambitious Marianne Scott, who had enjoyed some minor success on Broadway and was now en route to Hollywood. An hour later Marianne was sharing his compartment.

"I've got a hankering to put my nose into this moving picture business," Leon said casually. Marianne's eyes lit up. "You going out there under contract to somebody?"

"No," she acknowledged, "but I got terrific reviews on Broadway last year." She didn't mention that she had not worked since.

"You got great boobs, too," he grinned. "In pictures that's a hell of a lot better than Broadway reviews."

"It's scary," she said with calculated wistfulness. "I mean, going to a strange town where I don't know a soul." Her huge dark eyes invited him to know her better.

"Stick with me," he urged, "and you'll do fine."

In three minutes she was stripped to the skin and flat on her back. Her boobs, Leon congratulated himself, were even better with her clothes off. What had threatened to be a dull and dreary train trip was all at once most interesting. Marianne Scott, he told himself as he shucked off his pants, was twenty and hot. What better diversion could he ask for?

Nearly a full day after the Twentieth Century Limited pulled out of Grand Central in New York it arrived at Chicago's La Salle Street Station. Here Leon and Marianne changed for the Santa Fe Railroad's deluxe California Limited.

Five days after he left New York Leon stepped down from the train at the small Los Angeles railroad station. With Marianne Scott hanging on his arm he felt like an adventurer. If she was an indication of what he would find in Hollywood, then this town must be one perpetual party. After all the dull years in shipping, he told himself ebulliently, he was ready for this.

Leon decided they would stay at the lush Potter Hotel in Santa Barbara and commute via the Cadillac he would buy at the earliest possible moment. Hollywood was a nice little town, full of flowers and palm trees, but he preferred more luxurious living.

Marianne was happy to indulge his taste. She "needed" more clothes, jewels, furs and entertainment than Johanna had had in her life. The would-be star went shopping every day and spent hundreds.

She always remembered to bring a present for Leon.

This delighted him. So what if he would pay for it himself. It proved she was thinking of him, not just of his money, didn't it?

Within three months everybody who mattered knew that a New York millionaire named Leon Raisa was in Hollywood with a hot little number he was determined to make into a screen sensation. By spring Leon, brash and charismatic as ever, his mustache now a pencil-thin line, was head of his own film studio. He was unperturbed that money was flowing out like the proverbial water. Leon felt himself king of the world. By June he had produced two Marianne Scott feature films and was looking for a distributor.

In New York Michal worried about Leon's activities in Hollywood. Over dinner he confided this anxiety to Johanna. "He's running through an awful lot of money. What does he know about making movies?"

"Michal, it's a new business." Johanna was relieved that Leon was in California. She wanted him far away in case he got in a scandal with one of the women who filled his life. Though Michal had tried to keep it from her, she knew that Leon had had to buy his way out of two scrapes in the past three years. At forty-eight Leon played like a rake of thirty. "Movie producers are still feeling their way. But they're making money. Look at how people are flocking to see Mary Pickford, Charlie Chaplin and Dorothy or Lillian Gish." She waved away the succotash.

Michal smiled wryly. "I guess I should be relieved he's not trying to join up with the Polish Falcons." These groups, in cities with large Polish-American communities, were training companies for what many young immigrants believed was a coming struggle for independence at home.

"Michal, don't talk about the Falcons when Bernie is at home." Johanna continually feared that Bernie, still with a year of college ahead of him, might decide to fight for liberation. For too many years he had listened to his father and Leon reminisce about their own politics in the homeland. Helen and Bernie had been particularly impressed that "Mama and Papa were spies in Warsaw."

"Leon's after me to invest in his company," Michal said tentatively. "It never hurts to diversify our interests."

"Go ahead if you want to," Johanna said, "but don't expect much." Leon, she knew, was a very poor businessman without brother Michal behind him.

"Leon will be in New York for two weeks in the fall. He has to do something about distributors for his films. We'll talk about it then. How about more coffee, Johanna?"

In late June of 1914 Archduke Francis Ferdinand was assassinated in Sarajevo. Europe stood on the brink of war. Germany declared war on Russia August first and on France two days later.

Johanna and Michal were distraught but not surprised when Poland became a central battleground. The Germans conscripted men from Poland, as did the Russians. This was the very worst of being a partitioned country. Though it was not their war, Polish brother was fighting brother. An independent Poland, dreamed of for so long and seemingly almost within reach, now appeared more necessary and more unattainable than ever.

The country was soon trampled under the boots of the opposing armies, neither of which cared about Poland. Crops were trampled, stolen, burned and livestock requisitioned to feed the invaders. Soon the land of the Raisas' birth was a barren, smoking ruin.

Both Johanna and Michal moved heaven and earth to raise funds for the Red Cross and for the Polish War Relief Committee. When Leon arrived in New York for a brief visit in November, they were shocked that he appeared more concerned about his movie studio than about what was happening in Poland. He fingered his nearly bare upper lip and made jokes while they worried themselves sick over Casimar. For the first time hostility arose between Leon and Michal. Three days after he arrived Leon slammed out of their house and back to Hollywood. No word from Warsaw came through.

In January of 1915 Leon pleaded with Michal to come out to Hollywood and see firsthand that the studio would be a wise investment. Mainly to ease the tension between them Michal agreed to go.

"Come with me, Johanna," he urged. "The change will do you good."

"I have too much to do," she objected. "Besides, I wouldn't want to leave Helen alone, not even with Melissa." Sometimes the nurse had more control of Helen than her parents did.

"I worry about Leon, the way he's throwing everything into his studio. He ought to have kept a reserve, held on to some stock in the company. I don't have much time for this, though. I'll just stay out there a week."

New York was bleak and grey under several inches of dirty snow. "You'll enjoy all that sunshine and the Pacific Ocean."

"One week," Michal repeated. "Even if I work on the train I can't spare more time. Ten days on the road—that's over two weeks in all. I'll miss you, Johanna."

Her eyes filled with tears. Michal almost never spoke of his feelings.

When he got off the California Limited Michal spied Leon standing beside a chauffeured Cadillac. "Leon!" He opened his arms wide to embrace his brother and grinned over Leon's shoulder at the wooden-faced driver.

"You came," Leon chortled with pleasure and held

Michal by the shoulders to look at him. "Until you hopped down from the train I wasn't sure you would."

Leon swept him off to the new house he had just bought for himself on Franklin near La Brea. "Like it?" They got out of the car and stood before the rather grand Spanish hacienda. "I had an interior decorator furnish it for me. Come on, let me show you."

In addition to his Cadillac Leon now owned a Rolls-Royce and had ordered a Leon Bollee roadster in yellow with green leather upholstery. "Out here, Michal, you have to put on the dog," he said, an arm about his brother. "Appearances mean everything. I've got a cook-house-keeper, two maids, a butler and a chauffeur. I order my suits from a tailor in Savile Row." He grinned wickedly. "And a barber comes every day to trim my mustache."

Leon showed him the studio the following morning; it was clear that the producer was highly respected in his company. Leon introduced him to the comptroller, John Novak, and for the rest of the day Michal went over figures. He was very pleasantly surprised at them. He remembered his brother had always been a master salesman. Maybe Leon had found his niche.

"Well, you know," Leon said, "we were good because you were smart. Novak's smart, too. I made sure of that."

In the evenings Leon took him from party to party. How could movie people put in a day's work when they partied so much? Michal marveled. He was impressed when he met Douglas Fairbanks, whom he had seen on Broadway. He was less impressed by the wild party at the home of Mack Sennett, where it seemed that anything bizarre was available.

At a dinner alone with Leon on his final night in Hollywood Michal saw a lovely young actress named Claudia Sherwood.

"You want to meet her?" Leon asked with a glint in

his eyes. Michal's head kept turning to the table across the room where a vivacious and lovely young brunette held court for four fascinated men.

"Leon," Michal protested, striving for an air of amusement, but Leon was already on his feet.

"Come along," Leon insisted. "I know two of the fellows with her. One's a director at Essenay and the other's a stunt man."

Michal reminded himself that he was leaving in the morning. He'd never see Claudia Sherwood again. But when he stood at her table and stared down into her provocative blue eyes he knew he wanted nothing more than to make love to her.

An hour later Michal and Claudia, Leon and Marianne piled into Leon's Rolls-Royce and headed for his house. Leon and Marianne disappeared into an upstairs bedroom. Michal and Claudia sat on a leather sofa before a fireplace in the den and sipped champagne.

"I wish you didn't have to go back to New York tomorrow," Claudia said wistfully. Michal felt a stirring in his loins. "I was hoping we'd have a chance to get to know each other."

"I'd better drive you home." He stood up, clearing his throat self-consciously. He guessed why Claudia was ready to throw herself into his arms. He was Leon's brother and she was admittedly ambitious. "You probably have to be on the set early tomorrow."

"I'm not on a picture right now," she said frankly and rose to stand before him. "Michal, there are a lot of bedrooms upstairs. Can't we share one?"

Michal delayed his return to New York for eight days. Via the brand-new transcontinental telephone service he explained to Johanna and to his office that he was arranging to invest to Leon's movie firm. There were few hours that he was out of Claudia's arms, and when they finally did part it was arranged that he would come back to Hollywood in two months, ostensibly on film business. Meanwhile he set Claudia up in the Alexandria Hotel, where his comings and goings would be far from prying Hollywood eyes.

Michal commenced a year of transcontinental commuting. Claudia was beginning to get work, though not at Leon's studio. She was on her way up and still she claimed that Michal was the only man she wanted in her life. She was always tender and passionate and Michal ignored Leon's blunt disclosure that Claudia slept around when he was in New York.

All that year Michal was a dynamo. Back home he spent a dozen hours a day at the office. He raised funds for Polish relief, for the Red Cross. He was elected secretary of his club and took on all its correspondence and half its management. Only his family he could not find time for.

In Hollywood he installed a secretary in a hotel comfortably distant from the Alexandria in Los Angeles, where he continued to keep Claudia. In saner moments he realized he was crazy to allow himself to be obsessed by a woman young enough to be his daughter, but in bed he forgot all about that.

On a trip to Hollywood three weeks before Christmas he carried with him a diamond and ruby bracelet, Claudia's Christmas gift. He felt himself rise as he anticipated her excitement when he gave it to her. He had never known anyone as uninhibited as Claudia. In bed she was often the aggressor, the opposite of Johanna. She egged him on to use all his strength and left him spent. He let himself go with her as he never had before, even with easy, comfortable Betsy Connelly, his only other mistress.

On the day he arrived in Hollywood Claudia was shooting a film. He went to see Leon at his studio, one eye anxiously on his watch. At six he would walk into the suite at the Alexandria and find Claudia waiting to welcome him.

He arrived at the hotel before her and changed into one of the fine silk robes he kept there. He stretched across the bed and visualized her blond hair spread over the maroon jacquard. He shifted restlessly on the bed, already impatient to have her in his arms. At the sound of a key he got up and strode toward the door.

"Michal," she crooned and threw herself at him. "Darling, I missed you terribly." She wore the pearls he had brought her on his last visit. They lent her a special air of elegance, he thought with satisfaction.

"Prove it," he ordered. "And don't take off the pearls."

Her lips parted in a promising smile. She linked her arm through his and led him into the bedroom.

"Lie down, darling," she ordered, knowing he was naked beneath the robe. "Tonight I'll make you very happy."

Johanna gently opened the door to Helen's bedroom to see if she was sleeping. Her face softened at the sight of Helen's slender body curled like that of a child beneath the covers. She had insisted last night that Helen not go to school today, although this was her senior year and every day important. Helen had a heavy cold that she had picked up ice-skating at Central Park with Rudy Conrad.

Johanna closed the door and went downstairs. The morning mail had already been brought in and put on a table in the entrance hall. She skimmed through, as always, in hopes that there would be some word from Casimar. Last August Warsaw had fallen to the Germans, but Casimar was safe in Paris after a hair-raising escape. Twice he had been able to get letters to them. Today there was nothing.

She settled herself in the parlor and began to open the mail. All at once she was cold and hot with discovery. Michal had bought a bracelet three days before he left for Hollywood. She stared until the words on the bill before her began to blur. "Engraved C.S. MERRY CHRISTMAS."

She sat motionless while the bill fluttered from her hand to the floor. Those initials belonged to some actress in Hollywood. It wasn't business that sent him tearing across the country every two months. Johanna intended to find out who it was.

She hurried upstairs to Helen's room. Her daughter slept soundly, her breathing faintly noisy from her cold. Across the room lay a stack of *Photo Play* magazines. Devoted to the movies, Helen collected newspaper columns and movie magazines and pored over them with religious fervor.

Johanna took the magazines to her room to go through the pictures and captions. It took no more than ten minutes to spot Claudia Sherwood. Her throat growing tight with anguish, she gazed at the lovely vivacious face of the rising starlet, who looked no more than three or four years older than her own daughter.

Now she read in minute detail every item where Claudia's name was mentioned, growing sick at the innuendoes about the various stars. And then she saw the page that she had feared to see. Claudia Sherwood smiled at her—Claudia between two men, Leon and Michal. The photograph had been taken at a Hollywood party. The report hinted that one of the men with Claudia was her secret romance.

Didn't Michal understand that Helen would surely see this item? How could he be so careless? Johanna told herself she was angry for Helen and Bernie, but she knew she suffered most because she had lost her husband.

Conscious of the time difference between New York

and California, Johanna telephoned Leon at his home, impatient with the delays entailed in a transcontinental phone call. At last Leon was on the phone.

"Hello," he snapped. He hated to be disturbed early in the morning.

"Leon, it's Johanna." Her voice was hoarse with urgency.

"Is something wrong? Michal has left early for the studio," he lied.

"I don't want to talk to Michal, I want to talk to you." Her voice sounded odd to her ears. "About Claudia Sherwood."

There was a slight pause. "What about Claudia Sherwood?"

"I know Michal's having an affair with her—"

"Not Michal," he blustered. "I have something going with Claudia. What's the matter? You been reading the gossip columns? It's me, not Michal. You know him better than that."

"Leon, stop lying," Johanna said tiredly. "I have a bill for a jeweled bracelet with the initials C.S. Leon, if the children find out, I'll never forgive him. If he keeps on with this affair," she said with a touch of hysteria, "he's committing himself to everlasting hell."

"Calm down, Johanna. I'll have a talk with her."

"A talk! What good will that do?"

"You'd be surprised. Miss Sherwood will listen, I promise."

"Leon—"

"I'll take care of it," he promised. "Michal won't even have to know."

"How?" she probed, her throat tight again. She realized he would just find another woman, but as long as they were discreet and she wasn't a celebrity, what could Johanna do?

"Trust me, Johanna."

"How?" she insisted.

"This is a clannish business out here," he told her seriously, "for all the competition. I'll tell her to break off with Michal or I'll personally see to it that nobody hires her. I can do that, Johanna, and Claudia knows it. She's an ambitious little slut. She'll drop Michal like he was poison." Unexpectedly he chuckled. "Which for her he is."

"Thank you, Leon."

"You know I'd do anything for you." She was surprised at his sentimentality. "You know all the Raisa boys wanted to climb in your bed."

"Michal?" she asked bitterly. "He hasn't been in my bed for years."

"Honey, you know what's wrong with your marriage?" Leon said with characteristic bluntness. "For years every time Michal got in your bed, Casimar was there between you."

Chapter 14

Helen stood before the full-length mirror in her bedroom and anxiously surveyed her reflection. Her gown of palest green chiffon was cut with the fashionable high waist that lent it an air of belonging to the era of Regency England. The neckline was modest enough, yet she was deliciously aware that the line of the gown emphasized her high, full bosom. She was sure Rudy would be fascinated by her appearance.

Tonight she was to graduate from Miss Lodge's School for Young Ladies. Last night Rudy had graduated from his school. At Rudy's party he pulled her into the library when nobody was looking and kissed her. They'd sneaked kisses before, but last night was different. She shivered in delighted recall.

Mama was happy that Rudy and she were friends. Rudy's family was Polish, too. That made them special. She had to carry on like crazy to be allowed to go to Miss Lodge's School instead of to a Polish parochial school.

Papa had helped her persuade Mama to allow her to go there.

She sighed. Mama was going to be so upset when she told her she wanted to marry Rudy before he left to join General Haller's Blue Army, fighting in France on the Allies' side. Rudy said there were already thousands of Polish-Americans fighting in France. When the war was over, Papa kept saying, Poland would be an independent country again.

Helen started at the knock on her door. "Yes?" Her heart pounded. She couldn't bear to have to talk to anybody just now. She wanted to stay here all by herself and think about being married to Rudy. It didn't matter that she was only seventeen. Her mother got married at sixteen. Rudy would be eighteen next month.

"Helen, are you almost ready?" her mother asked anxiously. "We mustn't be late."

"Mama, we don't have to be there for an hour. I'll be out in a little bit. It only takes ten minutes to drive to school."

"All right, darling, but keep an eye on the clock."

"Are my flowers here yet?" The girls were to carry roses.

"They're here," her mother assured her, "and they're lovely."

"I'll be downstairs soon," Helen said, impatient to return to her daydreams.

She had been disappointed not to have a graduation party. Instead Mama and Papa contributed the money it would have cost to Polish War Relief. Sometimes she thought her mother and father forgot they were Americans now.

She dropped to the edge of the bed and closed her eyes to think about kissing Rudy at the party last night. Mama would die if she knew how Rudy kissed her. She could feel it all the way down to the pit of her stomach. When he touched her breasts that way, she nearly died. But it wasn't wrong; they were going to be married.

It was exciting to think about Rudy and going off to France to fight under General Haller—along with that whole battalion or whatever the Falcons called themselves— but it was scary too. She would never admit to Rudy that she wished he weren't going.

When she went to confession she wouldn't tell the priest about Rudy's kissing her and touching her breasts. She'd be too embarrassed. Did Papa tell the priest he was running around with that movie actress in Hollywood last year?

She knew Mama and Papa loved each other; she could tell by that special way they looked at each other sometimes. So why didn't they share a bedroom? Rudy's parents did. Maybe Mama and Papa figured they were too old to do those things now. Helen shrugged. She didn't think she'd ever be too old.

Lita's father was a doctor. When he went away with Lita's mother to Palm Beach last winter, the girls sat up half the night reading his medical books. He even had some books about what married men and women did together. Lita said it made her feel funny inside just reading about it. She said when she was little, she could hear the noises from her parents' bedroom when they were making love.

Maybe Mama was so busy with volunteer work and all that she didn't have time anymore to think about those things. Lita said she was sure her parents still did it, especially when her father had a few belts of Scotch inside him. Did Papa run around with that actress—Claudia Sherwood—because Mama wasn't interested anymore?

Uncle Leon said his niece was pretty enough to be an actress. Now she searched her reflection again, finding fault with the cloud of shimmering fair hair that framed the perfect oval of her face, the expressive grey-blue eyes that were exactly like her mother's. She didn't want to be an actress. She wanted to be Rudy's wife. She'd have to tell Mama and Papa tonight. That was when Rudy was telling his parents.

Soon she left her bedroom to go downstairs and collect her bouquet of roses. Her father swept her into his arms for a tender kiss. "You'll be the prettiest girl on that stage tonight," he said proudly. "And for the prettiest girl your mother and I have a present."

Her father pulled a red velvet box from his jacket pocket. She opened a box and gasped at the splendor of the pearls that lay on the satin padding.

"Oh, Papa—Mama—they're lovely. Thank you." Helen kissed her father and her mother and put on the rope of pearls. "Mama, you look so beautiful, like a movie star," she said effervescently and saw her mother wince.

"I'll be escorting the two most beautiful ladies there tonight," her father said with an air of pleasure. Nonetheless, it was obvious that he was conscious of her bad choice of words.

By the time they arrived at the school the auditorium was already filling with smiling parents and relatives. Helen's eyes searched for Rudy and his family. Backstage the air was heady with the scent of roses.

Carla Raven looked as though she had been crying. Everybody knew she was in love with some boy who was flying with the Canadian Air Corps. Helen hoped she didn't have bad news.

After the graduation exercises she could squeeze in only a few words with Rudy. "You're telling them tonight?" he demanded.

"As soon as we get home," she promised.

On the way home her mother fretted because Bernie couldn't be home for her graduation. "Mama, he doesn't get out of school for another week." After graduating from Columbia Bernie had gone on to the Harvard Business School. It irritated her that Papa carried on so about a Polish student making it into Harvard. Bernie was an American.

"Besides," she giggled, "he knows that every girl in my class is mad about him. They nearly stampeded at my Christmas party when he looked in to see what was happening."

"He's such a handsome boy," her mother said tenderly.

"The image of Casimar," her father said—as he always did. Now he sighed. "I wish we had some word of him."

Mama was afraid Bernie would want to join up and fight with General Haller. She forgot how Papa and she and Uncle Leon had worked with the young rebels in Poland all those years ago. Even Uncle Casimar, whom she remembered vaguely from their trip to Paris when she was little, had been part of that rebel group. When people got older they forgot. Mama was already forty-three years old, though Papa always said she still looked like a girl.

Josip left them in front of the house and drove on to put the car away for the night. Her father put an arm around each of them and walked them to the house.

"I have a fine bottle of wine waiting to celebrate tonight," he said ebulliently. "And it's about time, young lady, that you decide about college."

Helen waited for Papa to pour the wine. "I have something very important to tell you," she began, her voice uneven, her hands cold despite the warmth of the night. "Rudy's asked me to marry him."

"Oh, darling." Tears welled in her mother's eyes. "I knew you two were close friends, but marriage?"

"Why didn't Rudy come to me?" Her father seemed mildly irritated.

"Papa, they don't do it that way in this country," Helen sniffed.

"It'll be a while before Rudy is free to marry you," her mother put in, "and I know his parents expect him to go on to college."

"Mama, Rudy is going to France and we want to be married right away." Helen tensed, anticipating a battle.

"That's out of the question." Her mother seemed terrified. "You're only seventeen and Rudy's the same age."

"Rudy will be eighteen next month." Helen lifted her head in shaky defiance. "He doesn't want to go away without knowing I'm his wife."

"No." Johanna shook her head determinedly. "When Rudy comes home if you both still feel the same way then you can be married after a suitable interval."

"Not when he comes home, Mama, now!" Her eyes filled and her lips trembled. "Papa—"

"Darling, Rudy and you are hardly more than children," her mother broke in. "You're both carried away by this horrible war—"

"Mama, you were a year younger than I am when you married Papa," she insisted, "and Papa was only twenty."

"Those were different times, Helen," her father said impatiently.

"How different? Rudy's going off to fight for Poland. Mama and you were running for your lives from Poland."

"There will be no wedding before Rudy leaves," her mother said firmly. "You can be sure Rudy's parents will agree with your father and me."

Tears filled Helen's eyes and spilled over as she turned from her mother to her father. This time they were lined up against her. "We'll see. It's ridiculous to treat us as though we were children. If Rudy's old enough to fight, he's old enough to marry."

"It's late," her father said brusquely. "We're all going up to our rooms and to sleep now. There's been enough said tonight."

Helen charged up the stairs into her bedroom and slammed the door behind her. She hurried to the telephone, her private line, a coveted sixteenth birthday present, and asked the operator for Rudy's number. It was late to be phoning, she thought guiltily, when Rudy didn't have a phone of his own.

Mrs. Conrad answered it herself; the servants must have retired for the night.

"Mrs. Conrad, this is Helen," she said apologetically. "I know it's late, but may I please speak with Rudy?"

"He's gone to bed. He'll call you in the morning," Mrs. Conrad replied. From the brusque tone of her voice Helen knew that Mrs. Conrad was upset. Rudy had talked to his parents and they had reacted the same as hers.

"Thank you, Mrs. Conrad. Good night."

Helen knew she would have trouble sleeping tonight. Rudy wouldn't go against his parents' wishes. In that one frustrating way he was old-fashioned—that and going off to fight for Poland. He had been born in New York; he was an American, like her. Of course she felt sorry for the Poles. She felt sorry for the poor Polish-Americans. She felt sorry for *all* poor people.

Mama and Papa clung so ridiculously to the old ways— like insisting Bernie and she keep up their Polish, even though they never used it. Mama was forever running downtown for some meeting or do-gooder's errand. Uncle Leon was more American than Papa and Mama, even though he came to America later than they did. Helen sighed and hung up her white graduation dress.

Tomorrow Rudy would come over and explain that

they'd have to wait until he got back from fighting in France. All at once Helen was cold. Suppose he didn't come back? He didn't *have* to fight. The United States wasn't at war. She laid her pearls back in their case.

She wasn't going to college, not if Rudy was off in France fighting with General Haller. Mama and Papa couldn't force her to go to school. When Rudy left, she'd ask them to send her out for a visit with Uncle Leon. She'd meet Mary Pickford and Douglas Fairbanks and Charlie Chaplin. Uncle Leon knew everybody in Hollywood.

Helen buried her face in the pillow and tried to sleep. If Rudy weren't so old-fashioned about listening to his parents, they could run off and get married. Now they'd have to wait until he came back—she wouldn't think about his not coming back.

When Helen awoke in the morning, deliciously late because school was over, she heard voices downstairs. She blinked, sat up and leapt out of bed. Rudy's mother had just arrived and Mama was taking her into the library.

She reached for the phone. Why hadn't Rudy called by now?

She asked the operator for the number at the Conrad house and waited. Mrs. Conrad had come over to talk to Mama about Rudy and her wanting to get married. Helen could just see it—the four parents against Rudy and her, and Rudy always so quick to do as his folks asked.

A lot of the girls at school thought fighting in the war was romantic, but Carla didn't feel that way. Carla knew that every time her boyfriend went up in his plane, it might be the last.

"Hello?" Rudy's voice was thick with sleep.

"Rudy, your mother's over here."

"I know. Papa and she had a fit when I said we want to get married before I go away."

"If you're old enough to fight for Poland," Helen repeated doggedly, "then you're old enough to get married."

"I tried to tell them that. They said we'd have to wait until after the war. Then we'll have the biggest Polish wedding this city ever saw."

"Rudy, I don't want a Polish wedding. I want an American wedding—right now." All at once an audacious plan was taking root in her mind. "Rudy, your mother will be here all morning talking to Mama. You know how it is when they get together. I'm going to dress and come right over."

Within twenty minutes she was ringing his doorbell. Mrs. Conrad would be at Helen's house all morning. Mr. Conrad left for the office at eight. There'd be nobody in the house except Rudy and the servants.

The Conrads' downstairs maid admitted her with a wide smile.

"Mr. Rudy's having breakfast in the breakfast room," she said. "Shall I bring you coffee, Miss Helen?"

"Please," Helen said politely.

Rudy sat at the table looking groggy and unhappy. He glanced up with a start of surprise as she walked into the room. "I didn't hear the doorbell."

"Rudy, we could go down to City Hall, or wherever it is that people go to get married, and do it secretly." Helen grabbed his ears and kissed him. "Later we can have a church wedding."

He pulled his head back a little. "We're both too young." He took her hands and kissed them.

"It's not fair," she said, her voice rising, and then forced a smile as the maid came in with a cup of coffee for her.

"The minute this rotten war is over we'll get married," he promised. "Nobody can stop us then."

"You don't want to go to France," Helen exclaimed. "Rudy, why did you sign up?"

"Papa expected it of me," he confessed. "He'd go himself even if he is forty-seven, but there's nobody to handle the business. Helen, I have to go for the sake of the family. After that dinner last year when we met Paderewski and his wife, I knew I'd have to go once I was out of high school."

"Our parents live with one foot in Poland." Helen beat her fist in frustration. "Why do we have to live that way too?"

"You want to see Poland independent," Rudy said reproachfully.

"Yes," Helen conceded, "but I don't want to see you die for her."

"Helen! What a thing to say. When I come home we'll be married and I'll go to college." We'll have an apartment or a little house near the campus." She saw the glow in his eyes. "I wish we had a place of our own right this minute."

"So do I," she said tremulously. "Rudy, let's go up to your room."

His eyes widened. "You mean it?"

"Why not?" All at once she couldn't wait to have Rudy kiss her again, to touch her breasts. "Nobody's home except the servants, and they won't stop us."

Caught up in young passion that neither had expected to be satisfied until their wedding night, Helen and Rudy sneaked upstairs to his bedroom. If she got pregnant so much the better, Helen told herself. Then he reached for her, clumsy but ardent and tender, and she forgot the rest.

Johanna felt tears sting her own eyes as she stood with Rudy's mother on the dock. Rudy kissed Helen good-bye with passion that Johanna found disconcerting. She had been years younger than Rudy when she gambled her life for Poland, yet she seemed to have been much older than Rudy. Was it because she had not grown up pampered and cherished, or did all parents feel like this when their children grew up?

"His father is so proud of him," Mrs. Conrad said tearfully, "but I wish he didn't have to go. Johanna, I'm so frightened for Rudy."

"God will watch over him." Johanna spoke with confidence she didn't feel. "This madness will soon be over and Rudy will come home to us."

"They're only children," Stella said bitterly. Helen and Rudy separated and he headed for the uniformed young men waiting to board the ship to France. "They shouldn't even be making the crossing when it's so dangerous." She waved a last good-bye and headed for a taxi.

Johanna turned to Helen. "We'll go to the Plaza for tea," she said with an effort at cheerfulness. "I have a surprise for you.

The headwaiter made a ceremony of seating them and effaced himself. Johanna cleared her throat.

"Leon has a magnificent house that he has always said is at our disposal. Let's go pay him a visit. We can leave at the end of the week." Now that she knew Michal had broken off the affair with Claudia Sherwood, she could bear to go to California. Claudia was engaged to marry a steel magnate far richer than Michal.

Helen looked at her with wide reproachful eyes. "I'm not sure I want to go."

"Helen, we're going." Johanna tried to be patient; she knew how upsetting it had been for Helen to see Rudy off to war. "Uncle Leon is expecting us. You know how fond of you he is."

"All right," Helen sniffed.

"Darling, you adore the movies." Johanna tried to coax her daughter into some enthusiasm. She understood how Helen felt. She lived in uneasy fear that Bernie might decide to go to war. "It'll be such an exciting trip."

In an effort to lift Helen's spirits Johanna swept her up in a frenzy of shopping for their trip. Bernie arrived home from Harvard the day before Helen and she boarded the Twentieth Century Limited for California. Remembering Rudy on his way to a battlefield in France, Johanna tried not to show her anxiety about Bernie's future. In September he was returning to the Harvard Business School. With God's help the war would be over by the time he graduated.

Michal's secretary had reserved a drawing room for them on the train. Always interested in what made travelers happy, Michal encouraged Johanna to make notes about the train's appointments. "The service is always subject to change. See what you think of the food, too."

"Come on, Papa, that's a lot of work," Helen objected. "This trip is supposed to be fun."

"The train carries stenographers," he said mildly, trying not to show his unhappiness at Helen's downcast face. "You can dictate your notes to one of them."

"I will, Michal," Johanna promised.

Then the all-aboard sounded. Michal kissed Johanna good-bye and reached to hug Helen to him before he kissed her cheek.

The train pulled out of Grand Central Station and headed north toward Harmon. Michal said this was one of the rare American trains not affected by the war effort. It continued to run as in peacetime.

From the moment the train left the station Helen kept her nose in a book, reluctantly putting it aside only when Johanna insisted she was hungry.

"What are you reading?" Johanna asked with an effort to draw Helen away from morbid thoughts.

"The Theodore Dreiser book." Her eyes challenged her mother to reproach her. Dreiser's novel *The Genius* had been banned in New York state.

Johanna was a little shocked. "Where did you get it?"

"Carla lent it to me. A visiting cousin left it with her."

"Let's go in to dinner." Sometimes Johanna felt her daughter was far more sophisticated than she. The girls of Helen's generation seemed to know so much, and yet, she mused as they left the drawing room for the dining car, in other ways they were very young.

She watched worriedly while Helen toyed with an excellent dinner. Everything she said seemed to be wrong. Johanna commented about her pleasure that President Wilson had declared last New Year's Day Polish Day and Helen looked as though she been slapped across the face. Since Rudy left Helen had resented every reference to Poland.

It was scarcely nine o'clock when Helen prepared for bed. She didn't want to make this trip, Johanna mused. Maybe it had been wrong to force her to go to California. She lay awake far into the night listening to her daughter toss and turn.

The train spend across country. Each day seemed just like the previous one. In Albuquerque Johanna tried to persuade Helen to do some fast shopping from Indians displaying their wares at the station.

"I don't want to buy anything," Helen shouted. "Leave me alone, Mama."

"I just hoped you'd see something you liked," Johanna stammered. Ever since they left New York she had been on the defensive. She searched Helen's face. Clearly her daughter had slept very little in the past days. Dark crescents underlined her eyes and her face was set in misery that seemed worse each day. "I love you," Johanna said desperately.

"Mama, please." Helen turned her face to the window.

"Oh, darling." Johanna reached out as she realized Helen was crying. "Darling, I want so much to see you happy."

"How can I be happy? Rudy's away and I don't know when he'll come home." She hesitated. "And now I know I'm not pregnant."

"Why should you be pregnant?" Johanna froze.

Helen swung about to face her.

"For the usual reason." Color flooded her face. "I hoped if I was pregnant, then his father could make sure Rudy was sent home. But I'm not." Her voice broke. "This morning I knew for sure."

"How could Rudy put you into such a position?" Johanna blazed with anger. "We always thought he was such a—"

"It was my fault. I went to his house the morning after graduation when his mother was with you. I wanted to be pregnant so he'd come home right away."

"Oh, my baby." Johanna pulled Helen into her arms and rocked her as though she were a little girl again. "My sweet little baby. Rudy's signed up, darling. Even if you were pregnant—and I thank God you're not—he couldn't come home."

"I can't do anything right," Helen cried. "I just wanted to make sure he didn't get hurt."

"Everything will be all right," Johanna promised. "When Rudy comes home you two will be married. Maybe both of you will to go college. You're so young." She hesitated, visualizing Michal's shock if he knew his little girl was no virgin. "We won't say anything about this to your father. It's better he shouldn't know."

"I won't say anything to anybody," Helen said in a scared little voice, "not even to the priest."

It seemed to Johanna that in Hollywood Helen drew close to her again. Leon took them on a tour not only of his own studio but of several others. He introduced them to actors and actresses whom Helen knew only from *Photo Play* and the other new movie magazines.

On their last night in California Leon took them to dinner at the Ambassador Hotel. When Helen excused herself to go to the ladies' room, Leon took Johanna's hand in his.

"How are things with Michal and you?"

"All right." She lowered her eyes. "Thanks for what you did for me last year."

"You mean Claudia Sherwood." He shrugged. "She's an overambitious little slut. She was easy to handle. What about Michal and you?" he asked again. "Is he back in your bed?"

"Leon, you ask impertinent questions." She tried to laugh.

"I don't understand my brother," he sighed. "If you were my wife, we'd be screwing three nights a week." Unexpectedly he grinned, ignoring her glare of reproach at his vulgarity. "More than that I can't handle anymore. I can't believe it. I'm fifty years old."

Back in New York Helen began to work with the suffragette movement. Letters from Rudy were sparse in the ensuing months. With the arrival of 1917 Americans talked already about the strong possibility of the United States entering the war.

Johanna and Michal were poignantly pleased, like Poles throughout the country, when President Wilson said in an address on January 22, "I take it for granted that statesmen everywhere are agreed that there shall be a united, independent and autonomous Poland"—meaning at the end of the war.

On April fourth Polish patriot and world-renowned pianist Ignace Paderewski spoke so eloquently on behalf of Poland that the Union of Polish Falcons at a convention in Pittsburgh voted to muster an Army of Kosciuszko. It would consist of a hundred thousand men who volunteered to fight by the side of the United States Army. When Secretary of War Baker pointed out that he could not legally accept their offer, the American Poles went ahead on their own, opening two enormous training camps.

Michal ached to be part of the action. "What am I doing here in an office?" he railed over dinner the night after Paderewski's impassioned speech. "I'm not an old man. I can fight."

"Michal, you're fighting," Johanna insisted, relieved that Helen was off tonight at a suffragette meeting. "You're providing vital supply lines. Your ships and your running the company are far more important than for you to carry a gun."

"I hear that it's expected that thirty-eight thousand Polish Americans will enter the American army. Another twenty-two thousand will go to join General Haller in France." His smile was wry. "The way I hear it, there'll be some Polish communities in America where the male civilian population will disappear."

The following day the United States declared war on Germany. Every Polish-language newspaper pleaded for young men of draft age to register for service. The priests made the same appeal on Registration Sunday.

On the following Monday Stella Conrad called Johanna. "Johanna—" Her voice seemed lifeless. "We've had word of Rudy—"

"What is it?" Fear caught at her throat.

"He's gone." Stella's voice swelled to a wail. "Rudy's dead. My son is dead."

Johanna heard the click of the phone at the other end. She felt encased in ice. How do I tell Helen? I am about to lose my daughter.

Chapter 14

"If you'd let me marry him, I might have been pregnant before he left. He'd have come home. He wouldn't have died. It's all your fault. Why did you do this to me, Mama?" Helen's voice was hoarse and out of control. Her face was white blotched with red; her eyes were so puffy the skin of the lids looked translucent. She had been pacing and raging for hours between bouts of abandoned weeping. Her theme was always the same: it was Johanna's fault Rudy had been shot from the sky.

Johanna was beginning to be really terrified of Helen's anguish and rage. If this kept up she would have to call Dr. Abramowiez. She had let her daughter carry on in the hope that she would wear herself out and feel better, but instead Helen was working up to real hysteria.

"Listen, darling, don't carry on like this. It wouldn't have made any difference. They just don't send soldiers home—"

"His father knows everyone in Washington," Helen said wildly. "He could have brought him home, he could

161

have, he could have! Go away. You wanted this to happen.
I don't want to have to look at you."

Johanna went downstairs to the telephone. She feared
that this breach could never be mended, but she would do her
best to make peace with Helen.

The doctor had far less patience. "What's it to be,
Helen, a shot of sedative or a little self-control? Make
yourself sick if it will gratify you, but decent young ladies
don't speak to their mothers like that, so stop it this
minute."

Astonished at such a tone from an old friend, Helen
subsided to mere sullenness. Melissa, back at last from her
afternoon out, added her opinion to Dr. Abramowiez's and
tucked her pet into bed with a hot toddy.

"That'll be the last of that kind of talk," she said a
few minutes later to Abramowiez and her mistress. "I told
her I'd smack her silly if I heard that nonsense from her.
'Do your grieving decent,' I said."

In the days that followed Helen moved about the house
like a wraith, speaking to no one except Carla. Helen behaved
as though her father and mother were the enemy, Johanna
thought bitterly. It was Carla who finally persuaded Helen
to go out again by insisting that Johanna had a duty to
join in the war relief effort.

Johanna knew the extent of Michal's pride in the
young Polish-Americans who rallied in support of the
American military effort. Forty thousand of them were
among the first hundred thousand Americans reporting for
service. From the steel mills and the mines and the docks
they rushed to enlist.

Many of them had left Poland in hopes of escaping
army service for a hated nation, but when America needed
them, they came forward, many knowing they might meet
brothers, cousins, uncles in the enemy trenches.

Bernie graduated from Harvard and came home to tell

his mother and father that of course he must go into service. With a Harvard buddy he left the house early on his second morning home and went off to enlist. Johanna smiled until he left and then locked herself in her room to cry. Helen grinned crookedly and punched him on the arm. Michal shook his hand, gave him a well-filled wallet and a hug and pushed his son out of the house.

Within a shockingly short time Bernie came home for a twenty-four-hour furlough to tell them he was standing by for active duty in Europe. Johanna hugged him to her, vowing not to let him see her cry. She would pray for him every day, she promised.

"If you get to Paris," she said with an air of bravado as Bernie bent to kiss her good-bye, "remember to look up your Uncle Casimar."

Bernie kissed his mother, then his father, and disappeared into the night. Johanna knew that within hours he would be on a blacked-out ship headed for the war zone.

Late in 1917 Johanna went to Helen's room to see why she had not come to dinner. She discovered that her daughter, along with her friend Carla, had secretly left New York that morning. They were headed for overseas duty with the American Red Cross. Her hands trembling so that the note almost fell from her fingers, Johanna read and reread the message.

> *Weeks ago Carla and I signed up for service with the American Red Cross. We gave our age as twenty-one and said we wished to go overseas to serve. By now we'll be on a troopship bound for Europe. Please don't worry, Mama. I must do this. Papa and you worked for Poland and now I work for America."*

Slowly, already feeling the emptiness of the house, Johanna walked downstairs to tell Michal what had happened.

"I'm not surprised," he said. His eyes were compassionate for Johanna's distress. "The children grew up hearing about our intrigues in Warsaw. Though he seems to have little concern left for Poland these days, Leon never spent any length of time with Bernie and Helen without talking about the old days."

"Why did we talk like that, Michal?" Johanna wept. "Why did we make it seem such an adventure?"

Michal held her and stroked her hair. "Helen knows it's not an adventure. Rudy's death taught her that. And wasn't Carla's boyfriend reported missing after a flight over France?"

Numbly Johanna nodded. "I wanted so to protect the children, and now they're both off at war." She pulled away and sniffed.

Michal took her trembling hand between his own. "We'll survive this too, Johanna."

London in 1917 was not the London of Helen's childhood. She walked through the streets with Carla and realized that America was a world away from the war.

They saw craters here and there along the Embankment, buildings that had been hit by the zeppelins and bombers that descended over the city on every moonlit night. The street lamps were painted black, every window blacked out. Anti-aircraft guns showed up everywhere.

Helen and Carla were assigned to work at a canteen for American soldiers. They made and poured coffee, cleaned the premises, bought the supplies and smiled cheerfully all day long. The faces of the young American soldiers who appeared at the Red Cross canteen were all the same, Helen thought, too young to die.

Carla asked every soldier she talked to about George's regiment; the Canadians were moving off to France in hordes now. A cynical doughboy from Boston told Helen that the only Americans thus far in France were Congressmen on inspection tours. He was impatient to be in France and finish the war.

Worn out from a long, demanding day, Helen and Carla usually went straight to the small room they shared. One night when they were about to go off duty Carla said she had promised that they would go to a pub with two American doughboys. "Why not? They're lonely and we're lonely."

"I can't." Panic seized Helen. She'd seen the hungry stares of the hordes of young men in khaki who poured each day into the canteen. "I know some of the girls go out—"

"Honey, we're not safe in New York. We may not be fighting, but we could be dead tomorrow."

Helen closed her eyes in pain. Rudy was dead, George missing. If they could give a little happiness to two soldiers who might be dead tomorrow, was that wrong? "All right, I'll go." She forced a wry smile. "If my feet hold out."

Helen and Carla made their way through the darkened streets to the pub where they were to meet the American privates. She was touched by their pleasure in the company of two Red Cross workers. Like Rudy, they could be dead tomorrow.

It didn't seem wrong when PFC David Mitchell, who had one more year at a small college in the Midwest, kissed her in a dark corner of the street. Eight nights later, when David whispered word that at dawn his company left for France, it didn't seem wrong to go with him to a cheap hotel where no questions were asked.

Nobody back home would understand, though, Helen

thought while she lay at rest in David's arms; only the soldiers and women like Carla and herself, who saw it firsthand.

Helen and Carla went out with a string of American servicemen in the ensuing weeks and hardly ever said no. They gave and received a great deal of short-term pleasure in a world like none they had ever dreamed existed.

The October Revolution put Russia out of the war and Germany could concentrate on France. Early in 1918, spurred by tales of vicious fighting, Helen and Carla contrived to be sent to France.

Despite her sixteen-hour work days on the war effort, Johanna found sleep hard to come by. She worried about Bernie, somewhere in France. Letters came at long intervals. Bernie was the kind of son who'd write often to alleviate her fears. The daily newspapers carried fearful casualty lists, but his name was on none of them. And now, at the end of a long day on a fund drive, Johanna sat at the dining table and read and reread the latest brief note from Helen.

> *Don't worry if you don't hear from me for a while. I'm fine. I'm glad to be part of what's happening and to know I'm helping.*

When Michal arrived she was still sitting at the dining table, though it was past eleven. Like her, he was engaged in volunteer work after office hours. Michal was jubilant that the Russians had rebelled. He was convinced that the Russian proletariat would understand the need for an independent Poland. Still, he was aware that the loss of the support of the Russian army was costing the Allies dearly.

"A letter from Helen?" His face lit as he saw the envelope with the familiar finishing-school penmanship.

"I think she's going to France." Johanna struggled to keep her voice even. "Of course with censorship she can't come right out and say so." She handed the note to Michal.

"It's been awhile since we've heard from Bernie." She voiced his own anxiety.

"Everybody knows how slow mail is to arrive these days," he replied gallantly.

"We'll hear soon," Johanna agreed.

He smiled up at Molly as she served him a plate of savory hot stew. Molly had good food waiting no matter how late Johanna or he got home. "Molly, how would we ever get along without you?"

"You don't have to," she said briskly. "Will you be wantin' coffee?"

"No, thanks. Not at this hour." He turned to Johanna. "The word that's coming through is encouraging." Michal reached for a fork. Because of his business on behalf of the government he often received classified information. "Our convoys along with the British fleet have destroyed over thirty submarines in the last year. The Germans can't replace them that fast. Johanna, we're going to win this war."

"But at what cost?" Johanna's face was tight.

"I wish there was some way to get word of my sisters and their families." Though Michal frequently begged them to leave their farms in German Poland, they were reluctant to uproot themselves. Already their children were married and raising families of their own. "Johanna, my sisters' sons could be fighting in a trench against Bernie." He pushed the food around on his plate.

"Michal, I've been thinking about going over with a Red Cross unit," Johanna announced. Thus far she had only thought about it, until Helen's note galvanized her into action. "I've had a lot of experience these past three years in organizing and serving. I could be useful."

Michal dropped his fork and stared at his wife. "Johanna, you do enough here."

"But over there," she said softly, "I might run into Bernie or Helen."

"Do you know the odds against that? One chance in a million that you'd see either of them."

"I want to take that chance." She spoke with deliberate slowness. "Helen went away blaming me for Rudy's death." Johanna gave a tiny sob. "I want my daughter back. I'm going to Europe to try to heal the breach. It's the only thing I can think of."

"She was a hurt little girl then," Michal said gently. "She knows better now. And you have duties here."

"Michal, I'm planning to go to France as soon as possible. Please don't try to stop me."

Michal stared long and hard at her, as though trying to memorize every contour of her face. "I won't; I know you feel you must. But don't ask me to like it." His smile was rueful. "I'll be scared to death every minute you're away."

Johanna began arrangements the next day and on a dreary dark night shortly before dawn she boarded a once-elegant transatlantic liner now transformed into a military grey troopship. She had allowed Michal to believe that her service would include nothing more hazardous than setting up canteens for troops in transit or well behind the fighting lines. In truth Johanna had been trained to drive an ambulance as well as to work in a field hospital.

Despite his Washington contacts Michal had not been able to locate either Bernie or Helen. But at least, Johanna told herself as she stood on deck in the blackout each night of the crossing, there was a chance that she might see one or both of her children. Michal and she knew that Casimar was somewhere close to Paris; at one point he had been serving in a French hospital.

Everyone in the convoy knew that they lived in nightly danger of attack despite their escort, yet Johanna felt oddly protected. She was traveling closer each night to Bernie and Helen—and closer to Poland.

While the collapse of the Russian Army had led to peace between the Central Powers and the Bolsheviks, the Bolsheviks still had not admitted Polish delegates to the deliberations on the peace treaty now being drawn up. It mattered little that the Bolsheviks recognized in theory that the Polish had the right to independence.

Like Michal, Johanna clung to President Wilson's "Fourteen Points" message to Congress just two weeks ago. In it he declared that Poland should be provided "with an outlet to the sea and an international guarantee of its independence and integrity."

At last the troopship arrived at Liverpool and Johanna's Red Cross group was billeted about forty miles southwest of London. When the fog did not sit heavily over their camp, the sharp January wind blew hard, and the bone-chilling damp never relented. Johanna waited impatiently to leave for France.

They entrained for London after four days and arrived at Waterloo Station early in the afternoon. The streets were thronged with officers and enlisted men of many nations trying to cram a year's worth of good times into the two or three days before they were hauled without warning back to France. Johanna was glad to be going with them at last.

In Paris the civilian population was being regularly exposed to aerial attack; the Germans were frantic to move into Paris before American troops began to arrive in numbers. At this point the United States had only a few divisions in France—and of those, two lacked combat experience.

Johanna was stationed at a base hospital just behind the lines in the vicinity of the Somme River. She and her colleagues were told this was a relatively quiet time, though the general assumption was that the Germans were preparing for a massive offensive.

Johanna settled in as best she could, frustrated that she could not be in Paris, as she had reason to believe Helen was based there. She was at a complete loss as to Bernie's whereabouts.

Late in February American forces began to arrive in impressive numbers. At the same time the workers at the field hospital became aware of an increase in German shelling.

One dark night in early March it started in earnest. Thousands of flashes of light punctured the sky, each immediately followed by a thunderclap. The Germans were on the offensive again.

Red Cross ambulances moved into action as the heavy barrage continued. Load after load of wounded arrived; Johanna never got used to seeing them. Ever-conscious that a scattering of American troops was stationed in the vicinity, she looked for Bernie on every stretcher. So far she had seen no one with the insignia of his regiment.

Dawn came but the shelling did not stop; it went on for days, weeks. The wounded kept arriving in staggering numbers, the fatalities agonizingly heavy. Ambulance drivers worked without sleep for days at a time, until they could no longer sit behind the wheel. Everyone—nurses, doctors, aides—worked until he dropped.

On a fog-laden night when the German bombardment was especially intense, a young driver collapsed after helping his aide remove the wounded from the ambulance.

"Stretcher," Johanna called out briskly, leaning over

the twenty-two-year old Midwesterner, who had driven for forty-eight hours without a break. "Stretcher!"

"There're lots more out there," his aide, a young Polish-American from Brooklyn, said apprehensively. "We've got to go back."

"You'll have to drive, Jake," Johanna said, wondering who on earth she could send with him.

"I'm afraid I can't, ma'am. Trick knee. Never manage the clutch. That's why poor Blaney packed it in. No help with the driving."

"I'll go with you," Johanna decided. "I can drive."

"You can't do that, ma'am." He was shocked. "You don't know what it's like out there."

"I'm about to find out. Wait while I find someone to take over for me. Refuel and stand by—and don't forget to get the keys from Blaney."

Jakob was terrified, not at going back into the field but that a woman was driving. Cursing her inability to make any speed through the heavy fog, Johanna inched ahead.

"Begging your pardon, ma'am," Jake said, "but all hell's breaking loose now."

"Then it's a good thing we came. If it weren't for all hell being loose, neither of us would be here. Cheer up, boy. I can't get any deader than you can."

Around them the shelling was devastating. As they moved ahead the aide shouted a warning that an ambulance loaded with wounded was approaching through the fog. Her heart pounding, Johanna slowed yet more. In the dense fog they just scraped each other.

"It's pea soup tonight," the other driver yelled through her window on his way past. "Take it easy."

"The trenches are just ahead," Jake said nervously. "You'd better stop now."

He was clearly shocked when Johanna jumped down

from the driver's side and moved forward to help with the stretcher. "Ma'am, you best stay in the ambulance."

"Stop ma'aming me, Jakob Kanski," Johanna told him impatiently. "We've got work to do. My son might be out there. Now get cracking!"

They moved ahead in a crouch, aware of alarming silence from the dugout just ahead—no answering fire to the Germans, who were fearfully close. Kanski went ahead, looked into it and then moved back.

"They're all dead," he reported, crossing himself. "Let's move on."

"We'll just take a look over there," she said, pointing.

"Ma'am, the Huns are moving in like cockroaches," he stammered. "Let's get out of here."

All at once he threw his hands above him and yelled. Johanna tried to catch him, but she was too small and slim to do more than break his fall. She leaned over him. Jakob Kanski was dead.

Johanna ran for the ambulance to flee. She could do nothing alone. About to climb behind the wheel, she heard a voice in low prayer. Best see if he could walk to the ambulance. Johanna crawled to a nearby dugout.

A bespectacled priest knelt beside a wounded soldier.

"I have an ambulance just beyond but no aide," she called to him. "We'll have to carry him without a stretcher."

"He won't be needing an ambulance," the priest said gently in English. His accent disconcerted her; he clearly was Polish.

Heart hammering, she stared in disbelief as he said a final few words over the dead soldier. How often in a lifetime would she have these unexpected encounters? Leon in New York, when they had believed him dead. Casimar in Paris, when she had no idea he was coming. Now—

"Casimar?" she whispered. "Dear God, is it really you?"

He gazed at her in the shadowy darkness. "Johanna—" His voice was deep with astonishment. "I must be dreaming."

"No, Casimar. It's Johanna." Were they to die here together on a battlefield in France? Alarm surged through her. "Casimar, look!"

A German soldier advanced on them, bayonet held high, death in his eyes. Casimar grabbed the dead man's gun and shot him when he was just closing in. The German soldier fell and Johanna turned away from the sight of the gaping wound in his head.

"He was sent ahead to scout," Casimar said, visibly stunned. As though burnt by the touch he dropped the gun to the dirt.

"Let's get out of here. Casimar, please come."

Casimar and Johanna sprinted for the ambulance. He slid behind the wheel. The fog hid everything.

"All I know is that we're driving away from the Germans," Casimar said grimly. "I'm billeted in a village somewhere to the left. My commanding officer expected me to stay behind the lines. I joined the British forces when the French turned over this area to them. I came to administer to the wounded," he said tightly, "not to sit in a village." He sighed, anguished. "And now I find myself with a gun in my hand and a dead German at my feet."

"He would have killed us both." Johanna was more shaken by Casimar's presence than by the brush with death.

"Johanna, I can't believe you're here. The years go by and you change so little."

All at once they were aware of heavy shelling. With recklessness born of necessity Casimar swerved off the road and drove across the fields away from the guns. They were going nowhere near the hospital, Johanna realized. It was less than a quarter mile away, but at this moment it might have been out of reach by a thousand miles.

Casimar drove without speaking for a while, caught up in the necessity to seek shelter.

"There's a village just ahead," Johanna said at last, seeing the outline of small houses.

"That's not where I'm billeted," he said uneasily. "We're lost, Johanna."

"The Germans haven't been here," she opined. "It hasn't even been shelled."

Casimar stopped the ambulance before a small frame house.

"I think the whole village is deserted. Look at the houses beyond. There's no smoke coming from any of them."

"At this hour they're all asleep," Johanna suggested as they left the ambulance.

But Casimar was correct. The inhabitants of the tiny village had fled.

"The shelling is coming so close they were afraid to stay." Casimar led her into the nearest house. "We'll stay here until daylight."

Casimar pushed open the front door, which no one had taken the time to lock, and held it wide for Johanna to enter. He groped in the dark until he found a kerosene lamp and Johanna produced matches from the pocket of her coat. The modesty of the house evoked memories of Johanna's Fall River.

"It's cold," he said. He was reluctant to take his eyes off her even for a moment. "I'll start a fire in the grate if there's wood." He looked in the box beside the fireplace. "And there is."

"I suppose it's all right if I make tea," Johanna said after watching him work to coax a flame from the chunks of wood piled into the grate.

He lifted his face to hers and she trembled at the intensity of his gaze.

"See if there's any food," he said gently. "They left too fast to take everything with them."

In the kitchen Johanna found a lamp, lit it, looked about for something to eat. On a shelf she found a box of tea, flour, lentils, a loaf of still-fresh bread. On another shelf there was jam. A bin on the floor was piled high with potatoes.

"The other room will be warm in a few minutes." Casimar's voice whirled her about. "Is there tea?" Johanna knew he was clutching at everyday routine to push away the horror of having killed a man.

"I'm just getting it now." She reached for the box of tea. "And there's bread and jam to go with it." Despite the dank chill of the kitchen she glowed with heat because she stood alone here with Casimar. Alone all night long . . .

"Where's the bread? I'll slice it."

For a few minutes the tension relaxed, as they were engaged in preparing a modest meal for themselves. Now and then the sounds of shelling reached them through the night silence. For now the deserted village seemed safe. What was happening at the hospital? she wondered anxiously.

"We'll eat before the fire," Casimar said, taking the bread, the jam and a pair of knives in his hands. "It'll be warmer there."

"All right," Johanna agreed, picking up the two cups and the teapot from the table, remembering that Casimar liked it without sugar but with a spoonful of jam on special occasions.

Casimar had brought two chairs close to the fire. Now he pulled a small table between the chairs.

"It's not quite Maxim's in Paris," he said, "but it'll had known love until tonight.

"Casimar, I can hardly believe I'm here with you." Her hand was unsteady as she lifted the cup to her mouth.

"I thought you were in Paris. I wrote Helen to look after you."

"I *was* with the Polish army in Paris," he began. "Then I was a chaplain at a field hospital. They sent me to the village because the Germans are so ruthless."

All the while he spoke, Johanna was conscious that she was with Casimar, whom she adored, who grew almost handsome with the passing years, full of warmth and compassion. Johanna ached with tenderness.

"Would you like jam in your tea?" she asked as casually as though they sat at a table in Maxim's of Paris. "I'll get a spoon—"

"You remember." His voice rang with pleasure. "I'll get the spoon." Not quite knowing how it happened, Johanna found herself in Casimar's arms.

"I was so afraid for you," she whispered when at last they paused for breath. "It was so long since we had word from you."

"I was sure it was a mirage when I saw you standing there in that dugout, Johanna." He pressed his face against hers. "I'm an evil man. A little while ago I killed, and now I don't think I can live without loving you."

"Casimar, we may never get out of this place alive," she said urgently, aware of the shelling in the distance. "I don't want to die without having loved you. Casimar, please?"

He swept her off her feet without a thought for the vows he was about to break. Casimar carried her into the tiny bedroom and dropped her onto the high feather bed. Firelight lent a delicate glow to her face as he bent to kiss her again. Her arms closed about him. This was the night for which she had been born.

Johanna curled up beneath the thick comforter provided by their unknowing host while Casimar went out to throw more wood onto the grate. Her clothes lay in a heap beside Casimar's. She waited impatiently for him to come back to her again, thinking of the firm body that never had known love until tonight.

"You're cold," she whispered as he slipped beneath the comforter.

"How can I be cold with you in my arms?" He lifted himself above her again, content for the moment to rest between her thighs. "You don't know the demons I've wrestled through the years. You were never out of my mind or heart. In Paris I didn't dare spend another ten minutes with you because I knew my vows would be forgotten. But tonight my strength is gone. I can't deny myself."

"Sssh. Tonight belongs to us."

He set his mouth at her breasts with the fervor of a man famished for passion. All night long they took their pleasure, for as Carismar said with a laugh, "We can't sleep with all the shelling anyway."

Chapter 15

Johanna awoke in Casimar's arms and lay motionless lest she awaken him. She knew—as Casimar knew—that this one night was all they could have. If God willed it, they would be safe from the German advance. If not, then at least they had this last happiness. No one would ever know.

When Casimar stirred, she reached to kiss him and immediately he was awake. As though he were a boy of sixteen, he was ready again to make love. She gloried in his passion, which matched her own.

They lay clinging together for precious minutes, but at last they must return to reality. While Johanna dressed in the morning chill, Casimar went out to build up the fire. Johanna went to the kitchen to make a pot of tea and slice the bread left over from last night.

Casimar stood in kitchen doorway, his collar conspicuously absent. "Johanna, I hear shells coming from our side, far to the west. I think we're pushing the Germans back."

"The ambulance should be out again." At the hospital they would suppose the aide and she were both lost and the ambulance blown up or stranded on the battlefield. "There'll be wounded to be picked up."

"I'll go with you," he said, "after we've had tea and bread. Later I'll go back to my village."

"Casimar," she said tenderly, thinking of his violated vows, "these last hours never happened."

"They never happened," he agreed, "except in the sight of God."

Johanna took the wheel this morning. It was possible to see fairly well through the light fog. Together they lifted the wounded into the ambulance and headed back for the field hospital. A British captain who had lost a leg asked Casimar to pray with him.

At the hospital Johanna found a joyous welcome. "Not only because we need you so," a doctor grinned. "We're damned short of ambulances."

Later in the day Casimar was sent back to his village and Johanna was caught up again in the frenzied work of the hospital. Everybody knew that the outcome of the war depended on this drive. If the Germans were stopped now, an Allied victory was assured.

March turned to April and the Germans launched a second offensive. Johanna fought against recurrent enervating tiredness. In the mornings it was difficult to arouse herself.

"Johanna, you ought to ask to be sent home," her worried assistant urged. "You look absolutely exhausted."

"I'll be all right, Corinne," Johanna insisted. It was late April and her stomach was in total rebellion. Corinne Williams, with whom she shared a room, was already dressed and dashing off for duty. No one in the hospital bothered with such formality as breakfast. They ate on the run. "I'll be on the floor in ten minutes."

Alone in the tiny room Johanna forced herself to her feet. This is absurd, she decided as her stomach churned. She would not be sick. And then all at once a suspicion crossed her mind. No, she thought, it can't be. She had just passed her forty-fifth birthday. She had missed a period because she was arriving at that age.

She stood beside her narrow hospital bed and forced herself to be realistic. She was always sleepy. She felt sick in the morning. She was constantly running to the bathroom. There was no need to ask the doctor; she was pregnant.

Giving no specific reason, Johanna asked to be relieved. Later she would consider what to tell Michal. It was not as though he had been faithful to her, she told herself guiltily. She knew about two women with whom she had shared her husband. How many others had there been?

Again Johanna was aboard a military grey ship on the Atlantic. She would not think about her last pregnancy. This child would live. She felt an odd sense of peace. With Casimar's baby her life would be complete.

She stood alone on the dark deck of the westbound vessel and tried to frame the words that must be said to Michal. He must never know whose it was. No one must ever know.

She arrived at the Fifth Avenue house with no warning. Molly cried with joy at seeing her home again.

Melissa rushed downstairs to welcome her. "Does Mr. Raisa know?"

"No, it's a surprise," she said shakily. The real surprise he would receive later. "Is he due home for dinner tonight?"

"He never comes home before nine or ten," Molly said. "Always he's working."

"I'll have dinner in my room and wait up for him," Johanna said. "I'm tired from all the days at sea."

"There's been mail from Bernie and Helen," Melissa reported. "Helen's in Paris and Bernie at some other place in France. I suppose he wasn't allowed to say just where."

"In France everyone says the war will soon be over," Johanna told them, but the three women knew that until peace was declared, neither Bernie nor Helen was safe.

Her bedroom looked impossibly luxurious after the austerity of the hospital room she'd shared with Corinne. She soaked in a warm tub until she heard a knock at a door and knew Molly was there with her dinner tray.

"I'll be right out, Molly," she called from the bathroom, patting herself dry with a large, thick bath towel. A hand rested for a moment on the still-flat belly where Casimar's baby was growing.

She was thrilled with it for herself, but how would Michal react? He would be upset, but how upset? Would he repudiate her? Instinct told her that he would not. For the sake of Bernie and Helen, Michal might accept the baby as his own.

She slipped into a filmy silk nightgown and robe and went out into the bedroom to have her dinner. Molly had lit a fire in the grate and pulled a small table up to it. Johanna stared into the orange-red blaze and thought about that night in the small house with Casimar. An open fire would always remind her of it.

Casimar lived for Poland's independence. He was convinced that the day was close at hand, thanks to the efforts of Polish-Americans who had not forgotten their homeland. Their dollars poured into the Liberty Loan drives, into the coffers of the Red Cross and into Liberty Bonds. Polish workers in America denied themselves to help the war effort, knowing that Poland's freedom was to emerge from the Allied victory.

Johanna finished her dinner and rang for Molly to remove the tray. For a little while Molly, who had been with them so long, sat with her and reminisced about Bernie and Helen. Molly would be surprised and delighted that she was pregnant again, but even to her most faithful servant the birth would be "premature." Only Michal would know part of the truth.

She was dozing in the chair before the embers of the fire when Michal knocked on the door.

"Come in." She remained in her chair, fearful that her legs would buckle if she dared to stand. Her throat tightened when she saw her husband.

"Johanna." His face was bright with pleasure. "Thank God you're home. I've worried about you every moment."

He bent to kiss her with passion that startled her.

"It's good to be home, Michal." It was true. Michal and Casimar were both part of her life, but now she knew Casimar was the love of her girlhood, brought late to fruition. In some strange way it seemed to her that this baby completed their relationship, put an end to the passion she felt for him and left behind only poignantly sweet affection. It was Michal who had shared the years with her, Michal who would forever be by her side—unless he rejected her now.

"Did Molly tell you I've heard from both Bernie and Helen?" He dropped into the chair across from her own.

"Yes. I tried hard to find them in France, but you were right. There was one chance in a million."

"You look wonderful." His eyes held hers, the air electric with unspoken emotions.

"Michal, there's something I have to tell you." She swung her face to the burning logs as though to draw strength from the blaze. "It—it'll hurt you."

"What could be so bad when you're safe home?" He smiled lovingly.

Johanna took a deep breath. "Michal, it was awful in France. Winter, and no proper housing, only tents and sheds. We were always cold, always tired—an eighteen-hour day was a luxury. When we were off duty we couldn't sleep for the shelling. Life was so grim it made us forget to be scared. Our bodies always remembered, though. Everyone was jittery all the time. No, don't speak.

"When we were terribly short on ambulance drivers, I went out one night to drive. The shelling was fierce. My aide was killed. There were Germans everywhere. A British officer and I were lost in the fog. We landed in a deserted village—"

She paused for breath, then hurried on so he could not interrupt. "We both would have been killed if he hadn't shot a German scout. We stayed for the night in a house in that village. The Germans were advancing and we expected to die. Michal, it was wrong—but we made love. And now—now I'm pregnant."

"You're what?" he shouted, knocking over his chair as he bounded to his feet. He loomed over her with knotted fists. She had never before so strongly felt the difference in their sizes; it made her cringe a little. "My wife, screwing a stranger! Johanna, how could you?"

At that she sat up straight. "At least," she said bitterly, "my daughter hasn't read all about it in her favorite movie magazine. Who are you to talk to me like that?"

He slumped. "I suppose you want a divorce to marry him."

"No, Michal, I don't. It was only that one night; I'll never see him again. He's married anyway; I couldn't have him if I wanted him—and I don't. I want you."

"Just a minute, Johanna. I need to sit down." Moving like an old man, Michal righted his chair and carefully lowered himself into it. "Now, what were you saying?"

"If you will have me under the circumstances, I would like very much to go on as if the baby were yours.

It is only that I won't have you throwing adultery in my face, now or ever.

"Michal—Michal, you need not fear its looks will be embarrassing. Its father reminded me forcibly of you." That was all true enough as far as it went, and now it was time to be frank about another matter.

"You know, Michal, I love you. I have been missing my husband very deeply these past years. If you find you can make me and the baby welcome, then I will be happier than I have ever been before." Now her voice broke. "Michal, do *you* want a divorce?"

"No!" He crossed the short distance between them and took her in his arms. "Johanna, I wouldn't want to live without you. But to have another baby?" He pulled back to gaze into her eyes. "My darling, how can I stand to see you go through that again? That's why I've never come near you all these years. I was afraid of losing you."

"Oh Michal, I thought you felt nothing for me. All those lost years." She clung to him. "I was overzealous, in my religious faith, Michal. What happens in bed should be between man and wife. A woman can go to confession and *not say* what is not the priest's business."

"My wife has come home to me." She saw the tears glowing in his eyes. "As for the baby's father—apparently I am the father." He swallowed hard and managed a real smile. "Shall we hope for a boy or a girl?"

"Michal, I've been so scared that you would turn against me."

"You should have known better," he scolded. "When will our little one be born?"

"Late November." Thank God for Michal's generosity.

"We'll tell everybody sometime in January," he decided. "So the baby will arrive six weeks early," he shrugged. "It happens."

"Michal, I love you."

He did not reply, but took her in his arms and kissed her passionately. At last he spoke. "Johanna, my darling, let's go to bed."

"Yes, please." She pressed her body to his.

Michal and Johanna were enjoying the honeymoon they'd never had. Each night Michal rushed home to be with her. She knew he was anxious about her welfare and sought at every moment to reassure him. As in the early years, he talked over business problems with her and listened to her ideas with heartwarming respect.

Together they rejoiced when on June third the prime ministers of Great Britain, France and Italy declared they were in favor of independence for Poland. Like most Americans, they felt a deep sense of pride that by late July over six hundred thousand American troops were in France to fight for peace. This was a war to end war.

Johanna and Michal each tried to conceal from the other their fears for their children. Until Bernie and Helen were safely home their pleasure in the reconciliation must remain incomplete.

In May they announced that they were expecting in January. If Molly and Melissa suspected otherwise, they gave no inkling of it. Johanna kept telling Michal that she had never gone through a pregnancy with so little discomfort. This delivery, she insisted, would be easier. Yet he was uneasy because of the child they had lost and because she was already forty-five.

When an extended heat wave settled over the city in early August, Michal talked about renting a house at Southampton for a month. Sitting by a window after dinner, he grew persuasive.

"Michal, you can't get away from the business for a

month,'' she protested, thinking of the miserable summer at Newport.

"I can run into the city once or twice a week and be back home in time for dinner.'' He rose to push a window wider open. Perhaps they could catch a breeze from the park across the way. He knew the heat was particularly oppressive to Johanna, now almost seven months pregnant.

"Michal, I don't think I could cope with the footmen,'' she said, trying for lightness, "though I hear at Southampton they don't wear knee breeches.''

"We won't be having any parties.'' He reached for her hand, knowing that she would never entirely forget the insult at Newport. "We'll find a house with a private stretch of beach. We'll sit on the porch and watch the waves roll up to the sand. I know how uncomfortable you are in this damnable weather.''

"Michal, what would I ever do without you?'' It still brought tears to her eyes when she thought how he had rallied to her side. An ordinary man would never forgive a woman for what she had done no matter how he had behaved.

"You'll never have to do without me as long as I'm alive,'' he promised.

The month at Southampton was a blessed relief to Johanna. She sat on the porch, which hung almost over the ocean, and watched the waves for endless hours. Each time Michal came back from a trip into the city he brought her a new novel and a trinket—a bracelet, a music box— from Tiffany's. She read Willa Cather's new book, *My Antonia*, and Booth Tarkington's latest, *The Magnificent Ambersons*. After dinner they walked along a solitary stretch of beach and talked. Once on a moonless night when it was very late they made love in the sea, feeling deliciously wicked.

The best days were those rare ones when Michal came back from New York with a letter from Bernie or

Helen. Johanna avoided reading the newspapers because the casualty figures, with peace presumably so close at hand, were appalling.

Back in New York the talk everywhere was of the second Battle of the Marne and the Allies' belief that they had reached the real turning point in the war. Over a million U.S. troops were in France. Their main objective was to cut off the German supply line, the Sedan-Mezieres Railroad, and thus force the Germans into retreat.

On September twenty-ninth Bulgaria signed an armistice. The following day the Ottoman Empire signed. On November third Austria signed. The abdication of Kaiser Wilhelm on November ninth hinted at an imminent German capitulation, especially on the heels of a false report of an armistice.

Finally on November eleventh the news broke. In a drizzling rain in the early morning of that day the German delegates walked to a railway car on a siding at Compiègne to sign the necessary documents. The most terrible war the world had ever known was over.

In the Raisa house on Fifth Avenue Johanna and Michal clung to each other, dancing with joy. Molly and Melissa were in the kitchen to show the other servants the extra that Michal had bought on the corner. WAR OVER! it proclaimed.

"Michal, they'll come home safe now." Johanna was out of breath from twirling about the room in Michal's firm embrace. "Bernie and Helen both."

"Molly's putting breakfast on the table," Melissa called from down the hall. "She's crying so hard I told her she'd make the coffee salty."

"Let's all sit down to breakfast together this morning," Johanna said. "Tell Molly to set the table for the whole household."

Everyone at the breakfast table rejoiced at the victory of the Allies. The world could return at last to normal.

"A free Poland," Michal said with pride. "Let's drink a toast to Poland's independence." He held his coffee cup aloft and everyone at the table joined in.

"Michal, stay home today," Johanna pleaded in mid-morning. He was thinking about going to the office. "Nobody's working today. Your building won't even be open." She told herself she was excited about the wonderful news of the armistice; it was just excitement that caused the intermittent odd pains in her stomach.

"Johanna, are you all right?" He looked at her searchingly.

"I'm fine," she smiled; then she frowned in concentration. "Michal—" She tried to smile again. "I'm sure it's just that I'm reacting to all that's happening."

"Johanna, I'm calling Ladislas."

"Not until we're sure," she insisted. Dr. Abramowiez was getting on in years. Why drag him uptown if it was a false alarm?

"You're going upstairs to bed." A trifle pale, Michal rather imperiously reached for her hand. "Come on, I'll walk you up before I phone."

Protesting all the while, Johanna allowed Melissa to help her into bed. The maid, young and frightened when Helen was born with only Leon and her to help, was calm and firm this time.

"Mr. Raisa's calling the doctor, and it's just as well. It'll take him forever to get here in today's traffic. It sounds like the whole city's going wild."

Suddenly Johanna's eyes widened. "I hope not too long. My water just broke." This one might be even faster than Helen, she realized. Already her contractions were rapid and severe.

"The pains are coming fast," she gasped, trying to stifle an outcry. "Melissa, tell Michal I want him."

In moments Michal sat at the edge of the bed holding her hands.

"Michal," she gasped, "it's going to be all right. Don't look so frightened."

"Ladislas is on his way," he announced. "He'll get here if he has to ask for a police escort."

Melissa and Molly were involved in preparations for the birth. Johanna was glad to be alone with Michal.

"Michal, I love you—"

"I love you."

"I'm glad this baby chose today to be born," she managed between pains, "now that the world is at peace."

They heard sounds of arrival. Then Ladislas Abramowiez, despite his advancing years, was bounding up the stairs. He too remembered Helen's birth.

"All right, Michal, go on downstairs and have yourself a stiff drink," he ordered.

"I'm staying with Johanna," Michal insisted. "I want to be here when our baby is born."

With remarkable speed Johanna pushed her third child into the world. She lay back exhausted from the effort and barely heard the doctor.

"You have a second son, Michal," he chuckled. "But you already know that, don't you?"

"Nicholas Raisa," Johanna said weakly.

BOOK TWO

Chapter 16

Helen lingered at the deck to watch the sunset over the Atlantic. Though the day was raw and bone-chilling, it was a relief to stand here with Carla and breathe fresh air. In their overcrowded stateroom the air was stale and suffocating. No one had any elbow room on a returning troopship. They were loaded to the gunwales with human cargo.

"I wonder what it'll be like to be home again," Carla mused. "We're different now, you know. We've both been through a war and lost a lover."

"Remember the trip coming over?" Helen shivered. "It was crowded worse than this. Summer, too. Everybody threatened to sleep on deck, but nobody dared. Not when we were scared to death of submarines all the time."

"We'll make better time going home," Carla predicted. "We won't be skulking along for any nine days this trip. No evasive action; we can just *go*."

"What'll we do back home?" Helen wondered.

"Have fun," Carla said with determination. "God knows, we've seen enough hell to last us a lifetime."

"I wonder if Bernie got through this all right." Helen frowned. "The way mail wasn't coming through these last months, I don't know anything."

By now both young women were seasoned nurses. They had advanced from serving coffee and doughnuts behind the lines to working in the field hospitals. The first time she saw a young soldier with his leg blown off, the stump bleeding through the emergency bandage, Helen had had to run out of the room to throw up.

"My mother couldn't get over your mother coming over and working in a hospital," Carla laughed. "Mama always said your mother was the most elegant lady she knew. And we know about working in field hospitals."

"Do you think we'll see any of the others again?"

"I'm not sure I want to. That was a whole different world out there. We did things there we'd never do at home. At least, I don't think we would."

"My mother nearly died when I told her I'd slept with Rudy." Helen had long since come to terms with her loss. "She'd turn green if she knew how many soldiers I've been to bed with since then. But I don't think it was wrong," she said defiantly. "None of us knew if we'd be dead or alive twenty-four hours later. You know, when we signed up for overseas service, I didn't even realize civilians were dying in the war too."

"I know. It was the romantic war to make the world safe for everybody." Carla was unexpectedly cynical for one a few months short of twenty. "What's it going to be like for all those fellows coming home without arms or legs?"

"Sssh," Helen cautioned, glancing over her shoulder. "What if one of them hears you?"

"Sorry," Carla said. "The first thing I'm going to do

is soak in a full hot tub for an hour. And then, I want a steak this thick"—she gestured extravagantly, glowing with anticipation—"and a big baked potato and a salad. And a quart of chocolate ice cream."

"Do you remember Tony Corelli?" Helen asked after a moment.

"Sure. He was the good-looking kid who caught a bullet in his shoulder his first day under fire. He'd been shipped out with about five weeks' training. Straight out of his junior year at New York University." She squinted appraisingly at Helen. "Even with his shoulder shot up, he couldn't keep his good hand off you."

"I remember one night when he practically pulled me into his bed. He was off in a corner of the ward and everybody around him was out cold for the night." Helen paused. "He gave up a little too soon. I liked him a lot," she admitted wistfully.

"Maybe you'll see him again in New York," Carla suggested.

Helen sighed. "Not with my luck. I'll probably never see him again. Just as well, I guess. He'll seem a whole lot different when he's back at NYU and working for his degree."

"What in hell do you do after you've been through a war, go to college?" Carla demanded. "Well, maybe I will. That would shock my parents as much as going to France."

Johanna was nursing Nicky when Michal came into the nursery after a long day at the office. "The most peaceful sight in the world," he said softly, sitting across from her, "is to see you with our son at your breast."

Johanna knew that in some fashion it was arousing to Michal. She saw the look in his eyes and felt herself stirring.

"Here we are at the age to be grandparents," she teased, "and in bed we act like twenty." She always pitied women her own age who said that bed had become a place for sleeping and nothing more.

"If you looked like a grandmother," Michal countered, his eyes dwelling on her delicately veined breast, "I might not feel that way."

"That would be too bad. There's a letter from Casimar on the dresser." Though Michal often told her to open Casimar's letters as soon as they arrived, Johanna always waited for Michal to open them and read them to her.

Nicky was falling asleep at the nipple. In a minute or two she would put him into the crib.

"I wish we'd hear from Bernie and Helen. They should be home any time now," Michal said wistfully as he slit the envelope, which bore a Warsaw postmark. Casimar had returned to Poland immediately after the armistice. "Oh, Lord." Michal frowned at the words scrawled on the flimsy slip of paper in his hands.

"What's wrong?" Johanna put Nicky on her shoulder to burp him. "Is Casimar all right?"

"He's talking about leaving the priesthood. He believes he is no longer worthy to lead."

"He mustn't quit." Johanna was ashen. He must have calculated that Nick was his son. "He's needed."

"He says he picked up a gun and killed a man in France. He says he lost his soul that night. He considered himself no longer fit to remain in the church." Michal gave Johanna a penetrating look and stood up to pace.

"Michal, we can't let him leave the priesthood." He had killed a man, yes, but that was only an excuse. It was Nicky who was driving him out of the church. She mustn't let it happen. "Tell Casimar you won't send money to the Polish church if he leaves it. Tell him you'll only supply funds as long as he's serving and you know the money is being properly handled." Why had Michal looked at her like that?

"You know I can't do that. I mustn't punish the church for Casimar. Tell you what, Johanna. You write to him. Once he made a choice for both of you—for all three of us. We let him do it, and we should make him stick to it. You write and tell him so. He'll listen to you if you say it right."

He shot her a furtive glance. "It—it doesn't matter what he has done or how he regrets it. He must not forsake his vows. Do you understand?" His voice was getting a little high and thin.

Astonished, Johanna stared at Michal. What on earth was making him sound like this? She laid Nicky in his crib. "All right, darling, of course I will if you think it will do any good. You know, you've just made a pretty good case yourself. Why don't you write to him and I will too? We'll mail the letters separately so he doesn't know we're in cahoots."

Michal was looking a little better, but his manner was still strange. "All—all right. We'd better read each other's letters so we don't give ourselves away with repetition."

It was Johanna's turn to go pale. "Whatever you say, Michal."

He turned to face her fully. He gazed at her searchingly for a moment and then nodded as if satisfied. Suddenly he smiled blindingly. "Well, that's settled."

December 12, 1918

Dear Casimar,

Michal tells me you are thinking of leaving the church. I hope the events of the war have not affected your faith.

I believe that all of us who served were sometimes shocked by close brushes with death and occasionally by the behavior of our own associates. I myself did a few things of which I am not proud, but I have put them behind me and I suffer no regrets. We took consolation where we could at the time and must continue to do so in peacetime.

Surely, Casimar, your consolation is the church. You have been married to her for thirty years; to leave her now would be to find yourself alone in a harsh world, as I know you will never come to America. Please reconsider before you make a decision that will affect the rest of your life.

Nicky is thriving and he is the image of his father. Michal says it's about time one of them looks like him; Bernie and Helen are all Boguski in spite of Bernie's size and coloring. We have not heard from Bernie or Helen, but Michal tells me I must have patience.

Casimar, please think carefully about the future. I could not be happy if I knew you were alone, as I fear you must be if you take the course you have laid out.

> With all sisterly affection,
> Johanna

Michal sighed and stared at the ceiling. He had known, of course, from the moment Nicky was born and Casimar looked out of his newborn eyes what happened in France. It was only to be expected in the circumstances, he thought, and just his own good luck that Nicky had been the result, considering how Michal had denied himself and Johanna the possibility.

Casimar's letter was another matter. Michal was in blind panic until he saw that Johanna's dismay was as great as his. Johanna's reply was more soothing to his soul than he could ever have thought possible. It told him everything he wanted to know: his suspicions were correct and Nicky was a Raisa; Johanna did not regret her escapade.

What made his heart swell, though, was the last sentence. He was not to lose his wife to his brother after all.

Johanna waited impatiently for word of Bernie and Helen. Michal kept reminding her that there was no way of knowing when they would get home. Troopships arrived all the time. The children would turn up sooner or later and that was that. Then he would spoil the effect by saying, "They're good kids. They probably offered to go last."

Johanna knew it had been unrealistic to expect them to be home in time for Christmas; still, it was a joyous Christmas because the war was over. The New Year 1919 Johanna and Michal celebrated at home, drinking their toasts in the nursery. Nicky's first New Year was full of hope.

Later, though, the days and weeks dragged. Johanna had not yet returned to her heavy volunteer schedule because she was nursing Nicky. She roamed restlessly about the house and spent a lot of time talking on the telephone when a friend or someone on one of her committees called.

Each morning when she sat down to breakfast with Michal he exhorted her to go back to sleep; Nicky was still demanding a nighttime feeding and by six lustily wailing again. Johanna fed him before she joined Michal at the breakfast table.

"I don't want you to become a wraith," Michal scolded on an early February morning. "Go back to sleep until it's time to feed that ravenous son of ours."

"I will," she promised. After breakfast she saw Michal off to the office and started up the stairs to their bedroom.

Melissa came down the hall to answer the phone. "I'll get it—" She waved Johanna on her way but a moment later was calling her back. "Mrs. Raisa, it's Bernie!"

"He's home?" Johanna almost stumbled in her rush down the stairs. Her hands were shaking when she took the phone from Melissa.

"Bernie?"

"In the flesh. I'm home, Mama. I'll be there as soon as I can find a cab."

"Oh, I can't wait to see you."

"I'm starving," he said ebulliently. "Tell Molly to have a double batch of pancakes and a quart of coffee ready for me. I can't wait to see you all."

"Welcome home, darling." Tears welled in her eyes as they met Melissa's. "It's wonderful to hear your voice."

Within forty-eight hours both Bernie and Helen were home. Johanna could not see enough of them. She was aware that they were not the same son and daughter who had left New York to go to war. She was glad that she had been in the war, though only for a few months. It gave them a new bond.

Johanna sensed shock in both Bernie and Helen about Nicky. They seemed to think it was a little vulgar to be having a baby in the forties. Nonetheless, both Helen and Bernie adored their tiny brother.

Bernie announced just days after returning from France that he was ready to come into Michal's business. He could not wait to put the war behind him and resume his normal life. Only now did his parents realize he had been wounded in a run-in with a nest of machine guns and had spent weeks in hospitals, first in France and then in England.

Helen talked vaguely about going out to Hollywood to visit Uncle Leon. "Maybe I could get a job at his studio," she said over dinner one night in early spring.

Johanna gaped in astonishment. "Do you think you'll like California?" She tried not to show her hurt that Helen talked of leaving again so soon.

"Leon is having problems with the studio," her father said somberly.

"You didn't tell me." Johanna turned to Michal with uplifted eyebrows.

"I didn't want to spoil the homecoming. He's in financial trouble. He's spent a fortune trying to build that no-talent Marianne Scott into a star. Leon won't listen to anybody anymore. I talked to his accountants. He's living too high, acting like a sugar daddy."

"Oh, Papa, don't worry about Uncle Leon. I'm sure he knows what he's doing. At least he's having some fun. I can't wait to see his movies. What are they like?"

Johanna exchanged an uneasy glance with Michal. "Er, I'm afraid we haven't seen the last few," she confessed. "They're, ah, not quite our taste."

"Mama, you sound like such a prude. Does Uncle Leon make smutty pictures?"

"Helen, what a thing to say! Of course not. Your uncle is not a pornographer, after all. It's just that your father and I do not particularly care for movies about drinking, gambling and dueling. We went to see them all for a while, but we got tired of the same things over and over."

"Where's Bernie tonight?" Michal asked, clutching at a safe topic.

"He's taking Wanda Reszke to the theater." Johanna smiled. She was delighted that Bernie was seeing a Polish young lady. "They went to see some operetta—*Apple Blossoms*, I believe."

"Who is she?" Helen was mildly curious. Mama always got that fatuous look on her face when she talked about Bernie, and now it was the same about the new baby. "I don't remember any Reszkes."

"Wanda's father was a member of the Polish National Committee," Michal explained. "He's just returned to Warsaw. Wanda has been in America since she was three. She has no memories of Warsaw, so she preferred to stay at school in New York.''

"Why should she want to go back to Poland?'' Helen shrugged. "She's an American." This was a constant sore point between her parents and herself. She considered that they lived with one foot still in Warsaw; what happened in Poland was more important to them than what happened in this country.

"We have to remember our heritage." Johanna gave Helen a stern look.

"Mama, you are no longer a Pole who happens to live in the United States," Helen said, fighting exasperation. "You're an American of Polish descent. You became a citizen long ago."

"That doesn't mean we can't love the country of our birth," Johanna snapped. Then she paused. America was the country of their children's birth.

"Every citizen except for the Indians has roots in an old country," Michal put in. "We cannot shed loyalties that have been bred into us."

"Poland should not dominate our lives," Helen insisted.

"It doesn't dominate our lives," Johanna countered, "but we mustn't forget our roots. It was hard to feel wholly American when even now there were people who referred to the Raisas as "those Polack upstarts."

"Helen, you must accept that your mother and I will always be part of Poland," Michal said soberly. "We fought for Poland. We wouldn't be here if it had been safe for us to remain there."

"You don't try to go back."

Johanna and Michal looked shocked. "Our business— our lives—we are part of this country now. It's too late for us to go back," Johanna protested. Many Poles had come to America to save up money and return to their homeland; most of them stayed. "But we can share Poland's agonies and its successes." Her eyes turned to Michal. "At least we can see ahead to the freeing of Poland."

"How can your mother and I not feel committed to Poland?" Michal demanded. "Your uncle Casimar lives there. My two sisters and their families are still there. Helen, part of you always remains in the country that saw your birth."

"Okay, okay. Let's change the subject. Is Bernie serious about this Wanda Reszke?"

"I'd be happy if he is," Johanna said fondly. "She's a bright, lovely young lady."

Bernie and Wanda were walking to the car his parents had given him on his homecoming. He kept trying to tell himself that he was home and his life was normal again, but he still awoke in a cold sweat after a nightmare each night. All around him people behaved as though there had never been a war. How did he wash what he had seen in France out of his soul?

"It was a wonderful show," Wanda said softly as they settled themselves in the black Pierce-Arrow.

"I enjoyed it too." He had never been so drawn to a woman as to little Wanda Reszke, who looked at him as though he were modeled on some Greek god. "Would you like to go to the Ritz for a late supper?"

"Oh yes," Wanda said with shy eagerness. "I've never been there."

They parked the car and headed for the Ritz-Carlton at Forty-sixth Street and Madison, Bernie's hand possessively on Wanda's arm.

"Are you warm enough?" he asked, conscious of her lush body beneath her fashionable short squirrel coat and long full skirt.

"Oh yes, Bernie."

She lifted her face to his and he felt color flood his own as his mind filled with erotic images. At college and graduate school he had allowed himself little social life. Even in the Army he had had little experience with women. Now he hoped to make up for lost time.

They walked through the crisp coldness of the night with a keen awareness of each other. They paused briefly before the elegance of the Ritz, then went inside to the charming Louis XV dining room. He smiled in secret pleasure at the envious masculine eyes that focused on Wanda as they were led to a table. He had never liked the new bobbed hair until he saw Wanda's.

Bernie prolonged their supper as long as possible. It was the only way to stay with her. Although this was 1919 and the young were in postwar rebellion, Wanda was a well brought up Polish lady and he mustn't take liberties.

"Bernie, it's past midnight." Wanda lifted limpid blue eyes to his. "I think you'd better take me home."

Wanda lived in a tiny apartment on Waverly Place. Her older cousin was out of town to speak before a suffragette meeting, she explained.

"Would you like to come in for a glass of wine?" she asked.

"Yes, but don't you understand you shouldn't ask strange young men into your apartment?"

"You're not a strange young man, you're Bernie Raisa."

He was mad about this small beauty who looked as though she had just come from a convent. "I mustn't stay long if your cousin is away," he said.

With a quick smile Wanda disappeared into the Pullman kitchen and returned with two glasses and a chilled bottle of wine.

"Pour for us, Bernie." She sat at one end of the small leather sofa littered with colorful cushions. As she tucked her slender legs beneath her, he caught a provocative glimpse of them.

"Sure." He forced a smile, too conscious of the thrust of her breasts beneath her lustrous taffeta frock. When she leaned over to take her glass, the neckline dropped to reveal the velvet rise of her breasts and the valley between them.

He cleared his throat and tugged at his collar, aware of embarrassing sudden tumescence. It had been a long time; practically never, in fact. He could think of nothing but her flesh and his.

"Bernie, tell me about the war," she crooned.

He frowned, jarred into reality.

"It's not good conversation," he said tersely. "Not even good to think about."

"I used to think about it." She put down her glass and moved toward him. "I wished I could go out to fight."

He drained his glass and set it down. "It was rotten. Be glad you stayed home."

"I wanted to go over with the Red Cross, but Papa wouldn't let me. He said I was too young. I'm not that young, Bernie. I'm twenty."

Without realizing how it happened, he was holding Wanda in his arms and kissing her as though he could never stop. A hand crept to her breasts and moved inside her dress. He felt a surge of excitement at the touch of satin flesh, a nipple hardening beneath his fingers.

"Bernie, wait," she whispered urgently and drew away from him.

"Wanda, I'm sorry—" His voice was uneven as he sought for self-control.

"Stay there," she whispered. "I'll be right back."

Bernie poured himself more wine. He was lucky Wanda hadn't slapped his face. His face burned as he remembered the taste of her mouth, the feel of her breasts. He ought to get out of here; he stood up. Wanda wasn't some slut a man picked up at a tea dance. She was a nice girl—like Helen.

He crossed to the chair where he had left his overcoat and reached for it.

"Bernie?" Barefoot, wrapped in a watered silk kimono, Wanda stood in the bedroom doorway. "Bernie, I'm so lonely. Don't leave yet." The invitation in her eyes was unmistakable.

With a low moan he went to her. Her slightly parted lips met his and her arms clung to his shoulders as he kissed her. She rubbed her small body against his tall, lean frame and excitement ripped through him.

"Wanda," he gasped when they at last parted, "I'm mad about you."

"And I'm mad about you," she whispered. "Bernie, isn't it wonderful?"

He untied the kimono and let it fall about her. She was naked underneath. He lifted her and carried her into the bedroom. The bed was already turned down for the night. He had not been this passionate since London, he thought, when that pretty English nurse taught him so much about making love. He lowered her onto the bed and shucked his clothes.

"Bernie, I never did it before," she whispered as she drew him to her. Her breasts pushed against his chest. "But I'm not scared with you."

He warned himself not to rush, but to make sure she was ready for him. His mouth nibbled at a nipple while his hands fondled her hips, her thighs, moved to caress the hot velvet inner thigh.

"Bernie, touch me there," she pleaded. "Oh, please, darling."

His hand moved between her thighs while her own

clutched at his shoulders. She was thrusting beneath him, her breath hot and sweet. He couldn't wait any longer.

She cried out for a moment when he entered her, and then they were moving together in a frenzy that seemed insatiable. "Bernie!" Her nails dug into his bare shoulders. "Oh, Bernie!"

For a little while afterward they lay limp and immobile. Then her lips found his cheek and kissed him.

"We'd better get married right away," she murmured, "in case I'm pregnant."

"Right away," he agreed, already stirring again within her. "Returning soldiers don't waste time. It won't seem strange at all."

Not until dawn did he dress and prepare to leave Wanda's apartment. Tomorrow, he promised, he would tell his parents about his engagement and she would write her father in Warsaw. By the time her father responded they would already be married.

"Bernie, where will we live?" she asked as she stood at the door with him in her kimono.

"We'll talk about that tomorrow," he promised, his head in a whirl. He was taking a wife. Mama and Papa would be pleased that he had chosen a Pole. "We won't bother with a big wedding—just family. All right? Please, not one of those big Polish weddings that last three days."

"A small wedding," she agreed demurely, lifting her mouth to his. "It's going to be such fun to be married to you, Bernie."

He walked out into the grey dawn in an aura of unreality. Even if Wanda wasn't pregnant from tonight, he was glad they were getting married. With a wife he'd be able to put the ugly memories of France behind him. He'd make love to his wife every night and sleep without nightmares.

He hoped Wilson's League of Nations would go

through. The world must never know another war like the one just behind them. Already he felt the need to protect his family.

He walked swiftly. Tonight he had slept without nightmares for the first time since the first enemy shells burst around him.

Wanda stood at a parlor window and watched the first pinkness of dawn streak across the sky, hugging herself and giggling. Bernie never guessed he was not the first. She had played her little scene just right. Papa would never tell the Raisas that he had thrown her out of his home; he'd be relieved that she had found herself a husband.

He'd said awful things: "*You're no better than one of those girls on the street. It makes no difference that you don't take money.*"

A secretive little smile about her full mouth, Wanda went into the kitchen. Today she'd treat herself, beginning with breakfast. She had caught herself a big bear just now. Bernie's father was a very rich and influential man. She would be very rich now. She had known when she went to the social hall to that dance that Bernie Raisa would be there. She had a bet with herself that she'd marry him within three months and it had taken her only one month to land him. She began to prepare a breakfast of caviar and champagne.

Chapter 17

Helen stood at the improvised altar during the elaborate nuptial mass. To Papa it was important that his son be married by a Polish priest. Someday, Papa vowed, there would be a Polish archbishop in the United States. Someday maybe the pope would be Polish.

Helen tried to conceal her annoyance at the length of the service. She couldn't understand why Wanda had asked her to be maid of honor. She hardly knew Bernie's bride. In fact Bernie hardly knew Wanda, Helen thought with cynicism not shared by her parents.

Helen looked over the guests. Wanda's friends were all artists and writers from Greenwich Village. Her cousin was out of town, as usual. Wanda ran with a fast crowd, she surmised. Was Bernie rushing the wedding because his bride was pregnant?

Helen made an effort to hide her boredom at the wedding banquet. Dutifully she did the polka—after kicking off her shoes—with Papa and then with Bernie. Men were so stupid. She'd lay odds Wanda wasn't a virgin when she met Bernie, even though Bernie acted as though his new wife were fresh out of the convent.

On Friday Helen was leaving for California, though her parents were not happy about it. They knew Uncle Leon had his girlfriend living with him. Helen would stay at the Alexandria Hotel in Los Angeles. It was the most expensive hotel in the city so of course Mama was sure it was the best. They refused to allow her to stay with Uncle Leon.

She wasn't sure why she was going out to California except that she was so bored in New York. All of a sudden Carla had developed a social conscience and was going back to school to get a degree in social work.

Saturday night while she was packing her steamer trunk her mother knocked and came into the room. "Helen, I wish you'd change your mind and go to White Sulphur Springs instead."

"I hate White Sulphur Springs. I want something to do besides sit around a resort. Uncle Leon will show me how to make movies. That *will* be fun."

"He'll be busy all day," Johanna warned, nervous about the scandalous Hollywood parties people talked about— drinking and drugs and sleeping around. "What will you do with yourself?"

"Drive around and see the sights." Helen abruptly turned her back. Nicky was adorable, but she couldn't get used to the sight of Mama with an infant in her arms. Oh well, at least Papa had stopped running after other women.

"When you get back, we'll have a dinner party to introduce Wanda to our friends. Be nice to her, Helen."

"What makes you think I won't be nice?"

Mama acted as though she were still a little girl, she thought impatiently. When did your parents realize you were grown up? Away from home she had known she was a woman. Now she was getting confused.

"I suppose it's too late to try to persuade one of your friends to go along," her mother said uneasily.

"I hardly see anyone except Carla," she explained patiently, "and she won't be out of school for a month yet." She didn't want to go to California with Carla anyway. This trip was personal.

"I can't get used to young girls dashing around by themselves." Johanna smiled apologetically.

"Mama, I've been to war and I'm not a young girl any more. What's so bad about a train trip?" Her constant impatience showed through again.

"All set for tomorrow?" Her father stood in the doorway.

"Just about."

"I'll probably be gone by the time you get up in the morning," he said indulgently, "so come kiss your father good-bye."

Johanna looked in on Nicky before she joined Michal in their bedroom. Though Melissa slept in an adjoining room, Johanna always came in to see that he was covered well before going to bed. While Michal forever insisted Nicky was the image of her, she knew he had inherited only her coloring. His face was Casimar's face—and Michal's—the two younger Raisa brothers bore a strong resemblance.

Michal was already in bed by the time she walked into the bedroom.

"You're worried about Helen," he guessed.

"We never seem to spend more than ten minutes together without a wall of hostility rising up between us. I'm glad she's home again, but I can't really reach her."

"Give her time. She's been through a rough two years."

"Michal, I wish I could help her."

"All we can do at this point is stand by. Come to bed now."

When at last she slid beneath the covers, Michal pulled her into his arms. "Helen will be all right in California," he promised. "Everybody in this country is crazy about movies. Leon will show her everything."

"Not everything." Tartness crept into her voice. "We hear such awful stories about social lives of the movie people. I hope he has sense enough not to throw her into that."

"Leon has little time for parties these days," Michal said. "He's in a pretty precarious financial condition."

"Can't you talk to him?"

"I've tried and his accountants have tried. He's furious with me right now." He hesitated. "He wanted me to put a million dollars into the company."

Johanna stared. "What did you tell him?"

"Let's just say he wouldn't accept my conditions. Too bad; I couldn't invest that kind of money without some controls." Michal's arms tightened about her. "Leon was particularly enraged with me when I told him how a million dollars could help the poor in Poland."

"What did he say?"

"He said, 'Fuck Poland.' I don't think I can ever forgive him for that. All Leon cares about is living like royalty, dissipating his life away. Nothing ever satisfies him. But I'd always been so sure that Poland was etched on his soul. My God, Johanna." He sighed in frustration. "Remember how it was with us when we were young in Warsaw? Leon was a firebrand."

"Michal, that Leon is long gone. People change. We all change."

"But not our sense of values."

"Stop blaming yourself for not doing what your older brother asked. What you did was right."

"Then why do I feel so rotten?"

"You shouldn't," she said vigorously, resenting Leon's hold on Michal. "He didn't even come East for Bernie's wedding," she complained.

"He couldn't." Automatically Michal went on the defensive. "It was such short notice, and he was embroiled in a distribution dispute."

"If he had wanted to come, he would have." He always made a fuss over the children when they were little, and they'd adored him. Helen still did. Bernie acted very respectful, but Johanna suspected Bernie didn't like his Uncle Leon. "It'll seem strange to have both Bernie and Helen gone again."

"Bernie and Wanda will be back in another week." They'll probably stay with us for quite a while—until they find a place of their own."

On Friday Helen settled herself in her compartment aboard the train. She had brought along copies of the new Joseph Hergesheimer novel, *Java Head*, which everybody was talking about, and Sherwood Anderson's collection of short stories, *Winesburg, Ohio*. She would hole up and read until she got to California.

It was a relief to be away from home, from familiar, prying faces. She wasn't comfortable with anyone except Carla, and Carla was running like mad from those last months in the hospital. It had been different when they were just serving coffee and doughnuts to the soldiers, but at the field hospital it was as though somebody had jerked away the fancy wrapper on life and showed them reality.

She wouldn't feel lost this way if Mama hadn't stopped her from marrying Rudy. Even with Rudy dead, if they'd had a child she wouldn't feel so lost. What was she going to do with the rest of her life? Helen was a war casualty.

When she ordered dinner brought in from the dining car, she'd asked for a cocktail. A drink or two each night with dinner, she promised herself, to help her sleep. She had not had a really satisfying night of sleep since London.

Helen kept to her compartment for the entire journey except for changing trains in Chicago. She read. She watched the passing scenery. A good-natured porter brought her a pile of movie magazines. At last, when she was fighting claustrophobia, the train pulled into the small Los Angeles railroad station.

Her uncle had dispatched his chauffeur to drive her to her hotel. He would meet her there for dinner; everybody important in pictures could be seen dining at the Alexandria sooner or later. Unexpectedly she felt a flurry of excitement as she followed the bellman into the luxurious hotel.

She took in the crystal chandeliers, the fine Oriental rugs, the marble columns. Potted plants made a lavish display. The first thing she saw when she entered her suite was a vase of her favorite red roses. Leave it to Uncle Leon to remember.

Tomorrow Leon would take her for a tour of the studio. She had allowed Papa's secretary to reserve a return in two weeks. However, she had no intention of returning until she was bored with Hollywood.

She was soaking in a warm tub, reveling in the solitude, the feeling of independence, when the telephone rang. She climbed out of the tub in perilous haste, clutching at a towel as she hurried to the phone.

"Hello?"

"You're looking gorgeous this afternoon," said Uncle Leon's ebullient voice.

"Isn't it wonderful how we have movie screens hooked up to our telephones?" she giggled, all at once feeling gay and carefree. Uncle Leon did that to people.

"I'll pick you up at nine. Wear something shocking. This is California."

She tried on every dress before she decided on the bias-cut black; it covered her from throat to toe yet managed to appear daring. Mama hated it. She said it looked like something the vamp in a movie would wear.

Helen sat down to make up her face. Mama would hate that too, but the movies had inspired sophisticated women everywhere to use cosmetics. She couldn't go to dinner at the Alexandria with a bare face. Her efforts completed, she smiled in pleasure. Carla said she looked like a movie star when she wore make-up.

She had been born with dark hair, but by the time she was a year old it was its present reddish blond. At intervals she considered coloring it black. She adored Gloria Swanson's black hair, so beautiful in *Don't Change Your Husband*, which Helen had seen the day before Bernie's wedding.

Carla and she had gone to the Strand on Broadway and then to the Ritz for tea. All Carla could talk about was college—one more reason to make this trip.

Her uncle phoned from downstairs to say he was on his way up. She took a final anxious glance in the mirror. Uncle Leon was famous. She mustn't disgrace him when they walked into the Alexandria's dining room.

Leon's eyes swept approvingly over the black jacquard, which clung to every inch of her lissome body. "Baby, you look magnificent, as though you just stepped off a movie set." He grinned and reached to kiss her. "My beautiful niece." Even though he was fifty-three years old, he was terribly handsome, Helen thought. "Remember, I know you longer than anybody else in the world. I saw you even before your mother."

When she was little it had embarrassed her to hear

Uncle Leon's story about being the midwife at her birth, but now it amused her.

"We were sorry you couldn't come to Bernie's wedding," she said dutifully, instructed to convey her parents' regrets.

For a moment his face clouded, so briefly she thought she might have been mistaken. "I was working my ass off on a picture. The director was out of his mind." Helen was oddly pleased that he no longer cleaned up his language for her benefit.

As they entered the luxurious dining room an orchestra began to play soft dinner music. "As if just for us, Uncle Leon," Helen giggled.

"Helen," Leon whispered, "Er—don't call me uncle, please. I'm just Leon, an old family friend."

"Leon," she said throatily and clung tighter. They were both enjoying the game. Where was Marianne Scott? He must have told her he was taking his niece out to dinner.

The headwaiter came forward to greet Leon by name and seated them at one of the best tables.

"This is a real mix, movie and society people," Leon told her. "Five years ago there were a lot of places closed to movie makers. Now they're all welcome except at some of the snob holdouts like the Pasadena Country Club. All that money," he chuckled, "it makes even movie people acceptable."

They were having coffee when a tall, rather heavy man with an air of authority stopped by their table.

"Leon, we haven't seen you around for weeks," he said. "Where have you been keeping yourself?" Helen was aware of considerable tension beneath the smiles being exchanged.

Leon introduced Marshall Rankin, a major film distributor.

"Are you arriving or leaving?" Leon asked.

"Leaving. I'm with the party over there at the entrance." His eyes lingered on Helen, wondering if she was Leon's new girl. This was a lot more fun than New York and the Polish National Committee.

"Why don't you drop by my house in about an hour?" Leon suggested. He spoke casually, but his mind was racing. "We'll have drinks and conversation. Helen's a family friend from back East." Now she realized her uncle had introduced her only by her first name. "I'm taking her home to meet Marianne." In spite of his other women, her other men and their quarrels, Leon and Marianne never stayed apart long.

"I'd like that," Marshall agreed, his eyes resting on Helen's breasts. "Say about an hour." He moved away briskly.

"Honey, I'd like you to turn on the charm for Marshall," Leon said overcasually. "There's something big happening between some of the top producers and the exhibitors and I haven't been able to get it straight. See what you can dig out of Marshall tonight." His eyes rested appraisingly on his niece. "Your father says if you'd been a boy, you'd be a fine businessman or a lawyer."

Helen was startled. "He never said that to me." She had always thought he couldn't wait to see her married. He was already talking about how wonderful it would be to have a third generation in the business. "And why can't a woman be a fine businessman or a lawyer?"

"Now why would a beautiful girl like you want to waste her life in an office? Tell you what, I'll put you in business myself. Come back to me with some real information from Marshall and I'll buy you the prettiest diamond bracelet you ever saw." He smiled, but his eyes were serious.

"I'll try," she promised. It exhilarated her to know Uncle Leon thought she could do something important for him. Mama and Papa thought she ought to spend her time working in the Polish community and then get married, have children and keep on with the volunteer work. She was only twenty; she had a lot of years ahead of her. She would have some fun with Leon before she settled down.

Forty minutes later they were in Leon's Spanish mansion high in the Hollywood hills. It seemed to Helen that every light in the house was on as they walked up the broad stone steps to the portico.

The door flew wide. A tall, sleek woman a few years older than Helen stood there in a ruffled red velvet robe cut audaciously low. Masses of dark hair hung about her shoulders. She was beautiful under her sulky expression.

"Leon, where have you been?" Her voice was shrill. "I called the studio and they said you'd been gone for hours."

"Marianne, I'd like you to meet my niece Helen. Marshall Rankin is coming over in a very few minutes. He's not to know Helen's a relative. Make sure the decanters are full. The more Marshall drinks, the more talkative he'll be." He leaned forward to kiss Marianne and smacked her on the rump. "Go on, see to the drinks." He turned back to Helen. "Don't ever tell your mother and father I brought you here. They still think you're a little girl. It wouldn't do for you to know I'm keeping the next big Hollywood star."

"I won't say anything."

Still sulky, Marianne retreated down the hall. Helen disliked her on sight. At least Uncle Leon hadn't married her.

Leon was pacing and stroking his mustache. The last time Helen saw him he had been slightly grey, hair and pencil mustache both. Now he was aggressively dark again. His mustache was fuller, too. Helen suspected he had to keep it longer to be able to dye it.

He showed his age in other ways—wrinkled hands, pouchy eyes, a slight stoop and a hint of potbelly. He had lost none of his charm and energy, though. And his clothes! He was as fashion-conscious as any woman and he dressed like the most successful young actors in town.

"Let me show you around the house," Leon said expansively, putting an arm about her waist. "God, I look at you and see your mother twenty years ago. The resemblance is incredible."

"Only on the outside. Mama and I think alike about nothing." Mama didn't even like her to have a cocktail before dinner. Mama and Papa thought anything but a glass of wine was suspect. The Prohibition Amendment wouldn't ever go through, would it? Even Papa admitted he thought it was absurd.

Soon they heard a car drive up. Marshall had arrived. They gathered in what Leon referred to as their French salon and settled on a white velvet sofa while Marianne, whose expression appeared to be perpetually sulky, poured the drinks.

Most of the conversation—sparring, it seemed to Helen—dealt with the movies. As though reading Helen's mind, Marianne leaned over to whisper to her.

"That's all people in Hollywood talk about, even at parties. What's happening on what lot, who's bringing in the biggest grosses." She shrugged and went over to settle herself on Leon's knee.

Helen wasn't going to learn anything from Marshall if he sat here and talked to Leon. She'd have to get him out of here. She rose to her feet, pretending to yawn. "I'm tired from five days on the train. I should be getting back to my hotel." She saw the swift glint of approval in Leon's eyes.

"I'll see you to your hotel." Marshall leapt to his

feet. "I have a heavy day tomorrow. I should get some sleep myself."

The night was cooler than she expected. She hunched her shoulders in protest against the chill as Marshall hurried her to the car. She was glad he had a chauffeur behind the wheel. She didn't trust him to drive after four brandies.

"I know you're tired, Helen, but there's a great party on about five minutes from here. You'll see some people you've never seen before except on the screen." He laid his hand on her knee.

"I can't stay long," she told him. "Maybe half an hour?" She made no effort to pull away from him.

"Half an hour," he promised and leaned forward to kiss her. "How did Leon let you get away?"

"We're old family friends. Besides, there's Marianne."

His chuckle was derisive. "She'll ruin him. She's the world's worst actress, and she photographs like a dog. She must give him a great time in bed."

"Ruin him? Is his studio in trouble?" she asked innocently.

"Yes, and it'll be in worse trouble soon," he predicted.

"How?" His hand crept near her breast. This was almost incestuous, she thought with a touch of humor. He was old enough to be her father. She'd never made love with anybody over thirty. "What's he done now?"

"Just trouble," he said vaguely.

"I know he's concerned about something that's happening between the producers and exhibitors," she said and then clapped her hand over her mouth. "Marshall, don't tell Leon I told you!" That should fool him.

"I won't tell if you won't. The major producers are out to gain control of distribution. As soon as we exhibitors heard about that, we got together to make plans of our own. We're out to sign up every theater owner in the country for a five-year deal. The small companies can close up shop.''

"Marshall, how tricky!" She laughed and took his hand away from her breast. "Leon will be devastated.''

"Let's don't go to the party," Marshall suggested. "Let's just have a few drinks all by ourselves.''

"Oh, I don't think I can stay awake another five minutes," she said apologetically. "Call me tomorrow night. But right now, take me back to my hotel, please. I'm just exhausted from that awful trip across country.''

In her suite at the Alexandria she phoned her uncle. He answered immediately. She could hear Marianne screeching in the background.

"He talked," Helen said immediately.

"Don't say anything else," Leon admonished. "You're on a switchboard. I'll send the car for you right away.''

Leon opened the door himself. The servants had all retired for the night. Marianne was stretched on the white velvet sofa, her red robe fastened only at the waist. She displayed spectacularly long legs and a lush white bosom.

"All right, tell me," Leon demanded. "What's up?''

Helen reported, aware that Marianne had abandoned her sulkiness to listen intently.

"The goddamn bastards!" Leon slammed a fist onto the arm of the sofa. "That's not shrewd business, it's piracy.''

"What does it mean, Leon?" Marianne asked. Helen looked askance at her silken sweetness, but Leon seemed not to notice the mood change.

"It means we won't find one movie house in the country to show our pictures." He was white with rage. "Only the majors will stand a chance.''

With deliberate slowness Marianne swung her feet to

the floor and pulled her robe closed. "You're not going to make me a star," she said contemptuously.

"We'll figure a way out of this mess," he blustered. Alarm overtook him as he realized his precarious position. Marianne was about to walk out on him and his whole way of life was in danger. "I've got angles."

"Of course, Leon." Helen stared at Marianne.

"That's what you think, honey. When a producer is through in this town, he's through. You're too old to start over again," Marianne said with brutality that made Helen wince. Poor Uncle Leon. "I'm moving out in the morning. There's a director dying to set me up in a place of my own at Court Corinne. Maybe it isn't much compared to this place, but Johnny Moss is on the way up."

"Get out now," Helen commanded, "you little bitch."

"Don't you call me a bitch." Marianne threw herself at Helen fingernails first.

Leon leapt forward to pull Marianne from Helen. He pushed her with such force that she fell to the floor, cursing him in the kind of language Helen had heard only from soldiers brought in from the battlefield.

"You can stay tonight." Leon's voice was calm. "When I come back from the studio tomorrow, I want you out of my house." He turned to Helen. "Are you all right?"

"I'm fine. I'll be over early tomorrow to watch her pack."

"I'll drive you back to the hotel. Tomorrow you'll move into the house. With Marianne gone for good, your mother and father can't object."

They drove in silence to the hotel. When they arrived, Leon insisted on seeing her up to her suite.

"I didn't want to expose you to Marianne's temper," he apologized. He gazed at her with unnerving intensity.

"Don't mind that I stare. I haven't seen you in so long. I'd forgotten how much you resemble Johanna. The last time I saw you you still seemed a little girl. Now you're a woman."

"Leon, if I can do anything to help—" she said impulsively.

"You've helped already. Now I know what I'm up against." His face tightened. "I asked your father for a loan of a million so I could make a real dent in this business, but he'd rather send the money to Poland than to his own brother."

"Papa turned you down?" Helen was stunned. She had always believed that Papa put family above everything else in the world.

"He turned me down. Now it may be too late to bail myself out." He forced a smile as he leaned forward to kiss her good night. "But don't worry your pretty little head about me, sweetie. Leon Raisa is a survivor."

Helen lay sleepless far into the night. Why had Papa failed to come to his brother's rescue? Uncle Leon had always been the most colorful man she knew. He walked into a room and suddenly all eyes were on him. It was hard to believe that he was three years older than Papa; he seemed twenty years younger.

She fell asleep at last to chaotic dreams about Leon and herself in a desperate escape from a gang out to kill them. Awaking, she thought carefully about his circumstances and her own. They were both in trouble of a kind; maybe they could help each other out.

She wasn't going back to New York, that was for sure. She would stay here in Hollywood and help Uncle Leon get his life together again. What was there for her back home? Mama was determined to see her married and raising a family and she wasn't ready. There would be nothing but strife.

She would never love again, she vowed, but despite her conviction she found herself thinking longingly of Tony Corelli, who had tried, but not hard enough, to get her into his hospital bed in France.

Chapter 18

Melissa brought Johanna the morning's mail at the breakfast table. "A letter from Helen," she reported with a smile.

"Oh, good." Johanna reached for the mail with one hand and stifled a yawn with the other. "How's Nicky this morning?"

"Much better. I always get so frightened of croup, so I've been sleeping in his room. That's why I'm a little late this morning. He had a couple of coughing spells. Nothing severe, but it cost us both some sleep."

"Melissa, you do too much. I swear I'm going to hire a lady's maid for myself. You'll be old before your time doing for both of us."

"Don't you do that, Mrs. Raisa. I don't have time to train nobody. Besides I like it."

"I'd meant to go downtown to sit in on Mrs. Zabriskie's sewing circle. She's a wonderful old lady. I can't believe she's past seventy-five already. But she still fights for every Polish cause that comes along." Johanna paused as she read the brief letter from Helen. "Oh, no."

"Problems?"

"Helen's staying in California indefinitely, she says. She's left the Alexandria to move in with her uncle." Johanna sighed. "What can we do? She considers herself a woman now."

"The excitement of living in movieland will wear off soon," Melissa predicted.

"I can't help worrying about her, though," Johanna admitted. The movie magazines and gossip columns were full of lurid stories about the movie people in Hollywood.

"That's a mother's privilege."

"I thought once the war was over we could settle down to a calm way of life, but I don't suppose that ever really happens. We just change our worries."

"You're expecting Mr. Bernie and Miz Wanda home tomorrow, aren't you?" Melissa asked.

Johanna nodded. "We'll have a special welcome home dinner. I did hope Helen would be here for it."

She paused in thought. "We're happy to have Bernie and Wanda here as long as they like, but Wanda wants a place of their own right away." Michal had raised Bernie's salary on his marriage, but not so high that the newlyweds could afford a house anything like this one.

"I'm sure they'll find something soon, Mrs. Raisa. Excuse me, it's time for Nicky to get dressed."

Bernie tried to ignore Wanda's sulking as they checked out of the fabulous Royal Poinciana Hotel and followed the porters to the train at the tiny Royal Poinciana Station. They would be departing in ten minutes.

Wanda was furious at him on several points. It had been more than generous of Papa to foot the bill for their Palm Beach honeymoon, but Bernie was sure he had not expected Wanda to spend a fortune in the smart little shops. Wanda spent more time in the shops in the hotel than she did sightseeing or with Bernie. One day of traveling about in the Afromobiles, wicker chairs propelled by attached tricycles at the rear, and she lost interest.

She had been fascinated by the Beach Club, where most guests at the Royal Poinciana went in the evening to gamble. The gambling room of the Beach Club, resplendent in an emerald and white interior, appeared a simple white clapboard house from the outside.

During their two-week stay Wanda gambled nightly. Bernie felt sick when he thought about her staggering losses at roulette. He had drained his private checking account. All their other expenses were billed to his father.

Wanda slouched in a corner of their compartment, silent until the train pulled out of the hotel station. "You acted like an awful prig last night," she told him, her blue eyes smoldering reproachfully, "after I wangled a special invitation to that party."

"It wasn't our kind of party."

"Did you expect to be taken up by the Stotesburys, the Munns and the Phippses?" she drawled. "A couple of first-generation Americans?"

"Wanda, I'm not ashamed of being first-generation American." Bernie was seeing a Wanda he hadn't known existed. Wanda thought she could make him forget everything in bed, but that was no longer true. "I have no aspirations to be one of New York's Four Hundred."

"I know." Her tone was bitingly superior. "In your family it's enough for your father and mother to be the uncrowned King and Queen of Polish America." She crossed her legs and reached for a cigarette. "You humiliated me last night when you insisted we leave that party."

"I don't smoke opium," Bernie said tersely. "I don't find it amusing to hole myself up in a room with the doors and windows covered with wet sheets to smoke a drug that I know is harmful and addicting. I had no intention of staying for the second round.''

"I've sniffed snow," Wanda said loftily. "Down in Greenwich Village it's considered amusing.''

"I don't call cocaine amusing." Bernie was feeling grimmer by the minute.

"Everybody in Hollywood uses opium and snow.'' Wanda shrugged.

"I don't care what they do in Hollywood.'' For a moment Bernie thought about his uncle out there. Wanda was dying to meet Uncle Leon; he was a movie producer, therefore important. "In our family we don't take drugs.''

He would have to find a place for them to live as soon as they got back to New York. His parents would be shocked and distraught if they saw this side of his wife. Nor would they be having grandchildren any time soon. Once they were married Wanda insisted he use protection when he slept with her. She had no intention of ruining her figure with children.

"You were different before we were married,'' Wanda asserted.

"No, you were different, Wanda.''

In Hollywood Helen became her uncle's constant companion, both at work and after hours. Only now did she realize that he was not the sole owner of the studio. He had four partners, all frantic because of the exhibitors' ploy. Now they understood why Mary Pickford and Douglas Fairbanks, Chaplin and D.W. Griffith had started their own distributing company. No movie theater in the nation could buy except from the trust.

Marianne had walked out on Leon, but the studio workers, still on salary, treated him like the king of Hollywood, and Helen received royal treatment as well.

She was tickled pink by the stories racing around Hollywood about Leon Raisa's "gorgeous new mistress." Rumor insisted he was keeping her under wraps until he sprang her on the movie world as his brand-new star. Only his intimates knew the desperate state of his finances.

Late one evening, when the studio employees were gone for the day and the movie set quiet, Helen sat across the desk from Leon in his office and watched him juggle figures.

"We'll bring in this picture," he said tiredly, "but I had to mortgage the house to the hilt to do it."

"I don't really understand everything that's going on," Helen replied. She was troubled. "I know about the exhibitors' circuit and that they're producing their own pictures now, but they can't make enough to satisfy demands. Can they, Leon?" She had never called him uncle since the first night at the Alexandria.

"No," he conceded, "but now they're plotting a deal with the giant film companies. They'll squeeze small outfits like mine—like Clara Kimball Young's—right out of the business."

"But if you have a really great picture," she protested, "wouldn't it be to their advantage to buy it?"

"I don't have a great picture. What I have was good enough four or five years ago, even three. But this business is growing fast." He looked at her quizzically. "I'll bet with some careful planning I could make you into a star. God knows you've got the looks and the style. If I could find the right script and the right director—"

"No, Leon." Before the war she would have been thrilled to death if anybody had suggested such a thing, though even then she was sure she wasn't an actress. All the girls at Miss Lodge's had nursed secret fantasies about being a movie star. "Besides, you have enough on your hands to finish this movie." It was the best picture he had ever produced—everybody at Raisa Films agreed to that—but today it wasn't good enough.

"I'm not giving up on you. I think you could be another Gloria Swanson."

"Leon, is there some way you could cut costs? The picture is running days over schedule." Everybody said Leon Raisa thought he was King Midas the way he threw money around on the set.

"I told you, Helen, I've got the money now."

"But you need to hang on to some of it," she said earnestly, alarmed at hearing that he had mortgaged the house, which was more a symbol of success to him than the studio.

"Maybe it's time to move on to another business. We'll see."

"What about going back into shipping?" she asked. "Papa would find a place for you with him again."

"I'm not interested in that penny-ante stuff," Leon said impatiently. Helen refrained from pointing out that her father was one of the richest men in New York. She understood what Leon meant. He wanted excitement and color. He enjoyed seeing his name in gossop columns, his photograph in the movie magazines with his arm around some beautiful actress. "Stay with me, baby. I'm not through yet."

This happened to be the day Johanna had Helen's first letter from the West Coast. When they finally got home the phone was ringing off the hook.

"Helen, what is this nonsense about your staying on in California?" Her mother was trying to sound amused, but Helen sensed the alarm in her.

"I like it out here. I like working at the studio." Mama was scared to death she was playing the party scene. She wasn't. She went to parties with Leon, but they rarely stayed long and never drank more than a beer. He just wanted everybody to see he was still not defeated. He enjoyed showing her off, having everybody think they were living together. In Hollywood Helen Raisa had become Helen Reynolds. "Uncle Leon says I'm catching on to the business fast."

"It's not quite the environment you should be in, Helen."

"I'm not a wide-eyed little girl, Mama. How's Papa?"

"Papa's fine except that he worries about you out there in Hollywood." Papa and Mama never approved of Leon, Helen thought. "Nicky's teething like mad and Bernie and Wanda have their own apartment."

"Uncle Leon's having a rough time financially." Helen allowed a hint of accusation to color her voice. "There's some rough action out here that's shaking the movie business up. He could use some help," she said bluntly.

"He could have had help if he had been willing to do business sensibly. Your father lent him a lot of money to start up. If Leon wants more he will have to sign a contract, not ask for a handout."

Helen cast up her eyes and tapped her foot. "Mama, doesn't Papa trust his own brother? It's only a short-term loan."

"Your father's gone into it thoroughly. No one lends a cool million with no guarantees—or when it can never be repaid. This is something Papa and Uncle Leon's accountants have gone into at great length." Now she chose her words carefully. "If Leon decides he'd like to come back into the firm, I'm sure Papa will find a place for—"

"You know he won't do that. Look, Mama, I have to get dressed now. Leon is taking me to a party at the Ship Café. It's the birthday of some movie star he knows. Kiss Nicky for me. I hope the teething doesn't give him too bad a time."

Late in the summer, with the studio all but closed down and no new picture scheduled, Helen received a letter from her mother saying that she was coming out to visit for a week and bringing Nicky along. They'd stay at the Alexandria.

Leon insisted, as Helen knew he would, that her mother and his new nephew stay with them at the house. "Your mother's scared to death I'm introducing you to the sordid Hollywood life," he drawled. "She thinks I take you to a different orgy every night."

"She's coming out to persuade me to return to New York." Helen was oddly pleased that her mother would go to such lengths, even though she felt her parents and Bernie were strangers.

"Are you going back with her?"

"No." Leon would need her when the roof fell in on Raisa Films, and they both knew it would happen within weeks. His four partners were frantic to salvage what they could. They wouldn't gamble on his wild goose chases.

Helen went to the railroad station in the chauffeured Rolls-Royce to meet her mother and baby brother. She tried to tell herself she wasn't excited, but her heart pounded as she saw her mother emerge from the train followed by Nicky in Melissa's arms.

"Mama!" With warmth she had not shown her mother since Rudy's death she ran forward to greet her.

"Helen, you look marvelous," Johanna admitted grudgingly after an anxious scrutiny. "All this sunshine must agree with you."

On the way to the house she told her mother that things were going badly at the studio. "Not just for us, but for all the small companies." She hesitated. "I don't think Leon can hold on much longer." Helen saw her mother start at her use of the bare first name and for distraction took Nicky in her arms and kissed him enthusiastically.

"What's happening with Bernie and Wanda? Is Wanda pregnant yet?"

"No." This was unexpectedly terse.

"Is anything the matter?"

"They seem to be happy."

"They're young." Helen shrugged. "Why rush to have children?" Again she asked herself if Mama had deliberately gotten pregnant to make sure Papa didn't wander away again. They were sharing a bedroom again. Were they still sleeping together? Why was it so disconcerting to think of your parents doing *that*?

Later, in Johanna's room—she had consented at last to stay with Leon—Helen explained that out here she was Helen Reynolds. "This is a crazy business. It keeps up Leon's image of being the 'flamboyant Raisa' to have people think he's keeping a young mistress."

Johanna sniffed with distaste. "Helen, that's ridiculous. Even for Leon it's absurd."

"If it makes him feel good, then why not?"

When her mother had unpacked and changed for dinner, Helen showed her through the house. "It's mortgaged to the hilt," she said bluntly.

"I'm sorry to hear that," Johanna said with a show of discomfort. "I suppose he mortgaged it to try to save the business?"

"That's right. Mama, it really isn't Leon's fault he's in trouble. Honestly, if it weren't for this exhibitors' cartel—"

"Helen, I don't want to argue with you about your father's money. If there were the slightest chance to save Leon's studio, Papa would help. He's studied the situation thoroughly with his own accountants and with Leon's. They all agree there's no way to bail Leon out of this."

Helen was showing her mother a Gloria Swanson film in the projection room when they heard a car pull up before the house, then Leon's voice in conversation with the butler. Ramon would be telling him they were here in the projection room.

"Johanna," he called out ebulliently, switching on the lights, "do you know it's been over three years since I've seen you?" He charged forward to kiss her warmly. "Damnit, you never change. You look more like Helen's sister than her mother."

"You're looking well," Johanna said. "Filling out at last."

"I know, I live too well. Where's my new nephew? When do I get to see the little fellow?"

"Melissa has him out in the kitchen for his supper," Helen put in. "Come on. Let's go out there."

She led the way out to the kitchen, hoping to postpone the coming scene. There'd be a dramatic plea for her to come home, she guessed, and shouting and recriminations all around. Still, irritation was interwoven with a kind of pleasure that her mother was this anxious about her. Those first weeks back home from France it had seemed there was no thought in her mother's head but for Nicky—and of course Bernie, Mama's darling first-born son.

In the kitchen Leon knelt to scrutinize his newest nephew.

"Hey, he's a big boy. Looks a lot like Casimar." He laughed as Nicky, ever a cheerful baby grinned back at him.

Why did Mama blush like that? Leon was right. Nicky did look like Uncle Casimar. He and Papa were a lot alike except that Papa was much handsomer. Too bad for Nicky.

Soon Nicky was off to bed and Leon marshaled Johanna and Helen into the French salon of his Spanish house for preprandial cocktails.

"You'll want a sidecar." Leon nodded at Helen. "What about you, Johanna?"

"A little white wine," she said stiffly, wondering if Helen drank a cocktail before dinner every evening. It sounded like it.

"What's happening back in New York?" Leon asked while he went about preparing their drinks.

"About the same as the rest of the country. Returning soldiers are still running around after jobs. Too many of them are not finding them—"

"Come on, Johanna," Leon scoffed good-humoredly. "There are always a lot of people who can't find jobs. The country's on the way toward prosperity like we've never seen. All those damn wartime restrictions have been lifted. People are spending money like never before." He handed her a glass, quite full.

She took a sip and put down her glass, then sat where she could not reach it. "And we've got wild inflation," Johanna pointed out.

"It's going to stop," Leon argued. "The new taxes Congress is going after will check it. Of course Wilson is so damned concerned about peacemaking he can't see what's happening here at home."

"Michal's concerned about the Bolsheviks in Europe." Johanna sighed. "We've had some hysteria here about the Communists, but I don't think we have anything to fear. It's Europe that's in danger from Bolshevism. When the Soviets organized the Third International last March, they made no secret that they were after world revolution."

"Can't three people in this country ever get together without talking about war?" Helen's color was high. "That's what I like about Hollywood, Mama. People out here know how to have fun."

Not until after dinner did her mother launch into a long urgent plea for her to return to New York. Johanna had meant to wait until she'd been here a day or two, but she couldn't hold off.

"Mama, I love it here. The weather is magnificent and the people are great." Now faint hostility welled up in her because she knew her mother disapproved of Leon's associates. "I just may stay here forever."

Helen went along with Leon in his efforts to pretend that all was well at the studio. Together they showed her mother the more respectable side of Hollywood social life. They took her to dinner at the fabulous Pasadena mansion of one of the studio partners; they introduced her to Leon's accountants; they lunched at the Alexandria. Helen and Johanna took Nicky to the four-year-old San Diego Zoo and stayed with the mayor; his wife's brother was one of Leon's partners.

Much of the table talk at the dinner in Pasadena concerned fears that prohibition of liquor would soon be a reality. The states were ratifying the amendment with speed that would have sent Leon to hoarding a cellarful of his favorite beverages if his credit had been in less dismal shape.

Helen was relieved when her mother's visit was about to end. This week had been difficult, evoking memories she would have preferred to keep buried. Mama was a constant reminder of Rudy and what her life might have been like if he had lived.

In the overdecorated white, pink and gold Italian guest room where she had spent the past week, Johanna locked her steamer trunk. She could hear Helen in good-humored exchange with Nicky downstairs in the foyer. Helen was relieved that she was leaving, Johanna thought wistfully. Michal had known it was futile for her to come out here to persuade Helen to come home; maybe she should have listened, but she must make the effort.

Neither of the children was happy. Bernie said not a word about trouble in his marriage, though it was clear to anyone who loved him that all was not well. Michal said it was just the rough first year that all newlyweds went through; Wanda was a lovely wife. Bernie seemed in love with her, so what was wrong? Maybe everything would be all right, as Michal kept saying, once they started a family.

There was a knock on the door. Thinking it was Ramon to pick up her trunk, Johanna called, "Come in, please."

The door opened and Leon came into the bedroom.

"I thought you'd be at the studio." They had said good-bye last night.

"I figured I could come home to see my beautiful sister-in-law off," he said. As he moved closer, she smelled whiskey on his breath; he started his drinking early. "It was great having you here, Johanna." His eyes trailed over her with the sensuous approval that had always disturbed her.

"I enjoyed being here, though I'd hoped to persuade Helen to go back home with me." She hesitated. "Remember, Leon, for all her air of sophistication Helen's only twenty. I don't think she ought to stay out here in this kind of atmosphere."

"Johanna, relax." Leon chuckled and reached for her hand. "I've never had a chance with my beautiful sister-in-law. Let me at least have the pleasure of the company of my beautiful niece."

As she recoiled in distaste from a lecherous smile, Ramon knocked and asked if he might come in for her trunk.

"Yes, please," she cried with relief.

She was unnerved by what she felt in Leon. She knew there were moments when he looked at Helen and saw her. She must not allow her daughter to remain in Leon's house.

Chapter 19

Bernie sat at the perfectly appointed dinner table and ate Molly's perfect roast beef without tasting it. He managed to display respectful interest in what his father was saying, though his mind dwelt on the absence of his wife.

Wanda had refused to come. "Bernie, I don't care if you lie or tell the truth. Say I have an awful cold if you want to, but I can't bear another of those stupid dinners. There's never a drink to speak of—and all that dull talk about what's happening in Poland."

Michal cleared his throat and put down his fork. "I have an announcement to make. Casimar wrote to say he is staying in the church. He says many persuasive friends added their voices to ours, but no one but you and I could have been so eloquent and so convincing."

"Michal, that's wonderful. Does he seem happy about it?" Johanna asked.

"Very happy. He said he had always known he chose right for us back in Warsaw and was glad to be reminded of it. He renounced the world over twenty years ago. He is of no age and in no position to enter it again even if he wanted to, and now he knows he doesn't." Michal smiled briefly and picked up his fork again. "He didn't even mention the man he killed, just spoke of the church and the family.

"The only other thing he has to say is that since January the Russians have increased the number of troops on the Polish border from seven divisions to twenty. They'll have to act soon or the Russians will attack."

"I thought we'd have peace when the Armistice was signed." Bernie felt a nerve quiver in his left eyelid. "Didn't enough people die in the war?"

"We'll have peace only when we have a world government with teeth," Michal said grimly. "It grieves me that the United States Congress voted against our joining the League of Nations."

"Enough of this gloomy talk," Johanna ordered. "I'm going to order tickets for that marvelous new play *Beyond the Horizon*. Would Wanda and you like to go with us, Bernie? We could have dinner at the St. Regis first."

"I don't think you should count on us." Bernie forced a smile. "Wanda says this cold looks as though it might drag on for a while."

"Make her see a doctor," Michal urged him. "At her age she should be able to shake off a cold with no trouble. All you young people seem to go out in cold weather without enough clothes on."

"She's going to the doctor tomorrow," Bernie said quickly. How could he tell his parents Wanda wouldn't go out to dinner unless it was at a speakeasy? "What do you hear from Helen?"

"She still likes California," his mother replied. "I don't say any more about her coming home because I think that just makes her more determined to stay there."

"Uncle Leon still making those brainless movies?"

Every time he was over he heard that Uncle Leon was on the point of going under.

"His company has been taken over by his partners and the property is up for sale." Michal shook his head. "I suspect that happened some time ago and it took your uncle a while to tell us about it. But he's enthusiastic about some new business venture he's into now. Helen's even gone out to take a typing course so she can help him in the office."

"What kind of business?" Bernie asked. Wanda thought business was the dullest thing in the world. She couldn't understand how he could get excited about what happened at Raisa Shipping. If he listened to her, he'd be running around Greenwich Village playing at painting or poetry reading or some such damn silly thing. How would they live if he listened to her? "Papa, you used to say Uncle Leon was a sensational salesman."

"That he is," his father confirmed.

Bernie noticed that his mother's mouth was set. Whenever Uncle Leon's name came up in conversation Mama looked upset. She thought Uncle Leon was coming between her and Helen. She didn't understand that staying in Hollywood was Helen's way of cutting loose from the family. A lot of young women were going through that.

"I'm not sure what Leon's line is this time," Michal went on, "but that's Leon's way. He takes it for granted I know what he's doing. His mind is always a mile ahead of himself."

Bernie hated not being entirely honest with Mama and Papa, but what was the point in upsetting them over his trouble with Wanda? It was bad enough Wanda had run up all those bills in Palm Beach, which Papa had said were to be charged to him.

Earlier than normal, using Wanda's supposed cold as an excuse, Bernie left the Fifth Avenue house and headed toward his own apartment in the East Sixties. The night was crisp and cold, the trees in the park gaunt in the night shadows. He walked north along Fifth Avenue to Sixty-Third and turned east.

Nothing seemed to please Wanda—the apartment, the maid, the occasional friend he invited for dinner—except her friends from Greenwich Village. She wanted to run around every evening to the speakeasies, then sleep half the day away. He had a job to go to five mornings a week. He couldn't sit around swilling booze in a speakeasy every night in the week, and in truth he didn't want to.

Approaching his building, he looked up at the seventh floor. Every light was on; Wanda hated coming into a dark apartment. Bernie supposed she was off somewhere with her screwy friends. They were all so pretentious; he didn't believe there was a real talent among them.

Maybe if they had a baby, Wanda would change. When they got married so fast that way, he'd hoped she was pregnant. He looked at Mama with Nicky in her arms and felt himself suffused with tenderness. If Wanda had a baby, she'd settle down, forget about the speakeasies, stop babbling nonsense about Sigmund Freud. She'd be too busy with the baby to talk all the time about what a rotten world it was and how nothing made sense but to try to have whatever fun they could.

He was sick of hearing the kind of things Wanda's friends said all the time. Not everybody thought like them, though they were the ones that got all the attention. They called themselves the New Generation, but there was another new generation of people like himself, who worried about what was happening to people in Europe, who only knew about speakeasies from reading about them in magazines. Not every college student had a car to take his ''sheba'' to roadhouses where they'd get drunk and then go neck in the back seat.

Bernie laughed silently. Any fellow knew that if he were ossified he'd be useless on the back seat.

Suddenly he knew a way to get past Wanda's insistence on a condom for making love. He shuddered. She even carried one in her vanity in case they were out somewhere and got passionate.

He'd get her drunk and then start to make love. Wanda was the most passionate woman he'd ever known. With a few drinks in her she'd forget all about protection. It was deceitful, but he had to do something to save their marriage.

As he expected, Wanda was not home. This was Friday night and he didn't always go to the office on Saturdays. He could wait up for her tonight.

What would his parents think if they knew he let Wanda go off without him to speakeasies? Or—face it— couldn't stop her. They wouldn't understand a liberated woman. Well, sometimes he didn't himself.

He showered, pulled on silk pajamas bought for the honeymoon and settled himself in an armchair in the living room, conscious more than ever of the contrast between the elegant furniture in his parents' home and the ultra modern stuff Wanda had crowded into their apartment. He hated all the chromium-plated handles, the wild designs on the upholstery fabrics. It jarred his senses.

Despite his determination to remain awake until Wanda arrived, he dozed off until he heard her, slightly off-key, singing "Japanese Sandman." He jerked upright in time to see her drop her new raccoon coat on the floor. She stretched her arms above her head in a languorous gesture that lifted her short skirt above her knees.

In moments like this, when she was neither sulking nor complaining, she seemed utterly desirable. Her eyes met his and she smiled the provocative little smile that always started a pulse hammering low within him.

"You missed a whole evening of whoopee," she purred, "and guess who we saw at the theater?" Her voice was muffled as she pulled her dress over her head. A second later she stood coyly before him in her pale pink silk teddy. "Elinor Glyn."

"Who's Elinor Glyn?" Wanda was already drunk. He should have realized she would be, but most nights he was already half asleep when she slid into bed beside him.

"Darling!" Her eyes widened in reproach. "She wrote that absolutely marvelous book that everybody's reading—*Three Weeks*."

"I guess I've heard of it." Bernie pulled her into his lap. "Isn't it supposed to be terribly shocking?" He nuzzled her neck.

"Oh yes." Wanda snuggled against him. "It's about this noblewoman who seduces a young man—much younger than she is. They have a wild love affair, but afterward she has no regrets. She admits she enjoyed it."

"How about seducing this older man?" Bernie coaxed.

Wanda giggled drunkenly. "Darling, you're only five years older than me."

"Pretend I'm forty," he coaxed.

"No." She yawned widely.

"Then I'll seduce you." He slid his hand under her teddy and then put her up on the arm of the chair. Sliding from under her legs, he thoroughly kissed one knee. "Did I ever tell you that you look just like Mabel Normand?"

He swept Wanda up in his arms and carried her to the bed. She was half asleep already by the time he had her out of her teddy, but when he caught one pink nipple in his mouth and slid a hand between her thighs, she roused. "Honey, got your protection?"

"Sure, just relax. We're going to have a wonderful time." He stroked her flanks with his fingernails and she sighed.

Somehow her vulnerability at this moment enhanced his passion. How he loved her when she was sweet like this. Her hands clutched at his shoulders when he thrust within her. Now she was fully awake, moving with him, her passion matching his.

"Oh honey, make me go crazy," she whimpered, an insatiable tigress beneath him. He felt the ripping of her nails across his back. "More, honey, more."

Her savage cry of pleasure blended with his own, and then she lay limp beneath him. He didn't move for long moments, knowing that soon he'd be ready to make love again. But then he heard the faint even sound of her breathing and knew she was asleep.

Gently, so as not to awaken her, Bernie pulled himself away from his wife and tiptoed in the darkness to the bathroom. Tomorrow she would not even remember this. She'd sleep till noon and last night would be a fuzzy memory.

Twice a week, when Wanda stayed at home with her husband, they made love in her approved fashion. At least two other times a week, when Wanda came home from carousing with her "artistic" friends, they made love in what Bernie thought of as the good Catholic fashion.

Before Wanda suspected it, Bernie was sure she was pregnant. He kept an eye on her and knew she was late. She was too wrapped up in having fun to notice. Then on a balmly spring evening Bernie came home from the office to find Wanda in a stormy mood. She waited until their housekeeper had served dinner and left the apartment to give vent to her rage.

"Wanda, you're not eating," he said warily as he heard Millicent close the door on her way out of the apartment.

"I'm pregnant," she screamed. "We did it and you weren't wearing anything."

"Wanda, you know they're not entirely safe," he told her, fighting remorse. Still, he believed Wanda would be happy when they had a baby. It was because she was running around with those goofy friends of hers that she was behaving this way. "It happens sometimes." He spoke with a hard-earned calm.

"I won't have a baby," she shrieked. "I'm too young. Do you know what it'll do to my figure? I'll look like an old woman."

"You'll look wonderful." He put his arm around her. "My mother has had three children and she has a lovely figure."

Wanda jerked away. "Your mother wears expensive clothes that would make anybody but a toad look good. I'm not having this baby, Bernie. I know a doctor who'll take care of me. There are lots of them around."

For a few seconds Bernie was too stunned to speak. How could she think of such a thing? Still, he temporized. "It's dangerous to have an abortion. You could die."

"I won't die; this is a competent surgeon. And don't you dare say anything about the church," she warned. "The church isn't going to walk around looking a zeppelin, it'll be me. I don't want a baby." Her voice soared hysterically. "I hate you, Bernie. You wanted this. You don't care about me. All you care about is yourself!"

"Wanda, please—" He was shaken by the sight of her in wildly hysterical sobs. "Baby, don't carry on this way."

"I won't have a baby!" She picked up a plate and threw it it across the room, and then another and another while Bernie backed away, stricken.

"That's enough of that, Wanda." He forced himself into action. "You'll make yourself sick like this."

He picked her up and carried her into the bedroom. She lay with her face buried in a pillow while Bernie stroked her back and tut-tutted. Then the sobbing ebbed off into silence. Wanda was asleep.

Bernie went out into the dining room to clean up the shattered dishes. Then he cleared the table and washed up. He had to talk to Mama, he thought. If anybody knew how he could manage his marriage, she would. He respected Mama's wisdom tempered with compassion.

He left a note for Wanda on the bedside table, though he suspected she would sleep all night. Tonight he was too impatient to talk to his mother to walk. He took a taxi. He hoped Mama would be alone. He didn't want to face both of his parents with the problems of his marriage.

"Bernie—" His mother strode into the foyer to welcome him with outstretched arms.

"Mama, I have to talk to you. Could I see you alone?"

"Papa's at a meeting tonight and he won't be home for hours. Let's go up to my sitting room."

In silence they walked up the staircase to his parents' suite. This was where Mama always brought him for what she used to call their growing-up conferences when he was a boy. Mama might not always have agreed with what he had to say, but she always listened and offered practical advice. He could never fully understand Helen's resentment.

In the bedroom his mother settled herself in a chair by the fireplace while at her instructions Bernie applied a lit match to the ready-laid fire.

"Have you had dinner? Shall I have Molly bring up a tray for you?"

"I ate." He had barely touched the food on his plate, but just now the thought of eating made him queasy.

"You're having problems with Wanda," Johanna guessed.

He stood before the fireplace and gazed at the grate. "Is it that obvious?"

"Every marriage has problems, darling, particularly in the first year."

"I didn't know Wanda until after we were married. She lives in an entirely different world from me. She doesn't like my friends, the few that she's met, and I don't like hers. But I know we have to get past that, particularly now." He took a deep breath. "Wanda's pregnant."

"She'll settle down now," Johanna exclaimed, her face suffused with happiness. "A baby will make all the difference in the world."

"Mama, she doesn't want the baby." His throat was tight with anguish. "She—she wants to have an abortion."

He saw his mother's face drain of color. She sat very still and silent for a moment. Then she gathered her wits. "She said that in a moment of shock. She can't mean it, Bernie."

"She means it. She's said ever since we were married that she didn't want to have children for a long time."

"Her mother died in childbirth, as I recall." Johanna's voice deepened with sympathy. "When Wanda was only four. Bernie, she's frightened right now, but it's far less dangerous to have childbirth now than it was sixteen years ago. Let me talk to her."

"Talk to her, but it won't help. I don't know what will help, and it's my fault. I—I disregarded her wishes." He felt color warm his face. How could he talk to his mother about contraception? "I promised her we'd take precautions."

"She mustn't try to lose the baby. It could be dangerous if she did—"

"Wanda wouldn't do that," he said confidently. "She wants an abortion by a competent physician. I heard her talk about a friend who had one last month. She said with the right doctor it was less than having your tonsils out."

"And you think she'll go to this man. I'll talk to her

in the morning. Don't tell her I'm coming, but let me have a real talk with her. I just might change her mind.''

Johanna slept little that night. She had thought Wanda a lovely sweet child and welcomed her as a daughter-in-law. She had been furious when Helen, clearly more perceptive than she in this instance, made snide remarks about Wanda and her friends. Michal wondered that her father made no effort to come to the wedding. Johanna pointed out the shortness of the time and the need for him to be active in Polish politics, but never once had she heard Wanda talk about her father, nor had anyone ever met her ''cousin the suffragette.''

They were living in chaotic times. She had thought that once the war was over the world would settle down again. Instead here in America they fought inflation, unemployment and absolute terror of Bolshevism. In January a nationwide raid on so-called Reds resulted in the arrest of six thousand people, most of them neither foreigners nor Communists. Fewer than six hundred were eventually deported, but only because Secretary of Labor Wilson insisted they all receive fair trials.

In Europe the war was supposed to be over, though already there were fresh troubles in Poland. Border skirmishes threatened to become worse. Casimar was far less optimistic than Michal and she about the future of their homeland. Michal was concerned about who would be elected President in November and he was uneasy about the fate of the League of Nations.

While Michal and she were both saddened by the attitudes of the more vocal of the young people in the country, Johanna could understand and sympathize with their disillusionment. They had gone to war with such idealism to fight the most terrible war in the history of mankind, yet the world was still unsettled and unhappy.

The entire world was shocked by the brutal murder of the Russian royal family in July of 1918, and that shock colored the world's attitude toward the Communists even in 1920. Red menace hung like an ominous cloud over all Europe and Asia.

"You were restless last night," Michal remarked as they prepared to go downstairs to breakfast.

"Did I disturb you?"

"No, dear." He smiled gently. "But after all these years I know when you're upset. You're worrying about Helen."

"Well, yes," she said. No need to worry Michal with this other problem. "She ought to be back home and meeting young men of her own age. She ought to be thinking about marriage."

At the bottom of the steps they paused to look outside and check the weather. The sun shone but it was cool and windy.

"Typical mother," he teased, pulling her into his arms for a moment. "You can't wait to hold the first grandchild in your arms."

"Are you any different?"

"I've got Nicky." He kissed her warmly. "I thank you every day of my life for our third child. You don't know how I enjoy my second son."

Remembering Bernie's warning that Wanda slept late, Johanna forced herself to wait until past eleven to call. She deliberately did not phone ahead, knowing the value of a surprise attack. Still, her heart was pounding as she pressed the doorbell of the apartment.

In the long dark night she had arrived at an unflattering assessment of Wanda, reluctantly because this was her son's wife. Michal had been outraged at the bills from Palm Beach. She knew that Bernie invariably made excuses for Wanda's absences from family dinners. From others in their circle she knew that Wanda was caught up in hard-drinking café society. But Wanda carried Johanna's own son's child, and she would pay almost anything to prevent an abortion.

"Good mornin', Miz Raisa," Millicent greeted her with a wary smile. "Miz Wanda didn't sleep too good last night. She's just gettin' up."

"Bring me a cup of coffee, Millicent, and I'll wait for her in the living room." Johanna smiled warmly.

"Yes ma'am."

Millicent brought steaming hot coffee in a cup of Haviland china from the elder Raisas' other housewarming gift. A few moments later Wanda, looking beautiful and defiant in a feathery white chiffon negligée, came into the room.

"Good morning, Wanda. You're wonderful as always."

"I feel lousy," her hostess snapped. "Millicent, bring me a cup of coffee," she yelled.

Where was the shy, sweet young thing who had married Bernie little more than a year ago? They should have checked into her background, Johanna thought. But Wanda's father was one of them, a fine Polish gentleman. What had happened to his daughter?

"Wanda—" She forced herself to smile. "I'm so delighted with the news."

Wanda's eyes widened and she seethed. Bernie had run straight to his mama and tattled about the baby she meant to get rid of.

Johanna saw her rage. How could she be so unfeeling? To want an abortion was beyond Johanna's comprehension. "Of course," she forged ahead before Wanda could make a reply, "I told Bernie's father this morning that an apartment is no place to bring up a child. You'll need a house of your own and a nursemaid—a wet nurse—as soon as the baby arrives." She paused to allow this to sink in.

"Bernie won't care where you live, but I thought you ought to tell the real estate broker whether you prefer Fifth Avenue or Park." It would cost a fortune, and for a while Michal would be shocked at bribing Wanda, but it was a small price to pay to save their grandchild. "Which *would* you prefer?"

"Park," Wanda said at once. She envisioned herself as the dazzling mistress of a house on Park Avenue and smiled greedily. "Fifth is really passé."

"Then Park it shall be," Johanna assured her. "Make sure the broker shows you a wide selection before you choose. We'll deed it to Bernie—in trust for the baby."

Wanda understood her perfectly. No baby, no house.

"We should be in the new house before the baby comes," Wanda said. "I'm going to be so busy. All that furniture to buy—" Her voice trailed off. She knew the limitations of Bernie's salary.

"That'll be our gift in honor of the baby," Johanna said, hating herself for caving in to Wanda this way. At least there would be no abortion. Wanda and Bernie—with God's help—would present Michal and her with their first grandson in approximately seven months. Bernie's marriage would be on safe ground after that—or at least she must hope so. Meantime, no house would be bought until it was far too late for an abortion. She would pick the broker herself and have a chat with him about several points. Who pays the piper calls the tune, she mused, smiling rather grimly.

She listened for an agonizingly long time to Wanda's prattle about what she wanted in a house and furniture. When she could take no more and rose to flee, Wanda kissed her enthusiastically; she now regarded her mother-in-law as delightfully useful.

"I'll call a broker right away," Wanda cooed. From the glint in her eyes Johanna knew she was dying to spread the word among her friends. "I don't want to be running around looking when I'm popping out like mad."

"I'll take care of that for you, Wanda," Johanna offered firmly. That way she could control which houses the broker would show. "I know how tired you'll be in these first weeks."

"That's right." Wanda's eyes widened with curiosity. "You had Nicky less than two years ago."

"Nicky will be two on Armistice day." Johanna's face radiated tenderness. "I'll have the best brokerage in the city calling you within the week," she promised.

While Josip drove her downtown to see Mrs. Zabriskie, Johanna debated about how she was to tell Michal what she had done. At times like this she was conscious of the drawbacks of being a woman. While Michal always said everything they owned was hers as well as his, she still had to ask Michal for anything she could not buy out of the household money.

Michal always said she was a part of the business and used her for his sounding board. He respected her opinions, but Johanna believed he would be profoundly shocked if she asked to be taken into the firm or even to have money of her own.

It looked quite certain that postwar politics called for ratification of the Nineteenth Amendment, granting women the right to vote. The right result for the wrong reasons, she thought cynically. She felt a surge of excitement at the prospect of going to the polls to vote. Odd how Michal seemed to think she would meekly vote as he did all the time.

The car pulled up before Mrs. Zabriskie's building and Johanna walked with her usual swiftness up the stoop to the entrance. Despite her age Mrs. Zabriskie continued to take in boarders. She had been thrifty through the years—a trait of Polish women that Michal said made it possible for the men to strike so stubbornly—so that she was financially secure and too proud to accept more than an occasional gift.

To Mrs. Zabriskie, who knew more secrets than any other woman in the city, she could confide the problems of Bernie's marriage. What she couldn't tell the priest at confession she could tell Mrs. Zabriskie.

"Johanna, you acted right," Mrs. Zabriskie said vigorously in the kitchen over coffee and cake. "You have to use the means at hand sometimes. Women have to take power; men never give it to them. If I were you I'd never tell Michal it's a bribe. In fact, lead him to think it's his idea."

"It'll cost a small fortune," Johanna admitted. "It would make it a lot easier for him to spend it if he thought of it as a gift."

Mrs. Zabriskie hesitated. "Johanna, I think I have to say this to you." She stared at the table for a moment, then met Johanna's eyes. "I know people who are friends of Wanda's father. He has never had an easy time with his daughter. He—he put her out of his house because he refused to tolerate her behavior. You must always watch out for Wanda. For Bernie's sake, keep an eye on her."

Johanna waited impatiently for Michal to come home from the office. When he got home he came directly into the library as usual, knowing she would be there waiting to have a glass of wine with him. Despite Prohibition their wine cellar was sufficiently stocked to see them through years of the very light drinking done in this household.

"I was down visiting Mrs. Zabriskie today," she told him as she handed him a glass of sherry.

"Then you picked up a copy of *Narod Polski*." He smiled with satisfaction.

"And *Nowy Swiat*." Michal knew she never went

downtown without bringing home at least two in their native tongue. "I'll give them to you after dinner, but right now let me tell you what has happened today." Despite what Mrs. Zabriskie said Bernie would not expect her to keep any of this from his father.

"I knew you were worrying about something. When you're restless like last night, you're upset."

"Michal, I made a huge commitment on our behalf," she began slowly. "Only because it was necessary."

Michal flinched when she told him about Wanda's insistence on an abortion. "So I—I promised her a furnished house on Park Avenue if she has the baby. I've fixed it with the realtor and all—a price limit, a delay so she can't double-cross us, a specific amount for furniture and no more. I had to move fast, Michal, she already knows an abortionist."

"Johanna, I figured we would give Bernie a house in five years. Besides, you should have told me this morning so I could say how much to spend. Money is a man's business."

"Michal, there was no time for scruples. I tell you, she could have had it done today." She took his hand and he covered hers with his own.

"Then thank God you were smart enough to know how to cope with this. On Wall Street, if you were a man, you'd make a fortune with that sharp head of yours."

"Then it's all right that I made the promises?"

"It's all right, my darling." Unexpectedly he grinned. "And I don't doubt for a moment that you'll control Wanda as you see fit. Bernie should say thanks every day that he has a mother like you."

Chapter 20

In the small office that adjoined her uncle's Helen typed up the bills of lading for tomorrow's shipments. Business was good; Leon didn't have to tell her how good. She was now in full charge of the books and was paid a substantial salary.

"Helen," Leon called from his office, "have you arranged for the trucks to pick up tonight?"

"They'll be there," she promised. "On the dock at four a.m."

"What time are we to meet the guests at the yacht?"

"We sail at six this evening," Helen said, enjoying the details of her job. "Cocktails will be served immediately, dinner at eight. The entertainment will begin at ten. By midnight everybody should be in bed. At two we rendezvous with the delivery ship. We dock to unload at four and will sail again no later than five, just before dawn. Breakfast will be served on deck at ten."

This was a ritual they went through with each consignment. Leon said they could not afford one minor slip-up; one tiny mistake and Raisa Enterprises would be out of business. He loathed the details, though, and greatly appreciated her ability to handle them.

Only Leon would have dreamed up this method of operation, she thought with a mixture of admiration and affection. With his connections it was perfect. To all the world Leon Raisa was still trying to regain his foothold in the movies. It was assumed that his small parties aboard the yacht, rented from the banker who had granted the mortgage on his house, were given in the hopes of acquiring fresh financing.

The studio was gone, but Leon clung to the house. Helen had tried to persuade him to take a bungalow at the Beverly Hills Hotel; it would be a very good address and cost far less than maintaining the house and staff. In these last months she had become aware of the value of each dollar, but to Leon his mansion in the hills was an indispensable symbol of success.

"Wear something with sequins. That's always sexy. You must have something like that from wardrobe," Leon said with his satanic grin. Before the studio was wrested from his hands, he had taken her to the wardrobe department and ordered her to try on everything she liked. The results filled a room at the house.

"Black silk crepe with sequins, cut so low and slinky Mama would turn green," she laughed. "You'll approve."

"We'll serve coffee and pastry before the guests go to their staterooms," Leon said, his eyes aglint with amusement. "That always seems to put them to sleep."

What did Leon instruct the chef to put into that coffee to ensure their sleeping? Helen didn't dare ask. Even she, plagued by chronic insomnia, slept through both the delivery and the removal of the cargo. She felt terrible the next day, too.

"Maybe we ought to arrange for a private delivery to

your father," Leon drawled. "How do you think he would react to a case of the best Scotch to come down from Canada?"

"I don't think you should consider it," she said firmly. "Papa might not understand."

Almost everybody they knew, including her father, thought Prohibition was ridiculous. Almost everybody in the country acted as though it didn't exist, but her parents would insist that the Constitution should be respected. It was difficult to realize that her mother and father, like Leon, had been rebels in Warsaw. Unlike Leon, Mama and Papa had mellowed into stuffiness.

Early in the afternoon Helen drove to the house to make her elaborate preparations for the party. She spent a long time at the mirror. The black sequin dress, designed for a vamp in Leon's last movie, came barely past her knees and dipped low in front and back. Narrow sequined strips fringed the skirt. She pinned a silk rose to one shoulder and wore the pearls that had been her graduation gift. They added the carelessly rich touch that Leon would like.

Humming her favorite new song, *Whispering*, she went downstairs to wait for Leon, pleased with what she liked to call her working costume. There was nothing wrong about Leon's bootlegging operation. He was making scads of money supplying something people wanted. The wrong was in the law, she thought.

Downstairs she noticed the mail. She frowned at the envelope that bore her mother's large scrawl. Sometimes Mama sounded absolutely paranoid about her staying out here with Leon. She'd die if she knew about his new business venture.

She ripped open the envelope as she waited in the small sitting room Leon and she used at home. The French salon was to impress guests; they both felt more at home here, in the English-style parlor. Her eyes scanned the widely spaced lines on tissue-thin airmail paper. For two months now, since July, there had been airmail service between New York and San Francisco. Mail to southern California came down by rail.

Wanda expected her baby sometime in December. So she hadn't been pregnant when she married Bernie. Helen shrugged. She knew her brother had not been Wanda's first. Wanda had been out to marry rich. Helen wondered why Mama and Papa had bought them a house on Park Avenue. Papa always swore he would not keep grown children in luxury. A house for the baby was one thing, but Park Avenue?

Each time Mama wrote about Wanda's baby, Helen was upset for days. Except for Mama Helen would have given them their first grandchild. Except for Mama she wouldn't be living in exile out here in California; she'd be married to Rudy and raising a family.

Wanda stood naked before the full-length mirror in her green marble bathroom. She hated looking like this. She wished she had gotten the house in time for an abortion. All at once she reached for a bath towel and draped it across her swollen torso. From the breasts up and thighs down she was still gorgeous. Billy Kingston was wild about her, even when she looked like this.

God, she was dying for a drink. It was rotten of Bernie to throw out everything in the house. He had even gotten at the cooking wine. She was so damned tired of his fussing. She was only having this stupid baby because she had to get the house and furniture. Living for the brat was too much to ask.

Bernie wouldn't be home tonight, she reflected with a silken smile. He had gone with his father to Boston on a business trip. Bernie had insisted Millicent sleep at the house tonight so she wouldn't be alone; months ago she had scotched his ideas about having live-in help. Who wanted lousy servants snooping around all the time?

With only the towel draped about her she left the bathroom, crossed the bedroom and went into the hall.

"Millicent," she called sharply.

"Yes ma'am." Millicent came nervously up the stairs. Millicent was scared of her ever since Wanda had just missed hitting her with the coffeepot last month. Millicent was so infuriatingly stupid.

"I'm tired. Tell everybody they can leave right now. Forget about dinner."

"I'll fix you something later if you get hungry."

"No, you won't. You're going home too."

"But Mist' Raisa said I was to stay overnight so you wouldn't be alone in the house."

"Forget what Mr. Raisa said. Mrs. Raisa is giving you the night off. I want to be by myself."

"Yes ma'am. I'll tell the others."

She waited until she was sure everybody was out of the house, then telephoned Billy. She didn't know exactly what he did for a living. He painted a little and wrote bad poetry. Somebody said he was kept by some rich old biddy on East Seventieth Street, that he had his own apartment in her townhouse and was free to do what he wanted—most of the time.

"Hello?" Though it was only four in the afternoon Billy already sounded as though he'd had a few drinks.

"Hello, Billy." She used what he called her super-sexy voice. "You busy?"

"Not too busy for you," he said.

"I'm all alone in this old house without even the makings of one drink. Come over and keep me company?"

"How long will you be alone? So I'll know how much to bring."

"All night. Bernie's in Boston and I've got a terrible thirst."

"I'll be right over. Bring out the ice."

She went to the closet and pulled down a black georgette negligee trimmed with feathers. Bernie hated it, but it made her look sexy, even when she was all bloated like this. She looked like a movie star, she told herself complacently.

She hadn't seen Billy in almost six weeks. Would he be disgusted? She'd really blown up since then. But at least he'd bring her something to drink. That dumb doctor kept filling Bernie's ears with all the things she shouldn't do—like drinking and smoking. He wouldn't even let Bernie sleep with her now; he was afraid she'd lose the baby. She giggled. Fat lot of good that did with men like Billy around.

She was just bored to death. She hadn't been inside a speakeasy for almost two months. She talked on the phone to people, but that wasn't like being with them. It was a good thing Billy was coming over with a bottle. They'd have a few drinks and she'd feel lots better. She wished she could stay drunk till the baby was born—till after it was born. She didn't want to think about the birth.

Now she went to her dressing table to do something interesting with her face. She stared hard at her reflection when she finished. With her negligee hanging loose this way, she didn't even look pregnant, and the make-up made her look great.

She went downstairs to the kitchen to chop up ice for their drinks. She had just finished when she heard the bell. She left the kitchen and went up to the foyer. Billy was leaning on the bell.

"All right, I'm coming," she called, cursing at her awkwardness in late pregnancy. "Billy, be quiet."

She pulled the door wide. Billy stood there with a

brown bag in one arm. He looked a lot like that new actor that everybody was raving about, Rudolph Valentino. Even pregnant she got all excited when she saw him in *Eyes of Youth* with Clara Kimball Young.

He didn't walk across the screen. He kind of slunk. He was so sexy just to look at that she started to flutter. Maybe he made her think of Billy because she knew Billy was kept by that old lady who must be pushing sixty, and Rudolph Valentino looked like the perfect gigolo.

"Aren't you going to ask me in?" he mocked, his eyes sweeping over her, undressing her. She suppressed a giggle. Didn't it matter to Billy that she looked like the fat lady in the circus?

"If you're carrying what I think you're carrying, rush inside," she invited ebulliently. "I have a terrible thirst."

"We miss you, poor baby." He brushed her mouth with his. "Now lead me to the ice."

When the drinks had been made and sampled, Wanda suggested they go up to her bedroom. Just in case her stupid in-laws happened by, let them see the lower floors dark. They'd think she was in bed reading and not ring the bell.

"For a woman with child," Billy said with mock solemnity, "you look gorgeous."

"Do I look sexy?" she asked wistfully, starting up the stairs.

"Of course you do."

"Maybe with another drink I'll feel sexy." Wanda paused on the stairs. "Pour me another, Billy."

They stood there drinking for a few moments, then continued upward. She saw the way Billy's eyes lingered on her breasts, not really best for the dresses that were fashionable now, but she wasn't going to flatten her bosom even for fashion. Men loved them big and soft like hers.

Billy could probably see through her negligee right to her nipples.

"What's happening around town that I'm missing?" She was faintly breathless from the steps. "Any raids lately?"

"You know, Wanda." Billy clucked his tongue. "The police protection deal keeps most of the speakeasies open, but the Prohibition Bureau is something." He shook his head sadly.

"Billy, I'm so bored with everything," Wanda sighed. "Don't ever have a baby."

"If I ever do," he giggled, "I'll come borrow your maternity clothes."

"You don't know how miserable I've been," she moaned. "Everybody hates me when I look like this." She leaned toward him, knowing the neckline of her negligee would reveal the white rise of her breasts when she did. She saw his eyes focus there. He cleared his throat in that little way he did when he was getting excited.

"I don't hate you, Wanda," he said ardently.

"Let's go have another drink." She pushed the door open and walked into her bedroom. It was funny to see Billy getting all overheated even though she was pregnant.

In the bedroom she sprawled in the chair before the fireplace and held up her glass for a refill. Her eyes moved down to his crotch. Even seven months pregnant, she gloated, she had him raring to go.

"Ooh, I feel giddy," she laughed, draining her glass. "Billy, let's make ourselves comfortable on the bed." Was he too drunk? No, there was proof positive right there between his legs.

She pulled the pillows into a heap behind her and stretched out on the bed, the black negligee parting to her thighs. Even now her legs were gorgeous, long and slim and white.

"Wanda, you are something," Billy said hoarsely. Not like that old lady he had to make happy.

"You're sweet, Billy." She reached for his hand and brought it to her breast.

His hand slid beneath the black georgette and fondled the nippled whiteness. A groan escaped him as he leaned forward to kiss her. His tongue pushed between her parted lips and dueled with her own. She groped for the hard, throbbing mass between his thighs.

"Billy, take off your clothes," she ordered when they broke for breath.

"Is it all right now?" he asked, staring at her swollen belly.

"Would it make you sick when I'm like this?"

"No, baby." His eyes were smoldering. "There are ways, you know. We don't have to disturb that little guy."

Her eyes didn't leave Billy while he stood stripping beside the bed. It was a shame to waste that on a rich old biddy.

"You look like Rudolph Valentino," she murmured as he picked up his clothes with unexpected neatness and hung them across a chair. He was doing that deliberately, she thought, to make her passionate. Didn't he know she was ready to go through the roof right this minute?

"Who's he?" He came to stand beside the bed wearing only a provocative grin.

"That new actor in *Eyes of Youth*. Every girl in the audience is dying to get him into her bed."

"So I'm Rudolph Valentino and I'm standing by your bed—like this." His voice was hoarse with anticipation. "Does it give you any ideas?" She leaned forward and put her hands on his hips. He groaned and clasped her head between his hands while she made love to him. She was driving him crazy, she told herself triumphantly as his hands moved to her shoulders with painful force. She took him deeper when she heard the low rumble in his throat. "Oh God," he gasped, "oh God."

She lay back against the pillows and pushed aside the negligee.

"Kiss me here," she coaxed, lifting her breasts toward him. "Kiss me this minute."

She closed her eyes while his mouth and tongue toyed with first one nipple, then the other. Bernie hadn't touched her for two weeks. Maybe that's why this was so good. She could feel a muscle low within her reaching for what wasn't there.

"I want you," she said sweetly. "I want you in me." She reached between them to fondle him into fresh readiness and found it hardly necessary.

"Honey, it may be awkward," he warned, lifting his mouth from her breasts.

"No," she said smugly, "not this way."

She pushed him onto his back beside her and lifted her cumbersome bulk above him until she found the heat of him.

"It'll be so good," she promised, beginning to move with him. "Billy, help me. Help me!"

She dropped her hands to his chest and closed her eyes as they moved with painful intensity, reaching for the ultimate satisfaction. Wanda cried out with savage release as she felt herself bathed in his passion. A muscle within her seemed determined to drain him.

"Oh God," he muttered, bathed in sweat, "Wanda, you are something."

She sat still on him, her breath coming in gasps. Bernie didn't know what he was missing. Stupid Bernie always listened to what the doctor said. She wasn't supposed to smoke, she wasn't supposed to drink, she wasn't supposed to fuck.

"You all right?" he asked.

"Just trying to get my breath," she laughed. "I'm going to need some help getting horizontal."

Laughing at their awkwardness, they managed to move Wanda onto her back.

"And I was afraid you might be too drunk," she jibed. "Billy, you're not half bad yourself."

"I'm going in to bathe." He strolled leisurely toward the bathroom. "I can't stay too late tonight. I have to be home in another couple of hours." He turned back at the bathroom door. "Pity I can't stay the night."

"Billy—" She frowned uneasily. "Throw me a towel, will you?"

While Billy bathed, she tried to cope with frightening suspicions. She was all wet down there. Was that what the doctor meant by her water breaking? That wasn't supposed to happen for two more months. Even as she thought this, she felt a contraction. Was it a contraction? No, she was crazy, she told herself. It was that rotten gin Billy had brought over.

She lay tense against the pillows, telling herself it was silly to be scared. She wasn't having contractions, just that one silly little pain. Then she felt another hardening in her belly, stronger this time.

"Billy," she shouted, "Billy, get the hell out of the bathtub. Billy, I'm in labor!"

Chapter 21

The phone rang in the library, where Johanna sat writing to Helen. "I'll get it, Melissa," she called and reached for the receiver. "Hello?"

"The baby's coming," Wanda cried. "I'm all alone at the house and I'm having contractions."

"I'll be right there," Johanna said. Where were the servants? "Be calm, Wanda. With a first baby it's always a long time. I'll phone Dr. Lindsay and be right there."

"It hurts," Wanda snarled. "I told Bernie I didn't want to have a baby. He did it on purpose. I know he did."

"Wanda, just lie back and rest." Alarm shot through Johanna. "How will I get into the house?"

"The door is unlocked," Wanda said after a long pause. "A girlfriend was here visiting me, and she let herself out because I didn't want to take the stairs again. Hurry! I'm scared."

In ten minutes Johanna got out of the car and sent Josip to Dr. Lindsay's office for reinforcements. She let herself in and hurried up the stairs.

The door to Wanda's bedroom was open wide. Wanda lay writhing on the bed, a sheet pulled up to her neck. Her negligee lay on the floor beside the bed.

"I've sent Josip to pick up Dr. Lindsay," Johanna said, noting the pair of long-stemmed glasses on the mantel. "He'll be here in a few minutes."

"It's not supposed to be happening yet. The baby isn't due until December. Oh God," she shrieked, "I hate that Bernie! I hate him!"

Johanna tried to remind herself that Wanda was very young, in pain and scared. "Let's get you into a fresh nightgown." She pulled back the sheet and saw that Wanda was naked beneath it. "Well, let's get you into a nightgown."

"The baby was supposed to be born in a hospital. Dr. Lindsay promised."

"So it has other ideas." Johanna rummaged in the dresser drawers for a suitable nightgown, then realized Wanda owned no such garment. She brought out a white silk one and walked to the bed with it. "Babies often come early, Wanda, and they and their mothers do well nonetheless."

She helped Wanda into the nightgown and went into the bathroom for a towel to wipe the sweat from her. Returning, she saw a pair of men's fine Parisian drawers lying on the floor. They bore the finely embroidered initials *WK*. She glanced at Wanda, whose eyes were screwed shut. Johanna whisked the glasses and the underwear out of sight so the doctor wouldn't see them. Then her hands trembling, she dried Wanda's face and pushed her hair back.

Again Wanda was fighting a contraction. "I don't want this thing in me. I want Dr. Lindsay to take it out. I'm the mother and I come first."

"Sssh. Dr. Lindsay will be here soon. Before the

night is over you'll hold your baby in your arms." Why were the servants away? Bernie had not gone away overnight since Wanda got pregnant without insisting that one of the three servants sleep in the house. "You'll love the baby when it comes," she said tenderly, remembering her own joy with the arrival of each child, her grief when their second son arrived stillborn. Wanda's baby would be fine, she promised herself.

Wanda had wanted no part of Dr. Abramowiez. She insisted on a Park Avenue doctor who would deliver in a hospital. Johanna was relieved that she been able to reach Dr. Lindsay. The way Wanda's pains were coming one on top of another, she knew delivery was close.

At the sound of the doorbell Johanna charged downstairs to admit Dr. Lindsay. "I was unable to arrange for a nurse on such short notice," he announced without preamble.

"I'll help," Johanna promised.

"It's the mother's help we need most," he said with a flicker of humor. "I hope Wanda will be cooperative."

Two hours later Johanna held her first grandson in her arms. Bernie had decided as soon as he knew Wanda was pregnant that the baby would be named Johanna or Jason. What a tiny little morsel of humanity, she thought, enveloped in love and recurrent wonder at the miracle of birth. Jason weighed perhaps five pounds, but he filled the air with lusty cries.

Lindsay managed to find a nurse after all. She already bustled about the room preparing it for her new charge. Jason would need extra care during his first weeks, but everyone was optimistic about his survival. He had Raisa blood, Johanna told herself with pride. He would be strong.

"I'll take the baby now, Mrs. Raisa," the nurse said briskly. "He's a lively one even if he is so early."

Wanda lay pale and angry against the pillows. In

truth it had been an easy birth with amazingly short labor, but Wanda felt terribly put-upon. She would soon be asleep in spite of her rage.

Dr. Lindsay was preparing to leave. "Mrs. Raisa, there's nothing else you can do now. Go home and have your dinner." He chuckled. "For once my wife will see me at the dinner table at a decent hour. Why do most babies insist on arriving in the middle of the night?"

Dr. Lindsay hailed a taxi and dropped her off at the Raisa home before going on to his own. Johanna suspected the obstetrician disapproved of Wanda. Thank God he had not seen the glasses and the garment wrapped around them, now safely hidden at the bottom of her capacious handbag.

At home she called the hotel in Boston to tell Bernie he had a son.

"She had the baby alone," Bernie gasped. "I shouldn't have come up here this late in her pregnancy."

"Bernie, she's fine and the baby's fine. Keep your appointment in the morning and take the next train home. Everything's under control."

She told him all about it again and then talked to Michal. "Remind Bernie that you were clear out of the country when Helen was born, and we did fine." Johanna wished Michal were home so she could show him what she had found. This evidence obviously accounted for Jason's early arrival. She needed her husband tonight.

At midday Michal arrived at the house. He had stopped off for a moment to see his new grandson.

"Wanda was asleep," he reported. "The doctor's sent a wet nurse." Wanda had no intention of spoiling her figure by nursing. "Darling, even at this stage, you know that baby's a Raisa." He glowed with jubilation.

Thank God for that at least. No need to tell him about her suspicions.

"How was the Boston trip?" Johanna asked. "Come into the library until luncheon is ready."

"Good," Michal said with satisfaction. "I see a definite upswing in business, though I worry about what'll happen in the elections next month. I'd hate to see Harding elected. I don't think the man's qualified for the job." He frowned a little, then sighed and settled in his chair.

"You don't believe the Democrats can win with Coxe?" Johanna tucked her feet under her and leaned into the corner of the big leather sofa.

"Not a chance." Michal shook his head decidedly.

"Because of the mood of the country?"

Michal nodded.

"Luncheon is served," Molly announced.

"We'll be right there," Johanna promised.

Over the soup Michal relayed a message: Wanda and Bernie wanted Johanna to arrange the christening.

"Bernie doesn't want it for at least three weeks," Michal added. "He said Wanda had a terrible time. She needs to regain her strength."

"That's ridiculous. It was the shortest, easiest first birth I've ever heard of. If she'd behaved herself it would have been even easier. She fought her contractions the whole time."

Thrusting aside her misgivings about Wanda's conduct, Johanna made arrangements for Jason's baptism following Sunday services three weeks hence. She thought about bringing out Nicky's christening gown, but Wanda might reject it as second hand, ignoring the sentimental value. Johanna ordered a handmade costume from an exclusive Madison shop. And all the time she worried about Bernie's marriage.

In November, as Michal had predicted, Warren G. Harding was elected, but affairs in Poland were causing

Michal and Johanna more concern. In October 1920 in Moscow Lenin said, ''By attacking Poland we are attacking also the Allies. By destroying the Polish Army we are destroying the Versailles settlement.''

Early in 1921 Casimar wrote that he was now a bishop. In honor of the occasion Michal and Johanna sent a lavish contribution to the church in Poland. Johanna kissed Nicky good night with a special feeling of pride on the night the news came.

Johanna worried about Helen's continued absence from New York. At intervals she talked about going out to California for a visit, but she feared Helen would look upon this as interference. Michal said in her own time Helen would come back to them.

Johanna made a habit of dropping in to see Jason each afternoon. Wanda was always out. Johanna wondered more and more uneasily where she went.

Bernie came over for dinner every week, usually without Wanda. He stopped making excuses after a while. He looked haggard. Johanna went through each day with a sense of waiting for disaster.

Bernie sat at his desk and ignored his sandwich and coffee. He had to do something about his wife. It was dangerous to Jason for Wanda to drink so much. She would fly into tantrums for no reason at all. Thank God Mrs. Greene was so devoted to him. He had cautioned her never to leave Jason alone for a minute when he was away from the house.

Now he pushed back his chair and went to the window. He knew Mama and Papa would be devastated if he tried to divorce Wanda, but under proper circumstances he could force Wanda into a separation. From Mrs. Greene he knew that she left the house every day at three. Today he would see where his wife spent her time—and with whom.

*   *   *

Wanda stood before the mirror in her bedroom scrutinizing her reflection. Having the baby hadn't damaged her figure so much. Once the body knew she wasn't nursing her breasts had gone back to normal. With a sense of pleasure she cupped her breasts in her hands, teasing the nipples pressed flat beneath the brassiere fashion decreed she wear.

She liked the new long necklaces that hung to the wide belt around her slim hips. If Bernie saw this dress, practically up to her knees, he'd have a fit. But the daring in New York and Paris were always way ahead of other women, she thought complacently.

She looked at the clock on the mantel. Almost three. She had to meet Glory Adams at Bergdorf's at three. So she'd be a few minutes late. Glory would wait for her. After they'd shopped, they'd go down to the Village to that new speakeasy Billy had told them about. Who knows whom they might not pick up down there, she thought with a flicker of anticipation. These days the richest people went down to the Village.

Wanda suppressed a giggle as she looked into her purse to see that her vanity was supplied in case her pickup was careless. Billy had given them the password. It was, "Fuck the baroness."

Looking for a taxi, Wanda thought about the Rolls-Royce *cum* chauffeur that took her mother-in-law about town. Why couldn't they have a chauffeur? Oh, well; another servant would just be in the way.

Glory, married to a wealthy stockbroker, divided her time between shopping and slender young men. She said her husband was lucky if he could get it up once a month. He was fifty-four and Glory was twenty-three. Wanda knew how she felt. Bernie could get her all excited when they first got married, but now she just pretended. Men were so stupid.

Wanda found Glory waiting for her. For an hour and a half they roamed Bergdorf's, buying at whim and ordering everything sent. Then they left the store to take a taxi to the Village.

Feeling guilty and ashamed, Bernie followed their taxi. His black Maxwell was inconspicuous enough to go unnoticed, he supposed. He felt faintly sick at following his wife in this clandestine fashion. So far she had done nothing except shop at Bergdorf's. He winced as he anticipated yet another bill. When he tried to explain to Wanda that his salary didn't cover such extravagances, she threw a temper tantrum.

Bernie straightened behind the wheel. The taxi was turning west on Ninth Street. He'd have to follow fairly closely so as not to lose it. He was less familiar with the Village than most well-to-do men of his age. His teeth set, he stayed behind them. He could see Wanda and her friend—unknown to him, as were most of Wanda's friends—in avid conversation.

Then the taxi pulled to a stop before a small, neat brownstone house with fresh black trim. The two women got out, glanced in both directions and walked to an iron grill at the basement entrance. After some communication they were admitted. It was one of the endless speakeasies all over the city, Bernie gathered.

He drove around the block, almost getting lost in a maze in the attempt, but at last drove up to park at the curb three houses away from the grilled door. From here he'd see Wanda come out. He had to see for himself what he suspected. He sat sweaty and miserable at the wheel of the car.

He watched a score or more arrive in the course of the

next hour, most of them young. Some pretty young women were with middle-aged or older men. What would he do if he saw Wanda come out of there with a man? No need to start a scene, he warned himself. He just had to know.

They were two strangers in bed now, and she infuriated him by her lack of interest in Jason. Occasionally when he had business associates over for dinner she would play at being the devoted mother if it suited her mood. In bed it was like going to a whorehouse and paying two dollars—as if that had ever appealed to him.

Bernie stiffened to attention. He could hear Wanda's light laughter before he saw her. That laugh meant she was pleased with something. She came into view clinging to a tall, thin, hard-looking man in his early twenties. Glory and another even younger man followed. Her escort led Wanda to a Hispano-Suiza. She didn't take her eyes off him; she had no idea her husband was following her.

Bernie sat still in a cold sweat. So now he knew. His wife picked up strangers in bars. He now doubted that she was a virgin when he met her. Straight out of the army and hot, he had fallen for her line. All she wanted was to marry rich, and neither he nor his money could keep her satisfied.

He'd go to a lawyer tomorrow and ask about a legal separation. Wanda wouldn't want Jason; he was a toy that bored her in five minutes. But first he'd have to tell Mama and Papa. Maybe they would have some advice.

He went home. The office was closed and he knew Wanda wouldn't show up for hours. He would have another solitary dinner and she would come home hours later with a story about the exhibit of a friend downtown or the rehearsal of a play by someone she used to know. Wanda's excuses were all familiar now; she used them several times a week.

At the house he went directly up to the nursery to see Jason. Was it wrong to deprive Jason of his mother?

Wanda wasn't much of a mother, simply a woman who had reluctantly carried him for seven months. She hadn't even provided the customary nine months, he thought, throat tight with rage.

When Jason was fed, bathed and put to bed Bernie decided to forgo dinner at home. He sent his apologies to the cook and headed for his parents' house. Molly always cooked for an army.

He found his parents in the library. Neither remarked about his dropping in for dinner. Bless Mama and Papa for never asking questions. He saw their concern at unwary moments, though; to Mama and Papa marriage vows were sacred.

For a while, over glasses of sherry, they talked about the business. It always amazed him that his mother was so perceptive. At regular intervals Papa asked for and took her advice, even when the board disagreed. Mama's insight sometimes was uncanny.

"I have something unpleasant to tell you," he said finally, to get it over with before Melissa summoned them to dinner.

"What is it, Bernie?" his mother asked.

In halting, painful sentences Bernie told them about his afternoon. He had suspected Wanda was seeing other men for some time.

"It's not that I'll be depriving Jason of a mother," he said bitterly. "Maybe it's for his own protection too. When Wanda drinks too much, she gets nasty. If she hurt the baby, I'd kill her."

"The house is yours and Jason's," Michal reminded him. "You must not allow her to keep it. You don't owe her a house and staff."

"Come home and bring Jason with you," Johanna offered. "I promise you, Bernie, he won't miss his mother."

"He has to stay there till she's out," Michal stated.

"You'll give her an allowance, but don't start it until she moves. And close all her charge accounts early tomorrow. You can keep the house yourself if you like or sell it and move back home with Jason. I'll ask Henderson to act for you in the separation."

"No, Papa," Bernie objected. "It's going to be ugly. Henderson would be lost in this kind of case. Let me find somebody who is up to Wanda's weight."

"Bernie, there's something I should tell you." His mother stared at her lap. "If necessary I'll testify to this. The night Jason was born Wanda called me. You remember, she was suddenly in labor and terrified. When I got to her bedroom I saw two glasses on the mantel. They reeked of gin. On the floor was a pair of men's drawers." Bernie saw the color rise in his mother's face. "They were mono-grammed *W.K.*"

"Thank you, Mama. I'll tell the lawyer."

"Tell him I brought them home and I still have them."

She looked up and smiled. "I had a letter from Helen yesterday." His mother seemed determined to brighten the mood in the library. "She asked for pictures of both boys. I'll send some out in my next letter."

"Any word about when she's coming home?" Michal asked.

Johanna sighed. "Not a word. She seems all wrapped up in her job. It seems her uncle is a very generous employer."

"What exactly is Uncle Leon's business?" Bernie had never heard anything more specific than that Leon was "doing very well."

"He says he's selling bottled water," Michal said carefully. His tone and his look told Bernie he suspected something else. Was Uncle Leon a bootlegger? In the first months of Prohibition people had been apt to laugh about that, but not now, when moonshine and adulterated commercial liquor were reported to be causing deaths and blindness. In this week's *Literary Digest* there was an article about it.

Helen sat across the desk from Leon and tried not to show her astonishment as he outlined their new operation.

"Baby, what we've done so far is small potatoes. We're going to operate on several levels now."

"Besides the cutting plant?" She didn't care for this new routine of bringing in whiskey from Canada and cutting it in Leon's new plant. Their customers now received a mixture of whiskey, water and cheap grain alcohol to make three gallons out of every gallon that came in from Canada. "Leon, maybe you're moving into dangerous territory."

"Helen, I pay all down the line. Now in addition to the cutting and bottling plants I'm arranging to buy a vineyard about eighty-five miles east of here. We'll have a press adjacent to the vineyard to make perfectly legal grape juice, which—" he paused to grin—"we'll store in a cellar. Sixty days later we'll have wine. In addition I'm buying one of those distilleries that the government lets stay in business to make denatured alcohol."

"Leon, what are you planning to do with denatured alcohol? Are you going into the pharmaceutical business?"

"For the time being."

"Leon, be careful," she pleaded. The Treasury Department had a small army of Federal agents sniffing out bootleggers. While everybody thought the whole subject was a joke, people were going to jail. What had first seemed like an amusing adventure was now worrying her sick. "You won't enjoy wearing prison clothes."

"I won't go to jail. I'll make five million in the next year and ten the year after," he prophesied. "You'll have a sable bedspread on your bed and wear diamonds as big as rocks.''

Two days later Leon drove her to see the vineyard he had just bought. It seemed to spread endlessly. The former winery was being set up to make grape juice. Leon showed her the vast expanse of the cellar, where the juice would be fermented into wine.

"Suppose Federal agents come to inspect?" Helen asked, increasingly nervous about Leon's operations. "You're supposed to be selling grape juice."

"We will be," he grinned. "We've contracted the whole crop to Casipol, Inc. We ship on Fridays." He held up a hand for silence. "Casipol contracts storage from Helanna Co. And I rent my cellar to Helanna. I own all three firms, of course, but they'll never dig that tidbit up.''

Helen tried to tell herself this was just another business venture. Everybody knew the Eighteenth Amendment was nonsense. Yet it seemed to her that Leon and she were socializing with increasingly unsavory people. He no longer made any pretense of interest in movies. His mustache was waxed now and he had let his sideburns get longer. He looked more and more like a gangster.

Instinct told Helen she ought to pull out of Leon's venture and go back to New York. She had a comfortable bank account. She didn't have to go back home and live with her parents. She could take an apartment and find a job. She had acquired good office skills in California. Yet the prospect of returning to familiar scenes was unappealing. She wasn't yet ready to go home.

Chapter 22

Bernie sat nervously in a chair before the huge executive desk of Victor Corelli while the attorney carried on a cryptic telephone conversation with a client. A college friend had steered him to Corelli as being an astute matrimonial lawyer.

At last Corelli put down the phone. He smiled apologetically as he turned to Bernie.

"I'm sorry for the interruptions, Mr. Raisa, but my partner is in the hospital recovering from a heart attack. I've had to take on his clients as well my own." He leaned forward with an air of sympathy. "I understand your situation, I think. It's going to require time and a lot of legwork. I'd like to turn it over to my nephew Tony." His next words showed his pride. "He's a bright eager young attorney, fresh out of NYU Law School. He'll do a fine job for you."

"All right." Bernie strove to hide his disappointment. Jim had recommended Victor Corelli, not some nephew. "Will he be able to get on the case right away?" He was miserable under the same roof with Wanda. They still shared a bed, though he made no effort to touch his wife, nor she him. In the early weeks it had often been Wanda who made the first move.

"I'll call him in and introduce you right now," Corelli said briskly.

Bernie liked Tony Corelli on sight. The elder Corelli had been well advised to turn the case over to him. Bernie and Tony spoke the same language. Both had fought in France, though Tony humorously admitted he caught a bullet in his shoulder his first day under fire.

"I saw plenty of action after that shoulder healed," Tony said, "to make up for a slow start."

"Let's hope they don't have another one next week."

"They may," Tony muttered, suddenly grim. "But let's talk about your case. Are you sure you don't want a divorce? It doesn't sound too likely that you'll reconcile."

"I want a separation and my son," Bernie said stubbornly. "I'm willing to give her half my salary but no rights in the house. The house is in trust for my son and she can't have it."

"It may take time," Tony warned, scanning a list of private detectives, "but we'll move in as fast as we can."

While they lingered over dinner at the Alexandria Leon told Helen they were taking the train to Chicago on Sunday. It was time to move the pharmaceutical firm into their regular operation.

"How do you mean?" Helen asked, more sharply than she intended.

"You'll see." He smiled mysteriously.

"How long will we stay there?" The prospect of seeing Chicago was appealing. Though she never admitted it to her family, she was tired of perennial sunshine.

"A week," he said. "Just long enough for me to set

up the operation. I'll have to do some hiring, buy a couple dozen trucks. You'll be busy," he promised.

On Sunday they boarded the plush California Limited. Each had a drawing room. Helen soon realized that Leon meant to spend little time in his own. He dawdled with Helen in the dining car over meals that included such items as fresh mountain trout, put on board just before the train pulled out. He patronized the train barber and checked the stock market news at every station. He dragged Helen to the observation car at regular intervals.

They sped along at ninety miles an hour except on the steep grades and dangerous curves in the Rockies, marveled at the vast sameness of the Plains. Restless at being confined to the train, Helen tried to occupy herself with books from the train library, but they were outdated and dull.

She was relieved when at last they arrived in Chicago, where a rented limousine and chauffeur whisked them to the elegant Blackstone Hotel. Leon had reserved a two-bedroom suite. They had dinner in the sitting room. Leon was in an expansive mood. Tonight he talked about the early days in Warsaw. He told her about his life in Siberia, his escape and arrival at New York.

"Helen, you never saw anybody so surprised as Michal and Johanna when I knocked on the door of their flat on East Seventh Street." He never referred to Mama and Papa as her parents, but always as though they were contemporaries. "It was like a ghost had walked into the house." He viewed her speculatively. "If I hadn't got so damned impatient in that church in Warsaw and sneaked out on my own, it might have been me Johanna married. My baby brother Casimar insisted on the marriage. Michal admitted it to me." He reached for the bottle of whiskey that was always close at hand and poured another drink into his water tumbler. "All three Raisa boys had a yen for Johanna, even Casimar the Saintly."

All at once Helen was cold. Now she understood Leon's discomforting way of staring at her sometimes when he'd had more to drink than was good for him. He liked to keep her around because she looked like Mama.

The waiter came in to clear. He cast her a speculative look. That made up her mind. "I'm for bed, Leon. See you in the morning."

"I left a call for seven-thirty," he told her. "I want to be out at the plant for a meeting by nine sharp."

Helen locked her door and went to bed, but she couldn't sleep. She reached for the novel on the bedside table and began to read. Tonight Edith M. Hull's popular new novel *The Sheik* left her cold. It was going to be a movie with Rudolph Valentino; she remembered hearing about it over dinner one night at the Hollywood Hotel. Ever since *The Four Horsemen of the Apocalypse* women were screaming for Valentino.

In the morning after a quick breakfast, Helen and Leon went downstairs to their waiting limousine. As the car sped to the edge of the city, Helen saw that autumn had arrived in Chicago. On the outskirts they saw trees in magnificent shades of red, orange and yellow. Leaves blanketed the ground. Not until this moment did Helen realize how desperately she missed New York.

She had grown up enjoying the sight of the changing seasons in glorious Central Park from her bedroom window. With poignant nostalgia she remembered her father pulling Bernie and her on sleds over hard-packed snow in the park. She remembered her father taking them into the park with their bicycles. Later, because Bernie was five years her senior and considered himself too old for such things, Mama took her to the zoo in the park.

"You're quiet this morning," Leon observed.

"Sleepy. I never sleep well the first night in a hotel."

"I'm interviewing all day tomorrow and the next day," he said briskly. "I'll need you to help. You make sure the men are able-bodied, speak decent English and have driving experience."

"How do I know they're able-bodied?"

"You're a woman." His eyes mocked hers. "Look at them. You'll know."

Helen turned her eyes away. At moments like this she was uncomfortable with Leon. It was almost as though he forgot for a while that she was his niece and looked at her as though she were the young mistress he liked to pretend she was.

The pharmaceutical plant was impressive, Helen admitted as they stepped from the limousine. Leon still hadn't told her how he expected to use medicinal alcohol in their regular operation, though he kept telling her not to worry; he was legitimately in the business of making and selling it.

Leon went through the plant and held a meeting with the staff, all of whom had been in the employ of the previous owner. Subsequently he led her back to the limousine and directed the chauffeur to another address.

"We won't be hiring there," he explained, again with that glint in his eyes.

"Leon, tell me what's going on," she demanded impatiently.

He leaned toward the chauffeur. "Find a place for us to have coffee and wait for us."

In a family restaurant nearby Leon ordered coffee for Helen and himself and waited for the waitress to leave before talking.

He leaned forward and gave her a wink, then cast a suspicious glance around. Finally he whispered, "You saw the huge inventory there in the plant?"

"Yes." Helen spoke in a normal voice.

Leon shushed her violently and continued to mutter. "Well, those three hundred drivers and helpers we're hiring tomorrow and the next day will go to the plant at midnight on the third day and steal the inventory. They'll take it to a new plant right here in Chicago, where we'll be cutting. I'll collect two ways, on the insurance and on all that booze we'll have to ship to our thirsty customers."

"Leon, you can't do that. Denatured alcohol is poisonous. You know that." She was cold with alarm.

"This stuff hasn't been processed yet. It's still just good old grain.

"Listen, I never gave you that diamond bracelet I promised you way back when you helped me with Marshall Rankin. Before we go back to the Coast you'll have it."

Helen tried to tell herself she was here on a job. She tried to concentrate on hiring drivers. They wanted big, healthy men who asked no questions.

For two days they interviewed and hired. Leon called the men together at the end of each day and explained what was required of them. On the third day Leon tossed Helen a roll of bills and told her to go spend it.

"Take your time," he ordered. "You have all day to shop. When you've finished, come back to the hotel and have dinner. I'll be out all evening. Don't wait up for me." He was in high spirits.

Helen went to Marshall Field immediately after a late breakfast. The day was crisp and cool, the sky a magnificent blue without a cloud on display. She stepped out of a taxi—Leon was using the limousine today—and walked into the elegant department store. She remembered hearing her father say that the two Field clocks, visible blocks away, were a favorite meeting place for Chicagoans, like the Biltmore Hotel clock to New Yorkers. Again she yearned for her native city.

She returned exhausted at four o'clock, burdened down with parcels. Leon would be both hurt and insulted if she hadn't spent all the money he had given her. On impulse she had bought presents for all the family members, even Wanda, to be shipped by the store. Belatedly she reminded herself to drop another of her brief letters to her mother and father, letting them know she was in Chicago on business.

She ordered dinner served in the sitting room. It was superb, but she ate with little interest. When the waiter had cleared, she tried to concentrate on reading. She had the new Pulitzer Prize Edith Wharton novel, *The Age of Innocence*, but despite its obvious charm she found it difficult to concentrate.

She fell asleep at last in a living room armchair, to be awakened around four by Leon's arrival.

"Why didn't you go to bed?"

"I was worried." Helen rubbed her eyes and sat up straight.

"What happened?"

"Everything went hotsy-totsy," he said smugly. "The trucks came and took everything they were supposed to take. And why not?" he grinned. "I was there to let them in. After they left I broke a few windows, made it look like a break-in. It'll all be discovered tomorrow morning. Then I'll hire a guard. When we have a full inventory again—" he snapped his fingers. "Another break-in. The Chicago police can't be everywhere."

"What about the guard?" Helen asked. This was getting out of hand.

"He'll be tied up for a few hours until the help comes in the next morning. If he quits, we'll find somebody else. I figure maybe a dozen break-ins and we'll have to close that operation. But in twelve operations we'll make a fortune."

"Leon, the police aren't going to sit by and let you maneuver a dozen break-ins," she protested.

"Baby, you've seen enough by now to know. Money paves the way for anything. With enough money you can buy anybody." He crossed to the chest where he had hidden his cache of Scotch. "I'm going to have a drink and go to sleep."

Shortly past seven in the morning the phone jarred Helen awake. Leon was already answering. She reached for a robe and went into the sitting room of their suite.

"I can't believe it," Leon said with an air of outrage. "Why would anybody steal our entire inventory?" He gestured for quiet while he listened. One eyebrow lifted in amusement. "I hadn't thought of that." He sighed. "We'll have to hire a guard to cover the plant at night. That's a heavy loss." He paused. "Oh, of course, the insurance. But you'll be back-ordered on all our accounts. The wholesalers won't be happy about that." He listened again. "I'll dress, have breakfast and be right over."

Leon decided it would be best if Helen came along with him. He cautioned her to appear properly upset. That wouldn't be a problem, she thought. She was damned upset.

At the plant the workers were at their accustomed places. The plant manager had already sent out for glass panes to replace the broken windows. The damaged window frames were in the process of being repaired. The police had come and gone.

"We've never had anything like this," the manager apologized. "Of course Chicago isn't what it used to be. With Prohibition we've seen a bad element coming into the city."

"I'd like to use an office," Leon said with an air of

distraction. "I never expected to walk into a situation like this. It's a little different out in California—"

"Oh, yes, Mr. Raisa. Use my office." He pulled the door wide for Leon and Helen to enter. "I'm so upset myself that I think I'll go out and have some coffee. If there's anything you want to know, just ask Lonnie. He's been here for twenty-two years."

Helen pretended to take notes. She wished they were out of Chicago and back in California already. She wished she were home in New York.

Forty minutes later Helen and he became aware of the arrival of half a dozen police cars. "Why are they back again?" she wondered.

"Helen, get out of the office. Go mix with the workers. No, go to the women's washroom and lock yourself in a booth. Get moving! Don't get caught here with me."

Her heart pounding, she hurried from the office to the washroom. Fortunately, the employees were too busy watching the cops to notice her. In the women's washroom she hid in one of the stalls, sitting on the tank with her feet on the seat. For a long time she waited in silence.

At last she could hear noisy conversation outside. Leon had been taken away by the police. Two women came in.

"Can you believe somethin' like that happenin' here?" one asked. "That man who bought the plant is a gangster. A truck driver went right to the police when he heard about the robbery last night. He said it was no break-in. That there Mr. Raisa let them in."

"Yes, and his fancy-pants secretary left him high and dry. Ran right out the door and down the street."

There was a rush on the ladies' room before things settled down. Several times her booth was approached and the door rattled. Helen sat perfectly still and shook. Ten minutes after the last worker left, tense with fear, she sneaked out and hurried to a side entrance. It was very hard to walk nonchalantly off the premises.

Eventually Helen found a bus that would take her back to the Blackstone Hotel; there were no taxis in this neighborhood.

On the long bus ride back into the heart of the city she tried to calm herself. Leon had been arrested. What should she do now? She saw a woman gaze at her curiously and knew she looked distraught. She willed herself to think clearly. So far she was not involved. Leon had sent her away and covered her tracks. Would the others at the plant remember and mention her to the police? They couldn't find her. They knew her only as Miss Reynolds from Mr. Raisa's California office. That meant it was time to be Miss Raisa of New York again.

She watched anxiously for her stop. At last! Straining to retain her poise, she left the bus and pushed her way through the busy street to the hotel. Faintly breathless, she paused at the desk to ask for the key. The hotel didn't know yet that Leon had been arrested.

Upstairs in her room she went directly to the phone and placed a call to her father. She paced as she waited for it to go through.

"Good morning. American International Shipping."

"Marya, this is Helen Raisa," she said shakily. "May I please speak to my father. It's very important."

"He's in a meeting," the operator said uncertainly.

"Get him out."

At last her father's voice was on the line. "Helen, are you all right?"

"I'm in Chicago, Papa." Oh, it felt good to hear his voice. "It's Leon. He's been arrested."

"Where are you?" Her father showed no indication of what he must be feeling.

"At the Blackstone Hotel."

"How are you fixed for cash? Enough to settle your bills and buy a ticket home?"

"I've got plenty, and the room and car are paid in advance for four more days."

"Good. Don't pack. Tuck a nightgown and your jewelry into a nice big handbag and go straight to the station. Be on the next train even if you take a detour before you come home. Just don't go back to California. They'll look for you there too. It's time to come home, honey. So get cracking. I'll use the suite and car myself and bring your baggage with me when I get home.

"I'll be there first thing in the morning," he wound up. "Don't talk to anyone, just leave. I'll arrange for a Chicago attorney to go to Leon immediately. And don't worry," he said as though she were ten years old again, "everything's going to be just fine."

Chapter 23

Johanna stood by folding shirts for him as Michal packed for his trip to Chicago. "How long will you have to stay?" she asked, unnerved by the thought of her daughter in flight. Michal said Helen sounded terrified on the phone.

"Not more than two days, I judge. Henderson put me on to a Chicago attorney who is arranging bail. Of course he'll have to stay in the city until he comes up for trial."

"What do you think will happen?"

"He's guilty as hell," Michal said flatly. "I don't think he can buy his way out of this."

"Then he'll go to prison?" She felt cold at the prospect of Michal's brother in prison for bootlegging.

"Leon knew what he was doing. He knew the consequences." Michal was furious and he flung his clothes into his bag. "No matter how ridiculous a lot of people believe Prohibition to be, it's the law, and the law has to be respected."

"Maybe now Leon will learn he has to live by the same rules as other people. If he'd stayed on with you, none of this would have happened.'' She allowed her own exasperation to seep through.

"If he'd stayed with me he probably would have used my ships."

"Do you think Helen followed your orders?"

"If not I'll bundle her out of there, but I expect she did. If she's still at that hotel she'll be entirely too easy to find. Don't worry,'' he added hastily. "She'll be home in a day or so."

"I'll go with you to the station,'' she said. "Call me when you arrive in Chicago."

At Pennsylvania Station Johanna saw Michal off on the Broadway Limited to Chicago, then returned to the house. Surely now Helen would be ready to come home. Despite her shock at Leon's predicament she felt a surge of relief that Helen would be separated from him. On count-less nights she had lain awake remembering Leon's remarks to her when she was about to leave Hollywood: "Johanna, relax. I've never had a chance with my sister-in-law. Let me at least have the pleasure of the company of my beautiful niece." She was always afraid that one night, steeped in Scotch, Leon might forget Helen was his niece.

Back at the house she was pleased to find Bernie.

"Your father just left for Chicago,'' she told him. "Your uncle Leon is in terrible trouble, arrested for theft, fraud and bootlegging."

"Don't worry about Uncle Leon,'' Bernie scoffed. "An American prison will seem like a country club in comparison to the time he spent in Siberia."

"When he was in Siberia he was twenty-three and tough,'' Johanna reminded him.

"Mama, Uncle Leon still thinks he's twenty-three years old.'' Bernie tried for a touch of humor. "At fifty—what—one—"

"Fifty-five, though he'll never admit it, even to people who have known him all his life."

"At fifty-five," Bernie pointed out, "he's strong, healthy, good-looking. He'll come out of this as cocky as ever."

"At least he's learned he can't get away with anything he likes." She crossed to the library bar. "Let's have a glass of wine before dinner." Her face lighted with a touch of amusement. "And don't you dare tell me we're breaking the law. We've had this wine in the cellar for years. I'll be darned if I'll throw it down the drain."

"I hear that some of our most illustrious Congressmen have private stills in their basements." Bernie told her indulgently. "It's kind of hard to accept Uncle Leon's going to jail for breaking the same law."

"I worry about the kind of liquor he's selling." She handed him a glass and sank into her corner of the sofa.

"You read that article in the *Literary Digest* about bad liquor causing blindness and death."

"Let's talk about pleasant matters," she said firmly. "How's my favorite grandchild today?"

"Your only grandchild is just fine. It looks as though he's going to walk any day. I don't know what's taking him so long."

Until dinner was served they talked about Jason and Nicky. Johanna swore to herself she wouldn't ask Bernie what was happening with his attorney. When there was news, Bernie would tell her. She lasted through the soup course.

"Bernie, you're pleased with this lawyer you've hired?" she asked. "He's making progress?" She remembered her pleasure at Bernie's wedding—and now this.

"I have to sit tight until he has sufficient evidence to push Wanda into agreeing to a separation," Bernie reported. "He has a private detective on the case." Bernie sighed.

Poor baby, Johanna thought. He hated this sordid mess, but Wanda had fooled the whole family—except for Helen. Helen had never liked Wanda. "He wants to make sure he can convince any lawyer she may bring in that it's useless to fight the separation."

"Remember, Bernie. When this is all over—and if you like—we'd be happy to have Jason and you here with us."

"I know,"

Johanna worried about Bernie's future. He needed a home of his own, a real wife. Jason should have a sister or brother or both. At twenty-seven Bernie's life shouldn't be ending, but in the church divorce was not possible.

"How much is Helen involved in what happened to Uncle Leon?" Bernie asked. "She worked for him, didn't she?"

Johanna stared at him in shock. "Do you think she knew all about it and connived?"

"No, not about the raid necessarily, but she must have known he was a bootlegger. Probably doesn't see anything wrong with it."

"I know a lot of people consider it nothing," Johanna said. "Your father knows a man who boasted about being arrested for bootlegging. But it's not a big joke anymore, not when bad alcohol is being sold and people sicken, go blind, even die."

"Uncle Leon is out to make a lot of money fast, but he wouldn't sell poisoned liquor."

"Not knowingly," Johanna agreed, "but how can he be sure what he's selling? This can get out of hand. I don't want Helen mixed up in it. I could kill Leon for involving her."

"She's out of it now," Bernie pointed out. "The great adventure is over."

*   *   *

Johanna knew she wouldn't sleep tonight. From now on she hoped Leon would stay out of their lives. She tossed all night, was relieved when morning arrived.

She was kissing Nicky good-bye while Melissa waited to take him to the park for the morning when Michal called.

"How's Helen?"

"Cowed," he said. "I just put her on the Lakeshore Limited and told her to lie low to Fort Wayne. Leon is out on bail, but he has to stay here. The lawyers will try to delay the trial as long as possible, but it's unlikely that he'll get off scot-free." All at once Michal sounded tired. She guessed that he had slept little on the train last night. "I can't do too much more. I'll probably take the Lakeshore tomorrow. I can't stay away from the business any longer than that."

"Tell Leon it serves him right—no, don't, of course, but I wanted to get it off my chest."

Johanna's eyes filled with tears when Helen got off the train, her daughter's face was so pale and strained.

"Darling, it's so good to have you home again."

"Where's Nicky?"

"Out in the park as usual at this hour. Molly's standing by to make breakfast. I'll have coffee with you." It felt so good to have Helen home again.

Over breakfast Helen made a point of telling her mother that she meant to take an apartment of her own.

"I have office skills. I shouldn't have any trouble finding a job," she said matter-of-factly.

"Perhaps your father can find a place for you at American-International," Johanna said. "He would love to have another child in the Raisa shipping empire."

"I want to find a job on my own," Helen said,

avoiding her mother's eyes. "I want to manage my life myself, even it means making mistakes."

"I'm sure you'll have no trouble finding a job." Johanna must say nothing that would antagonize Helen. "Business is booming in New York. Where do you think you'd like to live?"

"In Greenwich Village, I think," Helen said uncertainly. Johanna winced. Wanda lived in Greenwich Village when Bernie met her. "Rent is cheap down there. I don't expect to earn the kind of money Uncle Leon paid me." All at once she was defensive. "Uncle Leon just got caught up in the times. He shouldn't have been arrested. Half the country is either bootlegging or buying from bootleggers."

"Bernie will be over for dinner tomorrow," Johanna said firmly "He's eager to see you."

"Bernie alone?" Helen knew when a subject was closed.

"Wanda and he seem to be having some difficulties. More than that I can't say."

After breakfast Helen went up to her room for a nap. She had slept poorly on the train, she explained. Not until close to dinner time did she emerge from her room. Johanna had not left the house. She meant to be available if Helen came down and felt like talking.

The next day Bernie arrived only moments before they were to sit down to dinner. He had gone home from the office to see Jason before leaving for the evening.

"You finally got smart and came home." Bernie kissed his sister with warmth.

"I don't know that it was smart. I loved California. I just didn't want to go back under the circumstances. Leon's arranging for his California attorney to pay off the servants and close up the house. I'm getting rid of everything out there. It was mostly clothes, and I can't use California clothes in New York this time of year.''

Johanna remembered that in California Leon was supposed to be a family friend rather than Helen's uncle. Thank God she had come home. That was not the right environment for a young woman.

"Jason behaving himself?" Michal asked with a grin.

"Mrs. Greene is spoiling him to death," Bernie laughed, "like his grandparents."

"Nicky and Jason have a wonderful time together in the park every day," Johanna told Helen. "Nicky feels very protective."

Over dinner Johanna made an effort to keep the conversation light. She aware of the tension in Bernie. She wished this awful business of the separation were settled, yet she dreaded to consider what lay ahead of Bernie, tied to a wife who was not a wife. The family would make sure, of course, that Jason did not miss out on love. It would be a joy to rear him with Nicky.

Bernie left early, teasing his father about being a slave driver who kept him charging to the office early in the morning. Johanna enjoyed the closeness that both Michal and she shared with Bernie. Someday, she prayed, they'd share that same closeness with their daughter.

Bernie left the office early the following afternoon to keep an appointment with Tony Corelli. Tony had called in the morning to say he thought they had matters well in hand and that it was time to move. Bernie walked briskly, trying to shut out of his mind the thought of how Wanda would carry on when he spurned her.

There was an early hint of winter in the air that oddly lifted his spirits. Bernie enjoyed the changes of season in New York. Helen and he had argued about that last night. Helen insisted she loved California and the eternal sunshine, but he suspected she was pleased to be home for the winter.

What did Tony have that would persuade Wanda to agree to a legal separation? Photographs, he supposed. Wanda in bed with other men. Whatever it cost he wanted Wanda out of his life. He wouldn't let her have Jason, he vowed.

Bernie strode into the lobby of Tony's office building. He rode up in the elevator with increasing anguish. How could he have been such a fool as to allow himself to be entrapped by Wanda? Still, Jason made it all worthwhile.

Immediately at his arrival in the law offices of Corelli & Weinstein Bernie was ushered into Tony's office.

"Sit down, Bernie." Despite his effort to be business-like Tony Corelli looked sympathetic. He reached into a manila envelope. Wordlessly he pulled out a handful of snapshots and spread them across the desk facing Bernie.

Gritting his teeth in distaste, Bernie inspected each one. He didn't ask Tony how he had gotten them. He didn't want to know. They showed Wanda naked in bed with five different men. In several of the photos she was pleasuring two men. He felt sick as he gazed at them. He didn't want Wanda touching Jason. His son would go to stay with his parents today, by God.

"Do you have copies of these for me to present to my wife?" he asked bitterly.

"I have a set right here for that purpose." Tony reached into a desk drawer and pulled out an envelope. "I haven't drawn up the separation agreement yet because I thought we should discuss the specifics."

"I told you. She can have half my earnings. I just ask that she get out of the house and leave Jason in my custody."

"Bernie, you have to play it smarter than that," Tony said gently. "First of all, you don't offer half your earnings.

You're on the way up. You'll be keeping her in royal luxury someday if you do. Offer her a set amount as long as she doesn't remarry.''

Bernie was startled. "Wanda's Catholic. She knows she'll be excommunicated if she remarries.''

"Come on, Bernie, do you think she cares? Mark my words, she'll take herself out to Reno and get a divorce plenty quick if someone else shows up looking like a better deal financially. If she remarries, then you're off the hook on support. If she had any religious convictions she wouldn't do that.'' He pointed at the pictures.

"And don't ask for custody of the baby. Now, don't get excited.'' Bernie was suddenly white. "From what you told me she won't want him anyway. You make an offer of support for herself and the baby, and I'll lay any odds she'll tell you she can't keep Jason on that amount. Don't let her use him to push up the ante,'' he warned. "Tell her you think your son belongs with his mother.''

"Suppose she agrees?'' Bernie's throat was tight with alarm. "I won't let her have him, Tony. I want to take him to my mother today.''

"Don't do that. His nurse will look after him. Besides, she won't agree; she's not the type—not unless she thinks the baby is a bargaining point. You've got to convince her you think an infant belongs with his mother. Can you do that?''

"For Jason I'll do anything. But I won't let her have him.''

"All right. Let's talk about money.''

For the next few minutes they grappled with financial details. When they had arrived at a suitable figure, Tony broached another point that he clearly knew would be repugnant to Bernie.

"If Wanda tries to call your bluff, you tell her you'll get a divorce if you have to. With these photographs you can win a divorce in New York with no trouble. She's not going to let these things hit the papers. She'd never hold up her head after that."

"I have to do it," Bernie said desperately, "for Jason and for my sanity."

"Wait while I get the separation agreement typed up," Tony said. "Present it to Wanda tonight."

An hour later with the papers in the breast pocket of his jacket Bernie left the office for home. As usual, he spent an hour with Jason before Mrs. Greene insisted it was time the exuberant but yawning baby was put to bed. He looked forward to this hour and the hour each morning that he was alone with his son in the nursery.

He went downstairs and waited to be summoned to dinner. Sometimes it bothered him that the servants must be aware of his wife's infidelities. Sometimes he caught a glow of sympathy in Mrs. Greene's eyes. She was far more of a mother to Jason than Wanda had ever been.

After dinner he settled himself in the library to listen to the Victrola for a while. Though Wanda ridiculed his passion for opera, he enjoyed listening to the phonograph records. He remembered taking Wanda to the Metropolitan Opera; she had pretended to be enthralled, but of course that was before the wedding.

Tonight he put on a Caruso recording of *Celeste Aida*, glad the nursery was two floors above and that the music would not disturb Jason. Caruso had made his final appearance at the Met just last year in *La Juive*.

By ten he was on the point of dozing. He roused himself to go up to the bedroom and methodically removed all his personal effects to the most distant guest room on the second floor of the house. Settled in his new bedroom, he prepared for the night there.

He waited with seething impatience for her return. She was not home by midnight, and he went down to the kitchen to make himself coffee. Though the house was now night-cool, he was perspiring heavily in anticipation of what lay ahead of him.

Shortly after one, while he sat in a chair before the fireplace in what had been their bedroom until tonight, he heard Wanda let herself into the house. She hurried up the stairs and into the room, surprised to find him awake.

"Glory took me to see this new play down in Greenwich Village," she said. "Afterward there was a party. It was still going when we left." She looked and sounded faintly defensive as she slipped out of her much-favored raccoon coat and kicked off her pumps.

"Sit down, Wanda. We have some talking to do."

"Now?"

"Now." He reached into the pocket of his robe and pulled out the snapshots. "Take a look at these." He handed them over and watched for her reaction.

Her mouth fell open in disbelief. "That isn't me," she shrieked. "How dare you think it is?"

"Come on, Wanda, it's you. Wearing nothing but the diamond and gold cross my parents gave you when Jason was born." He leaned forward. "I want a legal separation, Wanda. I'll pay for your support and the baby's. I don't care where you live as long as it's not in this house. And of course I want the right to see Jason whenever I like."

"You're crazy." But her eyes betrayed her alarm.

"I've gone over this with my attorney. We've arrived at a figure that will support Jason and you comfortably in a small apartment wherever you like. You won't need help. You'll have plenty of time to take care of Jason yourself."

"I'm not moving out of this house, Bernie." Wanda was getting over her shock.

"Then I'll go into court and sue for divorce on five counts of adultery. These pictures will be famous. I'll win,

Wanda, you know that." He was fighting to appear in total control.

"You divorce me? The nephew of the precious bishop in Poland? You wouldn't dare."

"Before the war I wouldn't have, but this is a whole new world. I want you out of my house and out of my life. Now, what'll it be? A separation with support for yourself and Jason or a divorce? If I ask for a divorce, you'll get nothing, not with the evidence I can bring into court."

Their eyes clashed. Bernie refused to back down, though he felt sick. Wanda's eyes focused again on the array of snapshots in her hand.

"How much?"

Bernie mentioned the figure.

Wanda flinched in disgust. "How am I supposed to live on that?"

"It's far more than you lived on before we were married. It's more than you deserve."

"I spend more than that on clothes."

"Then you'll have to stop. Remember, Wanda, if I go into divorce court, you'll receive nothing."

"I might manage if I go to work, but I can't work if I have to take care of Jason."

"You're asking me to take him? A baby belongs with his mother." He could feel nervous sweat beading on his forehead and trickling down his neck.

"I don't want him," Wanda said coldly. "I never wanted him."

"All right, I'll see what I can arrange. Perhaps my mother will take him." He struggled to hide his elation. Tony was smart. "I want you out of this house within two weeks. You'll give me your address and my lawyer will see that you receive a check each month." He reached into his pocket for the separation agreement, unfolded it, pulled a pen from his jacket pocket. "Sign here, Wanda."

She scrawled her signature and sneered at him. "Anything else?"

"Yes, as a matter of fact. I've closed all your charge accounts." He ducked out the door and slammed it just before Wanda began to smash her perfume bottles.

Chapter 24

Johanna was relieved when the separation was a fact. Within a month the house was on the market. Bernie and Jason moved into the family house on Fifth Avenue. Johanna would have been happy except she knew how Michal worried about Leon. And she worried about Helen, living alone in the Village.

Early in 1922 Leon came up for trial. He was sentenced to four years in the Federal penitentiary in Atlanta. Michal went to Chicago for the trial and returned baffled and uneasy. Over breakfast the morning of his return he gave Johanna a full report of the trial.

"He might have gotten off with a lighter sentence but for the fact that he filed an insurance claim the morning after the robbery. That wasn't bootlegging, that was fraud."

"When will he be sent to Atlanta?" Johanna asked. Knowing Leon, he would be out of jail before four years.

"He's on his way now—in a private club car he rented for himself and seven others headed for the Atlanta penitentiary." Michal shook his head. "Leon's a rich man.

304

He means to have life as easy as possible. He plans on having his meals sent in from one of Atlanta's best restaurants. He talked about a maid to clean his cell. An Atlanta florist is supposed to deliver fresh flowers every day."

"How long before he buys himself a pardon?" Johanna asked. Her cynicism startled them both.

"As fast as he can manage," Michal conceded. "But he can't even apply for parole for at least eighteen months. Even if he's a model prisoner, there's no guarantee his lawyers can manage parole even then."

Johanna knew Michal was upset at Leon's imprisonment and shamed that this could happen to a Raisa. He waited weeks before writing the unpleasant news to Casimar. He knew that Casimar was disturbed about the political and economic chaos in Poland. Now a recession was making life difficult for many Poles.

Nicky, who would be four in November, was delighted to have Jason living with him. Still, in moments of frustration Johanna wished Wanda dead and was then beset by remorse. She lavished the same love on Jason as on Nicky, vowing that he would never lack a mother's love.

Bernie was developing a close friendship with the handsome young Italian lawyer who had arranged the separation. Tony Corelli was brilliant, she and Michal agreed. Johanna encouraged him to invite Tony to the house for dinner regularly. Michal and she both enjoyed discussing politics with Tony.

As the months sped past, Johanna began a plot to bring Helen and Tony together. She knew she mustn't be obvious. Helen would resent matchmaking. But she worried about Helen's living alone in that tiny Village apartment. She and Michal had been invited there only once.

Johanna fretted over Helen's isolation from the family,

comforted only by the knowledge that Helen was still close to Carla. She knew that Carla was studying for her master's degree in social work. Carla was no flapper, who spent her life dedicated to fun.

Johanna struggled to understand the young women of the twenties. Outwardly Helen appeared one of them. They all tried to be exactly alike, Johanna thought with exasperation, wearing their skirts shorter each year, talking so knowingly about Freud and sex, smoking, drinking, dancing their crazy dances, obsessed by Paul Whiteman, and his jazz.

Each time she tried to have Helen at the house when Tony was there she met defeat. Helen talked vaguely about going to meetings with Carla. She was often "too busy" for dinner, though she dropped by for brief visits at odd hours. Most of her time at the house she spent with Nicky and Jason, as though she felt safer in their company than with her parents.

At the approach of Thanksgiving Bernie told Johanna he'd like to invite Tony to dinner. Tony's uncle, Victor Corelli, would be in Florida for the week. A bachelor, Tony's uncle had maintained for twenty-two years a liaison with his secretary, whom he didn't marry because she was neither Italian nor Roman Catholic. Tony's sisters and brothers were scattered about the country and he would be alone.

"Of course, bring him along. It will be a pleasure. We always enjoy having him for dinner." And Helen will be here, she thought triumphantly.

Leaving nothing to chance, Johanna made a determined effort to assure that Helen would not skip out on their traditional Thanksgiving dinner. "Bring Carla," she suggested, but Carla would be home with her family.

On the holiday morning Johanna and Michal took the

two boys to the park. The sky was overcast, heavy with snow.

"Mama, if it snows can we come to the park again?" Nicky asked, his eyes surveying the heavy clouds with hope.

"Can we, Mama?" Jason parroted. Despite their best efforts Jason followed Nicky's example when addressing his grandparents.

"Yes, darling," Johanna promised. "Both darlings."

"I was thinking of our first Thanksgiving," Michal reflected, his face tender. "You decided it was time we celebrated it. We were in that flat on East Seventh Street. You baked your first pumpkin pie from a recipe you copied from a cookbook in the library. You baked yams along with the turkey and cooked a potful of cranberries. I remember I felt kind of disloyal to be adopting an American custom. But even then I was grateful that this country was so good to us."

"Mama, squirrel," Jason cried delightedly and pointed.

"We can't stay much longer," Johanna cautioned. "I want to be home when Helen arrives." And Tony, she thought with a surge of anticipation.

By the time they returned to the house, Bernie was in earnest conversation with Tony in the library. The whole house was permeated with savory aromas from the kitchen. Mrs. Greene, who had become part of the household along with Jason, took the two children upstairs. They would be brought down to the dinner table when the family was prepared to sit down.

"We're talking about the possibility of running Al Smith for president on the Democratic ticket in '24," Bernie told his parents.

"He'll never make it," Michal predicted. "Not a Roman Catholic. Maybe in thirty or forty years, but not now."

"He's been Governor of New York since 1919," Tony said earnestly.

"New York is unlike any other state," Johanna argued. "The country at large won't vote for a Catholic. They figure his allegiance goes first to the church and then to the country."

"You've got a special interest in the political chances of Catholics?" Michal asked Tony.

"I don't have to worry about national politics. What I have in mind is eventually running for city council or the state assembly. There's a lot that needs to be done both in city and state government."

"Any time you care to run for office," Michal said, "count on me as a strong supporter. I deplore what this city has become. It's controlled by the syndicates and we seem unable to do anything about it. We're the richest and largest city in the country, and gangsters control our police, our public prosecutors, our judges, to name a few. I'm serious, Tony. You run for office and this family is behind you all the way."

Johanna heard the doorbell ring. Boleslav was going to the door. It would be Helen, she guessed. She listened expectantly while Helen exchanged small talk with the butler in the foyer.

"Yes, Miss Helen. The family's in the library," Boleslav told her. Johanna heard the carpet-softened click of her high heels as Helen walked down the corridor to the library.

"Helen." Michal rose to his feet with a bright smile of welcome and rushed toward his daughter. "That cold air brought color to your cheeks," he said, kissing her warmly.

"Rouge, Papa," Helen laughed and turned to greet her mother. "I'm not late, am I?"

"No, dinner won't be served for another twenty

minutes. Molly likes the turkey to be very crisp." Johanna paused. Helen was staring across the room at Tony as though he were a visitor from another world. "Helen, I'd like you to meet Bernie's friend—" Tony was on his feet and walking toward Helen with both hands outstretched.

"Helen," he murmured softly, "the prettiest Red Cross aide who ever set foot in a field hospital in France."

"Hello, Tony." Helen allowed her hands to be grasped in his. For a moment Johanna saw her excitement before Helen contrived to mask it. "I was on duty in the hospital when Tony was brought in with a wound in his shoulder. Tony, you were a rambunctious patient." Their eyes sparked with electricity.

"You never told me you knew my sister." Bernie accused Tony, but he was clearly pleased.

"I never knew her last name," Tony explained. "I knew you had a sister named Helen, but there are lots of Helens in this world." His eyes moved back to her as though he must reassure himself that she was here.

"Did you ever get back to New York University?" she asked, settling herself in a chair. She looked beautiful, chic, poised.

"I got my law degree and went on to pass the bar exam. Now I'm an Ll.D. I told you I'd do it. I was sure I'd make it back."

"Helen, he was my lawyer in the separation," Bernie explained. "That's how we met."

How Bernie respected Tony for working his way through college and law school. His father died when he was twelve, his mother in the flu epidemic four years ago. His uncle was of the old school and believed in making a young man work hard. He extended only meager financial aid but took him into his law firm once Tony had his credentials.

"They sent you back into action when you recuperated," Helen recalled. "I thought you should go home. That shoulder still wasn't right."

For a little while Johanna and Michal listened to the conversation of the three young people. Not until they were settled at the dinner table with the two small boys, proud to be sharing the holiday dinner, did the conversation become general. How charming Tony was to Nicky and Jason, Johanna thought with pleasure. She wished she could read Helen's mind. She knew Helen was happy that Tony was here, but how happy?

When Helen stood up to leave, Tony said he would see her home. Tony was a fine young man; Helen could hardly do better. They knew Tony and admired him. Not like Wanda.

"Would you like to go somewhere for coffee and conversation?" Tony asked while they searched Fifth Avenue for a taxi.

"Nothing's open on Thanksgiving," Helen said, although she was reluctant to part company with Tony. It was crazy to walk into the house that way and see him sitting in the library. "Unless you'd like to come up to my place for a little while. I make a fairly decent pot of coffee."

"I'd like that very much."

A few minutes later a few stray snowflakes began to hit the sidewalk and evaporate. Tony flagged down a taxi for them. Helen moved far across the seat, leaving a foot of space between Tony and herself. At odd intervals since the war she had thought about Tony, knowing the unlikelihood of their meeting each other in a city the size of New York. Fate was a sly old lady, it seemed.

"Tell me what's been happening all these years," she coaxed him. They sat at the kitchen table with their coffee;

the living room with its Murphy bed suddenly seemed dangerous.

"You know most of it. I finished up at NYU, went on to law school and into practice with my uncle." His eyes crinkled. "I went through the usual madness my first year back, chased everything in skirts. But I soon got over that."

She surmised he wanted her to know he wasn't going to try to throw her into bed. Good.

"I went out to California to work for my uncle. He had a movie studio out there for several years. You probably know—he's in the Federal penitentiary in Atlanta for various shenanigans connected with selling bootleg liquor on a rather large scale. Now I'm a secretary in a social service agency."

"Do you like it?"

"Yes." She thought about her job for a moment. "I like doing something useful."

"What do you do when you're not working?" Meaning, she gathered, was there a steady man in her life.

"The usual."

"I doubt there is anything usual about you." There was no mistaking the ardor in his eyes. Had she made a mistake in asking him up for coffee?

"I'm involved with the Student Volunteer Movement," she said, "not that I'm a student. My friend Carla—she was with me in France—is getting her master's in social work. She brought me into the movement."

"I don't know about it." His voice was alive with curiosity.

Over more coffee they talked with youthful intensity about the need for peace in the world. This was the goal of the Student Volunteer Movement. "We're not exactly pacifists," Helen said. "We believe war is immoral and the League of Nations is the best bet for keeping peace in the world. But if the league or the World Court can't bring about a settlement of some dispute, then we'd fight to settle it in the right direction."

"I wish the world could look at war and not see it all wrapped in glamor," Tony grumbled. "When the young people in this world make up their minds that there should be no more war, then we'll have peace."

At the end of the evening Helen invited Tony to join Carla and her at a meeting of the Student Volunteer Movement. "And talk to Bernie about coming along, too," she added self-consciously, lest Tony think that she was in pursuit. "He thinks like us."

When Tony said good night without making an effort to kiss her, Helen told herself she was relieved, but she lay restless far into the night. She had not slept with anybody since France. She felt almost like a virgin again. Tonight if Tony had been sufficiently persistent she wouldn't have refused him. She wouldn't have refused him in that field hospital if he had persisted.

It was just as well, she told herself. She didn't want to become seriously involved with anyone, and instinct told her that Tony was not interested in a casual affair.

The four young people—Helen and Carla, Tony and Bernie—began to spend several evenings a week working with the movement. Afterward they gathered at Helen's apartment for coffee and more conversation. Bernie was contemptuous of Henry Mencken's oft-repeated statement of four years earlier that war was "the most colossal experience" a man could encounter.

Gradually their small group was enlarged to include several other young people of similar commitment. As soon as he met Victoria Malloy, Bernie knew somebody of supreme importance had moved into his life. She was small, slender, with nearly black hair that framed a lovely heart-shaped face. Her skin was creamy white, quick to be suffused with becoming color, her expressive eyes an appealing blue.

Vicky's great-grandfather fought for the North in the Civil War. Her father fought with Teddy Roosevelt's Rough Riders at San Juan Hill. She lost her only brother in the world war. She hated war with a passion that matched his own.

Within weeks Bernie admitted to himself that he was in love with Vicky. Not the infatuation, the sheer physical attraction he had felt for Wanda. He could have been happy to spend the rest of his life with Vicky. He knew she loved him; it shone from her. She was perplexed that he seemed content to be with her without so much as a good night kiss.

By spring it was agony to be alone with Vicky without taking her in his arms. Like himself, she was Roman Catholic. She would understand that as long as Wanda lived he was a married man. Helen understood. She never once mentioned Jason in Vicky's presence. Still, he knew it was wrong not to tell Vicky that he was married and a father.

On a night in early March Bernie took Vicky to the theater to see *Humoresque*, based on the Fannie Hurst novel, with wonderful Laurette Taylor. Knowing that Vicky loved the theater but could not afford to attend often herself, he made a point of taking her at least once or twice a month. Two weeks ago they had seen *Laugh, Clown, Laugh* with Lionel Barrymore and last month Barrymore's sister Ethel in *The Laughing Lady*.

They emerged from the theater in their usual euphoria after seeing a fine performance to find that in the course of the evening a light snowfall had become a near-blizzard. Bernie's arm moved about Vicky's waist as they trudged through the blanket of snow to the car he had parked between Eighth and Ninth avenues.

"You're cold," he said as she huddled into the fur collar of her coat. They made slow progress to the car.

"I'm fine," she insisted. "I'm still warm with the pleasure of seeing the play."

After a few moments of struggling with the engine Bernie was able to move the car into the road and drive at an annoyingly slow pace toward Vicky's tiny apartment on East Nineteenth Street.

"Snow like this reminds me of home," Vicky said wistfully. "I was born and raised in a tiny steel town in Pennsylvania soft-coal country. Evans City, it's called. At eighteen I came to New York to seek a career as an artist. It didn't take me a year to find out I had no talent. I was tired of starving for my art, so I settled for a secretarial job in a department store." But at twenty-two she was in love with the city and rejected all pleas by her family to return to a village thirty miles from Pittsburgh. "Our house, surrounded by snow, looks like one of those rural postcards. Great for a visit," she laughed indulgently, "but not for the long term."

Bernie parked and they hurried from the car to the brownstone house just beyond, where Vicky lived in the top floor rear apartment. A closet had been converted to a kitchenette with a two-burner electric stove on top of a small icebox. Vicky's excellent taste had made the small bed-sitting room quite cozy. She had covered the plaster walls with red and gold Chinese tea paper and covered the double bed, set against the wall, with a red and gold coverlet. The improvised sofa effect was completed by a row of red velvet cushions lined against the wall. White drapes and pewter carpeting eased the eye.

"I'll make coffee," Vicky said as Bernie helped her off with her coat.

"I'll do it," he offered. "You get into something warm and dry."

Bernie took a few minutes to find the coffee and the pot. While it was brewing he reached into the breadbox, hand-painted by Vicky, for the homemade *stollen* Vicky's mother always sent at the holidays. Her recipe was particularly rich and full of nuts and raisins.

"The coffee is beginning to smell wonderful already," Vicky said in her light voice. "If the fireplace worked, this would be a marvelous apartment, even so tiny."

Bernie turned around to face her. Without heels, in a long red velvet robe, her hair loose, she was beautiful and sweet and vulnerable, he thought. "You're marvelous." He could not go on a minute longer without being honest with her. "Vicky, there's something I have to tell you." He spoke jerkily, did not look at her, fumbled with the chairs, the cups, the saucers. His hands shook. "Please, sit down."

"What is it, Bernie?" Vicky's eyes were like saucers. What had made him so nervous all of a sudden?

"I think you know, Vicky. I love you—but I don't have the right. I'm a married man, my dear. We have a legal separation. My son Jason is almost two and a half. You know I live with my parents; my mother is raising Jason."

Vicky stared at him for a minute, then looked away. Her lip trembled a little, but she controlled it. She took a rather ragged deep breath before she spoke. "You should have told me."

"I couldn't make myself do it. I was so stupid to marry her I was embarrassed to admit it to you. She was the first woman I met after the war and I was in a hurry for a normal life. Wanda saw me as a road to comfort. She never loved me; she didn't even want to have Jason. My mother, a very wise lady, persuaded her not to have an abortion." Vicky winced.

"Vicky, there's no point in divorcing Wanda. I can't remarry or I'll be excommunicated, and that would be too hard on Jason." He gave her a helpless look and put his bowed head in his hands.

"The coffee's boiling over." She leapt to her feet and rushed to the stove.

"Vicky, don't hate me," he implored.

She poured coffee into the two waiting cups, her small hand trembling. "Hate you, Bernie?" She laid a hand on his shoulder. "I love you."

"Vicky—" He got up and pulled her into his arms. "Vicky, how will I live without you?"

He brought his mouth down to hers. Her arms clung to him while their mouths fused. He felt the pounding of her heart against his. While the blizzard raged outside, Bernie carried Vicky to her Gypsy-bright sofa bed and made love to her.

Afterward she lay in his arms while he drew the covers over them. "I didn't mean to do that," he said unsteadily. It was plain that he was Vicky's first lover. "But you're irresistible. I never suspected it was possible to love anyone the way I love you."

"We'll take what we can have," Vicky said with complete serenity. "I don't intend to give you up, Bernie."

Two or three nights each week Bernie stayed at Vicky's apartment until early in the morning. He would tiptoe into his own home before anyone was awake. He continually feared that he was ruining Vicky's life, but the one time he spoke of it and mentioned giving her up, she turned on him with fury and scorn. "I'm a grown woman and no one, including you, makes my decisions for me." How different from Wanda she was.

He knew Helen suspected he was living with Vicky. His sister was seeing a lot of Tony, and that relationship was stormy. Tony was eager to marry Helen, but she wouldn't say yes or no. Damn his sister for putting Tony through this, he thought with recurrent irritation. She ought to marry him or stop seeing him.

In the summer his parents bought a place at Southampton, a large rambling house set right behind the dunes.

"We're not interested in the Southampton Club or the party circuit," Johanna sniffed. She had never forgotten the snub they received at Newport when he and Helen were little. "We bought the house to be near the ocean, and to your father and me that's one of God's greatest creations. There are a dozen bedrooms," she said with relish. "Come out and bring your friends whenever you like."

A heat wave bore down on the city a few days before Vicky's vacation was to commence. They lay across the bed in her apartment beneath the roof. An open skylight provided a draft, but the sultry sun had beat down through the glass all day and the place was an oven. A pitcher of iced tea on a table beside them would stay cool for only about half an hour. The small fan whirring atop a chest blew hot damp air across their bare bodies. Sweat had made their lovemaking hilariously slippery, and they were still giggling a little.

"Vicky, come on. Go with me to the Southampton house on Friday night after work. We'll stay there until Sunday a week. It'll be wonderful to have a whole week together on the beach." He ran his fingers from her waist to her knee. "We can do this every night. And you'll meet Jason."

This last was the deciding factor.

Their circumstances had prevented her meeting any of his family but Helen.

"Bernie, I'm not sure we can pretend to everybody that we're just friends for a whole week under one roof."

"My family will welcome you no matter what. Tony said he'd be out for weekends too." He snorted. "Helen's giving him a rotten time."

"Maybe she's scared."

"Of Tony?" He lifted an eyebrow.

"Of making a lifetime commitment."

"You wouldn't be afraid."

"No," she agreed, "but I'm not Helen. She has her reasons, whether we understand them or not."

On a sunlit Friday afternoon Bernie waited beside his maroon Stutz for Vicky to emerge from the department store she worked for. There was always a special feeling when the work week ended, Bernie mused. Too bad about people who had to go in on Saturday morning, especially in the summer, when the weekend meant for some an escape from the city heat. Even Coney Island or Brighton Beach was better than the treeless streets. It had been such a ghastly hot week that they would both enjoy the drive out to Southampton.

Women were hurrying through the doors laden with parcels, aware that shortly the store would close for the day. Vicky came in and left half an hour earlier than the sales help.

Mama had been delighted when he said he was bringing a new friend out to spend the week at the beach. Then he said his guest was a young lady and her smile froze. Mama knew he needed a social life, but she was very strait-laced about married people's behavior.

His face lit up at the sight of Vicky coming from the store with a suitcase. He hurried forward to greet her and take her bag.

"Have you been waiting long?" she asked. She smiled naughtily and flashed a little leg as she got into the car.

"Just a few minutes. I can't wait to get out of the city."

"Me neither."

Belatedly Bernie asked himself if it might not have been better to rent a cottage somewhere for Vicky and himself. But he was anxious for her to get to know Jason, and he could not take a small child to a tryst. Tony and Helen would be out for the weekends and Vicky would enjoy herself. During the week there would be just Vicky, Mama, himself and the two children. Nobody could be uncomfortable in that easy-going group.

With the top of the Stutz down they caught a little air as they drove through the streets, fast filling with homebound workers and resort-bound weekenders. Vicky was intent on keeping him amused with small stories of her day in the complaint department. Neither of them wanted to think too much about this first encounter between Vicky and his family.

When they were well out of the city Bernie began to watch for a restaurant. "My parents went out right after lunch. I told them not to hold dinner for us. They'll have eaten with the boys instead."

"We won't dawdle over dinner," Vicky smiled. "I'm longing to walk on the beach tonight."

They arrived at Southampton to find Bernie's parents sitting on the wide verandah of the house. Before they were out of his car, Johanna and Michal were coming forward to greet them.

"The boys were dying to wait up for you," Johanna said affectionately, "but with all the excitement and the sea air they're both falling asleep by seven."

"Mama, this is Vicky Malloy," Bernie said with strained casualness. "Vicky, my mother and father."

"We're happy to have you with us. Shall we sit down or would you like to go to your room? I'll bet you're thirsty—lemonade, iced tea, water? Bernie, put those suitcases down." Nervous as the young couple, Johanna made such a fuss that no one could doubt their welcome. Michal, behind her, was smiling broadly.

"It's so nice of you to have me. Let's just sit down. I gather we've beat Helen and Tony out of the city." She was just right, Bernie thought with pride.

"They should be coming along soon," Johanna surmised. "Have you two had dinner yet? Molly has something ready for you."

"We had dinner on the way out," Vicky said.

"We could manage dessert and iced tea," Bernie added. "Vicky, Molly bakes like an angel in heaven."

Boleslav appeared and took the luggage upstairs. Molly came through the screen door with a tray and set it on a wheeled stand. Conversation ceased as she poured coffee and served perfect individual baked Alaskas.

"Oh, my goodness," Vicky whispered, quite awestruck. "A pastry chef."

Molly smiled, bowed and withdrew.

"I had one at dinner and I'll have a third when Tony and Helen get here," Michal boasted. "Molly's baking is all that keeps me slim." He winked and dug in.

Bernie allowed Vicky and his mother to carry on most of the table conversation. Now that they were here, he knew that his mother, always so perceptive, would understand he was in love with Vicky and at a loss.

As soon as it was polite to do so, Bernie swept Vicky away from the house and onto the beach. There was no moon and the Milky Way arced overhead; the surf was calm, the tide out. They walked hand in hand on the packed wet sand in happy silence, for a little while caught up in the beauty of the night and being alone together.

When they returned to the house Helen and Tony had arrived. All at once Bernie was convinced Helen was in love with Tony. Nothing kept them apart except Helen's capriciousness, whereas an insurmountable wall towered between Vicky and himself. How could his silly sister be so stupid and unfeeling? He wanted to shake her.

Chapter 25

Johanna watched Bernie and Vicky with increasing apprehension as the days sped past. Their love was plain to see. It was very sad, but their future together seemed doomed.

It would have been easier if Vicky had been less suitable otherwise. Johanna felt a surge of tenderness when she saw Vicky with Jason and Nicky. They flew a kite, swam, made a castle, dug a nice big hole, buried Bernie and Tony and Michal.

On Thursday, sitting on the verandah beside Bernie while Vicky romped on the sand with the two small boys, Johanna longed for Michal. Tonight he'd be driving up from the city. They must talk about Bernie and Vicky, the daughter-in-law she would be proud to welcome into the family. Was there nothing at all to be done?

Earlier than normal, when Bernie and Vicky disappeared for their nightly walk along the beach, Johanna persuaded Michal to retire to their room.

"It was dreadful in the city," Michal admitted on the

way up the stairs to their bedroom. "Halfway out I could already feel the difference."

"Helen and Tony will be out for lunch tomorrow," she reported. "Tony has a meeting early in the morning. Then they'll drive out."

"When are Helen and Tony going to stop playing games?" Michal asked. "Tony adores her."

"When Helen is ready. It's Bernie and Vicky who concern me."

"I don't begrudge Bernie's pleasure in her company," Michal said, holding open the door to their room, "but damn it, Johanna, what future do they have together?"

"I think they're grabbing at whatever happiness they can find." She tried to smile.

"You think he's sleeping with her?"

"You think he's not?"

"That bothers you," he said gently.

"It's not that, silly. What bothers me is that I'm certain they want to get married. I can't see a happy ending for them."

"I suppose we could hire a thug to bump Wanda off." Michal strove for humor.

"Michal, that's not funny." But her eyes were tender.

"Knowing Wanda the way we do, I suspect she could be goaded into a divorce."

"Vicky was raised a Catholic. If she married Bernie, even though he had a civil divorce, both their souls would be in jeopardy."

"Johanna, what else is living in sin?" he demanded. "You always try to solve every problem the children have. You can't do it." He reached for her hand.

"It's so awful. Those poor children. When Bernie made the worst mistake of his life we were right there cheering him on." She sighed. "Now they'll both have to pay."

"Johanna, talk to Bernie. Perhaps we're mistaken. Maybe all Bernie expects is a short and happy affair. And don't look shocked." He grinned. "This is the twenties. We're living with the emancipated young. Talk to Bernie and see how he feels."

"And then?"

"Then we'll talk again."

The following morning before Helen and Tony arrived from the city and after Vicky took the two small boys to the beach, Johanna drew Bernie to the verandah for a private talk; it was always possible to speak openly with her older son.

"Vicky's a charming young woman, Bernie," she said softly. "Am I wrong in suspecting you love her?"

"You're not wrong." His sigh was a knife in her heart. "And Vicky loves me. But we have no future. Mama, I don't know what to do." He slammed a fist into his palm.

"Would you marry Vicky if you could?"

"In a minute, but there is no way."

"I don't know, Bernie, but your father and I will talk. We'll write to Casimar. If there is a way, the church will surely open it to such a devout—and generous—family."

"An annulment?" Bernie asked. "What about Jason? It's plain enough that the marriage was consummated."

"Bernie, give us time. That may not be the only allowable reason. The church will wish to oblige us if there is any possible ground at all. Let's see what we can do before you eat your heart out."

Johanna went into New York for two days the following week. She spent hours closeted with church authorities without discovering grounds to dissolve an established marriage.

We are concerned not only for their happiness but for their souls. . . . It is plain that Wanda Reszke did not make her vows in good faith . . . refuses to have children . . . abortion . . . adultery. . . . Casimar, can nothing be done?

Six weeks after she mailed off this anxious missive the reply came. No, it was not quite hopeless. Casimar gave definite instructions along with a promise to add his own pleas for speed in the matter, since it was well known that requests for annulment could be drawn out over as much as ten years.

At once Johanna was on the phone with Bernie. "Meet me for lunch," he urged. "One o'clock at the Sert Room?"

"One o'clock at the Sert Room," Johanna agreed. This kingdom in the Waldorf, where the famous Oscar still reigned, was one of the few restaurants in New York that was surviving Prohibition. Only its superb food—and the speakeasies' indifferent-to-poor food and service—permitted it to flourish.

Johanna was already seated when Bernie arrived. She knew the morning had dragged for him too. She wondered whether she had extended more hope than she should have, but she offered an optimistic smile as he approached the table.

"I asked Vicky to meet us here," he said. "Is that all right? It concerns her too."

"Of course it's all right."

In moments Vicky was with them, faintly breathless from the rush from her office to the Waldorf.

"Let's order. Then we'll talk," Johanna suggested.

Luncheon ordered and the waiter gone, Johanna explained what she had learned and what Casimar had added.

"This could drag on for years," she warned, "and there's no guarantee that it will work."

"We'll wait." Bernie reached for Vicky's hand.

"Casimar says an annulment may be approved eventually by the Sacred Rota if Wanda continues to refuse to have children. Wait." She held up her hand as Bernie started to speak.

"It may work in spite of Jason—if Wanda refuses to rear Jason in the church."

"Will she do that?" Vicky demanded.

"Under the right conditions Wanda will agree to anything," Johanna said flatly. "Meaning the right price, which we're prepared to pay. Before we make a move Wanda must attest on paper that she refuses to have additional children, that she did not wish to have Jason, and that she has no intention of bringing him up in the church."

"Mama, I have custody of Jason," Bernie reminded her.

"There are times to be silent, Bernie, and this is one of them. Talk to Tony about drawing up the papers. Go to Wanda and bargain with her. She shouldn't mind much; she'll be wanting a new man herself." Johanna felt a nerve quiver in her eyelid. Bernie's whole future depended upon this. No matter how much Wanda demanded, they must agree. "Then we'll be ready to begin the preliminary trials. You need approval to take your appeal to the rota. Your uncle Casimar is knowledgeable about these affairs. He'll advise us all the way and smooth your path. There's no guarantee," she concluded, "but with God's help you may someday be free to marry again."

Summer blended into autumn while Bernie doggedly bargained with Wanda. He was determined to keep the payoff as low as possible, though Johanna reiterated that they would pay anything. She knew Bernie hated to place his parents in this position. It upset him that Wanda showed no interest in their child, even while Johanna pointed out that this was better than having her always around.

Tony helped push Wanda into signing the agreement for a lump sum of fifty thousand dollars. One of Tony's tame detectives discovered Wanda was keeping a sculptor. He goaded Bernie to threaten a lawsuit. An adulterous wife could forfeit her support payments altogether, he pointed out. Faced with the prospect of nothing, Wanda acquiesced.

Johanna watched Helen and Tony with barely concealed impatience. Tony loved her, yes; but how long would he wait for her? She feared to try to talk to Helen, who still nursed her old hostility.

One week before Thanksgiving in the wee hours, the phone ringing on the first floor disrupted the silence in the Raisa house. Strident in the middle of the night, it jerked Johanna bolt upright in bed. "Michal, who could it be?"

Ever a light sleeper, Michal was already on his feet. "Probably a wrong number."

Her first thought was of Helen. "I'll go with you." She threw aside the covers and reached for her robe, her heart pounding in alarm. When she found her slippers Michal was already rushing down the corridor to the stairs. They must arrange for an upstairs extension, she thought.

She was just starting downstairs when Michal reached the telephone stand in the hall. "Hello?" She grasped the banister and froze at the turn in the staircase. It had been raining all night. The streets were slippery. A car going a bit too fast could skid. Somebody might have run into Tony and her. Or a fire? Lots of buildings burned in the heating season, especially if they had gas laid on.

"We'll be right there." Michal's voice overrode her visions. "Thank you for calling us."

"Helen?" Johanna descended to the hall, cold and trembling.

"Wanda. She's in St. Vincent's Hospital. They don't expect her to live."

"You wake Bernie and start dressing. I'll put the coffee on and be right up."

Within twenty minutes they were driving through the wet night-empty streets.

"Did they say what happened?" Bernie had asked this twice already.

"No," Michal said patiently, "only that she's probably dying. She asked them to call us. She must be terrified."

In her private room Wanda lay gaunt and colorless. She and three others had collapsed in a speakeasy. The others were dead on arrival. It was methanol poisoning from bad gin.

"She refused last rites," a pretty young nurse said unhappily, smoothing the cloud of hair from Wanda's face.

"Wanda?" Bernie reached for her hand and her eyes fluttered open.

"Bernie, I'm scared," she whispered. "I hurt so much."

Johanna turned to the nurse, who was very upset. "Please ask the priest to come to the room." She leaned over the bed. "Wanda, the priest will guide you. Don't turn him away."

"I don't want to die. I'm only twenty-three. I shouldn't have to die."

"Wanda, put your trust in God."

"I've done bad things." Wanda's voice trailed away, but her eyes clung to Johanna.

"When the priest comes, you must let him pray for you. You'll be all right, Wanda. You don't have to be afraid."

The room was heavy with death. As the priest came into the room to administer the last rites the nurse was checking Wanda's pulse. "Hurry," she mouthed.

A few minutes before four Wanda died. The pretty little nurse was fighting tears. She was thinking, Johanna guessed, that she might have been the body on the bed. So many deaths from bootleg alcohol. Leon might insist that his alcohol was the real thing, but how could he know? He didn't drink it.

"I'll arrange for the funeral," Bernie said, pale and drawn. "I'll have to write her father in Warsaw."

Bernie and Vicky waited six months to be married. It was a quiet ceremony in the library of the Raisa house, with only the family, Vicky's parents and her sister Anne. Tony and Anne were the best man and matron of honor.

As the priest said the words that united Bernie and Vicky, Johanna involuntarily turned to her daughter and saw tears glistening in Helen's eyes. Helen and Tony loved each other. What nonsense had Helen dreamed up to keep them apart?

After the ceremony dinner was served in the huge formal dining room, which was seldom used. The two little boys, not present at the nuptials, were elated participants in the wedding dinner. Jason had a mother of his very own now, Johanna thought sentimentally. He would soon get used to his new house without Nicky. When Bernie and Vicky returned from a brief honeymoon at the Greenbrier in White Sulphur Springs, they would move into a service flat only a ten-minute walk away.

As the weeks went past Helen's depression grew and showed more and more. Though Helen kept up her casual attitude, Johanna saw the lapses that betrayed her.

Tony was involved heavily in Al Smith's campaign

for the Democratic nomination. The convention was to be held in New York on July ninth. He was too busy to notice her misery, which to be fair she tried not to inflict on him.

When Tony went upstate for a long weekend of baby-kissing and handshaking, Johanna coaxed Helen into going with her to Southampton to prepare the house for the season. They would be alone; Michal was campaigning too, among the Polish-American community, and Vicky had volunteered to take Nicky.

Johanna looked forward to a weekend alone with her daughter. She vowed that somehow she would contrive to talk to her about Tony. Helen had insisted they wouldn't need Josip to drive them; he would take her father on his political rounds in New York while they were away. She would drive her mother and herself to Southampton in her new Stutz.

They arrived at the Southampton house at high noon. The help had been working to open the house for the past three days. A temporary cook had been installed; Molly remained at Fifth Avenue until the July Fourth weekend. After that Michal dined at his club when he remained in the city.

"Oh, smell that wonderful sea air," Johanna rhapsodized, emerging from the car. "It's so clean and fresh. Let's have lunch and go down to walk on the beach."

Inside the house they found a smiling staff and a cold buffet lunch. Places had been set on the porch facing the ocean. The chicken lobsters, she reported, had been brought in just that morning, the vegetables picked only two hours ago.

Johanna thought Helen was already losing some of the tension that was a constant part of her in the city; after luncheon Helen went upstairs to her bedroom to change into a pair of the gaily colored pajamas that were just appearing at the resorts this summer. Johanna changed into a wrap skirt and blouse. On the beach Helen discarded her shoes to walk barefoot over the sand, and moments later Johanna did the same.

They talked little as they walked under the brilliant June sun, pausing here and there to watch the waves coming in to shore, admiring the fluid grace of the airborne seagulls and laughing at their clumsiness on the sand. To Johanna Helen seemed a girl again, and the years since her high school graduation had never existed.

This was a quiet restful day, one both women needed. After dinner, when the servants had gone off duty for the day and Helen and she were alone, Johanna suggested they sit out on the west porch with coffee and watch the sun set and night fall.

The air was pungent with wild honeysuckle. In the distance they saw the running lights of a small vessel. Soon the first star appeared in the sky.

"Papa said he was thinking about taking up golf," Helen remarked. "Why don't you apply for membership at the club?"

"I don't think we'll do that."

"Why not? I hear the links at Shinnecock Hills are superb."

"Darling, at Southampton your father and I are still 'those upstart Polacks.' Not that it bothers either of us. We bought this house because we love the view. What's important to this family," Johanna said firmly, "are the magnificent sunrises and sunsets out here, the beach, the privacy. Not parties or clubs."

Johanna took a deep breath. "Helen, what about Tony and you?" The moment of silence seemed to last forever.

"What about Tony and me?"

"When are you going to stop playing games with him and marry him?"

"I'm only twenty-five. Women don't rush into marriage these days." Helen crossed and uncrossed her legs.

"Are you being fair to Tony?"

"Are you saying I should stop seeing him?" She tapped her foot.

"I'm saying you should marry him. You love each other. What is keeping you apart?"

Helen's fidgeting halted for a moment and then took up a furious pace. "Mama, I can't ever marry Tony, not the way I've lived."

"Rudy?" her mother protested. "Darling, that was years ago. Many girls make a mistake like that. Don't punish Tony and yourself for that."

"It wasn't just Rudy. In England—in France—when we didn't know if we'd be alive the next day—Carla and I slept with a stream of soldiers. Nothing mattered except feeling alive for a little while. After awhile everyone knew about us. It didn't seem to matter then—most of us were the same way. But now—" Moonlight etched the anguish on her face.

"Darling, Tony loves you—"

"How can I expect him to want me when he knows the truth?"

"Helen, if what you say is true, he must already know. He was in that field hospital a long time. You've said yourself there were no secrets. Bring it up with him if you must, but mark my words, he won't care. Give him the chance to prove that to you."

"I—I don't know," Helen whispered. "Suppose he doesn't?"

"You have to take the chance. You can't go on this way. It's bad for both of you."

On the Thursday after their return from Southampton Helen called from the office to say that Tony and she would be home for dinner.

"Tony's all excited about the political campaign. In another year or two he thinks he'll be ready to run for some local office himself. He thinks— Tony thinks it would be wise politically for us to have a huge Polish-Italian wedding. As long as we're going to be married, let's go after the votes at the same time."

"An autumn wedding, darling?" Johanna asked, suffused with happiness.

"Whenever you think best, Mama. Whatever will be good for Tony's career. And Mama, thank you."

BOOK THREE

Chapter 26

With her hand in Michal's Johanna listened to the nuptial mass on this glorious October day and thanked God for bringing Helen and Tony together. Though Vicky was already showing her first pregnancy, she was Helen's matron of honor and Bernie was the best man. Tears of pleasure filled Johanna's eyes. Helen was a vision of traditional Polish beauty in her long full-skirted gown with satin ribbon bands and a many-colored garland in her hair.

The church was filled with well-wishers, friends of the Raisas and the Corellis. Johanna was secretly relieved that Leon's parole had not yet come through. Michal insisted he hoped Leon could be at Helen's wedding, but Johanna was more realistic. Tony would not find his political future enhanced by any association with his wife's uncle.

The wedding banquet was served to six hundred rather motley guests in the Waldorf ballroom. In the course of the evening three orchestras played. The music included Polish, Italian and popular songs. Johanna was jubilant.

Her daughter had been successfully launched into married life.

After the wedding banquet Helen and Tony left for a four-week honeymoon. They sailed on the magnificent *Mauretania*, which in the postwar years was the darling of the fashionable younger set. Johanna and Michal, Bernie and Vicky saw the bridal couple aboard shortly before the midnight sailing. Gazing about at the hordes of young people, joyous in anticipation of the trip ahead, Johanna thought they looked like drawings from *Vanity Fair*. The scent of money was everywhere.

The Raisas stood ashore while the elegant *Mauretania* prepared to embark. Johanna cast her mind back to the ship that had brought Michal and her to New York thirty-five years ago. She remembered their second cabin accommodations, only a meager improvement on steerage. They met Jan on that trip, and he talked with such wonder about the first-class deck, where there were "bathtubs of white marble and a room for eating that is like that of a palace."

The Raisas had come far in thirty-five years, Johanna thought with pride. Now her daughter traveled to Europe first class. In less than five days the *Mauretania* would dock at Southampton. Michal and she had made the journey in the opposite direction in eight days. In London Helen and Tony would stay at Claridge's and at the Crillon in Paris.

Michal at the wheel of the Rolls-Royce, they dropped off Bernie and Vicky at their apartment. Before pulling away from the curb Michal turned to Johanna.

"Would you mind very much if we drove downtown before going home?" His smile in the shadows of the car was whimsical.

"To Seventh Street and Second Avenue?" she asked.

"Where else?" he chuckled. "I just want to look up at the old flat."

"I wish Mrs. Zabriskie could have lived to be with us tonight," Johanna said quietly. "She loved the children."

"She loved America," he added, driving with uncustomary swiftness down the deserted streets. "I remember her saying, 'One day we'll have a Polish president in America. One day there'll be a Polish pope in Rome.' "

"Tony sure was disappointed that Al Smith didn't get the nomination in July." They invited Tony's whole family to the wedding, but only three couples appeared. Tony and his uncle had been cut off from his family since they rose above their blue-collar origins. The rest of the Corellis were incorrigible snobs and disapproved of the rich and of "not knowing your place."

"Tony bounces back quickly," Michal laughed. "He's convinced Al Smith will win in '28. He's sure we'll soon have a Catholic president in the White House. But I don't think so. Not in '28. Maybe in fifty or sixty years. Not in our lifetime." He hesitated. "Mrs. Raisa, if we can find an all-night automat or some restaurant other than a speakeasy open at this hour, would you join me in a cup of coffee? After we've paid our respects."

Over coffee Michal confided his wish to buy out the estates of two of the partners in the business who had died in the last year.

"In time I'd like to buy out all of the others. I want the business to be family-owned, to be handed down to our children and grandchildren."

"I like that, Michal," she agreed, knowing he made no major decision without consulting her. Only because of her was Michal so moderate about buying on the stock market, when most of the country, from shoeshine boys to millionaires, was up to its collective neck.

"When Tony comes back, I want him to draw up the

papers to set up trust funds for you, the children and Jason. There will be another after Vicky has her baby.''

"Michal, are you keeping something from me?"

"Johanna, I only want to know you're all provided for no matter what happens to me or to the business. I worry about where we're going in this country financially." Johanna knew that he distrusted the flourishing economy. They'd discussed it often.

"A trust fund for you as well, Michal. I mean for all of us to be safe." Despite their wealth neither Michal nor she had ever forgotten the crisis that almost wiped them out in the very early years.

By December Helen was sure she was pregnant. Like her daughter and son-in-law, Johanna was ecstatic.

In February of 1925 Vicky gave birth to a daughter, Johanna Lucy Raisa. When Lucy was three days old, Michal settled one million dollars on her.

After much manipulation Leon was released from the penitentiary in early March of 1925. On a blustery evening at the Raisa mansion he appeared to be greeted with warmth by his brother. Johanna endeavored to mirror Michal's pleasure. "Helen will be thrilled," she said.

"Leon, Leon, why didn't you write?" Michal scolded, his face alight. "We would have been at the train to meet you."

"Have you had dinner yet?" Johanna asked. "I'm sure Molly can—"

"Relax, Johanna," he interrupted, in high spirits. He pulled her into a close embrace. "I had a very early dinner on the train. It helped pass the time." His kiss was like sandpaper. They had made him shave clean in prison, but already his upper lip was frosted with new growth.

"I'll have a room made up for you." Why did she

always feel that they were on the brink of disaster when Leon appeared in their lives?

When Johanna rejoined Michal and Leon in the library, they were deep in a financial discussion. Michal had taken charge of Leon's affairs while he was in prison. Now Leon felt ready to resume the reins.

"Leon, be sensible," Michal begged. "This Miami boom could fall flat on its face any day. It's dangerous to invest too heavily down there."

"Michal, there are millions to be made." Leon grinned. "Within the law. I've had all the Miami papers sent up to me regularly. I've got this bird-dog instinct about making money. I won't just buy and sell. I mean to develop. Come down with me. This time of year New York's a mess. Stay for three or four weeks and we'll look around together. Michal, we were a great team in our time." Leon switched on his high-voltage charm. "You remember how it was with us until I got bored and left the reservation."

"I could leave Bernie in charge of the office for a couple of weeks," Michal mused.

"The others just collect their checks and do nothing—as usual," Leon said wisely.

"I bought out Bill Grady and Max Sudbury. I wrote you they both died." Michal turned to Johanna. "Would you like to go down to Miami for a couple of weeks? We could stand some warm weather after this winter."

"It's terribly crowded down there." Johanna wasn't eager to spend two weeks in Leon's pocket. "People wait months for hotel reservations."

"No worry about hotels." Leon smiled expansively. "I've already arranged for a house down there, right by the water. It belongs to someone in residence in Atlanta for another year at least," he said whimsically. "Before I left I made the deal to take over the house. We don't have to go down right away. I can hang around New York for a month or two.''

"No." Not a month or two. "Why don't we go down right away?" Tony was awaiting an appointment as assistant to the mayor. It would be best to get Leon away from the city before he had a chance to attract any attention.

"March is such a rotten month in New York. I could be ready in three or four days.'' She was talking too rapidly. Leon would smell a rat. Take a deep breath.

"I sort of hate going away when Helen is pregnant, but the baby isn't due until July. I guess I can't stick around all the time.''

"Then it's set,'' Leon said ebulliently, slapping Michal on the shoulder. "Wait'll you see this house. It's a showplace. Right on the beach.''

"I'll have my secretary make our reservations,'' Michal said. Still the loving younger brother, Johanna thought unhappily. Nothing Leon did could eradicate that feeling in Michal. It would be better for Leon to be involved in some legitimate business—and in Miami—than to be sucked into bootlegging—or stay in New York. Tony had worked hard to win this assignment to the mayor's office. They must not allow Leon to embarrass him.

On the following Monday Johanna, Michal and Leon boarded the train in Pennsylvania Station. Johanna and Michal settled themselves in the drawing room and Leon headed for the smoking car. As Johanna had expected, Michal and Leon spent much time together reminiscing in the smoking car or poring over financial matters in the drawing room. As always, Leon seemed to gather fascinated people. It astonished Johanna that at fifty-nine and despite the hectic life he had lived Leon appeared a dynamic, distinguished as well as handsome man-about-town.

She was content to spend hours on the observation platform or in the drawing room with the new Sinclair

Lewis novel, *Arrowsmith*. Vicky had given her Dos Passos' *Manhattan Transfer* and young Fitzgerald's *Gatsby*, which she meant to read lying in the Miami sun while Michal and Leon pursued business.

As the train sped south the first green buds of spring appeared on display in Virginia. The grass was up in the Carolinas and vegetables and fodder were in the ground and the farmers were beginning to prepare the soil for the cotton crop.

Johanna was surprised to feel a sense of anticipation as the train chugged into the crowded, gloomy Miami railroad station. Excitement pervaded the place, sprung from the passengers about to get their first sight of Magic City.

With his customary flair for the expensive Leon had arranged for a limousine to meet their train. Johanna had been wise enough to leave her sables at home and bring only a light raincoat. While other wealthy New Yorkers sweltered in coats too valuable to entrust to a porter, Johanna looked and felt wonderful in her light blue two-piece knit traveling dress.

Traffic reminded her of rush hour in Manhattan. She noticed license plates from nearly every state in the union. Chuckling, Leon diverted her attention to a police officer directing traffic from beneath a beach umbrella. It seemed that the roads were too narrow for the flow of cars that traveled along them. She had never dreamed any city's traffic could be worse than New York's.

The house Leon had rented from a big-time gambler in the Atlanta penitentiary was said to have been designed by Addison Mizner, who had made Palm Beach into the haven of the ultrarich. It bore the Spanish touches for which Mizner was noted and of which Leon was fond along with an indoor swimming pool, gold-plated bathroom fixtures and an art collection more notable for its monetary value than for its aesthetic attributes.

A domestic couple remained on duty; absent or not, the owner valued his Miami domain. "I'll see to hiring a full staff," Johanna said briskly. "It will give me something to do."

Leon confided that his landlord intended to approach Michal's firm about building an ocean-going yacht after he was released. Johanna began to suffer some misgivings about this association.

Within twenty-four hours—in a town so crowded with new arrivals that people paid to sleep elbow-to-elbow on porches—Leon had bought a house to serve as his offices. Michal admitted he was mesmerized by the phenomenal turnover of real estate, the prices that escalated by the day.

On their second evening in Miami Johanna and Michal sat on the sprawling verandah to enjoy the view while Leon took a prospective client to dine at the prestigious Royal Palm Hotel. On his first day in Miami Leon had already scooped up a mass of land options.

"I don't understand this land boom," Johanna confessed. "To me it sounds more speculative than buying on margin on Wall Street."

"It's gambling," Michal agreed. "You saw the Ponce de Leon Hotel this afternoon. That's the headquarters of the binder boys. They buy options on land and then try to sell them before the first payment is due. They bid up the prices to a point of insanity. This town is full of promoters who're out to make a killing overnight and they're not too fussy about how it happens."

"Michal, let's don't get involved."

"No, I have no taste for this buying and selling in Miami. Still, I'd rather see Leon involved in real estate than bootlegging. From what I hear it's a major occupation in Florida. A perfect locale, Leon tells me, for rumrunning."

"Surely Leon won't try that again," Johanna said sharply. "Hasn't he disgraced the family enough?"

"Johanna, Prohibition is a joke," Michal protested. "Leon got caught; thousands of others haven't."

"It's against the law." Johanna's face set stubbornly. "If we don't respect the law, what kind of country will this become? Make Leon understand that he has to stay out of anything even faintly shady. Wasn't one term in the penitentiary enough to teach him a lesson?"

"You're being unreasonable. Leon is my brother. He won't do anything to disgrace the family." His eyes avoided hers.

"Michal, open your eyes. He already has. Bootlegging isn't protesting against tyranny in Poland. It is breaking the law of a land for which we have immense respect, our country and our children's and our grandchildren's. I don't want to go back home and be terrified of picking up a newspaper and seeing Leon's name on the front page again."

"He's my brother. What do you want me to do? I can't write him out of my life."

"Just make sure he doesn't wreck ours." Johanna shifted her chair to get the setting sun out of her eyes, also turning her shoulder to Michal.

"I think I'll take a walk on the beach," Michal said coldly. "Don't wait up for me." He stalked off the porch.

Johanna watched Michal disappear into the night. He was tired and troubled but loyal to Leon and now angry with her. How could he not see that Leon was dangerous, amoral, not even capable of personal loyalty?

Leon sat in the plush dining room at the Royal Palm while his guest eagerly wrote a check for a cool hundred thousand for a small parcel of land Leon had bought yesterday for twenty thousand. He was sure the check was good; his client was one of the richest men in America. This was the land of the supersalesman, and Leon was one of the best.

Jubilant at his success, Leon said good night to his client and left. That worthy retired to his suite upstairs to boast to his pretty young mistress, brought from Chicago in his private railroad car, about the shrewd deal he had just made.

On the long narrow porch of the imposing Royal Palm, Leon debated about how to spend the rest of the evening. He was hardly ready to return to his splendid rental and sit in a rocker beside Michal and Johanna.

He left the porch of the hotel to walk decisively toward the waiting limousine. "I'll be in the Seminole Club." This was a casino adjacent to the hotel and erected for the benefit of the tourist trade. Local residents, unless very wealthy indeed, were not permitted to cross the threshold. Leon strolled around the corner and down the club's red carpet.

He headed first for the roulette table, where he lost eight thousand within twenty minutes. He soon transferred his interest in roulette to a short bosomy blonde hustler in a sequin gown, who made no secret of her own interest in him. She was interested in anyone who could lose eight thousand and smile.

He rose from the table and walked to her side. "Why don't we go somewhere and talk?" he said without preliminaries. After months on end in the pen he was ready for a woman, by God.

"Talk?" she drawled, her eyes eloquent.

"For openers." He dropped an arm about her waist. It was crazy the way any woman who looked like Johanna made him horny. This one was quite a fair imitation of Johanna's youth. "We can go somewhere and dance first.

No Charleston," he warned with a chuckle. "I'm a tango or foxtrot man."

"We could go to Texas Guinan's," she suggested. "I'm Candy. I'm a dancer."

"You can dance with me any time. I'm Leon." At Texas Guinan's, his sources of information in Atlanta had told him, even a glass of cracked ice cost two and a half bucks, but the best Scotch in town was available there.

For a while Leon enjoyed himself at the club. He always enjoyed being in the company of a young and beautiful woman who was not averse to traveling hands. The entertainers—a pretty little dancer named Ruby Keeler particularly caught his eye—were excellent.

"Let's go," he said abruptly and signaled a waiter to bring his check. He had just recognized a pair of men who worked for Al Capone. What the hell was that bastard doing down here? Not buying real estate. All at once he was tingling with excitement. "We'll go to my place, Candy. We've got a liquor cellar there that's as good as anything the club can offer."

Rumrunning was a major industry in Florida, he remembered a source telling him. Nobody except the Feds ever bothered about bootlegging—they had more important interests. And for the right bait the Feds would look the other way.

When they arrived the house was dark except for the foyer chandelier and the wall sconces on the staircase. Michal and Johanna had retired already, as he had expected. The servants slept in the cottage behind the house.

"That's it for the night," Leon told the chauffeur as he helped Candy from the car. "Pick me up around ten tomorrow morning."

"Yes sir." The man tipped his cap and slid behind the wheel.

"This your house?" Candy asked. Leon draped an arm over her as they headed for the door.

"For now." He wished he hadn't had that last Scotch. But hell, he was still good for one round with this young slut.

"You're going to stay here for a while?"

"A while." He opened the door and pushed it wide.

"Feel like going for a swim in the pool?" He loved the pool and the tennis courts—necessary to his amour-propre. "Wait till you see the size of it."

"I have something else in mind," she murmured, pressing up against him. "Unless you're not in the mood."

"I'm in the mood. Let's do it in the pool."

Much later Johanna heard the door to the master bedroom suite open and close. Beside her Michal gently snored. It was ridiculous to lie here wide awake like this. Usually the sound of the waves lapping at the shore was sufficient to lull her to sleep.

Was she being too hard on Leon? Michal was convinced that the term in prison had made Leon see that he was not above the law.

"Make yourself comfortable, baby." From the next room Leon's deep voice jarred her into realizing he had not come home alone. "Want some more booze?"

"No." In the heavy silence of the night it seemed to Johanna that the wall between the rooms was nonexistent except to provide a screen. "Maybe later," a young feminine voice purred.

Johanna lay stiff against the pillows. First one shoe dropped, then another. Couldn't Leon have taken his—friend—to another room on the floor?

"Stop the sightseeing and take off your clothes," Leon scolded. "It's been awhile and I'm tired of waiting."

"Do I make you horny?"

"Get out of that teddy and come over here. Don't I look ready to you?"

"Oh, honey, do you ever." A giggle ended in a gasp. Johanna clenched her teeth in distaste. "I'm good," Candy boasted. "I'll do anything you like."

"I like a lot." Leon cleared his throat. For a few moments there was silence. "Yeah, baby. Keep that up. Sweet as candy," he said thickly. "You make me feel like sixteen again."

Johanna turned on her side, away from the wall between their bedroom and Leon's, and pulled the pillow over her head. Still she could hear the passion as it rose to fever pitch in the adjoining suite. Didn't Leon know they could be heard in the next bedroom?

"Oh, you are something," Leon grunted at last.

"You're staying down here for a while, aren't you?" Candy repeated.

"We'll see plenty of each other," Leon promised. "And tomorrow we'll go out and buy you some pretty trinkets to show you how much I like you."

A short pause was followed by the slow, rhythmic creaking of the bed.

"Leon, my brother would like to talk to you," Candy said after a few minutes of silence.

"Your brother?" The creaking stopped.

"He saw me watching you and recognized you at the casino. He just bought one of those old war surplus planes. Leon, he'd like to go into business with you bringing rum up from the Caribbean. He's got a sure-fire setup for bringing it in, but he needs you for distribution."

"Your *brother*?" Leon snorted. The creaking resumed.

"Actually, he's my brother-in-law. He's married to my oldest sister. Will you meet him tomorrow to talk about it?"

"Yeah, I'll meet him. Tell your *brother-in-law* if he

can bring in prime stuff in quantities that appeal to me we'll do business.''

That tears it, Johanna thought. Leon's going right back into business, and against some stiff competition. Al Capone maintained a magnificent home right in Miami. She and Michal would be out of there tomorrow, she vowed.

As always at the beach, Michal rose early.

''Sleep later, Johanna. I'll have breakfast and go for a walk on the beach.''

''I'll go with you. We have to talk.''

Michal didn't press her. He could tell she wished to be away from the house before she spoke. They dressed quickly and went downstairs to breakfast, Johanna uncomfortably aware who owned the luxurious house.

At the breakfast table, served by the rather obsequious houseman, Johanna felt personally soiled as a guest in the house of Leon's fellow convict. The servants knew their employer was in prison, and not just for selling illegal whiskey.

Leon's ''friend'' was head of a syndicate of loan sharks, gamblers, whoremasters—leeches. His name had been spilled across the *New York Daily News*, the *Daily Mirror*, the *Evening Graphic*—nicknamed the *Pornographic*. Johanna wondered what besides his house Leon had rented or borrowed—his contacts? His hit men? His business?

This morning Michal did not linger, as was his habit away from New York, over three cups of strong black coffee. He was on his feet at the first indication that Johanna had finished breakfast.

''It's a beautiful day again.'' He gazed out at the cloudless sky, the rolling ocean. ''No wonder the Florida climate enchants so many people.''

When they were a hundred yards from the house,

Johanna said she wanted to return to New York. Michal stiffened. "But it's so beautiful down here. I thought you were enjoying Miami."

"I might if I had not been awake when Leon came home last night. He brought home some girl he'd picked up somewhere."

"Leon's been in prison for such a stretch." Michal took her hand and led her north along the beach. "He'll calm down."

"Michal, he's going back into bootlegging. It was bad enough before, but now gangsters control every bottle of liquor sold in this country." Johanna swung around and planted herself in Michal's path. She gazed fiercely into his face. "Listen to me for once. Nobody will ever stop Leon from doing exactly what he wants to do. He's meeting a man with an airplane that will bring up rum from the Caribbean. Leon is going up against some tough competition. He'll get himself killed, Michal."

"I'll talk to him."

Johanna shook her head. "Don't bother. He'll go ahead no matter what you say. Please Michal, let's go home tomorrow. You can make up some excuse about the business."

Johanna turned and reached for Michal's hand. "Come on. Let's get in some good beach time while we're here." Michal followed meekly. He was remembering Leon as a young revolutionary thirty some odd years ago, Leon's heroic escape from a labor camp in Siberia.

"Not tomorrow, love. The day after. I'll tell him tomorrow night that I've talked with the office in New York." Michal's eyes were dark with pain. "I'll tell him we have to go straight back."

Chapter 27

Back in New York Johanna tried to put Leon out of her mind. Tony's appointment as an assistant to the mayor came through. She gave a family party to celebrate, including Victor Corelli and his Caroline. She knew that Tony regarded Caroline as his aunt, though Victor could never bring himself to meet her at the altar.

In May came the arrest of John Scopes, who dared teach the theory of evolution to his students. At the same time the Florida House of Representatives passed a bill requiring daily reading of the Bible in all public schools in the state. Mrs. William B. Ross, the first woman governor in the United States, was running Wyoming in high style.

In mid-June, slightly earlier than anticipated, Helen's son Joseph was born at Lying-in Hospital. Tony was ecstatic. When tiny Joseph was a month old, Johanna pursuaded Helen to bring him to Southampton for the summer; Vicky and her children were coming too. The men would drive out for long weekends. Johanna took deep pleasure in her children and grandchildren. It was a tranquil summer, marred only by continued political problems in Warsaw.

As always, Casimar kept in close touch. Leon was not one for correspondence, but late in the summer he wrote an unexpectedly long letter about his real estate dealings in Miami. He was pouring a fortune into building a hotel on the beach, catering to the wealthiest of tourists.

"You see, Johanna," Michal said, obviously relieved, "Leon's in real estate. You've been upset for nothing."

But signs were pointing to the end of the boom. Late in the summer prices of land dropped in half, then surged up again; but people began to be uneasy. In addition Miami was hit by critical freight congestion. Building materials were lost in transit. Embargoes were declared on everything from lumber to cattle feed. In some parts of Florida a doctor's prescription was necessary to buy ice. Mail service broke down.

Early in September Leon appeared on their doorstep. He admitted to some financial difficulties but was confident he could come about. He had come to New York to negotiate for funds.

"I'm not asking you for money, Michal," he said grandly. "I've got fine connections here. That hotel will make me a fortune. There'll be nothing to match it in the whole state by the time it's finished."

"Leon, maybe it's time to pull out of Florida real estate," Michal said over dinner. Johanna listened with apprehension. Perhaps Michal was right and Leon was involved only in real estate, but Johanna didn't believe it for a minute.

Leon seemed to conduct his business operations in the evenings—probably in choice speakeasies, she thought sourly. On his fourth evening in New York he appeared for dinner jubilant. Things were working out exactly as he had planned, he confided as they lingered over dessert and coffee.

"Let's go out on the town tonight," he said expansively. "You two act like a stodgy old couple. Johanna, you're still a beautiful woman."

"Thank you, Leon." She managed a faint smile.

"Go upstairs and put on something dazzling," he commanded her. "We're going to the Club Gallant."

"Go on, Johanna," Michal said good-humoredly. "Let big brother show us the poshest club in Manhattan."

To please Michal Johanna went upstairs to change into a chic gold brocade and the diamond and emerald necklace that commemorated their thirty-sixth wedding anniversary. The brocade would not be too warm, she told herself, as this was an unseasonably cool evening.

On occasion Michal and she had been in the smartest of the New York nightclubs. They had gone to small, select Les Ambassadeurs to see Jimmy Durante, Eddie Jackson and Lou Clayton. They had enjoyed Bea Lillie at the Sutton Club, Libby Holman at the Lido, Fred and Adele Astaire at the Trocadero. But they were not part of cafe society. None of the New York Raisas, now that Wanda was gone, were part of that mad social world that considered getting drunk a requisite of fashionable and happy life.

Johanna was aware that Leon would probably have chosen a less urbane club than the Club Gallant on Washington Square if he were pleasing himself. Here was none of the splash and glitter so reminiscent of Hollywood. Here good taste was expected of the patrons.

They knew, too, that the champagne served them was the best obtainable. It was inconceivable that Barney Gallant would serve his patrons anything else. When the orchestra played Michal's favorite hit of last year, *I'll See You In My Dreams*, Johanna asked him to dance.

Returning to their table, they saw a man leaning over in whispered conversation with Leon. As they approached the man left hastily. Leon seemed upset, though a moment later he was smiling again.

"I have some unexpected business to take care of tonight." He signaled their waiter to bring the check. "I'm sorry to cut the evening short this way."

"Is something wrong, Leon?" Michal gave his brother a penetrating look.

"No, everything's fine." His bluster was a shade too heavy.

Johanna had never seen Leon afraid of anything or anyone, but look at him now. Tonight he was scared. The sagging jowls, the heavy lines in his face, the paunch that even the finest tailoring could not conceal—tonight they all exuded fear.

With no display of haste Leon walked with them from the club and out into the night. She saw his eyes sweep along the street. He had insisted that they take a taxi to the club rather than have Josip drive them. No point, he'd said grandly, for Josip to sit around in the car for hours. They'd take a taxi home when they decided to call it a night.

Moonlight spilled a silver glow about them as Leon moved toward the curb to flag down a taxi. A black limousine was approaching slowly. Then all at once Leon was shouting at them, "Get down!" Leon charged away up the lightly populated street. "For God's sake, Michal, duck."

For an instant Michal and Johanna froze. Then Michal flung his wife to the sidewalk and dropped beside her. Johanna, trained in hundreds of air raids, was already rolling into a sheltered corner. They heard a blast of machine gun fire as the black luxury car screeched to a temporary halt. Then the gunfire ceased and the limousine skidded around a corner and was gone.

"Leon," Michal yelled, running toward the sprawled figure of his brother, "Leon."

"Call an ambulance," Johanna shouted to a man leaning out of a nearby house. "He's still alive."

Michal was on his knees beside his brother. The street was filling with people. How long would it take for an ambulance to come? In her Lanvin gown Johanna crouched beside Michal, flinching at the gaping wound in Leon's chest, the blood seeping out to soak his shirt. All at once she felt herself back at the field hospital in France. Was this not war of a kind too?

"It was a gang murder," a woman said excitedly to her companion. "Do you know who he is?"

"One of those bootleggers—Al Capone?" another guessed.

"Naw, it was Leon Raisa. But you're right; he used to be a big-time bootlegger," put in a pretty little blonde.

"He's not dead," Michal said grimly without looking up. "Did anybody call for an ambulance?" A siren shrieked across Washington Square and a police car approached the crowd that surrounded Leon, who remained unconscious.

"Move back," a policeman ordered briskly. "Everybody move back. Make room for the medics."

Michal stayed beside his brother and Johanna spoke to the police officers. She urged Michal to his feet while the ambulance crew fetched Leon. "May we ride with him?" Johanna asked uncertainly, clinging to Michal's arm.

"We'll drive you to the hospital." The officer jerked his head at his partner, who advanced on the avid onlookers.

"Move on," he ordered. "Go on about your business."

Within minutes of arrival Leon was in surgery. "Why did it have to happen?" Michal railed. "*Why*? He'd put the past behind him. He was in real estate, Johanna." He slumped and put his head in his hands. "Why was he gunned down that way?"

Johanna knew Leon had not put the past behind him. Anger welled in her. Knowing what lay ahead of him, why hadn't Leon left them at the club and gone on his way alone? Why drag them into it? Never mind the danger; look what the horror of it had done to Michal.

They had been waiting for almost two hours when the newspaper reporters began to arrive. This was what made headlines for the *Daily News*, the *Mirror*, the *Evening Graphic*. When the photographers showed up Michal pulled Johanna to a window and stared resolutely out into the night. Both refused to answer questions.

"Hey, Michal Raisa's daughter is married to Tony Corelli. What do you suppose the mayor thinks about having an assistant who's related to Leon Raisa?" Michal's arm tightened about Johanna.

"Michal, I'm going out to find a telephone," she whispered. "Tony had better hear about this. Besides, Helen must be told."

"You can't; they'll follow you."

"Oh, no, they won't. I'm on the board of this hospital. I know it inside out. I'll place my call from the conference room. I have a key. Trust me."

"Don't be gone long. Soon Leon will be out of surgery. He'll want to see you."

"He's in God's hands, Michal," she said softly. She knew if Michal didn't that Leon's life hung by a thread.

St. Vincent's Hospital was a maze, and Johanna had friends all over it. Leaving the most persistent reporter scratching his head in the cafeteria, Johanna let herself into the conference room and dialed Helen and Tony's number, knowing they would be frightened at a call in the middle of the night. The phone rang half a dozen times. They couldn't hear it, she thought, and decided to let it have twenty more rings, but on the next the receiver lifted.

"Hello?"

"Tony, I'm sorry to disturb you at this hour, but Leon's been shot. I saw the wound and I don't think he's going to live. He's in surgery at St. Vincent's and the place is crawling with reporters asking about your relationship to him."

"Oh, my God. I'll be there in twenty minutes."

"You stay home. You didn't know him and I will not have a passel of newsmen see you show up at his deathbed. Here's what I want you to do. First call Bernie. Tell him to bring Helen to the hospital. I know she'll want to come and she'll never forgive me if he dies and she doesn't make it in time, so tell Bernie to hurry."

After very little further conversation Johanna hurried back upstairs. The reporters eyed her with new respect but did not let up their badgering. She hurried to the window where Michal still stared out into the night.

"Tony's calling Bernie to bring Helen," Johanna whispered. "I expect them in a few minutes."

Half an hour later the doctors approached Michal and the reporters and photographers charged.

"Is he alive?" a reporter demanded. "Does he know who gunned him down?"

"Mr. Raisa?" A doctor, ignoring the reporters, addressed Michal.

"Yes," Michal said. "How is my brother?"

"You may see him now." The surgeon firmly shut the corridor door in the face of the fourth estate.

Johanna and Michal followed him down a hallway. He waited until they had turned a corner to speak. "He's conscious now but he has only hours to live, maybe less. He's anxious to talk to his family."

"Thank you, doctor." Johanna said quietly. A tremor shot through Michal.

The surgeon gestured to Leon's nurse to leave.

"Hey, you're all right," Leon said with a shaky smile.

"We're fine." Michal reached for Leon's hand. "And you'll be fine."

"No, little brother," he drawled, "this is the end of the line, but I had a good run for my money." His eyes settled on Johanna. "Old Henderson has instructions about what to do with my money. Except for a couple of items it all goes to Casimar for the church. That should be something in my favor, shouldn't it?"

"Leon, you should rest," Johanna urged. All the years seemed to disappear now, and Leon and Michal and she were back in the house in Warsaw with Casimar and Mama Raisa. Leon was the hero of the household, the one the young people in revolt considered their leader. What had gone wrong?

"Casimar can say a lot of prayers on my pile. All I'm holding out is enough for a sable coat for Johanna." Leon coughed. "You have to take it, Johanna, or the taxman gets it all, including the church's share. Remember me when you wear it. I always had a thing for beautiful blondes."

The door opened and Helen and Bernie came in. Bernie shook Leon's hand but could think of nothing to say. "Cheer up, nephew," his incorrigible uncle grinned. "If you ever manage to have half the fun I've had you'll smile on your deathbed too. Now clear out of here and let me speak privately to my favorite niece."

Michal ushered out Bernie and the rather reluctant Johanna.

"Oh, Uncle Leon," Helen gulped, "why did it come to this?"

"Stop sniveling and bring me my vest. I don't have much time, and sure as God made good Scotch whiskey your mother's going to clutter up my room with a priest any minute now."

Helen, accustomed to far odder Leonisms than this, meekly fetched the garment and sat on the edge of the bed as he indicated. He fished in the vest lining near a side seam, going by touch, since he was too weak to hold up either his head or his hands.

"Ah, here it is." He panted a little, resting, then held out his closed fist. The vest dropped to the floor. "Great little hiding place. Slide things in under the half-belt, where the bulge is never noticed. Come on, hold out your hand."

Helen reached out as if to take the object, but Leon gripped her wrist in his feeble fingers and slipped something around it. It was a bracelet, a simple string of very fine half-carat diamonds. "There," he gasped, "I've owed you that for a long time. I was saving it for your birthday, but I guess I'd better not wait. Good thing that damned incompetent hit man missed it. It'll look great with your pearls."

Helen was weeping openly. "Uncle Leon—"

"Damnit, girl, I told you never to call me that. Now look, I don't want your mother to know about that bracelet. She's always been the only woman in the world for me, but there's no getting around it, she's one hell of a prude and she'd never understand. I don't want her sniffing disapproval all over my last earthly act. We've had a lot of secrets, young Helen, and that bracelet is just the last and the best of them. Hear me?"

Helen nodded, and just as Leon had predicted, Johanna came in with a priest.

"I figured you'd be along," Leon sneered. "Can't let the bishop's brother leave without a proper sendoff. Michal, don't let the damned undertaker touch my mustache. Get my barber in."

Within the hour, while Michal clasped his brother's hand, Leon died. There would be no gangster's funeral for Leon, Johanna vowed, but a quiet private service and an equally private burial. Leon Raisa had returned to his family.

The morning tabloids carried lurid stories of the gangland battle that had cut down Leon Raisa. The papers reported he had been out to cut in on Capone's business on the Eastern Seaboard from Florida to Maine. The murder was regarded as a warning to any other ambitious entrepreneurs.

After Leon was laid to rest in a Westchester cemetery, the family returned home to receive calls. Friends of Michal and Johanna filed in and out of the house to pay their respects. Telegrams came from Leon's associates in Hollywood—and one from the Federal facility in Atlanta.

Late one evening about a month later when the family sat alone in the library over coffee and pastry, Johanna forced herself to broach the subject that had been disturbing her for the past three days.

"Tony, what's happening with you and the mayor?" she asked without preliminaries.

"There's the usual problem," Tony admitted. "All kinds of graft and corruption go on under cover, but any hint of association with—" he hesitated.

"With a criminal element," Johanna supplied, avoiding Michal's stare of reproach.

"I'm guilty by association," Tony said unhappily, "and I never even met him."

"Tony's being pressed to resign," Helen told them. "How dare they."

"Go ahead and resign, Tony," Johanna said with resolution. "Don't give them the chance to fire you. Announce that you're going to be busy preparing to run for city council in the next election. People forget fast. You run a strong campaign and they'll forget all about Leon.''

"Mama, you have a way of coming forth with the wisdom of an elder statesman," Bernie said tenderly. "Of course that's what you have to do, Tony. You'll have the whole family behind you."

"Papa?" Helen asked tentatively.

"I think your mother's right. Now's the time for Tony to run for public office."

The family drew together to prepare for Tony's campaign. It was understood that money would be no object. After a decent interval Johanna would begin to entertain on a wide scale. First they would concentrate on the Polish and Italian votes; then they would spread out. After all, the Raisa family was highly respected in New York.

Helen's grief was more manageable than her family expected. To be sure, they all made it very easy for her, but the important factor was that Helen thought her glamorous uncle had gotten exactly what he had coming. It was a hard thought and it made her feel like a monster sometimes, but really, Leon had begged for it. Helen had never been sure he wasn't getting ready to sell methanol-alcohol booze; if he hadn't been in the slammer he might have been responsible for Wanda's death.

She loved her bracelet, which curiously enough Tony never asked about, and at first she took a child's delight in a secret. But one night she woke up from a dream that her parents had been shot too, and over a cigarette in the dark cold-bloodedly concluded that Leon Raisa was really too selfish to live. After that she wore her bracelet for the early days in California—and because she had earned it— and put the death of Leon Raisa in the back of her mind.

Johanna knew Michal would mourn long and hard for Leon. Her own grief astonished her. She remembered only the very early years, just like Michal.

On late autumn weekends, well past the season, she insisted they drive out to Southampton for a quiet time alone. Nicky was always pleased to spend a weekend with Jason and Lucy or with little Joseph.

At Southampton Michal and she would walk for hours along the deserted beach. Michal's love for the ocean matched her own. In the sea he would find comfort.

Shortly before Christmas Helen confided that she was pregnant again. "We hope it'll be a girl, but if it's a boy we won't send him back."

"You've given your father and me the grandest Christmas present in the world," Johanna told her, eyes brimming with tears of joy. "Our grandchildren are our real riches."

"Mama, do you think Tony will win the election next year?"

"If praying—and money—can do it, Tony will win. Most of all, remember, Tony deserves to win. He'll be a fine councilman."

A new grandchild plus his son-in-law on city council might ease Michal's mourning for Leon. Michal was spending a small fortune trying to locate his sisters in what used to be German Poland. Casimar had been able to do nothing, but Michal, bereft of a brother, was desperate to find the rest of his family.

Chapter 28

Early in 1926 Johanna began to give important political dinners. Despite her advancing pregnancy Helen was a co-hostess at luncheons for the wives of New Yorkers who could be helpful in Tony's election. Bernie was active among the young Democrats of the city with an eye toward promoting Tony's nomination for City Council.

In May Johanna and Michal were upset when news came through that Marshal Jozef Pilsudski had entered Warsaw at the head of troops and had been labeled a rebel by the government. After two days of heavy street fighting Pilsudski took over the government with almost dictatorial power.

"When will Poland be a republic?" Michal railed.

"It's called a republic," Johanna reminded him. "Anyhow, there'll be another election in a year and half. It's better in Poland now than in our time."

Late in June Helen gave birth to a second son, Henry. Vicky had suffered an early miscarriage only weeks earlier, and Bernie was determined that she refrain from future childbearing. They had two children and that was a cozy family, Bernie insisted.

Tony never saw much of his family while campaigning, but Helen did not complain. Vicky and Johanna were aware of her loneliness and kept her company as much as they could. Henry throve with or without his papa.

Tony won a decisive victory, and no sooner had he taken office than Michal was planning his future in the state Assembly. Johanna was glad Michal had Tony's political future as well as the business to fill his mind, since the search for his sisters in Poland appeared to be hopeless.

At intervals Michal expressed anxiety about the economy, though business—except for the disastrous collapse in Florida—was booming. Production was up, demands for consumer goods strong. Corporate profits were rising even with the higher pay brought about by strikes. Everybody, it seemed, was buying on the installment plan, living like kings.

Over a family dinner at Southampton in the summer of '28 Michal again expressed his concern about the state of the economy. "In a way what's happening on the market reminds me of the Florida boom. Stock prices are artificially high. And this buying on margin is dangerous."

"Everybody's out to make a killing," Vicky contributed. "I read in the *Times* last week about a stockbroker's butler named Johnson who listened to market tips at the door and built up a fortune of almost half a million dollars."

"My uncle is going heavily into the market," Tony said soberly. "It's become a compulsion with him."

"For a lot of people," Bernie replied. "They're all so damned optimistic."

"Not all," Johanna objected. "Last week Roger Babson wrote that a crash is on its way and it could be devastating."

"Let's pray he's wrong," Tony put in.

"For most people," Michal pointed out, "credit is a way of life. How else can a working man pay for a new car or furniture or appliances for the house? Nobody seems to realize how much they're adding to the cost of everything by paying all that interest. At these interest rates actual costs can go up as much as forty percent."

"I suppose for some people that's the only way they can get things," Helen said compassionately. "I mean, have things right now instead of saving up for years."

"Thank God, in this family we can avoid credit buying," Michal said. He gazed at the young people. "I hope none of us is careless or greedy enough to buy stocks on margin."

"Not around you, Papa," Bernie said. "I learned more about business from Mama and you than at Harvard."

Johanna and Michal often baby-sat for the children when the two young couples went out in the evening; it gave them great pleasure.

"With grandchildren you have all the pleasure and few of the headaches," Michal confided to Bernie and Vicky when they came home from a performance of Philip Barry's new Broadway hit, *Holiday*, on a brisk October evening. "It's a gift from God."

"Jason and Lucy slept through?" Vicky asked.

"Like two angels," Johanna said sentimentally. "We kept the radio low, but sometimes their grandfather got carried away and sang along with Rudy Vallee."

"Missed my vocation," Michal boasted. "Should have been a radio star."

"Did you talk to Helen today?" Vicky asked. "Last night she was feeling so tired I thought she might be having a cold coming on."

"I called late this afternoon but she was out," Johanna said. "I'll call her when we get home."

Johanna phoned Helen late, but Tony was out at a meeting and Helen would be waiting up for him.

"How are you, darling? Vicky said you might be coming down with a cold."

"No," Helen said with a special lilt in her voice. "I ought to wait and tell Tony first, but I can't wait. I went to the doctor this afternoon just to make sure. Mama, I'm pregnant again, and this time it's going to be a girl."

"I'll pray for a girl," Johanna promised. "I'll ask Uncle Casimar to pray too. I'm so happy for you. I know Tony will be too."

"Tony would be happy if I stayed permanently pregnant. A large family is his idea of heaven."

"Is it all right if I tell your father?"

"Of course. But don't tell Tony I told you first."

When Michal suggested a six-week trip to Europe, Johanna insisted they wait until after Helen delivered. Her daughter was having an uncomfortable pregnancy, though Helen rarely complained.

By the sixth month Helen's doctor suspected twins. He insisted on naps in the afternoon, little nighttime socializing. She fretted at the inactivity; she liked to go to as many political affairs with Tony as possible.

Late on a May afternoon she sat sipping hot chocolate with Vicky and reporting on the birthday party she planned for Joseph, who would be four next month.

"Oh, God, I can't get comfortable," she fretted, trying to adjust her bulk in the upright chair that made it possible for her to rise without assistance. "I'm as big as a house."

"You don't have much longer. What does the doctor say, about eight weeks?"

"I hope I can survive eight weeks. Poor Tony, he's scared to death to come near me now. My hot Italian husband. It must be hell for him."

"I would love to have another baby," Vicky said wistfully, "but it doesn't seem to be happening."

"When it's meant to happen, you'll be pregnant again. I expect Tony and I will have a dozen before he's satisfied." All of a sudden she started, grimaced in unexpected pain.

"Are you all right?" Vicky asked overcasually.

"I'm not sure." Helen was aware of her heart pounding. "I—I could be feeling false labor." She shook her head. "No, it must be something I ate today. I'm not due for two months." But a hand rested on the huge mound that was her stomach.

"You ought to check with Dr. Rainy. Shall I call him? Twins are often early."

"At seven months? Vicky, they're still so little." She frowned, concentrating on another contraction.

"Helen, we have to get you to the hospital." Vicky was on her feet. "I'll call Dr. Rainy."

"Maybe they're not contractions," Helen said doubtfully.

Vicky's phone conversation was brief. When she hung up she sighed with satisfaction. "Dr. Rainy is sending an ambulance. While we're waiting, we'll get you into a nightgown and robe."

"I don't need an ambulance," Helen protested. Suddenly she doubled up in pain. "Vicky, the babies are coming *now*."

Vicky helped her into the bedroom. Thank God the children were out with the nurse.

All at once Helen was remembering Uncle Leon's story of playing midwife at her own birth. But she had been a normal, full-term baby.

White-faced but determined, Vicky brought out a nightgown, helped her out of her clothes.

Between contractions Helen managed to lie on the

bed. "They're coming," she cried out and pushed with all her strength.

By the time the ambulance pulled up before the house, Helen had twins, boy and a girl, born three minutes apart.

"They're here," Vicky said, vastly relieved. "Just let them lie there on your stomach. There'll be a doctor with the ambulance." Vicky raced to answer the door.

Five hours later Helen lay white and anguished in a private room at Lying-In Hospital. Twice before she had lain in a bed here, but with such joy. Helen's third son had died and the fate of the little girl, who weighed in at three pounds, was uncertain. Helen herself, following surgery, had been told there would be no more pregnancies. She lay with her eyes closed so she need not speak with Tony or her mother, sitting by her bed.

"That's right, Helen, go to sleep," her mother said. "Tony and I are going out for a quick bite. We'll be back in an hour or so."

"How can I leave now? How can you think of food when my daughter is dying?" Tony whispered angrily.

"Hush. There's an even chance that she'll live. The doctors are doing everything possible. Helen needs to sleep. Later she will need you, and then you must be fed and rested, ready to give her some real support. Now come on." Johanna herded him out of the hospital and into a quiet neighborhood restaurant.

Helen lay and let the tears slide down her face. Tony had said the other baby was dying. Now he would not have his large family and Helen would never have a daughter.

She watched dully as a nurse slid a needle into her arm, not caring whether she slept or woke.

*   *   *

In ten days Helen was released from the hospital. Tiny Sandra, whose fate was still uncertain, remained behind for around-the-clock nursing and emergency facilities. Johanna and Helen spent each day at the hospital with her. Rather alarmingly, Johanna thought, Helen showed a tendency to dwell on the loss of the boy.

Finally one day Johanna refused to describe the funeral again. "Helen, you must pull yourself together and put your mind on your living children and your husband. Just be glad little Leon lived to be baptized."

"But *why*, Mama?"

"Darling, he was too small to survive," Johanna said gently, as she had on dozens of other occasions. "Be happy that we have Sandy. In three days she'll be a month old."

"She's so small."

"The nurse told me she's almost five pounds now," Johanna pointed out. "The doctor says that's the turning point. Helen, she's going to be fine."

"And I can't even nurse her."

"You've nursed your two boys. Besides, that isn't the prime requisite of motherhood," Johanna said firmly. Tony was a nervous wreck between the baby and his wife. "I know that the doctor won't allow Joey and Henry to see their little sister, but they must not think that Sandy and Leon are all you care about now. They have to know you love them, too."

"Mama, I lost a son and my daughter's life hangs by a thread." Helen's voice rose and she bared her teeth. "Don't tell me about my duties." Her clenched fists shook and she jumped to her feet.

"You're not the only woman who's lost a baby, Helen. I had a stillborn son after a terrible delivery. And I was nearly out of my mind because at that time Bernie talked about entering the priesthood. Your father longed for a son to carry on the business. Thank God, Bernie fulfilled that wish—but for a while I hated myself because I thought I had failed your father." She leaned forward to take Helen's hand in hers. Her daughter was staring at her as though she had never seen her before. "Tony loves you, Helen. He's happy with his family. He's sad to have lost this third son, but very happy he has you and the boys—and now a little girl."

"Mama—" Helen's voice broke. "Do you think we'll keep Sandy? Do you?"

"We'll keep her," Johanna promised, pulling Helen into her arms. Her daughter sobbed against her shoulder like a small child. "The doctor is very optimistic. And we're all praying for Sandy to stay with us. You'll see, my darling, you'll have your daughter."

Three months to the day after Sandy's birth she weighed in at nine pounds and the doctor declared her healthy. Vicky gave a small party for Helen's children, Nicky and her own two. Nicky was nearly eleven, Jason almost nine. Johanna cuddled the newest grandchild in her arms while Helen cut the cake. Slices were set aside for father, grandfather and uncle.

Johanna had just arrived home when Michal appeared. She stared at him in surprise; she had not expected him for at least two hours. "Is anything wrong?"

"Good news and bad," Michal said around a kiss. "The search is over. We've located five nieces and nephews and a dozen grandnieces and -nephews. My two sisters and their husbands have died." His face saddened. "I would like to have seen them again. I remember their weddings, though I was only a boy then. There was a long space between my sisters and us three boys."

"Michal, just be glad you found so many. Does

Casimar know yet? You must write him with all the particulars.''

"He's already been notified. And in the spring," he promised, "we'll go to Warsaw for a whole month with Casimar and take Nicky with us. He can be tutored so he doesn't miss any of his schoolwork."

"In the spring," Johanna agreed, her heart pounding.

How could she take Nicky to Warsaw? How could she face Casimar? A joy to see his son, yes, but what if they reawakened the sense of sin that almost sent him out of the church once before?

Chapter 29

Johanna put out of her mind the problem of going to Poland in the spring. It was an exciting prospect to return to Warsaw with no fears of repercussions from the old days. Pilsudski, the old revolutionary, was at the head of the government. Still, Johanna was aware of the internal tensions, the increasing power of the socialists. Casimar was guarded in his optimism about the future of Poland.

Knowing that economic instability still haunted Poland, Johanna shopped extravagantly for gifts for Michal's nieces and nephews in what used to be German Poland. Michal sent lavish checks, ecstatic at finding his family again, caught up in childhood memories. Johanna herself had never met Michal's two sisters; they married and left Warsaw before her family came to the neighborhood.

While Michal was personally happy, he was concerned about the economy. It was October 1929. The stock market had been neurotic for the past several weeks. He distrusted the new President, though the general feeling was that he was a brilliant man and a great humanitarian.

Of course Hoover had been Secretary of Commerce and was considered pro-business.

After much soul-searching Michal sold his stocks and urged Bernie and Tony to do the same, "Though I suspect only those who trade heavily on margin stand in danger. They use credit to gamble on stock prices, and that's just asking for trouble. A lot of this market disorder is from panic sales to cover margin losses. The rest, of course, is price correction on overvalued stocks."

On Wednesday, October 23, prices on the New York Stock Exchange began to plummet. By the time the Stock Exchange closed at three a record number of shares had been traded, the second largest amount in history. The three radio networks reported devastating drops in prices. Even the top companies—General Motors, Kennecott Copper, Sinclair Oil—had dropped.

Driving to his office downtown Michal saw the crowds gathering before the brokerage houses—not wealthy stockholders, he judged, but clerks, shopkeepers, waiters, housemaids, mechanics.

At mid-morning Bernie arrived for a business conference. He looked tired and stern. "Bernie, you aren't tied up in the market?" Michal asked sharply.

"No, but Vicky's father was caught. He's a proud man. He had to fight himself to call us, I know. I wired him four thousand to keep him from being sold out. It's not going to get better, is it?"

"I doubt it, Bernie."

Marya, Michal's secretary, returned from lunch to report that police had cordoned off the entrance to Wall Street from Broadway. "Hundreds of police were moving out all through the financial district. I heard somebody ask why they were there. A policeman said, 'To make sure there's no trouble.'"

Word circulated through the offices of American-

International and reached Michal that trading was up again. From the elated faces of a number of his employees Michal realized most of them were embroiled in margin buying and some had been able to cover themselves. Yet he felt calamity coming. His heart ached for them.

The radio news that evening reported on a joint statement by thirty-five representatives of the largest wire house on Wall Street. They insisted that the market was "fundamentally sound" and reported to the American public, "The worst has passed."

At dinner Johanna also wanted to discuss the stock market. "Melissa was caught short this morning. When I saw her standing there with that brown envelope in her hand and a look of panic in her eyes, I knew she'd received a margin call."

"Melissa?" He stared at Johanna in shock. "After all she's heard in this house on the subject?"

"Michal, people look around and see others making fortunes. They can't help wanting to do the same."

"You covered for her?"

Johanna nodded. "It was only a few hundred and she'll pay me from her wages on a schedule. What's happening on the market won't affect the business, will it?"

"We're not sold over the counter, but business in general is bound to be affected. But don't worry. We can sail through anything without hurting much."

On Friday evening Vicky gave a family dinner party. Jason's ninth birthday had been celebrated at a children's party earlier in the week, but nine was deemed old enough for an evening with the grownups.

Of the children only Jason and Nicky would be present tonight. Jason would feel very important, Vicky told herself. It pleased her that Jason and Lucy looked so much alike. No one ever suspected they were half-siblings.

Vicky dressed for dinner with one eye on the clock. Bernie should have been home forty minutes ago, she thought uneasily. She suspected he had stayed at the office to talk with his father about the state of the stock market. Both were anxious despite—or because of—the unprecedented press conference yesterday afternoon by Thomas Lamont of the House of Morgan. Lamont reported that none of the brokerage houses was in difficulty, that all margins were being met satisfactorily. Wall Street was optimistic.

"Mama," Jason called from outside the bedroom door. "When will Nicky be here?"

"Soon, darling," she promised. "Go downstairs and practice piano till he comes."

"Do I have to?"

"You have to," she said firmly. "Grandma is expecting to hear your new piece after dinner."

"Can I listen to *Amos 'n' Andy*?"

"It won't be on until seven o'clock." She hesitated. "Practice till seven and then you can listen until people start to arrive. Are you all dressed? Hands and nails clean?"

"Mrs. Greene said I'm fine." Jason's voice ebbed away as he hurried down to the music room.

"Where are you racing so fast, young man?" Bernie's approaching voice demanded in high good humor.

"To practice my music and then hear *Amos 'n' Andy*."

Vicky turned to the door with a welcoming smile. "You don't have too long to get dressed." He looked tired. While none of the Raisas had much money in the market, what happened on Wall Street affected all business. He'd been so sympathetic about helping her father, she thought tenderly. Her husband was a compassionate man. "I've laid out your clothes for you."

"I'll be ready," he promised and grinned. "How does Jason feel about having two birthday cakes?"

"Great. He can't wait till Nicky gets here so he can crow."

Maybe tonight, when Bernie was feeling mellow after the party, she'd talk to him about going back to work. She tried to find satisfaction in volunteer work, but she had no patience with all the little egos that had to be coddled, the inefficiency and lack of real commitment. She yearned for a challenge. Listening to Bernie, who could be so fascinated by some project in the firm, made her eager to feel that same kind of satisfaction.

"You invited Victor and Caroline, didn't you?"

"Yes, of course. All the uncles and aunts will be here."

"Good. I saw Tony this morning. He was upset about the state of the market. Tony's afraid his uncle is deeply committed."

Bernie disappeared into the bathroom. A moment later the shower beat into the tub. Downstairs piano practice had ceased; Jason would be sitting on the floor before the radio.

Within twenty minutes Bernie was dressed and at the door to admit Helen and Tony. Vicky hurried out from last-minute consultation with the cook. While it was fashionable these days to serve only a few courses in deference to the new fad for thinness, Vicky always catered to the men of the family, who enjoyed a lavish dinner on such occasions. In addition to her father-in-law's favorite barszez and kolduny, dinner would include bigos and stollen in addition to baked potatoes, stuffed cabbage and the two-tiered birthday cake.

"Helen, I adore your dress," Vicky said. Her eyes swept over the simple turquoise shift with a matching jacket.

"I went on a spree again," Helen sighed. "I couldn't resist the new winter clothes."

"Tony, where did you buy that perfect shirt?" Bernie said with a twinkle. "And I'll just bet those precious cuff links are from Tiffany's."

"The shirt's very exclusive—Sears, Roebuck," Tony boasted, "and the cuff links came from the five-dollar tray at Woolworth's."

"All right," Vicky laughed. "No more talk of clothes. Helen and I only spend so much time on clothes out of boredom. What's happening out there in the world today?"

They strolled into the living room to talk about construction of what was to be called the Empire State Building.

"It may be a hole in the ground right now, but soon it's going to be the tallest building in the world," Helen said.

"Nobody here is going to be upset if I bring out a bottle of champagne?" Bernie glanced about the room.

"Am I having some too?" Jason demanded from the doorway. The presence of an uncle and aunt had won over *Amos 'n' Andy*.

"Certainly not," Bernie said sternly. "Drinking champagne is against the law."

"You do it."

"I am old enough to judge the law. You are not, but merely copying me and seeking a treat. When you have learned why to do things you too may drink champagne."

While they were toasting Jason's birthday the other guests arrived almost on one another's heels, first Uncle Victor and Aunt Caroline, then the senior Raisas with Nicky.

The apartment rang with conviviality, but Vicky was conscious of the anxious glances that Caroline bestowed on Victor at odd moments. While he seemed in high spirits, Victor had an anxious look. Bernie had said he was heavily into the stock market. Tonight, Vicky vowed, they would not talk business at all.

"Let's all go into the music room. Jason's going to play piano for us."

Everyone settled in chairs while Jason sat down at the piano. He might not be another Paderewski, but for nine years old he played exceptionally well. In the spring he was to play in a recital of Miss Attleborough's best pupils.

Dinner was scheduled to commence after Jason played his new piece, so they went directly to the dining room. Jason and Nicky were delighted to be part of a grown-up dinner party, and they spent the evening torn between high spirits and company manners. After the cake had been cut and served, Jason and Nicky were shipped off to Jason's room, where Nicky would sleep tonight.

Despite the efforts of the women to keep the conversation casual, the men kept returning to the growing menace of Mussolini and Fascism in Italy and of Hitler and Nazism in Germany as well as the troubles on Wall Street.

"The President says the business of the country is on a sound and prosperous basis," Victor Corelli asserted.

"Victor, it's time to get out now," Michal argued, "before the bottom falls out."

The evening ended on a somber note despite Victor Corelli's blustery reminder that *The New York Times'* reports indicated a sound economy. While Vicky and Bernie prepared for the night, Vicky questioned him at length. Mama—Johanna—had privately expressed her fears that things would get much worse before they got better.

"Vicky, we're going to be fine," he assured her, switching off the bedside lamp. "And did I tell you that you look very beautiful tonight?"

"Thank you, Bernie." She allowed him to pull her close beneath the covers. "But I can't get over the fact that somebody as conservative as my father could be in serious trouble. Bernie, it was sweet of you bail him out."

"He's family," Bernie said—magic words to the Raisas. "Vicky, you're all tensed up," he scolded, "but I know how to take care of that."

Helen awoke suddenly to find that there had been a sharp drop in temperature. She'd go look in on the children, make sure they were covered. Tony was not in bed. She reached for her robe and slippers and hurried out of the room without bothering to switch on a lamp.

She guessed that she would find Tony in the kitchen having himself a cup of tea. On the rare occasions when he couldn't sleep he went out to the kitchen so as not to disturb her.

"Tony," she said softly, and he turned toward her with a start. "I woke up cold and thought I'd check on the children."

"I'll go with you." Together they went into the bedroom shared by the two boys, pulled up rumpled blankets, tucked them securely about small frames. Helen looked into the nursery where Sandy slept in her crib, the nurse only a few feet away.

Hand in hand Helen and Tony hurried through the night-chilled apartment into the comfort of their bed. "You're worrying about your uncle," Helen guessed.

Tony drew the blankets up about them. "He says he's covered. He had to cash in his life insurance policies to do it, though. I don't know what'll happen if stocks take another dive. I've never seen him so distressed."

"Tony, if he needs help, we can borrow from the trust fund."

"Uncle Victor wouldn't take help. I already offered and he was furious that I even suggested it. He's built himself up from nothing, Helen. He shined shoes on Wall

Street when he was ten. He went to City College at night and worked during the day. He put himself through law school. He's too damn proud to take. I worry about him."

"Try to sleep, Tony." Helen dropped her head onto his shoulder. "Maybe the newspapers are right. Maybe on Monday the market will show itself firm again."

In the morning Tony warned Helen that he would be holed up all weekend preparing for court on Monday. She called her mother and Vicky and persuaded them to join her in the afternoon for a visit to the Metropolitan Museum to see the new Georgia O'Keeffe painting, *Black Flower and Blue Larkspur*, which had just been put on exhibit. Afterward they would have tea at the Plaza.

After breakfast, with Tony at work in the library, Helen sat down to read the papers. Here was encouraging word from financial leaders of the country. Charles Schwab, chairman of Bethlehem Steel, said he expected prosperity to continue indefinitely.

Walter Teagle, president of Standard Oil, announced, "There has been no fundamental change in the oil industry."

Alfred Sloan, chairman of General Motors, was said to regard Thursday's drop as a healthy adjustment.

The bankers also considered the situation well in hand. On Saturday call money was available at a comfortable six percent interest. During the two-hour trading period prices fell only slightly. Still, Trinity Church next day was jammed with worshippers praying for recovery on Wall Street. Sightseeing buses toured the district from noon on, with guides declaiming that it was here that "millions of dollars were lost last Thursday." One Wall Streeter was selling six-inch strips of Thursday's ticker tape to tourists at fifty cents each.

On Sunday evening Helen managed to pry Tony away from his legal papers to go with her and Vicky and Bernie to see the new Eugene O'Neill play, *Strange Interlude*, to see why Mayor Nichols of Boston had called it obscene and refused to allow it to appear there.

Underneath the pretense that this had been a normal weekend Helen was aware, as was much of America, that the supposed recovery of the stock market after Thursday's debacle had left tragedy in its wake. The tabloids were full of lurid stories of despair and suicide. The speakeasies were mobbed with the desperate, seeking to forget their troubles.

On Monday Tony left the apartment for court with a sober comment to Helen that he hoped his uncle, usually a cautious man, could realize it was time he got out of the market, no matter how high his losses. On impulse Helen called Carla to see if she was free for lunch. As a case-worker in a social service agency Carla put in a hectic working day, though she humorously conceded her clients were not personally affected by the shenanigans on Wall Street.

"You love your work," Helen said wistfully over lunch in a Childs close to Carla's office. "It shines from you." Carla was proficient at ignoring her parents' insistence that she remove herself from such shoddy surroundings and enjoy life.

"I love it, though my mother is convinced it's an evil force that keeps me from getting married. She can't conceive of any woman who doesn't need money insisting on working.

"I gather my father is taking a beating on Wall Street."

"Is it bad?"

"Oh, I figure they won't have to sell their apartment or get rid of the servants. Papa invests in the market, but Mama's money is all in real estate."

After lunch with Carla Helen went home to the children; on Mondays Ellen was off from two until nine the following morning. After a morning in the park Joey and Henry were content to nap for an hour. While they slept she sat in the nursery with Sandy in her arms. Her tiny daughter was a never-ending miracle to her.

After she put Sandy down in her crib to sleep, Helen went downstairs to listen to the Wall Street news. It was another disastrous day, refuting predictions of improvement. Many people had spent the weekend ruminating about their stock investments and decided to dump their holdings. Prices were skidding at a perilous pace.

On Tuesday morning, despite President Hoover's insistence that industry was on a sound basis, it speedily became clear that the stock market was in a panic. Helen called her father and was shocked at the report he gave her. Somehow talking to Papa made it real. Tony was in court; she couldn't see him until tonight.

She phoned Vicky; both young women were upset about the news on the radio. Hundreds of policemen were on duty in the financial district. A reporter, his voice trembling with emotion, talked about desperate brokers, their shirts and collars torn by panic-stricken clients, moving like "shell-shocked soldiers" around the ticker tapes. The Stock Exchange's medical department was accepting patients from the police; it had become an emergency station for sufferers from shock and nervous exhaustion.

Helen switched off the radio and gazed out at the dismal rain falling over the city. She wished she had gone to the visitors' gallery at the Stock Exchange to see for herself this historical day in American history. Then she remembered that the visitors' gallery had been closed since midday Thursday.

In the afternoon she went out to a committee meeting. Several of the women expected to attend did not appear. Gloom unrelated to the weather settled over the members present. Here too the panic was taking its toll. A doctor's wife reported that her husband was up all night treating patients suffering from strokes and heart attacks brought on by staggering financial losses. A latecomer arrived with the painful news that Western Union had hired taxicabs to speed delivery of margin calls. It was the worst day in the history of the stock market.

Disregarding their agenda, the women gathered around a small radio dialing up news bulletins. Men were crying openly on Wall Street. Regardless of their religious background men and women were pouring into nearby Trinity Church to pray. At this hour Wall Street was a solid block of distraught men and women from Broadway to the river. Shortly before six a reporter announced that the market had lost ten billion dollars.

Helen arrived home a few minutes past six to be told that Tony was tied up with a client and wouldn't be home until seven-thirty or eight. As she started upstairs the phone rang. "Hello?"

"Helen?" It was Caroline, very agitated.

"Yes, Aunt Caroline."

"I called Tony's office and he was in court. I tried again just now and there's no answer—"

"He's out with a client. Can I help?"

"Helen, I'm terrified." Her voice cracked. "Victor called me about four o'clock. He was babbling. He said he'd lost everything. He even cashed in his life insurance. He said we'd have to move out of the apartment—"

"Where is he now?"

"He came home about five minutes ago and locked himself in the bedroom. He won't let me in. He keeps saying he has to kill himself. There's nothing left from his whole lifetime of work. He keeps saying it over and over again—"

"I'll be right there," Helen promised. She didn't

know where Tony was. *Call Papa.* "Talk to him through the door. Tell him you love him. Ask him to marry you. Just keep his attention."

"I'll try. But hurry—oh God, please hurry."

Chapter 30

Helen dialed her father's office, praying that he was anywhere but on the way home. She knew that Josip always picked him up at the office with the car.

"Answer," she whispered to herself. "Please answer." The switchboard would be closed; she had dialed his private line.

"Mr. Raisa's office."

"Is my father there, Marya?"

"He's in conference, Miss Helen." All at once Helen remembered talking to her like this when she phoned about Leon's arrest. It seemed a million years ago rather than only eight. "They should be finished in half an hour."

"This is an emergency. Please get him to the phone." She could feel her heart pounding. In less than one minute Michal was there, sounding frightened. Helen had never before hauled him out of a meeting. When he had heard her out he was somewhat relieved. His imaginings had been far worse.

"I'll meet you at Victor's apartment," he said briskly.

"Josip is downstairs waiting with the car. Don't panic, darling."

Within ten minutes she was in the elevator of Victor's building. He and Caroline had lived on the eleventh floor here for twenty-two years. The elevator slid to a stop and she hurried down the carpeted hall to Corelli's door. She rang the bell and waited.

Caroline, white-faced and trembling, opened the door. "He's still locked in the bedroom. He just keeps on saying that he can't go on, that he wants to die—"

"What kind of lock is it on the bedroom door?" Victor's agonized mutterings were clearly audible in the living room.

"It's just an ordinary door. It locks by a key on the other side."

"I can't go on. It's too late. I can't go on. I have to jump. I have to do it—" Victor's almost incoherent words sent ice through Helen.

"Get a screwdriver," Helen commanded her hostess. "We'll try to knock the key from the door. And bring me a sheet of newspaper to slide under the door first to catch the key when it falls."

In a fury of frustration at the delay Helen waited by the door; Victor was unaware of her presence. Caroline rushed to her side with screwdriver and a sheet of the morning newspaper. Helen took the newspaper and slid it under the door.

"Talk to him," she whispered. "We don't want him to notice what we're doing."

"I'll try, but it doesn't help," Caroline stammered.

"Well, don't give up. Talk some more."

"Victor! Victor, listen to me." Caroline pressed her hands against the door. "I love you. I've always loved you. Who cares about the money. Let's get married. We can live anywhere, Victor, as long as we have each other. It'll be all right. Victor, please——'' Her voice broke.

The doorbell rang.

"There's Papa," she whispered. "I'll go let him in. Keep talking.''

Moments later her father dropped to one knee and reached for the screwdriver. "Let me do that, Helen.''

"Victor, please answer me. Is this all I mean to you? After all these years you turn your back. Victor, open the door and talk to me.''

"We'll get the key," Michal said with taut calm—— "There!" He cautiously pulled the newspaper from under the door. "Stand back.'' Michal unlocked the door.

Victor heard the door open. He stared wild-eyed at the three of them and lunged for the French windows. Michal charged him, but Caroline launched herself into a flying tackle, caught his waist and pulled him to the floor. Michal helped them both up and shepherded Victor to a chair far from the outside wall.

"Why did you stop me? It's all gone—everything's gone. I can't start all over again. I'm sixty-one years old.''

"Victor, you can't do this to me.'' Caroline was determined to bring him back to sanity. "What kind of a man are you to leave me alone after twenty-two years? No security, no insurance, no nothing. You can't do this to me, Victor.''

His eyes grew less wild and then he fell sobbing into her arms. "Victor, all I want is you, not the money, just you, darling.''

In the library of the Raisa house Johanna and Michal, their two children and their spouses gathered tensely around the radio. It was the night of October twenty-ninth. Estimates of the number of Americans affected by the crash ran from one million to three million. Many of those were reduced to destitution.

"It's tragic," Michal sighed, "that so many lives could be devastated in the course of a few days. The problem is that everyone—poor housewives and janitors, bankers and politicians—was speculating. They all got caught. We're on our way to being a nation of poor people."

"Did you tell Mama your news?" Bernie asked. Johanna turned to Michal.

"I was approached by the remaining members of the firm with an offer to sell. I think we'll toast my announcement in champagne. As of tomorrow, when Henderson completes all the paper work, American-International will be wholly owned by the family."

"Michal!" Johanna rose and threw her arms about him. "Bernie, you go for the champagne. This is wonderful. A company for Nicky, Jason, Joey and Henry to carry on along with Bernie."

"What about Lucy and Sandy?" Vicky protested. "They may want to go into the business some day." Johanna intercepted the secret look between Vicky and Helen. She suspected that both her daughter and her daughter-in-law were restless in their domestic lives. Both had worked for a living before their marriages. Afternoon teas and committees provided little challenge.

"There'll be a place for them," Michal insisted gallantly, "when the time comes." He spoke jovially and the three men smiled indulgently.

Johanna cast them an indignant look. Helen drawled, "As what? A secretary and a file clerk?"

In the following days desperate efforts were made to show faith in the United States economy. William Wrigley Jr. announced that he was buying stocks, as did Samuel

Insull. John D. Rockefeller Sr. said, "My son and I have for some days past been purchasing sound common stock." The Assistant Secretary of Commerce went on record as declaring that business was sound and only four percent of the families in the country were affected by the crash. The Stock Exchange would remain closed, however until Monday, November fourth, and then close again on Tuesday, Election Day.

Tony and his uncle were still partners; only Victor's private life was affected by his troubles. Caroline, long since retired, would go back to work at Corelli & Weinstein. They would move into a smaller apartment in the Bronx; the servants had been dismissed. All over America, Johanna thought unhappily, domestics were being thrown out of work as a result of the crash.

On Monday morning Helen and Tony stood up as witnesses at the ceremony that made Victor and Caroline man and wife. Victor said it was Caroline's proposal that really saved his life. Johanna gave a wedding dinner for the couple. Tears of pleasure filled her eyes when Helen hugged her and said she had never felt so close to her family and so proud of them all.

Johanna and Michal listened to the election returns on the radio Tuesday night. They were disenchanted with the performance of Mayor Walker. As a councilman Tony was always in conflict with the mayor, frustrated at the graft and corruption that permeated the city.

Johanna, Helen and Vicky had joined their men at the polls this morning to vote against Walker and for Fiorello La Guardia, a liberal Republican Congressman. Tony was convinced that La Guardia was just the kind of reformer New York City needed.

"Tony, I don't think your boy is going to make it,"

Michal said sadly about an hour before midnight. "The voters are going to put Walker back into office."

"They're making a terrible mistake."

"I think this means Tony should move on to state politics," Helen said. "He can't work effectively in opposition to the mayor."

"Not just yet," Michal said. Johanna nodded agreement, surprising the others; the senior members of the family had been talking for months about Tony and the state Assembly. "The country is in a bad state now, and the hackles at the back of my neck warn me it's going to be worse. Sit out the next primaries, Tony," Michal urged. "Bide your time."

The crash accelerated the growing economic crisis in Germany and pushed Hitler closer to high political office. By the end of the year more than two and a half million Germans were out of jobs. Banks were offering eight and three quarters percent interest on three-month deposits. Businesses were paying as high as sixteen percent for short-term loans; personal loans went as high as twenty-five percent.

At home steel production fell and orders for cars dropped drastically. To make matters worse, cash-strapped citizens dumped and glutted the used-car market. Radios, recently a fast-selling item, dropped off. Even speakeasy prices dropped. The Department of Labor in Washington predicted full employment in 1930. The public hooted.

Everywhere in the nation economies were being sought. Hotels offered rooms below operating costs and removed telephones to conserve a few cents a month. Electric clocks were disconnected to save on current. Bethelehem Steel fired six thousand workers and evicted them from company houses. The houses were torn down to cut down property taxes.

In New York the favorite diversion—it was free—was to line up and watch them build the Empire State Building. With the unemployment that was hitting the city and all of the nation the Empire State Building had thousands of sidewalk superintendents each week.

When 1930 arrived the Secretary of the Treasury told Americans to expect "a revival of activity in the spring." In March Hoover assured them that unemployment would be back to normal within sixty days, but a shocking number of Americans were fighting to keep a roof over their heads and food on their tables.

That year J.P. Morgan launched his new four-million-dollar yacht, the most expensive ever built. It included two separate sets of living quarters for Morgan, a lounge with an open fireplace and an elevator. It also provided employment for a crew of fifty-eight. While Morgan's business ventures showed a decrease in profits, he could console himself that he would pay no income tax this year.

Johanna listened with increasing anxiety to all the advice from the so-called leaders of industry, none of whom seemed to understand what epidemic unemployment meant to the average American family. Andrew Mellon said, "Liquidate labor, liquidate stock, liquidate the farmers." He was convinced that the country would recover automatically, as in previous depressions.

On a Saturday morning late in March Nicky went off with Jason, Lucy and Vicky to skate in Central Park. Johanna sat in front of a roaring fire in the library fireplace and sipped at one of her endless cups of tea while she read the *Times*. It had come to the point that she sat down with the papers each day with a sense of trepidation. The news seemed endlessly bad.

She looked up at sounds in the hall. Michal had come home early. "Michal," she called, "come into the library."

Looking tired and glum, Michal came into the room.

"Georgia's bringing me a cup of coffee," he said before she could ring.

"Cold out?" she asked. Michal worked harder than ever lately. Many of his workers were in dire financial straits, and he worked late analyzing their finances and advising them.

"Cold but crisp." He dropped into a tufted leather chair across from her own. "We ought to get out and walk on a morning like this." He forced a smile. "I haven't read the paper yet. Anything special?"

"Hoover came out with another of his asinine statements about how the recession is passing and how employment has improved. 'Only twelve states are in trouble,' " she quoted acidly. "He *alleges* that the worst effect of the stock market crash will be over in sixty days."

"I wish I could believe him, but I'm more inclined to believe Senator Wagner. He says the President is just trying to divert attention from the facts."

"Do you think this plan to cut personal and corporate income taxes will help the situation?" Johanna asked.

"Do you?"

"No." It pleased Johanna that most of the time Michal and she were so in harmony in their political thinking.

"Maybe the average family will have an extra six dollars a year to spend," Michal said contemptously. "What good will that do?"

"Michal, what's happening with the business?" Johanna asked after a moment. "Are we in trouble?"

"We're not making any money, and if things don't improve soon we'll start to lose. We can take that for a while, but I'm worried about the staff. I told them today that I was neither hiring nor firing, but the payroll can't possibly stay as high as it was. The price of job security is a pay reduction for everyone. I have stopped drawing my salary, but Bernie can't afford to, though of course he's taking his share of the cut.''

"Well, we can certainly stand to give up a little income. If things get tight we can always sell some real estate.''

"This is a bad time to sell. Prices are at rock bottom.''

"Still, the business comes first. For that matter Bernie and Vicky can come live here if we can't afford to pay them. We'll all be okay in the end if the Bank of America doesn't go bust.''

"And even then we'll be okay as long as the Penn Mutual is," Michal agreed.

"We can live on insurance and trust funds. Can the business make it, though?''

"We'll have to hope so, but even if it doesn't, we're lucky, Johanna." Michal stared into the fire. "We're in no real danger.''

As the Depression deepened in the following months, Johanna threw herself into relief work, drawing Helen and Vicky along with her. While the children had no recall of anything other than comfortable living, she still remembered the agony of the mill closing in Fall River. Hela's baby had died of poverty as much as tuberculosis. Across America millions of families were suddenly desperately poor.

Relief agencies were unable to cope with the level of unemployment that had taken hold of the nation. New York City boasted that its relief payments were more than in most cities, yet what could a family do with $2.39 a week? In two Texas cities blacks were refused relief. In the miserable winter of 1930–31 Detroit was forced by lack of funds to drop a third of its needy families from the relief rolls. Michal returned from a business trip in St.

Louis in despair. He had seen children searching for food in the city dumps.

"Never have we seen it this bad," he told Johanna on his return from St. Louis. "At our worst periods we were never hungry."

"In Poland the peasants knew hunger," Johanna said, "but never did I expect to see so much of it in America."

Chapter 31

Helen and Vicky emerged from a matinee performance of the recently opened Elmer Rice play *Counsellor-at-Law* and headed for the nearest automat for coffee. With trays in hand and nickels in readiness they picked up coffee and spice cake and found a table.

For a few minutes they were engrossed in discussion of the play. "And for a couple of hours," Helen summed up, "we could forget about bread lines and soup kitchens and evictions."

"Bernie's pretty upset about the bank closings." Vicky's face was suddenly less vivacious. "Three hundred and five last month and already five hundred so far this month. He says government bonds are selling at a discount."

"Thank God the Raisa fortune is secure." Helen hesitated. "So far."

Vicky frowned. "Last night I tried to talk to Bernie about going back to work. We all know how hard it is to find a job, but with all the people Bernie knows I figured I could come up with something. I was a damned efficient secretary before I married him." She smiled wryly. "Bernie pointed out that it would not be right for me to take a job from somebody who really needed it. That was the end of that idea."

"We put in a lot of effort with the charities. We work almost as hard as Carla." But she never felt the kind of satisfaction Carla felt, she thought. Helen had been struggling alone with a possibility that she was sure would shock everyone she knew.

"I think next week I'm going to start a free baby-sitting service for working women," Vicky decided. "I'll look after them myself. No, come to think of it, I won't have to. Mrs. Greene and Ellie know lots of women who will come for carfare and a good lunch."

"I know." Helen grimaced. "Mama has a whole string of them. You pay carfare and they walk. You double the carfare and they still walk. You double the carfare and send a car, and they ask you to give them more carfare and not send the car. Then they walk. It drives Mama crazy."

"I asked Tony how I could help the economy and he said, 'Pay someone to do something.' I never lift a finger anymore, but no one likes me for it. It's so discouraging." Vicky sniffed. "I can baby-sit free, though. Big apartment, lots of servants, park handy—why not?"

Helen was acutely conscious of the shabbiness around them and of the envious and resentful looks she and Vicky so often received. It was ridiculous, but sometimes those looks, justified or not, made her feel defensive. Helen was finding her self-esteem in danger and was seeking a way to restore it.

"Vicky, would you think I was crazy if I said I'd like to go to law school?"

Vicky thought for a moment. "No, why should I?"

"Well, it's a lot of work; first a B.A. and then law

school. Besides, plenty of people would say I should stay home with the children.''

"Oh, phooey. You don't have enough to do or you wouldn't be thinking about it. What's going to happen, your house will get dirty? The kids won't eat right? They'll forget what their mama looks like? Your husband will have to look elsewhere for companionship? I hardly think so. Why shouldn't you go back to school?''

"I don't know, but I have a feeling Tony isn't going to like the idea.''

"I have a feeling you're right, so here's what I'd do if I were you. Figure out where you want to go; pick two or three so you're sure you can get in somewhere you like. Find out how much it will cost. Then decide how much time you can afford to be out of the house for classes, library work, science labs and so forth. Don't forget commuting time, it's a big item. That tells you how many courses a semester you can take and how soon you can get your degree. Then it's time to talk to Tony, when you have facts at your fingertips.''

"Good heavens. Where did you come up with all that?''

"I'm a practicing feminist, remember? I know six married women in college, and that's the tested formula for getting your husband to go along. It's important to make him understand exactly what to expect and to consult him about your schedule. Generally you start with a light load, one or two courses. That lets you test the academic waters and lets him get used to the idea. A good man like Tony is bound to start cheering for you pretty soon. They always do if they love their wives.''

"That's more or less what I thought, that Tony would just need to get used to the idea. It's the law school part that I think will really get under his skin.''

"You've never talked about law school before.''

"I've thought about it, but it always seemed clear out of reach. Before I married Tony I was always at loose ends. I didn't know what I wanted to do with my life. That's why I liked Leon so much. He never got after me to settle down. I envied Bernie because once he started to grow up he was sure he wanted to go into business with Papa. Of course it never occurred to anyone that I might want to work for Papa too; not even to me."

"And then you got married and had children and that was supposed to be enough." Vicky nodded wisely. "A lot of women are dissatisfied with that. Ask a man how he'd like to be cooped up in the house with the kids all day and he gives you a blank look."

"Maybe it is enough for some women, but not for me. I know what I want to do instead. I want to offer free legal services to the poor. I plan to join the Legal Aid Society. There is no limit to the services they can use."

"Honey, don't be surprised if Tony's upset at first. He has such a passion for home and family. Let me know if you need help."

"Was Bernie shocked when you talked about going back to work?"

"He stared at me as though he'd never really seen me before," Vicky chuckled. "I keep wondering what his reaction would have been if the economy were sound. As it is, of course, I can't take a job from somebody who needs it."

"Some people think it's obscene to throw money around in the face of what's happening. They can't get over how Barbara Hutton's debut at that supper dance at the Ritz-Carlton last year cost sixty thousand dollars. Do they want the Ritz to close and put its people on the breadlines? They could have spent the same amount on a necklace or something. No one but a jeweler would have benefited and it would never have been noticed. Spread some money around where it's needed and they hate you for it."

"People look at us, with our big apartments and servants and cars," Helen said unhappily, "and they fill with resentment. It never occurs to them that the Raisas and Corellis employ fifteen servants who have no other hope of finding jobs. And somebody has to buy cars and clothes and steaks or no one will have a job long."

"Speaking of jobs, I know a dozen working widows with kids at the Polish-American Club. If Bernie says we can afford it I'm going to fill the whole apartment with poor Polish kids and lunch-and-carfare ladies to look after them. Think how they'll all eat. It makes me feel good to think about it."

"I'll have to talk to Tony pretty soon. I'm bursting with it now that I've actually made up my mind to go back to school. Want to tour Manhattan? This is a list of every college on the island that admits women. Let's go get some catalogs."

"I'm ready," Vicky said.

Dinner in the Corelli household was unfashionably early so that Joey and Henry could sit down to dinner with their parents. Before dinner Helen and Tony visited Sandy in the nursery until it was time for Selma to bathe her and put her to bed. Tony tried to avoid evening meetings that conflicted with these rituals.

It was three weeks after Helen's conversation with Vicky. When dinner was over and the two boys off to prepare for bed under the firm and loving care of Selma, Helen strolled with Tony into the library, which Tony used as an office. All through dinner she had been preparing herself for this conversation.

For relaxation, Tony insisted, there was nothing like *Amos 'n' Andy*. Helen sat quietly beside him on the sofa, shoes off and feet crossed before her, for the thirty minutes of the program. Tonight Tony would be in all evening.

"Good program," Tony grunted as he switched off the radio. He leaned back with an air of satisfaction. "I met a man today who I think is going to be the next President of the United States."

"Who?" Helen demanded.

"His name is Franklin Roosevelt."

"The governor?"

"He ran for vice president back in 1920. I think he's the kind of leader the country needs in these times, and there are already definite signs that he means to run." Tony reached for Helen's hand. "If Roosevelt runs for President in '32, then I'll run for the Assembly in the next primaries."

"It'll be wonderful to see you move up into state politics. You know the family will be behind you all the way." Helen hesitated. "There's something special I'd like to do, too, Tony. I want to go to college. I want to get my B.A. first," she rattled, "before I pick a law school. I think if I really work at it I can do it in three years—"

"Honey, what about the children?"

"Tony, as it is I don't see much more of them than you do. I'll give up all those committees. I'll have to be home a lot studying, and classes won't take more than eighteen or twenty hours a week."

"Helen, you have a home and children. I don't understand any of this—and what was that about law school?" He looked astonished; it had just sunk in.

Thinking of Vicky's acid remark, Helen said, "Tony, how would you like to stay home all day? Spend your time with menus, servants, shopping lists and bored housewives?" Hah! Vicky was right. He gave her a blank look. "That's why I want to go to law school."

"We'll think about it," Tony hedged.

"Why do we have to think about it? The admissions director at Barnard says I can start next semester."

The light knock at the door startled both of them. "Come in."

In coat and hat Selma walked into the library. Normally she left at seven. She'd stayed late tonight.

"I think Joey may be coming down with a cold. He has no fever, but he seems kind of warm. You'll look in on him before you go to bed?"

"I always do. Is there something going around?"

"I haven't heard of anything. It's probably just a cold, but we'll keep an eye out. Good night to you both," Selma smiled. "See you in the morning."

"Now do you understand how wrong it would be for you to go back to school?" Tony said gently. "Suppose one of the children were sick and you had an important exam at school?"

"I'd do what I do now when one of the children is sick. I call home once an hour and I stay in all evening to spell Selma. Tony, I can be a good wife and mother and still get an education. We're living in the twentieth century."

"You've been talking to Vicky," Tony surmised, frowning. "Bernie said she had some bee in her bonnet about going back to work. He convinced her that it was ridiculous."

"Vicky's ideas are not ridiculous. However, Vicky has nothing to do my wanting go back to school. I've been thinking about it for months. I don't like fund-raising and I'm sick of going to meetings. As a lawyer I could donate my services. Think of the tax deduction we'd get. I knew a long time ago that I expected more out of life than raising children, supervising servants and shopping.

"By the way, Bernie has not convinced Vicky that going back to work is ridiculous—only that this is a bad time. And wait till you hear what she has cooked up instead." Helen grinned. "Seriously, though, Tony. I want to do this."

"Think about it for another few weeks," Tony stalled. "You'll realize that this isn't the time of life for you to return to school."

"When?" Helen demanded. "When will be the time? When we're grandparents? Or when I was twenty-five and you couldn't wait to get married?"

"I have to make a phone call." Tony rose and bolted for the door. "I forgot about calling your father earlier."

Tony wasn't getting off the hook so easily, Helen promised herself. If he kept this up she'd register first and talk later. How could Tony be so narrow-minded?

On Nicky's thirteenth birthday, Armistice Day 1931, Johanna invited Helen, Tony, Bernie, Vicky and Jason to dinner at the Raisa house. Nicky and Jason were almost like brothers, she thought with sentimental pleasure. As part of Nicky's birthday present Michal had promised to take the two boys to the Army-Navy football game at Yankee Stadium on December twelfth.

After dinner and the ceremony of the birthday cake Nicky and Jason went to the old nursery, now the playroom, to listen to the radio. The grownups settled themselves in the library, which had long ago become the family sitting room. Johanna sensed Helen's restlessness and wondered what was bothering her. Bernie always came directly to her with his problems; Helen fretted in solitude.

Politics immediately took over the conversation. "All right, so Hoover's cut his own salary by twenty percent," Tony conceded, "and he's cutting government spending. But this isn't the time to cut, with thirteen million people out of work."

"Hoover's setting up public works programs," Michal

pointed out. "Not that I hold any brief for Hoover, but I have to admit the man's trying to ease the situation."

"It's not just America that's in trouble now," Johanna pointed out somberly. "Casimar writes that all of Europe is in deep trouble."

"When the Democratic Convention is held next summer, I'd take any bet that Franklin Roosevelt walks away with the nomination. And on inauguration day," Tony pursued, "he'll become the next President."

"Tony, have you come to a decision about running for the Assembly?" Michal asked.

"I figure on announcing my candidacy right after the national convention. That gives me plenty of time to get on the primary ballot."

"Tony, that's wonderful." Johanna radiated delight. "Helen, aren't you excited?"

"She's more excited at the prospect of going to college," Tony growled, his eyes on the fine Aubusson rug.

"Helen, you told me nothing about going to college," Johanna scolded, but she smiled approvingly.

"Tony doesn't want me to."

"Tony, why ever not?"

"I can't see how Helen can contemplate years of school. Not just an undergraduate degree, you know, but law school. We have three children and I'll be launching a political campaign."

"Tony, Helen was not cut out for domesticity. Suppose someone had told you you had to be a butler. It's the same thing." Law school, she inwardly rejoiced.

"Tony," Helen put in, "no matter what else I do I'll campaign for you. Just let me get a couple of semesters in first."

"How can you attend class and travel with me? Would

you be able to study on the road? And how will it look in the papers? 'Mrs. Corelli, a student at Columbia . . .'?''

"It will look as if your wife has brains and gumption," Johanna snapped.

Michal spoke up after a long silence. "Tony, it seems to me you can rely on Helen to know and do her duty. That's not your problem. What is?"

Tony resented having marital discord aired this way. Goaded, he talked frankly. "I spend all day with lawyers, politicians, powerful businessmen. When I come home at night I don't want to find another lawyer, I want a wife."

Helen was near tears. "No you don't. You want a contented cow. Before we were married you used to say you wanted to make me happy. Don't you still want that?"

"Of course I do," Tony conceded, seeming overwhelmed. All at once he chuckled. Johanna saw relief suffuse Helen. "You Raisa women are a formidable team. How can I object?" His face softened as he turned to Helen. "When you're ready for the bar exam I have some tips for you."

"And I promise never to run for public office." For the first time in weeks there was a lilt in Helen's voice. "At least not against you."

Chapter 32

Johanna tried to view the world with her usual optimism, but it got harder and harder as the months rolled on and the Depression deepened. Blindness seemed to affect the rich as well as hordes of public officials.

Like Michal, she was painfully conscious of the Hooverville right across the avenue from their own house in Central Park. It was a village the homeless had thrown together out of discarded packing boxes and scrap metal. There were Hoovervilles in cities all over the U.S.

Tony and Bernie both worked hard for the veterans of the World War, who in the spring of the year streamed into Washington with their wives and children to ask for an advance on the bonus scheduled to be paid in thirteen years. As many feared, the Senate voted against the bonus. Most of the veterans left Washington, but some stayed on in another Hooverville.

Roosevelt had the nomination; the Raisas and the Corellis focused on the coming primary. All the talk at the end of July was of how General Douglas MacArthur,

Army Chief of Staff, flanked by a Major Dwight D. Eisenhower, had paraded up Pennsylvania Avenue before a lineup of infantry, tanks and machine-gunners. The troops not only drove squatters from empty government buildings but also chased women and children across the Potomac and burned the shacks where they had lived for the past month.

Shaking with rage as she read the newspaper accounts, Johanna railed at Michal about what was happening. "This is the United States, not some dictatorship in Europe. How can Hoover expect to be re-elected when he sanctions military force against unarmed private citizens?"

Michal quoted bitterly, " 'A challenge to the authority of the United States of America has been met.' Doesn't that idiot realize that the people *are* the United States of America?"

"Wait till November," Johanna said smugly. "Everyone will remember and the tide will turn. Hoover will be out on his ear."

In November Franklin Roosevelt was elected President of the United States and Tony declared his candidacy for the state Assembly. Helen was in her second semester at Barnard College.

One year later Tony was elected to the state Assembly. His opponent, also a newcomer to state politics, ran on a platform of balancing the budget by reducing the state payroll and the dole. Tony maintained that Albany's duty was to ease its citizens' lot by whatever means was at hand.

At his victory party Michal took Johanna's hand and kissed it. "You know what we're going to do, Mrs. Raisa? In the spring you and I are going to visit Warsaw."

"Michal, can we?" Johanna was radiant.

"We have no reason to fear the government," he pointed out. "It isn't entirely a pleasure trip. I had a letter from Casimar today. I figured you'd rather read it tonight after all the celebrating.'' He smiled at Tony across the room. Helen clung to her husband's arm while well-wishers shook his hand.

"Casimar suggested the trip. He wants us to visit Berlin for a few days. As you know, Poland has a security agreement with Germany. Casimar is scared to death of this man Hitler. I can go to Berlin not only as a tourist with my wife but to also discuss business. Casimar expects it will be very useful to the Polish government to have a sympathetic outsider's ideas about what's happening there.''

"When will we go?'' Johanna had not seen Casimar in fourteen years. How did he feel about her now? He was no longer quite real to her. He seemed remote and perfect, like a saint.

"Not until spring, probably early April. We'll take Nicky with us.''

"We can't take Nicky out of school,'' she protested, her heart pounding. How could she face Casimar with him? Hard enough with Michal there.

"We'll take along a tutor,'' Michal said. "I want to show him Warsaw. Our Warsaw. I want show him off to Casimar.''

"No,'' Johanna objected, "I'd worry about his missing school. Besides, Germany is far too dangerous. We've read such fearful things about what's happening there. If we took Nicky with us, then we'd have to take Jason too. Those two are almost inseparable. Two children in Hitler's Germany would be more than I could cope with.''

"All right, we'll leave Nicky home. We can go back after Hitler is out of power. We'll go first to Berlin, then on to Warsaw,'' Michal went on. "Johanna, I'm all excited. We're going home again. I'll ask Casimar to arrange for the nieces and nephews to join us in Warsaw for a visit.

It'll be a big family reunion. Are you sure we can't take the boys?" But Johanna held firm and Michal, knowing her real reason, didn't argue too hard.

On the chilly grey morning of the fourth of March Franklin D. Roosevelt was inaugurated as the thirty-second President of the United States. All the Raisas and all the Corellis gathered in the library on Fifth Avenue to listen to the inaugural address on the radio.

Gloom invested everyone but the youngest children. At four-thirty that morning the new Governor of New York, Herbert Lehman, had declared a bank holiday. Governor Horner of Illinois immediately followed suit and word was that several other states were doing the same.

At the moment, however, the broadcasters' attention was on the front lawn of the White House. A hundred thousand men, women and children gathered before the inaugural platform, trampling forty acres of park and pavement. Some sought vantage points in the winter-bare trees. At the sound of a bugle President-elect Roosevelt appeared on the arm of his son James. The Marine Band played "Hail to the Chief." Roosevelt took his place before Chief Justice Hughes and placed a hand on a Dutch Bible that had been the property of three centuries of Roosevelts. The oath was administered and then the new President began his address.

Johanna reached for Michal's hand as Roosevelt began to speak. "My friends, this is a day of national consecration. . . ."

The next night Johanna and Michal, like most of America, heard President Roosevelt proclaim that March sixth through ninth would be a national bank holiday.

Johanna began to feel excited about the trip to Europe. Marya, Michal's secretary, was making all the arrangements.

They would sail on the *Ile de France*. In Paris they would stay briefly at the Crillon before boarding the Orient Express for Munich. From Munich they would take another train north to Berlin and the elegant Hotel Adlon. Then at last they would move on to Warsaw.

Johanna and Michal boarded the *Ile de France*—huge, black-funneled, elegant—early in April. Bernie and Vicky, Tony and Helen accompanied them to the midnight sailing.

"I love the bon voyage parties on a great ocean liner," Vicky said happily. "It's great when optimism is spreading."

"There is new hope lately," Johanna agreed. Most of the banks had reopened. The Civilian Conservation Corps had just been launched as a jobs program, and the President's buoyant confidence was contagious.

Still, while Michal and she prepared to sail for Europe amid much luxury, a sizable chunk of the population of the country was destitute, hungry, homeless. Michal, drained with efforts to keep the business from disaster without firings, was determined to relax and enjoy the four weeks ahead of them.

Their suite was magnificent. The main dining room was huge. The Parisian sidewalk cafe, complete with colorful awnings, was a delight. The trip, Johanna told herself, would be a timeless period of rejuvenation for Michal and her. On board the *Ile de France* they escaped their troubles for a while.

At Cherbourg they boarded the boat-train for Paris. Johanna told Michal all about the journey on this same train with Bernie, Helen and Melissa. She brought back their excitement at being in Europe and recalled her shock the morning Casimar presented himself at their hotel, the Crillon, then as now.

Paris was exquisite and Michal seemed to relax completely. He knew the city from business trips and recalled and sought out special small restaurants. They both felt young and romantic. Michal bought Johanna perfume, flowers, trinkets. She secretly ordered him a dozen silk lawn shirts and a pair of solid gold collar stays. They never went near a church or museum. The trip would have seemed like another honeymoon except that Michal and she were both aware of the foreboding undercurrents in Europe.

On the fourth evening they left Paris. A taxi took them to the Gare de l'Est, where they were to board the famous Orient Express. They would get to Munich early the next afternoon. Johanna was much impressed by the splendor of the train. Only last year had it been fully restored as a luxury train after years of a military run between Paris, Vienna and Warsaw. Their wagons-lits were as posh as a fine hotel, with wall-to-wall carpeting, plush upholstery, crisp white linen on the beds.

The train departed from the station precisely at seven-thirty. At eight Johanna and Michal went to the dining car, hung with Genoese velvet curtains. Gobelin tapestries covered the walls. Engraved silverware and fine crystal goblets dressed each table. The food was superb.

As the train raced toward Munich the next day, Johanna could feel tension building in Michal. Like her, he had only contempt for Hitler, and his feelings for Germany were bitter. He expected nothing to come of the two business conferences in Berlin, but they were good enough cover for his appearance in the city.

Johanna and Michal changed trains in Munich but did not stay. They slept that night in a luxurious suite at the Hotel Adlon, high above Unter den Linden. In the morning they went out for their first view of Berlin. Michal and she were sharply reminded that this country was plagued by unemployment. Where America had her Hoovervilles, German thousands lived in tent camps.

Johanna was repelled by the drab stucco and brick buildings, the widespread despair. She found it chilling to see the preponderance of military uniforms. Storm troopers, Brown Shirts, flagrantly homosexual officers. Johanna shivered. Instinct warned her that the world was gearing itself for yet another war.

It was a relief to depart Berlin for Warsaw. Johanna could think of nothing but the past. Mama and Leon were gone. Casimar was a bishop; Michal was convinced he would one day be a cardinal.

It was a miracle that Michal and she could return to Warsaw without fear of imprisonment. Yet even with the new government in Poland there was much tension. Many Poles were afraid the emerging new Germany would not respect the boundary with Poland. They were right to be uneasy; since the war Poland had held a rich industrial area, once German, now coveted by the Germans.

At the Warsaw railway station Johanna and Michal emerged from the train to find Casimar waiting for them. At sixty-two he was still erect and nearly handsome. Her heart flooded with love as he pulled her into his arms for a warm greeting.

"As beautiful as ever, Johannusya."

"Casimar, are we really here?" she whispered.

"You're here," he smiled and turned again to Michal. "I wish Leon had lived to be here with us. That would be something: the four of us together again."

Casimar had arranged for them to stay at a pleasant but modest hotel only five minutes from the seminary that Raisa money had built and Casimar lived in. Only in the hotel suite would they be able to speak in privacy.

Casimar marshaled Johanna and Michal toward a waiting car. Johanna thought fleetingly of her Red Cross ambulance, then of the small house in France, so close to the battlefield, where Nicky had been conceived. Casimar was inquiring about the next generations. He did not indicate particular interest in Nicky. Nonetheless, when Casimar mentioned Nicky by name, Johanna detected special curiosity.

The three spent every hour possible together. Casimar's heavy diocesan obligations magically eased when it was known his generous brother was in town. Casimar managed to show them nearly all the changes in the last forty-four years.

Michal and she listened attentively to Casimar's reports of unrest, of fears for the future; no European country seemed willing to fight the threatening Hitler regime.

"This is not a republic," Casimar said flatly, "it is a dictatorship. I hope we're able to sign a decent treaty with Germany, but the real question is, How long will Hitler honor it?"

Casimar listened with stern attention to every small detail of their brief visit to Berlin. What they told him confirmed the suspicions of many church leaders and would be passed on.

"Pilsudski is not well," Casimar noted. "When he's gone, I don't know that things will be better. I pray still that Poland will one day be a true republic. For over two hundred years we've waited and prayed for that day."

"Do you suppose you can come to New York for a visit?" Michal said hopefully. "You've seen only Bernie and Helen. You must meet Nicky and the grandchildren."

"Leaving Poland is very difficult these days," Casimar said. "Besides, it would feel like desertion. This Hitler Youth nastiness is invading Poland," he sighed. "Even in the universities I see disturbing outbreaks of intolerance. Some student groups are even demanding quotas at the universities in imitation of the German schools. That is not what I expect of Poland."

"Tonight," Michal said, an arm about Casimar's

shoulders, "we'll go out to dinner somewhere special and forget these things. We'll remember the early days, when we were full of ideals and hopes."

"We are still full of ideals and hopes," Casimar insisted. "We mustn't let the years rob us of that. But tonight we will celebrate and feel young again."

On their third day in Warsaw Johanna and Michal met seven of his nieces and nephews who came to Warsaw for this most special occasion. At first they were in a little awe of their American relatives, but Michal managed to put them at their ease.

"Manya, you're the image of your grandmother," he would marvel. "She was married just at your age and I was in the wedding." He raved about the food, he made them all drink vodka, he gave the teenage boys cigars. No one would ever forget rich Uncle Michal.

Over dinner in a fine new café where once the Okocim had stood, Michal's nieces and nephews talked about how it had been during the war. Poland was much worse than France, they all agreed. Johanna's eyes sought out Casimar's; France—the night with Casimar—was stark in her mind.

It was not possible to forget the scenes in Berlin that spoke so bluntly of the military mood of the Hitler regime. So much for all the hard work of the student peace movement; so much for the League of Nations and postwar reconstruction.

The days and nights in Poland sped past in an aura of unreality. Casimar clung to Michal and her as though to memorize their every feature. He held both their hands while he waited with them for the train that would take them away from Warsaw.

"Casimar, try to come to America," Michal pleaded affectionately. "Try."

"I'll see what I can do," Casimar said soothingly,

but Johanna knew this was to appease Michal. Casimar would never leave while Poland was in danger, and it seemed the mother country would always be in danger.

Back in New York Johanna was pleased and flattered when Michal was summoned to Washington D.C., along with other prominent business leaders, for a conference with the President. After seeing Berlin and Warsaw she thanked God over and over for America and her freedom and security. It would take time, as Michal kept insisting, but Roosevelt would lead them out of this terrifying Depression.

Helen plugged away at her schoolwork. Her children talked shop with her; they considered going to school first a skill and then an art. "You have to know when to pay attention." . . . "Listen for your teacher's 'important' voice and you'll be okay." . . . "Never lend a whole tablet, just a couple of sheets." . . . "A pen you have to give back. A pencil, maybe not. . . ." Joey was eight, Henry seven. Sandy at four couldn't wait to start school, she was so jealous.

Vicky was up to her ears in poor Polish toddlers. Bernie had given her a budget intended for twelve children and three helpers and it had become a game to stretch it out. No one took double carfare, some brought a little food, the children all "helped."

Jason and Lucy took rather a superior air at first, but this was soon diagnosed as language snobbery and dealt with. Vicky said, "Let's just see if you can learn good Polish as fast as they learn good English."

Nicky was growing up fast. Nearly fifteen and a quick and conscientious student, he was beginning to think about selecting a university. It never ceased to worry Johanna that so few Polish students were admitted to the more prestigious colleges. She had long known about the quotas in these schools. The Raisa money and power had found Helen a place at Barnard, and this magic would certainly work for Nicky if he continued to make good grades, but he would still be part of a quota.

Early in 1934 Tony was preparing to run for re-election in the Assembly when Johanna became aware that Michal was ill. He denied it, but she knew he was fighting pain.

"Michal, don't be a little boy," she scolded. "You're going to see a doctor."

"It'll go away," he insisted. "Turn on the radio. Isn't Fred Allen on tonight?" As Johanna turned away to the radio, pain clenched Michal and paralyzed him. After that night Johanna fought futilely to persuade him to see a doctor. Now she made a habit of going in to the office in the afternoon to make sure he left early with her.

"Johanna, do you have time to come in and learn the ropes?" he asked her one Friday afternoon. "I don't mean every day or even for a whole day at a time. But I'd like to know that you're familiar with operations."

"I can come in three afternoons a week if you like." Her throat tightened with anxiety. Michal was worried about his health. "But only if you promise to see a doctor. And don't put me off any longer. If you need treatment you're going to have it."

"At the end of the month," he promised. "Right now there's too much to do. Next week I go down to Washington for another conference."

Every afternoon at two Johanna appeared at the office. Michal gave her reports to study, went over figures with her, brought Bernie in to confer with them. The company was operating at a small loss, but not enough yet to be a threat to its health. Michal, one of the most generous employers in the city, had fired no one and was keeping wages at half-pay.

Johanna enjoyed being what Bernie called part of the team, but she continued to worry about Michal. Thank God, she thought, he was seeing the doctor at the end of the month. But at the end of the month Michal dashed off to a business conference in San Francisco with a kiss and orders to set up another appointment.

Bernie went with her to see Michal off to San Francisco. On the way home in the car he said uneasily, "Mama, do you think Papa looks all right? He seems awfully tired and grey to me."

"I'm worried to death, Bernie." It was relief to say so. "He absolutely promises he'll see the doctor as soon as he gets back from San Francisco."

"He'll go," Bernie promised, "if I have to carry him screaming all the way."

In ten days Michal returned exhausted from San Francisco. He was noticeably thinner than when he had left. Johanna went cold with alarm when she saw him.

"How're you feeling?" she asked casually on the way out of Grand Central.

"A little tired," he admitted. "Long train trips do that to me. Next time I'll fly."

"You're seeing Dr. Edison at three tomorrow afternoon. I'll pick you up and go with you. You're not weaseling out."

The next afternoon Johanna sat across the desk from the physician while Michal dressed in the examination room.

"I want Michal to go into the hospital for tests." Edison showed no sign of concern. "He'll only be there for two days"—he fixed her with an owl-stare over his glasses—"but let's get them over with."

"When do you want him there?" Johanna asked evenly.

"Tomorrow morning at eleven." Edison reached for a sheet of paper and began to scribble instructions. "No sense in wasting time."

The two days in the hospital stretched into four. Michal fretted at being away from the office, though Johanna and Bernie had the business well in hand. Every evening at the hospital they had a long conference; the rest of the family was encouraged to visit in the daytime.

On the fourth day Dr. Edison's secretary called.

"Can you come in this morning at eleven?"

"I'll be there," Johanna promised.

When Johanna saw Dr. Edison, his face was grave. She clasped her hands together to stop their trembling while she sat in a chair across from him.

"Johanna, I've tried to talk to Michal about surgery, but he refuses it. I'd like you to speak to him; it's urgent."

"How urgent?"

"I'd like to operate tomorrow. I'm sorry, Johanna. Michal has cancer of the colon."

Chapter 33

Johanna had a long, hard argument with Michal about the surgery. "Michal, you're always so realistic. Why are you fighting this?"

"Will you be happier if I let him cut?"

"The whole family will be happier. So will the internist and the two oncologists we've consulted, not to mention Dr. Edison."

Michal sighed heavily. "All right," he agreed. He had all the fears of a man who had never been sick in his life. "Tell them to get it over with."

Johanna leaned forward to kiss him. "I'll go start the ball rolling. I love you, my dear."

That evening there was no business conference. The family, except for children too young to visit, gathered around Michal's hospital bed.

Nicky and Jason made him laugh for the first time in a week with a carefully rehearsed pantomime: Michal (Jason) falls ill and Johanna (Nicky) drags him to the doctor (Jason). After much headshaking the doctor (still

Jason) operates on Michal (Nicky), who springs up from
his bed of pain, wrestles the doctor to the ground, raises
his arms in triumph and takes a bow.

"You'll go to the office every day, Johanna?" Michal
asked before the nurse shooed them out of his room. "You
promise?"

"You know I will."

"What's the matter, Papa?" Bernie smiled, "you
don't trust me? I'm almost forty years old and I've worked
for you for fifteen years." His face was suffused with
affection.

"Bernie, your mother was there beside me in every
major decision in the business. Sometimes she was way
ahead of me. Always listen to her." He nodded sagely.

Johanna slept little that night. She was at the hospital
a few minutes before Michal was wheeled out of his room.
An hour later both Helen and Vicky arrived.

After what seemed an appallingly long time, six hours
and more, Dr. Edison came down to Michal's room. Johanna searched his face as he approached them; he looked
tired but relaxed and pleased.

"Everything went very well, Johanna," he told her.
"We'll keep Michal in the recovery room for a while, but
all indications are that the operation was a success."

Life was beautiful again. Johanna divided her days
between Michal's room and the office. The patient seemed
weak and frail, but Dr. Edison had warned that convales-
cence would be slow.

Johanna expected Michal to come home at the end of
two weeks, but Dr. Edison judged that he needed further
hospital care. While the surgery had been successful, he
was recuperating even more slowly than anticipated.

Each time Johanna walked into his room, Michal's
face lit up. He enjoyed the children's visits, but it was his
wife who bolstered his spirits.

The expected two weeks became four and still Dr. Edison kept Michal hospitalized. Despite her determination to be cheerful, Johanna was plagued by worry.

At the end of four weeks Michal developed a slight cold. Johanna sat beside his bed while Edison examined him, his face impassive.

"I'll start you on medication and you'll feel better soon." With a faint gesture the doctor indicated he wished to talk to Johanna in the hall.

White-faced, Johanna followed him. "What is it?"

"I'm afraid it's pneumonia." he said bluntly. "We'll do what we can, but he is very weak."

Johanna stayed at the hospital night and day. She had a room on the same floor so that she could be in constant attendance. On the third night after his visitors left, Michal grew restless. He reached out for Johanna's hand when the nurse stepped out of the room.

"Johanna, I'll talk to Leon about buying the boat," he said with an anticipatory smile. Her heart raced. "We'll build ourselves a real business. You'll see, Johannusya."

Terror assaulted her. "It'll be wonderful, Michal," she whispered, her throat tight.

"You're a wonderful wife, Johannusya," he whispered, his voice weak. "I have always loved you. I'm very tired . . ."

His hand went slack, releasing hers. "Michal? Michal?" She reached for the buzzer to summon the nurse, but she knew he was gone.

The next few days were hazy. There was a funeral and a lot of callers, but no details at all. Johanna missed Michal in a thousand ways. She clung to Nicky, who was finding it difficult to realize his father was dead.

The children worried about Nicky and her being alone in the large house, it had been Michal's pride and joy and she would not think of selling and moving into an apartment. This house was the family seat and it would remain so.

Johanna went daily to the office. She had gradually taken over personnel management and such administrative functions as purchasing supplies and supervising the maintenance staff. "It's just another kind of housekeeping," she would laugh. But joking aside, Johanna's main job was to help set major company policy.

In summer she traveled to Southampton for extended weekends. The children, including Nicky, stayed at the house for the summer with Helen in charge. She was taking no courses, but Vicky kept her baby-sitting service open. Nicky found a pretty young girlfriend a few houses away from their own and was delighted to stay at Southampton.

Johanna treasured the letter from Casimar after Michal's death. He wrote that he had just received word from the office of the secretary of state. He had been nominated to be a cardinal. Now he was waiting for official word, a *ceremoniarus* of the pope.

Casimar would be a fine cardinal. Johanna visualized his presentation to the Pope and the investiture with the cape and the red biretta.

The pontiff would place the hat upon his head, saying the words that made him a cardinal, then make the sign of the cross three times over Casimar.

In the secret consistory the Pope would close the mouth of the new cardinal as a symbol of the discretion he must follow. Then he would be given the cardinal's ring. The final act, after the formality of consulting the Sacred College, would be the opening of the mouth to symbolize the right and obligation of the new cardinal to offer opinions and to vote on matters in his domain.

How Johanna wished that Michal had lived to see Casimar so honored.

Early in July she received another letter from Casimar, confirming that he was now actually a cardinal. Because of politics in Warsaw the ceremonies she had envisioned had not taken place. Instead the investiture took place in parts on two different days.

That Saturday night in Southampton Johanna announced to the family that Casimar was a cardinal "But most of his letter was about the future of Poland," she said. "He doesn't trust the Germans an inch in spite of the so-called nonaggression pact."

"Small wonder after Germany withdrew from the disarmament conference and from the League of Nations," Tony said somberly.

"That reminds me. Just before I left town I heard that the Austrian Nazis, probably including the German Embassy, have assassinated Chancellor Dollfuss and are attempting a coup d'etat," Bernie put in. "Sounds to me like thieves falling out."

"When did that happen?" Helen demanded.

"Apparently this morning, German time. I heard it around four."

"Mom," Nicky put in, "could I be excused now?"

"You don't want dessert?" Johanna asked. Nicky adored sweets.

"Not tonight. I'm supposed to meet Holly in ten minutes. We're going to a movie."

"Go along, darling," Johanna smiled. "Enjoy the evening."

She was happy to see Nicky interested in a girl. He had grieved too hard for Michal; Johanna was getting seriously worried when he met Holly and started to get back to normal.

The children would walk downtown to the theater in daylight and Holly's parents would send a car to pick them up.

* * *

Nicky hurried up to his room to change into his rubber-soled shoes for walking on the beach. Holly said if he came over early they could take a detour down the beach and still get to the theater on time. She was dying to see Clark Gable and Claudette Colbert in *It Happened One Night*.

Holly sure was pretty, he decided while he tied his shoelaces. He had never had a real date before he met her, but he was going to be sixteen in November; he was old enough. He paused to inspect his face in the mirror, relieved to see that his skin was still clear. Chuck kept saying if you didn't run around with girls and do things your face would break out, but his never had.

He raced downstairs and out into the sunny summer evening, glad Mom always insisted on an early dinner because of the kids. Holly's folks went to their club on Saturday nights and Holly usually ate dinner with the servants, though she said her mother would be livid if she knew. "I just don't understand her attitude," she sighed. "Anybody I don't want to eat with I don't want to be around at all. Our servants are very nice people."

Holly was sitting out on the verandah when he arrived. He felt sorry for Holly. Her folks were always running off to parties. In New York they were in café society. Funny; Holly seemed proud of that.

"I was afraid you'd be late, but you're not," Holly said approvingly. "Want a cigarette?" She reached for a pack of Lucky Strikes beside her.

"No thanks, I don't smoke."

"I'd better run up for a sweater. Sometimes it's cool at night."

"Yeah." He cleared his throat. When Holly looked at him like that, leaning over so that he could see right down the neck of her dress, he felt funny. He wondered if she did it on purpose. "We'd better watch the time if we're going to be at the theater when the picture starts."

"Want a drink before we go?" She winked. "I've got the key to the liquor closet. I stole the spare and had it copied. You can have anything you like."

He'd never before met a girl like Holly, who smoked and drank, but the guys at school talked about the kind who did, and he didn't think he was old enough to handle one.

"I don't drink," he said uncomfortably, "except at celebrations."

"Why don't you?" Holly stared at him as though she'd never known a boy who didn't drink. She moved in close to him and put a hand on his chest. "Are you afraid you'll get drunk?"

"I don't like it much," he said honestly, then crumpled before her contempt. "Besides, my father just died."

"Oh, nuts. You're not going to be any fun at all. Besides, what are you so upset about? He wasn't even your real father."

"What are you talking about?" Nicky began to wish he had never met Holly.

"I mean he wasn't your real father. Everybody knows that. I heard my parents talk about it. My father was one of your father's customers long before we were born. My father said your mother came home from France pregnant as hell. You were born six months after she got back from playing at Red Cross. I guess Mr. Raisa went along so as not to create a scandal." Holly shrugged. "But don't give me that goofy line about mourning for your father."

"I don't think I want to take you to the pictures after all," Nicky said tightly. "I don't think I ever want to see you again."

*   *   *

Johanna sat alone on the verandah in the comfortable quiet of the evening. With the ocean bathed in silver before her she could almost feel Michal beside her.

Jason was in the living room listening to the radio and the younger children were in bed. Their parents had gone off to a benefit at the Parrish Art Museum. Nicky must be feeling very grown up now that he was seeing a girl, she thought.

Looking at the children made her realize how the years were flying past. It was 1933. Jason would be fourteen in October and Lucy nine in February. In June Joey had turned nine and Henry eight. Sandy had just passed her fifth birthday.

The moon cast a pale gold glow over the beach. It hung over the right shoulder of the young man walking up the water's edge. Johanna was not at first sure who it was. Then the tall slim figure made a characteristic shoulder movement and she realized it was Nicky. Coming home early on a Saturday night?

"You're looking mighty handsome this evening," she said. Nicky walked up on the verandah, his shoulders drooping, his face shadowed. "Did you enjoy the movie?"

"I didn't go," he said shortly, reaching for the screen door.

"Nicky, sit out here with me for a few minutes."

"I'm tired." He kept his face averted. "I'd like to go up to bed."

"Five minutes," she insisted.

"All right." He sounded hostile and sullen.

"Was the theater packed by the time you arrived?"

"I tell you I didn't go. I've been walking on the beach."

"Nicky, what's the matter?"

"I had a fight with Holly," he said accusingly.

"You'll make up tomorrow."

"I never want to see her again, not after what she said."

"What did Holly say?"

"She said Dad wasn't my real father. She said—she said everybody knew I was born six months after you came back from France." Michal had always enjoyed telling Nicky and the grandchildren about her months in France during the war. He never mentioned dates, though. "Mom, it isn't true, is it?"

Johanna hesitated. She had never dreamed there was any gossip about her and Nicky. Michal was gone. What to tell the boy?

"Mom?" Nicky began to sound strident.

"You were born not six but seven months after I returned from France. Always remember, Michal Raisa considered you his own son. You were the apple of his eye. But no, he was not your natural father." Her voice was deep with emotion.

"He really wasn't my father? But I look just like him."

"You are a Raisa. Please, Nicky, let me tell you the whole story. I was on a battlefield in France trying to stay ahead of the Germans. I was driving an ambulance. I found Casimar praying over a dying soldier. Together we fled and took refuge in a deserted house. We didn't know if we would live through the night.

"Nicky, I learned to love Michal through the years and no husband and wife could be closer. But before I was married I loved Casimar. I married Michal because Casimar insisted. I think now that Casimar had private reasons other than my reputation. He wanted me well out of reach. It was a choice for him between priesthood and me—and he chose priesthood.

"That night in France, frightened and doubting that we would emerge alive, we rolled back the years and were a teenage couple very much in love. There was just that one night in all the years, Nicky.''

"Did Dad know all of this?" Nicky stammered.

"Part of it. I never told him it was Casimar. For that matter I never told Casimar you were his, but I think he knows." Johanna sighed. "After you were born he talked about leaving the church.''

"But he's a cardinal.''

"For one night he was a man. That doesn't prevent his being a treasure to the church. Remember, if we hadn't done it you wouldn't be here. And you made Michal very happy.''

"Will I ever see my real father?" Nicky asked.

"Michal was your real father and I never want to hear you suggest otherwise. However, someday I hope you will meet your uncle Casimar. I know he would treasure that moment forever. But for now, Nicky, you will honor Michal, Casimar and me by refusing to speak of or listen to anything on this subject. Michal was your father whether I committed an indiscretion or not. The rest is no one's business but ours.''

There was a long pause. "I'd like to go up to my room now.''

"Of course. Good night, Nicky.''

He hesitated a moment, then bent over to kiss his mother.

Chapter 34

Despite Nicky's apparent acceptance of the truth about his parentage, Johanna was occasionally troubled by doubts. It was difficult to know what went on in the mind of a teenager. Had she done wrong in telling Nicky the truth? During Michal's life she would have denied it.

Helen had almost earned her degree. She expected to graduate next February; already she was applying to Columbia College. Many difficulties unfortunately plagued the woman lawyer, but Helen was dogged; nobody and nothing would prevent her from practicing law. Johanna was proud of her daughter.

There appeared to be grounds for optimism about the economy, though Roosevelt made it clear the country still had far to go. Strikes erupted into violence even while the President was asking for higher pay and shorter hours.

Two of Tony's sisters had married Italians. They wrote from Palermo with extravagant praise for the good Mussolini was doing, but Tony was disturbed.

On Sunday morning at Southampton the family gathered at the breakfast table to discuss the Sunday *Times*. On this last Sunday in September Tony unhappily held forth on the rise of fascism in Italy.

"I don't know what's the matter with my sisters. They write me how Mussolini has built townships for former servicemen, built farms, drained the marshes, built roads. They don't understand that freedom is dead in Italy."

"He's threatening to drive women out of industry," Vicky added. "He claims the primary function of women is in the home. He just needs something besides his dog to feel superior to."

"Wait till he finds out how badly the women are missed," Bernie said. "I can't imagine trying to make do with no women in the labor force."

"Never mind what it will do to their families. Most women who work really need the money." Tony shrugged. "My sisters can't see anything wrong with it, though."

"What do you think Hitler and Mussolini talked about when they had that meeting back in the summer?" Nicky mused. "Wouldn't you all love to have been a fly on the wall in that room?"

"Whatever was said, it didn't bode well for the rest of the world," Bernie surmised.

"Grandma, you promised to walk on the beach with Joey and Henry and me this morning," Lucy reminded her. "You said we could feed the gulls."

"And so we will," Johanna promised. "I guess you're too young to want to talk politics."

"Babes in arms," Jason remarked, exchanging a glance of male superiority with Nicky. "Nick, let's go play catch out on the beach."

Nicky kept her feeling young, Johanna mused. Here she was at sixty-one with a son not yet sixteen. She didn't feel sixty-one—but how was sixty-one supposed to feel?

Michal was always proud of her appearance. Her figure was slim and her skin smooth; the grey that streaked her hair flattered her, he said. To Michal she had been beautiful till the last day he looked upon her.

Most of all Johanna missed Michal in her bed. Too often she woke up in the middle of the night because in her sleep she had reached out a foot to touch his or a hand to rest on his chest and all at once realized that Michal wasn't there. One of the worst nights was the one on which she realized she had probably made love for the last time; she lay awake until dawn and rose grim-faced, feeling cheated.

Early in 1935 Johanna attended Helen's graduation from Barnard. In June Nicky graduated from high school and in the fall he would start at Harvard. Jason was studying hard at Stuyvesant High, determined to enroll at Harvard before Nicky graduated.

At the end of the year the newspapers made much ado about William Randolph Hearst and Mae West. They had earned the two largest salaries in the United States in 1935.

At last the company was out of the red—showing no profit, but not losing money despite the payroll. Johanna rather relished trips to Washington, where she lobbied government officials on behalf of American-International and sought out government contracts, which eventually pulled the company back to its feet.

On the train trips to and from Washington Johanna skimmed novels. Helen would give them to her, insisting that they had much to say about what was happening in the country in these troubled times. She read John Steinbeck and James T. Farrell and Theodore Dreiser. She saw plays by Clifford Odets and Maxwell Anderson. They had their points, true, but they were just stories; Johanna did not quite see why Helen considered them so important.

Early in the spring of 1936 Tony called a family conference after much personal deliberation. On Easter Sunday afternoon he made an announcement that surprised no one.

"I think it's time I moved ahead," he said without preliminaries. Excitement glinted in Helen's eyes. "It's certain that Roosevelt will be renominated in June. I expect him to win in November. I think it's time I threw my hat into the national political ring. How do you feel about my running for Congress, folks?"

"Whatever you say, Pop," Joey agreed ebulliently. "Can I campaign for you?"

"Sure, son. Remember, my wife's going to be tied up with law school." He smiled tenderly at both of them.

"I'm glad to hear it, Tony," Johanna declared. "I was beginning to wonder if you had run out of ambition. I'll stump for you, and I'm sure the whole family will be behind you, as always."

"My brother-in-law Congressman Corelli," Nicky boasted.

"If I win," Tony reminded him, "only if I win." He hesitated. "I'm getting a late start, you know."

"You needed to wait until the economy showed definite improvement," Johanna pointed out. "Even though we still have eight million unemployed, things are looking up. We'll make it a whirlwind campaign. New York is in the mood for that."

The entire Raisa clan, including the children, were involved in Tony's campaign for a seat in the House of Representatives. The main plank in his platform was housing for the millions who were living in squalor.

Johanna Raisa was a name to conjure with among many women voters in New York. They flocked to hear her speak. One day at a women's luncheon at the

Waldorf-Astoria she spoke candidly about her own humble beginnings.

"In Fall River we lived in company-owned shacks—not much while you were there, and if you got fired you had till noon the next day to vacate.

"Then we came back to New York and took a flat on East Seventh Street. Our landlady was wonderful to us, but I know all about cold water walkups without a toilet, about sewer rats and no light on the stairs, about babies with tuberculosis and no money for a doctor." Johanna paused.

"Slums breed disease and crime. Tony Corelli knows it. Of the eleven million substandard homes in this country today, a shocking number are here in this state. Elect Tony Corelli to Congress and he'll fight for legislation to begin the long hard task of changing this picture."

Vicky organized the lunch-and-carfare ladies. She took over Johanna's string as well. They would walk to her place, handing out buttons and leaflets on the way. In Vicky's living room they would cover their coats with buttons ("Corelli Cares") and stuff their bags and pockets with leaflets. They would go out and flood the district and come back for lunch and more materials. Walking home in the afternoon they gave out yet more. No one in the district was allowed to ignore Tony Corelli.

Johanna was increasingly disturbed by her letters from Casimar. Pilsudski had died in May of 1935, but the government in Poland remained the same. There was much internal dissension about voting regulations as well as increasing fears that Hitler would invade.

Johanna let Nicky read all Casimar's letters. The official reason was that he was studying Polish, but he was deeply interested in Casimar and plainly intended to meet him someday.

Casimar wrote heatedly about the troubles in Spain. The civil war there increased his alarm about the future of the world. The attempt of the Spanish Fascists under General Franco to throw over the democratic government was loathsome to him, but he had no more use for the Communists.

Again the family gathered for hot summer weekends at Southampton. Johanna looked at Nicky and Jason, scared of another war. Joey and Henry were too young to fight. Johanna profoundly disagreed with most Americans who were more concerned about the state of the economy than the possibility of war. Congressional leaders heeded their wishes and vowed that America would not be drawn into another war.

On the last Saturday in August, just before Nicky was to return to Harvard for his sophomore year, the evening talk centered on the troubles in Spain.

"Nobody hates war more than me," Bernie declared, "but we know that fascism has to be stopped before it can spread around the world. Fascism and democracy can't survive side by side." He pushed away his plate.

"Bernie, enough talk about war," Vicky protested. "I'm still eating."

"Has anybody read *Gone With the Wind*?" Helen asked. "I don't dare start because everybody says it's compulsive and all I have time for is textbooks."

"I'm reading it now. Fascinating." Johanna patted her lips with her napkin. "Scarlett O'Hara is enormously good at getting her own way. In a man it would be admired if not approved, but it shocks people in a woman. Mitchell is rather wicked with all her characters. Everyone has feet of clay. I love it."

"May I have it next?" Vicky asked.

"Of course."

"When do you leave for school?" Bernie asked Nicky.

"Tuesday," Nicky said after a moment, startled out of a private reverie.

"Those are the good years, the college years," Bernie said wistfully.

"With what's happening all over Europe?" Nicky snorted.

"Nicky, do you have everything you need for school?" Johanna interrupted. "If you're not going to bother with laundry you'd better take plenty of everything. The next time I want to take you to dinner I don't want to have to buy you a shirt and a suit of clean underwear."

Tony won the Democratic primary and the family was jubilant. He could expect a landslide victory in November on the President's coattails. Helen was trying to figure out whether she would have to leave Columbia for a Washington law school. Johanna would miss the Corellis, but she was often in Washington on business, so would still see them regularly.

In mid-October Nicky came down from Harvard for a long weekend. He seemed troubled, but Johanna restrained herself from questioning him. Thank God he and Bernie, unlike Helen, freely confided in her most of the time.

As usual when Nicky was at home, Jason was constantly underfoot. The boys spent hours in heavy conversation in Nicky's room. Johanna left them alone as much as she could, but she noticed that the radio in Nicky's room was on for every news broadcast.

On Sunday Johanna went downstairs for her first cup of coffee, expecting to see no one. Molly and Melissa would be off to church and the other servants were off duty on Sundays.

She was startled to discover Nicky hunched over a cup of coffee in the kitchen.

"Good morning, Nicky."

He started violently. "There's hot coffee on the stove. I'll pour you a cup." He leapt to his feet with a smile, but his eyes were troubled.

"Nicky, you have something on your mind. I'd like to hear what it is."

"Mom, I have to tell you and it's going to upset you," he said awkwardly, bringing her a cup of coffee.

"Then tell me," she said matter-of-factly. "I hate postponing unpleasant matters."

"Mom, two fellows at school are leaving this week for Spain. They're joining the International Brigade that's being formed to fight beside the Loyalists."

"They would do better to stay at home and finish their education." Her throat tightened as she struggled to retain her equanimity.

"Mom, don't you understand? This is a fight for democracy, the greatest of all crusades. The youth of the world are going to Spain to fight." He took a deep breath. "I'm going too. My school friends and I are just waiting for word about how to proceed."

"Nicky, you're not yet eighteen years old." Johanna lost her calm. "I forbid it. You'll go back to Harvard and forget about Spain."

"On November eleventh I'll be eighteen," he pointed out. "You can only forbid it for a month."

"You see this as some romantic adventure," Johanna said impatiently. "War isn't like that. I know. I was in France—remember?"

Nicky rolled his eyes. "Yes, Mom, I remember. That's partly why I want to go."

"Nicky, war is ugly and painful. People die."

Johanna's voice was edged with desperation. "Don't go looking for trouble."

"I've thought it all out very carefully, Mom. I have to go. It's a matter of conscience." His face was alight with dedication. When he looked like that he was the image of Casimar.

"As soon as we know how to go about the arrangements, I'll sail for Le Havre with my two buddies from school. Committee headquarters is in Paris. I don't know much else yet, but they always listen carefully for news of Perpignan and Figueras.

"Don't look like that, Mama. I have to go."

Chapter 35

Johanna changed into slacks, sweater and a warm jacket and left the house to walk through Central Park. She felt she must remove herself from the house to think clearly. Her mind was in chaos at the prospect of Nicky's leaving to fight with the International Brigade.

On impulse she walked to the East Sixties to see Bernie and Vicky. It was well after eight; they would be up by now.

The doorman let her go straight up; he knew she would let herself in if no one answered the bell. She sniffed the pungent aroma of fresh coffee outside their door. Vicky made a small ceremony on Sunday mornings of grinding special coffee and brewing it in her mother's secret way.

"Mama," Vicky said with a warm smile of welcome. Vicky knew she wasn't here so early without a good reason. "Come in and have coffee with us. I was just getting ready to pour."

"Good morning." Bernie smiled and bent to kiss her.

"How're the children?" Johanna asked, sitting at the table in the breakfast room.

"Fine." Bernie chuckled. "Except that Joey and Henry are still Germany and Poland—mortal enemies who have signed a truce. I told them no more fighting or I wouldn't take them to the Army-Navy game next month in Philadelphia."

"I'll make you some eggs," Vicky said, opening the refrigerator.

"Just coffee."

"And bacon and eggs with Bernie and me. It isn't Sunday morning without bacon and eggs."

"What's up, Mama?" Bernie asked. "You didn't come here just for breakfast."

"I'm upset about Nicky. He says he's going to Spain to fight with the International Brigade."

"Oh, God." Bernie flinched. "He's only a baby."

"He'll be eighteen next month." Johanna shook her head. "I don't know how to convince him that he shouldn't go."

"If Nicky goes, Jason will be right behind him in two years," Vicky said dully.

"Maybe it won't last that long," Bernie suggested hopefully.

"We don't know how long it'll last," Vicky cried. "It could go on for five years."

"Can you two come for dinner tonight? Maybe we can knock some sense into Nicky's head. We'll have to be careful not to gang up on him or he'll dig in his heels, but let's see what we can do."

Johanna returned to the house. Nicky was upstairs in his room. Soon Jason would be over. She'd heard them talking yesterday about going to the movies.

It occurred to Johanna that Nicky might be turned down. Then she mocked herself. He was young and able-bodied. The Loyalists would take anyone able to fight; they were desperate.

Nicky felt endearingly protective of Jason. Perhaps this feeling for his nephew could be employed to make him reconsider.

The day seemed to drag endlessly. She dreaded the possibility that Nicky would not take the midnight train back to school. He belonged in Cambridge, in the classroom. How could she bear the thought of his crossing an ocean to fight another country's war?

Soon after five Bernie and Vicky arrived with Lucy. Johanna nervously inspected her watch. Nicky and Jason had not appeared yet. Because Nicky had no intention of returning to the campus? Johanna and the Corellis sat silent over their sherry in the library. Lucy shivered as she looked around at them and asked if she might go to the kitchen. Absent-minded permission was given.

Just as Molly announced dinner, Nicky and Jason arrived at the house. Despite Nicky's air of festivity he was on edge. He and Jason made it childishly obvious they had a secret. Even Jason was unwontedly excited and had red spots on his cheeks. Johanna's heart sank. Nicky's done it, then, she lamented.

As dinner was served they discussed the movie Nicky and Jason had seen.

Then, while they were waiting for dessert, "What do you hear from Uncle Casimar?" Bernie asked on cue.

"His last letter was mostly about Spain," Johanna reported. "He says the church is supporting the Nationalists because of government's efforts to dismantle Catholicism, but he can't in good conscience agree to support a Fascist regime." From the corner of her eye she saw Nicky's face brighten. "However, he can't support the Loyalists since they turned Communist."

"That's not true," Nicky said heatedly. "He's saying

that because the Loyalist government insisted on keeping the church out of government. That's as it should be.''

"But to refuse to allow religious orders to teach?" Bernie challenged. "Without them there is virtually no schooling. Both the Fascists and the Loyalists are killing civilians and murdering prisoners. Neither side cares about peace or prosperity; they're after power, pure and simple. If you ask me," he concluded contemptuously, "there's nothing to choose.''

"Franco is a dictator," Nicky demurred. "The Republican government was not Communist.''

"Nicky, we all would like to see a democratic government in Spain," Vicky said with disarming matter-of-factness, "but neither side is offering that. Idealistic people from a lot of nations are running to Spain because they want to see freedom there and they hate Fascism. But Communism is just as much a threat to freedom.''

"There was a democratic government in Spain until Franco overthrew it," Nicky persisted grimly. "They gave women the right to vote. They gave unworked lands to starving peasants—"

"And then swung sharply to the left," Bernie interjected. "No decent person admires Franco's Fascism, but Communism is no better.''

"Where do you get all your information?" Nicky asked with uncharacteristic arrogance. "It's not in the newspapers.''

"It's pretty plain if you think about it," Vicky insisted. "Democracies don't nationalize church lands, close their schools, burn their buildings.''

Johanna witnessed the debate with growing misgivings. Nicky was backing into a corner. At any moment he would realize they were deliberately working on him. This was going all wrong.

"I'm with you, Nicky," Jason declared. "Can I have

some more bigos? As soon as I'm old enough, I'm going over too." He stopped short and frowned. "It'll still be going on when I'm eighteen, won't it?"

Nicky froze for a second, then reached for another roll. He swallowed. "Hard to say right now."

"Oh, I expect it will, Jason," Johanna said. "It's going to be a war of attrition, you know. They usually go on for years, kill off a generation and leave nothing at all to build on." She could almost hear Nicky deliberate. He didn't care at all for the prospect of Jason perhaps dying in Spain.

"Maybe we ought to wait awhile and see what happens," Nicky said offhand. "I'm sure to get some reports soon from the International Brigade. The guys have promised to write to the *Crimson*." He turned to his mother. "What's for dessert?"

"Chocolate mousse."

After one of the most bitter political campaigns in history and despite the opposition of eighty percent of the press, Roosevelt swept into a second term in November on a Democratic landslide. The Raisa family rejoiced in the election of Representative Tony Corelli.

Johanna was aware that Helen was fighting an inner battle: law school versus Washington. On the Friday after Thanksgiving Johanna went to Washington with Helen to look at houses. On the train Helen confessed that she felt a little selfish.

"I'm not giving up law school and I'm not transferring at this late date. But Congressman's wife is a full-time job if you do it right."

"Rearrange your life to accommodate what's important to you," Johanna replied. "Don't feel selfish. Remember, you're Helen first and Mrs. Tony second."

"Law school is important to me," Helen said slowly,

"but I do have to consider Tony's career. And changing schools will be hard on the children." She squinted in thought. "There's no problem about finishing this term. Then I could ask for leave for the spring semester. That'll give me a chance to get organized in Washington. I can go to summer school and finish in the fall during Tony's adjournment. Then my biggest problem will be deciding where to take the bar exam, New York or here."

Under the Twentieth Amendment the new Congress was sworn in on January third. On January twentieth President Roosevelt was inaugurated for his second term. The whole family attended both occasions, though only the Corellis went to the Inaugural Ball.

These days when Nicky came home he said nothing about the civil war in Spain, but like Bernie and Johanna, he was anxious about affairs in Poland, which appeared to be headed toward authoritarianism. Casimar wrote that it held strange appeal for the youth of Poland and he feared the new leadership would be formed in the mold of Hitler and Mussolini.

In the summer of 1937 the family got together at Southampton several times. Jason graduated from Stuyvesant High and was accepted at Harvard. Joey, Henry and Sandy, gradually adapting to life in Washington D.C., were delighted to spend the summer at the beach while their mother went to school. Vicky and Johanna stayed there all summer too.

Johanna had a busy but calm fall; Congress was in adjournment and the Corellis were in New York, but the office was more demanding than ever. Then Helen finished school, Congress reconvened and Johanna began to go to Washington on weekends.

In March of 1938 she was touched and delighted when the family gave her a surprise sixty-fifth birthday party. Sitting at the resplendent table in one of the private dining rooms at 21, with all of the family, even nine-year-old Sandy, surrounding her, Johanna fought against tears of pride. Michal and she had done well in this great country. It would be fifty years in 1939. That would be something to celebrate too.

Johanna's birthday was toasted with Dom Perignon. Her eyes rested on the tiered birthday cake and its dozens of candles.

"I'm old enough to apply for Social Security," she chuckled. "Not that I ever will. I expect to go on working forever."

"Mama," Bernie said gallantly, "if you tried to apply for Social Security, they would throw you out of the office. You look twenty years too young."

"This is one of the beautiful occasions of my life," she said softly.

"When you walk into a restaurant," Helen told her, "men still turn to look at you. You're so beautiful and elegant."

Johanna laughed to refrain from tears. "These damn expensive clothes I can't resist. My worst failing—I'm a clothes horse."

Johanna's children were aware that prospective suitors appeared at intervals, and the Raisa fortune was not always the attraction. But there could never be another man in her life. From the day of Michal's death she put all thought of men and marriage behind her.

With the economy definitely on the upswing Johanna decided the company should buy some real estate. Bernie laughed and suggested that it was because Joey wanted to study architecture. "You'll keep the kids in the business any way you can."

"Actually it was Tony and all his ranting about the need for better housing in the nation." Tony was running for his second term in Congress and thinking about the Senate.

"You can't wait for Nicky to graduate next year and come to work for us," he mused. "I wish we could persuade him to go on to business school, maybe at the University of Pennsylvania."

"Nicky's impatient to prove himself." Her smile lost some of its brightness. Her youngest rarely talked about the civil war in Spain, but she knew it was often in his thoughts. At first it seemed he stayed home for fear of involving Jason. Now, however, he wrote frankly that the reports from Spain bore out his family's arguments.

". . . But still, Mom, there must be something we can do to save Spain for democracy."

Bernie, turning serious, interrupted her train of thought. "I worry sometimes about Jason. He's so impressionable, and whenever he's home he hangs around Columbus Circle and listens to the radical speakers on their soapboxes. He's down there every chance he gets, and when Nicky and he both come home from school they both go. Now he's talking about staying in New York for the summer instead of going to Southampton."

"Bernie, the boys have spent enough summers loafing," Johanna said briskly. "I'll write Nicky and you write Jason. This summer they come to work for the company."

Johanna knew that not only was the Communist Party drawing in many of the young, but plenty of parlor pinks were old enough to know better.

"That'll keep them out of Spain," Bernie's smile was wry.

"I don't think we have to worry much about the International Brigade anymore. Two of Nicky's Harvard classmates were somewhat disillusioned."

"Nicky told you that?" Bernie lifted an eyebrow in surprise.

"He told me that," Johanna nodded.

"Then why the hell are they hanging around those reds down at Columbus Circle?"

"They hear all the talk about the horrors of Nazism and Fascism, and I think that's how they rebel. And those soapbox orators are so earnest. They seem so sincere. I guess they believe what they spout—" Johanna gestured her incomprehension.

"Mom, have *you* been going down to Columbus Circle?"

"I like to know what's happening around the city," Johanna said apologetically. "Some of those eloquent madmen are quite appealing—no doubt about that."

"Jason and Nicky may balk at coming to work for the summer," Bernie speculated.

"I don't think so. I think they're bored. All this ramminess is because they don't feel useful. It's high time they got to work and I think they'll realize it."

In addition to Nicky and Jason's work for the company they were drawn into Tony's campaign. Polls were warning that the Republicans would make inroads on the Senate and House of Representatives this year and Tony was gearing up for a challenge.

The menace in Europe was more obvious each month. In September Johanna heard with shocked amazement that France, Great Britain and Italy had agreed to Hitler's demands for suzerainty over part of Czechoslovakia. This intensified the alarm of the Polish about their own pacts with Germany.

In the following March Nazi troops moved into Prague. England and France, at last aware of potential danger to their own countries, guaranteed to protect Poland in case of attack.

In August Germany and Russia, presumably deadly enemies, signed a nonaggression pact.

On Friday, September first at five in the morning Polish time German soldiers swept across the border and German planes attacked Gdynia, Cracow and Katowice. At nine German planes tried to bomb Warsaw, but newscasters reported they failed to reach the suburbs. At Southampton for a long weekend, Johanna spent all her time next to the radio, terrified for Poland and for Casimar.

Friday night the Raisa clan gathered about the radio to follow the happenings in Poland, none of which were good. The French and English were looking on helplessly, but on September third both declared war on Germany. In a fireside chat that night Roosevelt announced that the United States would remain neutral.

Johanna stayed beside the radio for the entire Labor Day weekend. Reports said the Polish forces were fighting on three fronts. Warsaw had been bombed four times. The fighting was heavy and the toll devastating. Many civilians were killed and wounded. Johanna prayed continually for Casimar's safety.

Within three weeks Poland was crushed. Russian troops, now in alliance with Germany, marched in to partition the country for the fourth time. No word came through from Casimar. Johanna was distraught. Nicky, part of the firm since his graduation last May, came home from the office every night to sit with her before the radio.

In October the entire Raisa family and the Corellis marched up Fifth Avenue with two hundred thousand other Polish-Americans in the Pulaski Day parade. The churches were filled with the children and grandchildren of Polish immigrants, all praying for Poland to be delivered from the Nazis and the Communists.

The Allies waited, poised for an attack, but not until April did the Nazis make their next move. They occupied

Denmark and Norway despite the resistance backed by British as well as Danish and Norwegian troops.

Early in May Nicky came to his mother in her office. From the grim determination on his face she suspected what he was about to tell her.

"Mom, the Polish are forming an army in Great Britain. A lot of Americans are leaving next week to join them. I must go. I can't stand by and do nothing." She saw the quivering of an eyelid, the pallor beneath his Southampton tan. "Please, Mom, don't try to stop me."

"I couldn't," she acknowledged. "Oh Nicky." She held out her arms to him. "Be safe. Please God, be safe."

Chapter 36

On a beautiful May afternoon, when to outward appearances the world was a lovely place in which to live, Nicky
said good-bye to his mother at Grand Central and climbed
aboard the Montreal train. Last night Bernie had chewed
his ear off for going off this way but had not changed his
mind. Not even Mom could do that.

He found his compartment, dropped his gear and
gazed out the window. There she stood, waiting for the
train to pull out, that warm smile slightly stiff on her face
by now. He knocked on the window to attract her attention
and waved. He had no way of knowing when—or whether—
he would see her again.

The train began the slow chug out of the station and
he leaned back in his seat, suddenly weary. Last night
after he got rid of Bernie he talked with Jason for almost
an hour, maintaining that his nephew was too close to
graduation to join up now.

He had not said so to Jason, but he had to go to

Europe not just to fight for Poland but to seek out Casimar Cardinal Raisa.

Restless, he left his compartment early, intent on lingering over dinner. While he waited to be served, he went over in his mind the few details he knew about the Polish army forming in Great Britain. He had thought that Polish-American volunteers would be racing to join up, but in New York he found that so far enlistment was light.

The dining car was filling up and a waiter asked permission to seat another passenger at his table. "Of course," Nicky said politely, though he would have preferred to be alone.

"This is a fine train," the middle-aged businessman said complacently. "Lately I seem to be spending more time on trains than in my office."

"Business has certainly showed a fast improvement." Nicky cursed silently; obviously small talk was required of him, and he was in no mood for that tonight. "I suppose it's all the trouble in Europe."

"Don't forget what Japan is doing to China," his companion went on. "Of course, we're two oceans away from the war, but I have to say it's gone a long way toward improving our economy."

"It seems that war is the biggest stimulant ever to the economy."

"Always like that." The plump man shuddered delicately. "I spent fourteen months fighting in the last one and I never want to see this country in another." He gave Nicky a quizzical look. "You on a business trip, young fellow?"

"For my mother's firm," Nicky lied. He refused to discuss his plans with a stranger. "I'll be in Montreal and Toronto for a few days."

Earlier than he had planned Nicky returned to his compartment to get away from his dinner companion. The man had fought in one war, Nicky thought impatiently, and been horrified, but did he have to stick his head in the sand and ignore all the threats that hung over America?

By the following afternoon Nicky was in the offices of the Polish recruiting center. In three days he was to leave for England. The news was that the Polish Army was already one hundred thousand strong and ready to move into action alongside Allied troops. The new group would be put through accelerated training in England. Nicky hoped to be a pilot.

Along with thousands of other recruits Nicky boarded a once-luxurious ocean liner bound for Southampton, England. The ship maintained a total blackout; all transatlantic vessels did since last September, when the British liner *Athenia*, with fourteen hundred passengers, including nearly three hundred Americans, had been torpedoed and sunk. Fortunately most of the passengers were rescued, but most ships traveled with a convoy and a crew prepared for trouble.

Nicky kept mostly to himself aboard ship. For the first time since the summer when he found out about it he could not keep his mind off his parentage. There had been periods when he felt isolated from his family, and at first he was shocked that a priest should father a child and go on to become a cardinal. He had long ago accepted his mother's point of view, that he should simply be glad for his own sake that they had done it. Now, on his way to war, he began to understand why they had. The driving force in him these days was to meet the man he called Uncle Casimar. The invasion of Poland, the death of so many in his mother's homeland, had lent this purpose special urgency.

From Southampton the recruits went to Polish headquarters and prepared to enter intensive training. "Have you heard what was happening while we were at sea?'' a gloomy-looking young soldier asked Nicky as they settled into their improvised barracks.

"No," Nicky acknowledged. "I haven't even looked at a newspaper."

"The Germans have driven through Belgium, Holland and Luxembourg and they're ready to push on into France."

"And Chamberlain's out," someone else said excitedly. "Winston Churchill is prime minister now."

With no delay the Polish volunteers were thrust into training. They worked each day until they were ready to drop. At the end of his third week in training Nicky was summoned to the office of the commanding officer for a special meeting.

He was kept waiting and in forty minutes he was supposed to hear a talk by a Polish officer who had managed to escape from Warsaw and reach London in disguise.

He scowled at the young woman, quite pretty, who sat behind the typewriter and served as receptionist to the commanding officer. Her soft fair hair hung to her shoulders, framing a delicate oval face. She appeared tired and grave, but here everyone did.

"Will I have to wait much longer?" Nicky asked impatiently.

"Until you're summoned," She frowned at his impatience.

"You're English?" he asked, puzzled by her accent.

"Polish. I went to school here in England. You're American?"

"I was born in New York, but my parents are from Warsaw."

"I was born in Warsaw." Her eyes, fascinating and blue, lighter than he had ever seen, were all at once dark with pain. "My father died in the defense of Warsaw and my mother, a nurse, got killed when her hospital was bombed."

"I'm sorry." He almost took her hand, then remembered she was a stranger. "My uncle was there. We've heard nothing of him. I have cousins also, but they were north of Warsaw. Perhaps you know my uncle—"

She smiled faintly. "Warsaw is a very large city."

"His name is Raisa. Casimar Cardinal Raisa—" Nicky spoke impulsively. He had never been drawn to anyone the way he was to this lovely Polish woman who spoke English almost as though British-born.

"Everybody knows Cardinal Raisa. He's really your uncle?"

"He's really my uncle," Nicky assured her. "I'm Nick Raisa."

"Your uncle is working in Warsaw. The Nazis were willing to allow him to go to Rome, but he refused. He knows how badly he's needed in Warsaw."

The commanding officer emerged from the office to order Nicky inside. Because their files on Nicky showed that he spoke fluent Polish and German as well as English, he was billeted as an interpreter. Aghast, Nicky fought against this. He had come to Europe to fight for Poland. He wanted to join one of the flying squadrons.

"Later maybe you can fly," the officer snorted. "Right now we need an interpreter. Report to this office at seven tomorrow morning. You'll work with Stefanie Cybis." He gestured to the desk outside. "She's an interpreter too."

Nicky was dissatisfied with his new assignment and surprised that he found such pleasure in seeing so much of Stefanie. Because he was unfailingly conscientious in the office, his commanding officer winked at Nicky's surreptitious flying lessons.

Over a late supper in a café one night in mid-June

Stefanie confided that their unit would shortly be shipped into London. "You're not supposed to know," she cautioned with a stern little frown that Nicky found endearing. "Be surprised when you're told."

"I wish it were Warsaw," he said recklessly. Stefanie flinched. "I'm anxious to find my uncle." It was clumsy of him to talk of Warsaw; Stefanie still grieved for her parents.

The door to the small café swung open and a Polish soldier attached to their company hurried toward their table. "You're to return immediately to the office," he said tersely.

"What's happening?" Nicky signaled for their check.

"You'll find out when we get there."

By the time they reached the office every available chair and corner on which to sit was filled. At last the commanding officer decided that everyone required for this briefing was present.

"Word has just come through that the Italians have entered the war on the side of the Germans. France's best troops are guarding the Italian border. Meanwhile, Paris has surrendered and the Germans are in occupation. The rest of France is expected to surrender within a week and then Great Britain will be without Allies in Western Europe. Hitler is boasting that he'll march into London in two months." He paused for breath. "We leave tomorrow morning for London."

Around eleven Johanna phoned home to say there would be guests for dinner. "Tell Molly I'd like her to have kolduny and bigos, but the rest is up to her . . . Yes, six of us. Bernie will be here but Vicky can't make it. . . . No, not the Corellis. . . . Any news?"

"There's a letter from Nicky," Melissa said. "It's postmarked London—"

"Have Josip bring it down to me," Johanna said. "I could use cheering up today." She hung up and sat motionless at her desk, thinking about Nicky in London. Bernie came into the office.

"Something's come up that I have to talk with you about, Mrs. Raisa." Bernie had always called his parents Mr. and Mrs. Raisa at the office. He dropped into a chair beside her desk. Bernie kept himself in good physical shape, she thought with pride. He would be forty-six in August, but he was firm and lean.

"What's the problem, Bernie?"

"I've been asked to work in Washington." Unexpectedly he smiled. "I suspect Tony has something to do with it."

"Doing what?"

"Some advisory post to do with shipbuilding. I don't like leaving the company. It sounds great the way Tony put it, but my first obligation is here."

"Take the job, Bernie. It's only until this damn war is over. I'm not so old that I can't take over till then. You go to Washington and enjoy it. I'll be fine."

"You're sure?" His eyes searched hers.

"I don't have to tell you how I'll miss you and Vicky and the children. Of course," she chuckled, "you all neglect me dreadfully anyway. I'll hardly notice you're gone." This was an old game. "I want you to take this post, Bernie. You'll do the family proud." She could feel his relief that she agreed.

"What do you hear from Nicky?" he asked.

"Josip is bringing me a letter right now from London. He must be there."

"I'll have to talk to Vicky about this move of course," said Bernie, returning to the subject at hand. "Still, she always sides with you. I think it's safe to say you have to run the company on your own for a while."

Alone again, Johanna tried to visualize New York with no member of her family. The prospect was daunting, but Washington D.C. was only a few hours distant, and she'd be working too hard to be lonely.

Josip arrived with the letter and Johanna closed her office door to read it. Because of censorship he could say little other than that he was in London and enjoying the city. Since 1938 and the Munich crisis air raid shelters had been appearing in London. Despite long hours on duty Stefanie and he had gone twice to the theater. British courage was admirable.

The letter was infuriatingly thin of real news. Were the British prepared for invasion? Was there any news from Warsaw? Were the Axis alliances holding firm? He gave no hint.

Johanna forced herself to concentrate on business. The shipyard was in operation around the clock, as Britain was in dire need of vessels. Johanna held her customary late-afternoon meeting with the plant superintendents, dictated two last-minute letters and left the office. As usual, Josip was waiting downstairs to drive her home.

The afternoon was hot and humid, typical July weather. Tonight Boleslav would serve dinner in the library before one of the French windows. That was the best place to catch a breeze from the park.

The butler had anticipated her wishes. A small table and a dining chair were set in the library. An electric fan rotated on a corner of the desk.

"Turn on the news, Boleslav," Johanna said.

"Why don't you wait until after dinner, madam?" Boleslav said, not quite meeting her eyes.

"Because I like to know what's happening in the world," Johanna said sharply. She turned it on herself. A newscast was in progress.

"We hope to have more news from England shortly,"

a mellow voice announced. "To recap what has happened, the Luftwaffe is attacking convoys in the Straits of Dover and the RAF is putting up a fierce battle. Dogfights light up the sky—"

Johanna switched off the radio and stood motionless for a moment, remembering London in 1918, the streets thronged with officers and enlisted men of many nations, all on brief leave from the battlefields. How had this happened again?

"Mrs. Raisa?" Boleslav said tentatively.

"I'm all right, Boleslav." She managed a smile as she moved back to her chair. "But hereafter let's not listen to the news until after dinner."

Chapter 37

Lucy announced that she wished to live with her grandmother, who was delighted, instead of moving to Washington with her parents. Lucy was reluctant to change schools and to leave her friends behind.

By the time school opened Bernie and Vicky were settled a block away from the Corelli townhouse and Jason was back at Harvard. Lucy definitely brightened up the Fifth Avenue house.

She had abandoned her yearning to act in the movies, though she had stood in line for over an hour to see *Gone With the Wind*. She wanted to be a singer. Johanna relished the light sweet voice singing popular tunes. Right now it was "I'll Never Smile Again"—such strong contrast to her effervescent personality.

On the night of September sixteenth Johanna was in an especially hopeful mood. Today there had been a letter from Nicky. For weeks now the news had been dominated by the battle of Britain and the courage and self-sacrifice of the British. Nicky wrote that he was fine but frustrated in his desk job. He was dying to get into the cockpit. Johanna thanked God his Polish and German were so good.

At dinner Lucy talked vivaciously about her new Bonnie Baker record, then embarked on some devious campaigning about her sixteenth birthday party in February.

"This family is awfully strict." Lucy sighed like the ingenue in a melodrama. "Some girls my age are already going to nightclubs."

"Ridiculous," Johanna scoffed.

"Carol, who's in my French class, says Mimi Baker was at nightclubs all the time when she was fifteen. She even went to the casinos."

"You can't afford it on your allowance, and I am not paying for you to sink into dissipation, so don't ask for a raise."

After dinner they went into the library to listen to the evening news. Lucy followed her grandmother's custom of avoiding the news during the day, and they always had their coffee at the radio.

"Today Congress passed the first peacetime Selective Service Act in history," the newscaster said crisply. Johanna stiffened in her chair. "All men between the ages of twenty and thirty-six will be required to register—"

"Grandma, that means Jason will have to register for the army?" Lucy asked.

Johanna felt cold despite the comfortable summer warmth of the night. "Not until his birthday next month. He's still nineteen."

"Well, it's good we're staying out of the war, then," Lucy said calmly. "It must be just a kind of—of precaution."

"I'm going to call Helen." Johanna put down her coffee cup. "She's probably a nervous wreck. Tony never expected that bill to pass."

Johanna spoke with Helen and then Tony about the prospect of war.

"I gather Nicky's letters to Jason are designed to discourage him from getting involved in the war," Tony said soberly. "Bless him for that."

Johanna clung to Roosevelt's assertion, "Your boys are not going to be sent into any foreign wars." There was no way she could have stopped Nicky from enlisting, but Jason felt no such pull to Poland. Not everyone who registered would be called up; perhaps Jason would never be in uniform.

Two weeks after Jason's twentieth birthday he came home from school to report that he had enlisted in the United States Air Force. He told his grandmother before he phoned Washington to tell his parents.

"It'll be a great experience," he said enthusiastically. "I'm hoping they'll let me fly. I'd rather be a pilot than a · bombardier or a navigator."

"When do you have to report for duty?" Johanna tried not to let Jason see her distress. The United States was not in the war, but the isolationists notwithstanding, how long would this be true?

"Tomorrow morning. I'll go down to Washington on my first leave. I know Mom and Dad will be mad at me for dropping out of school." He was trying to sound casual. "I can go back when this craziness is over, of course. It's not like they're throwing me out."

"Phone your mother."

Nicky wrote that Johanna must not be concerned if she didn't hear from him for a while. That surely meant he was on special assignment, but what on earth was it? Was he trained as a pilot and joining one of the Polish squadrons? The thought of another possibility made her blood run cold. What if they had seen his languages, his tenacity, his courage, and made him a spy?

Jason was jubilant; he had been accepted for pilot training. He yammered on and on about his pride in the Air Force until everyone was sick of it. Helen managed to fly out to Texas to visit him briefly while he was in training.

In the late summer of 1941, much quieter than when he left, Jason managed to come home on a four-day pass. The family gathered for the occasion at Southampton.

Johanna gloried in having Jason home, but he gave voice to her own suspicions about Nicky's role in the war. "He has to be in Intelligence. If he were still at a desk, even if he were flying, you'd have occasional letters from him, not just a note once every four or five months. But don't worry about Nicky. He can do anything. He'll be all right."

Nicky had been gone almost two years. It was eight years since he walked up the beach to the verandah and confronted her with Holly's ugly gossip. He had grown up fast after that. She could see his ardent face on that day when she saw him off for Canada at Grand Central. Many nights she dreamed of it at the compartment window as his train chugged out of the station.

At dinner on Sunday night Helen made an announcement. Tony had finally agreed to take a holiday in Hawaii in late November or early December.

"Then maybe I'll see you there." Jason grinned in anticipation. "There's a strong chance I'll be stationed at Hickam Field in Hawaii."

"That'll be fun." Helen sparkled. "Our handsome uniformed nephew can meet us for dinner at the Royal Hawaiian. I hear it's a terrific hotel."

"It'll do you both good," Johanna said approvingly. "You've been working too hard."

"I'm looking forward to four and a half days on a

Matson Liner between Los Angeles and Hawaii. I'm forever reading their ads. They're so enticing." Helen rolled her eyes. "I haven't a stitch to wear."

"The boys and Sandy can stay with us," Vicky offered. "It'll be good to hear young voices in the house again." Bernie and she were a little lonely without Jason and Lucy.

Whenever Johanna saw the family, the talk centered on the coming trip to Hawaii. Jason was stationed at Hickam Field, as he had expected, and his letters waxed lyrical about the beauty of Hawaii. Tony was juggling commitments to make time for the trip before he had to finish his preparations for the next session of Congress.

On Thanksgiving, when the family gathered for the traditional dinner at Fifth Avenue, Helen reported that they had flight reservations for Los Angeles early the following week. "At Los Angeles we connect with the *S.S. Lurine* with almost no delay, and four and a half days later we'll be at wonderful Honolulu."

Tony dropped an arm about Helen's slim shoulders while his eyes teased her. "The land of gorgeous maidens in grass skirts awaits us."

"You keep your eyes on your wife," Helen scolded, in high spirits at the prospect of a vacation. "We'll fly back; that way we'll have nine days in Hawaii."

Helen left New York wishing she had her mink coat but by the time their Pan American flight touched down in Los Angeles, she was glad she had settled for a light silk raincoat. She looked forward to the time aboard ship, with nothing required of her—no phones to answer, no domestic problems, no destitute clients, no parties on Tony's behalf.

Lying on a deck chair on the day before they were scheduled to come into harbor, Helen told herself the trip had been good for Tony. He had lost his pallor and he smiled a lot. Well, small wonder; this was almost like a second honeymoon. She had not even begun to miss the children, she was so busy with her ardent husband.

She had shopped with a rare extravagance for this trip. She adored the new ballerina length for evening. At dinner their first night in the islands, she promised herself, she would wear the black faille off-the-shoulder dancing dress. It had a net overskirt strewn with glittering gold paillettes. If it worked on Tony the second time as well as the first . . . He had not been able to keep his hands off her.

By evening they could see Molokai, low and dark to the south, and in the west the dazzling light on Mokapu Head. Helen was starting to get excited again after the languor of the crossing. Tony had made arrangements to rent a house on Koko Head looking east over the Pacific for their nine days in Hawaii. A domestic staff had been hired and a car was at their disposal.

In the morning they were packed and ready to leave the ship at sunrise. Together they stood at the railing of the top deck and tried to spot houses on Koko Head. The shadow of the ship on the water shortened as the sun rose and the sea turned emerald green. The war in Europe seemed to belong to another lifetime.

After breakfast most passengers went on deck to see the sights at docking. The sun was high and hot already.

"There's Diamond Head," someone said jubilantly. Helen was caught up in admiration for its majesty and beauty, though she had expected it to be much larger. It welcomed new arrivals with the air of a queen, the towering mountains behind serving as the queen's court.

Now the ship was moving past Diamond Head and the town of Honolulu came into sight, perhaps a dozen miles long. In the hills white houses clung to the earth.

Below was a mile-long strip of white beach that Helen knew was Waikiki.

They arrived with the traditional Hawaiian welcome. A band played thunderous music. A woman sang. People rushed forward to greet arrivals with the ritual leis. While they relaxed with the exotic newness about them, their host's chauffeur arrived to drive them to their house.

Settled in the car, Helen reminded Tony that tomorrow they were to have lunch with Jason. "We're to meet him at the dining terrace of the Royal Hawaiian. It seems incredible that he's an Air Force lieutenant. To me he's still little Jason, always tagging along after Nicky."

"They both tower over you," Tony laughed, "and the way Joey and Henry are shooting up they'll be past you in six months."

"Don't say that." She was unintentionally sharp. Joey was sixteen already, Henry fifteen. "I was thinking of the draft," she said in response to his stare of bewilderment.

"Hey, remember what you promised?" he chided. "We are here in Honolulu to have ourselves a high old time. No worry allowed." His sudden grin was contagious. "Can you imagine what the weather is like back in Washington?"

The house was small but charming, with a lanai overlooking the water. Hibiscus bloomed and formed a barrier between the garden and the surrounding guava grove. The staff consisted of the chauffeur-houseman and his wife, the housekeeper. They politely explained that they were off from Saturday afternoon until Sunday evening, but if Mr. and Mrs. Corelli should require service then, they would arrange for substitutes.

"No, we can manage, thank you," Tony said firmly. "We won't spend much time here. There's too much to see and do in the short time we'll be here."

Later in the afternoon they swam at Waikiki beach and drove home to change for dinner. The view from the house in the hills, Helen told Tony, was awesome. On the way to a neighborhood restaurant the housekeeper had suggested they paused to watch the sunset.

The next day's reunion with Jason was joyous, but it brought out Helen's longing for her own children. Seeing Jason in his uniform and knowing how close America was to war, she had to face the strong possibility that her two sons would soon be in uniform.

The days sped past with astonishing swiftness. Preparing for bed Saturday night, she was astonished to realize that tomorrow night would be their last in Honolulu. On Monday they headed back for Washington.

"I'm glad we came." Tony reached for her hand and drew her to him. "You're quite beautiful for an old bat of forty-two."

Helen tugged at the belt of his dressing gown. "Tony, darling, the servants are gone and we're all alone. Let's go out on the lanai." She kissed his ear and led him outside. They were there for quite some time.

Later Helen would think of making love in the moonlight on Koko Head as the last innocent pleasure of the good old days before the war.

Helen awoke next morning shortly after eight. For a few minutes she lay back against the pillows and planned the day. The packing had to be done tonight; she wasn't one to leave it for the last minute. Tonight they'd have a farewell dinner with Jason at a tiny native restaurant in Aiea. It was considered by the Hawaiians to be the best on the island.

Suddenly restless she left the bed, stood smiling down at Tony for a moment, then crossed to pick up a robe from the chair and went out onto the lanai. The sky was a glorious blue, though she had a hazy memory of fog in the night. It was Sunday. She ought to dress and go to mass, but she knew she wouldn't. She felt closer to God here alone in the hills than she often did in church.

She'd make breakfast for Tony and they'd have it out here, she decided. They'd take it easy, nothing but packing until it was time to go out to dinner.

As she was about to go into the house again, Helen paused. Good heavens, that sounded like gunfire.

She hurried inside. "Tony? Tony, I think you'd better wake up—"

He grunted, hugging the pillow as though settling in for the night.

"Tony, please."

He opened his eyes and turned to her. "Something wrong, honey?"

"I don't know." She hesitated. "It sounds like gunfire out there."

"Probably a drill. Remember, Jason said they were drilling a lot because of some recent alert. Turn on the radio."

"All right." She managed an uneasy smile.

She went to the radio, turned on KGU. There was a church service. "No gunfire," she conceded, feeling silly. "I'll go fix breakfast. You have time for a quick shower."

Helen went into the kitchen and stopped to gaze out the window over the sink. What was all that smoke down below? Nothing, she told herself. Probably practicing smoke screens. Jason had explained about that. If there was anything wrong down in the harbor, surely the station wouldn't be carrying a church service.

Helen put coffee on, brought out eggs from the refrigerator, dropped bread into the toaster and was drawn back to the window. The enormous cloud of smoke seemed to spread across the harbor. All at once the house shook. Was it an earthquake?

"Tony!" She hurried back into the bedroom. He stepped out of the shower. "Tony, did you feel that tremor?"

"No." He lifted one eyebrow. "You mean an earthquake tremor?"

"I don't know exactly." She squinted. Something was tickling her memory. It would come to her in a minute. "The house seemed to shake; the vibration went right through me."

The house shook again and Tony rushed toward Helen. "It's probably part of some military drill. Let's go out on the lanai and have a look."

"Put on some clothes first. It's still cool out."

She stood without moving until Tony returned in slacks and shirt. Helen had recalled why buildings shook like this—heavy artillery fire.

"Let's go outside," Tony urged.

Now the sky above the harbor was a blend of billowy grey smoke and yellow flames. They could hear planes roaring overhead.

"Look down there." Tony pointed at Hickam Field, where Jason was stationed. "Look at all that white smoke. Helen, it looks like Hickam Field is under attack."

With one thought they rushed back into the house. Tony switched on the radio. "Keep off the streets," a commanding voice ordered. "Do not use the telephone. Do not use the telephone."

The radio went silent but they left it on in case news bulletins came on.

"Why don't they say what's happening?" Helen demanded.

"Let's stay calm. We'll find out soon enough."

"I suppose we may as well have breakfast. How would you like your eggs this morning?" Helen didn't want to think about what was happening at Hickam Field.

"It's probably a drill. We haven't been around Honolulu long enough to understand how these things happen."

"There's no news on Sunday morning until nine-thirty. We'll have to wait till then, I suppose." It must be a drill; that's why they were ordered to stay off the streets and not use the phone. Still, even a drill could mean danger.

"Let's try the other station," Tony began, but he stopped short as a voice came over the radio.

The station was ordering twenty-five civilian doctors to report to Tripler Army Hospital.

"There's trouble, then," Helen said. "Injuries."

"Forget breakfast." Tony was terse with anxiety. "They'll need help down below."

"We're not supposed to be on the streets."

"I'm a Congressman, damnit. It's my duty to observe and lend a hand. Stay off the streets my foot."

In the library of the Raisa house on Fifth Avenue Johanna sat by the radio, twiddling knobs in her struggle to tune in clearly. "Lucy, you must have misunderstood. You probably heard Philippines and thought Pearl Harbor—"

The sound came in clear. Galvanized with shock, Johanna listened to the overwrought newsman. "Just a little over an hour ago Pearl Harbor in the Hawaiian Islands was attacked by the Japanese. The Pacific Fleet has been devastated. Hickam Field has suffered heavy damages—"

"Grandma," Lucy screeched in shock and rage, "Jason's at Hickam Field. And did Aunt Helen and Uncle Tony leave Honolulu yet?"

"They're scheduled to fly home tomorrow." She mustn't let Lucy know how frightened she was. Helen and Tony and Jason, all in the attack zone?

"Let's call Uncle Bernie." But it was impossible to

put a long distance call through to Washington. Johanna and Lucy sat together on a sofa and listened to bulletin after bulletin. The announcers made it sound as if survival would be a miracle.

Chapter 38

Helen and Tony put themselves at the service of the Red Cross. The auditorium at the University of Hawaii became a mass dormitory. People whose homes were intact took in as many as twenty or thirty evacuees each. Some families remained in their blacked-out houses. Radio reports were coming in not from the local stations but from as far away as Atlanta.

Helen was grateful to be busy. They knew that the Hickam mess hall had been destroyed, but they didn't know where Jason had been at the time of the hit. Vicky and Bernie would have heard the news by now and be beside themselves. Mama would be outwardly calm and inwardly a wreck.

They had gone through shock, terror and rage—and constant fear that the Japanese would return and take prisoners. Army and Navy wives stoically assumed they would not hear from their husbands for days.

Would Tony and she—and Jason—get out of Honolulu alive? All kinds of rumors were circulating: that paratroopers would be dropping on Waikiki at any time; that the Panama Canal had been bombed and blocked to cut off help from the Atlantic Fleet; that the Japanese had occupied Long Beach and were moving toward Los Angeles.

The city tried to return to normal despite the charred wreckage on Battleship Row and the airfield at Hickam. On Thursday a chaplain brought word from Jason. He was well; he had left the mess hall, in which no one survived the first hit, only minutes before the attack.

One week late Helen and Tony got aboard a plane for Los Angeles. In Washington Tony would report to the government on his presence at Pearl Harbor.

"At least I was able to get word through to Bernie and Vicky that Jason's all right," Tony said happily. He took a final glance back at the islands. "I wish I had been in the House to hear the President's speech last Monday. We're in the war now, Helen."

America was at war and suffering continuing defeats on the battlefields. From Pearl Harbor Day until the middle of 1942 America and her allies faced disaster in the Pacific. They lost Guam, Wake, Hong Kong, Borneo, Singapore and then the Philippines.

In Europe in 1942 the tide began to change. The Russians, now on the side of the Allies, were on the offensive, and Allied troops invaded North Africa.

It astonished Johanna in contemplative moments that life could go on so nearly normally in the face of what was happening in the Pacific, Europe and North Africa. Americans lined up regularly at the movies; on Saturday nights teenagers danced to hit records. Slumber parties were in fashion for teenage girls, though Lucy proclaimed herself "too old" for them. She was looking forward to her freshman year at Barnard in September, though most of her classmates at Stuyvesant thought women just "weren't college material."

But for all the outward look of normalcy Americans were very much part of the war now. As the men went into uniform the women moved into their jobs. The steel and clothing mills, the slaughterhouses and farms, the shops and wholesale houses were manned by women. No one had ever suspected it could be done.

The response of Polish-Americans to the war effort was tremendous. They contributed heavily to the armed forces and their women took their place in the labor force. At the Raisa house on Fifth Avenue two stars hung in the window for Nicky and Jason, but there were Polish-American households that boasted half a dozen sons in defense of America and hung a star for every one.

Frustratingly short, uninformative notes from Nicky arrived at intervals. So far he was all right, and so was Jason, though the situation in the Pacific terrified Johanna.

On a sultry June morning Jason climbed with his crew into a plane on the aircraft carrier *Yorktown*. A Japanese armada was approaching Midway Island.

"Let's get out of here," Jason yelled to the pilot in the plane beside him. "We've got torpedoes to unload."

"The fighters aren't manned yet," a voice reported.

Word came from the squadron leader that they must proceed without protection; there was no time to wait. The planes rose high into the sky before they sought out the Japanese war fleet.

Within minutes, it seemed to Jason, the sky was black with smoke, but he could see that the *Yorktown* had been hit. The Japs would pay for that!

*   *   *

The family knew only that Jason was in the Pacific and Nicky in Europe; they watched the progress of the war with nerve-racking anxiety. They got very little mail.

One day Vicky opened the door and walked into the house. No mail waited for her on the console table in the hall, but as she started up the stairs the doorbell rang. The maid Anya moved down the hallway to reply.

"It's all right, Anya. I'll get it," she called.

Her heart began to pound when she saw the Western Union boy on the stoop. She saw his look of sympathy and made a ritual of the search for a tip. Alone, she stared hard at the small yellow envelope before she opened it.

FIRST LIEUTENANT JASON RAISA IS REPORTED MISSING IN ACTION.

Jason is all right, she told herself; missing but all right.

There was no way Vicky could tell this to Bernie over a telephone, and she never knew when he'd be home at night. She would go to his office and then take a train to New York to tell Johanna and Lucy.

Jason must be alive; he was missing but alive, Vicky chanted to herself. Jason is alive, Jason is alive . . .

The war took on fresh urgency for the Raisa family. They made an unspoken rule against displays of pessimism; they won a close victory over Lucy's determination to join the WACS. The victory, her mother surmised, was not won on points, but by the handsome young naval lieutenant whom her father brought home for dinner one night. Lucy was in love.

The year 1943 brought fresh hope to the war-weary Allies. They were on the offensive at last. At home people complained about coffee rationing and sugar rationing and gas rationing. They ran to the movies to seek relief from reality. Ladies young and not so young flocked to the canteens to entertain servicemen.

In early June of 1943 in a shabby office in the center of London Nick and Stefanie sat waiting for the Polish intelligence chief to complete a phone call. They assumed they were here to be briefed on a fresh assignment and confident that they would be assigned together again. They were a team.

Sometimes Stefanie terrified Nick with her daring. He wished this damnable war were over and he could take her home with him. It seemed they had spent a lifetime together.

The chief hung up the phone. "All right, we'll talk now. I want the two of you to parachute in near Warsaw." He turned to Stefanie. "You know the city street by street?"

"Absolutely."

"You'll wear village dress. You'll be a young Polish couple from a farm, come to Warsaw in hopes of finding a job. Your identity papers will show that Nick is an epileptic, which will explain a seemingly healthy young man being left to farm. Your mission is to bring out Casimar Cardinal Raisa."

"Nick, your uncle," Stefanie said.

"Our contacts in Warsaw say it's urgent to remove the cardinal. He's in danger from the Gestapo. They know all about his activities against the Nazis."

"What are our instructions?" Nick tried to conceal his excitement. He was soon to come face to face with Casimar, a hero. This was their most dangerous mission to date. He was glad for the years he had spent in the study of Polish; he could pass as native-born.

Nick and Stefanie listened attentively, at intervals stopping the chief with questions. The war was going badly for the Nazis; they were particularly concerned about

Poland. That was why it was essential to bring Cardinal Raisa out of the country.

That same night Nick and Stefanie set off for Warsaw. Both were aware that there was no margin for error. Nick was caught up in anticipation of the encounter with Casimar Raisa; Stefanie knew only that this was his "uncle the Polish cardinal."

When at last the plane hovered in black night a hundred-odd kilometers out of Warsaw, mercifully undetected thus far, Nick and Stefanie prepared for the jump. She loathed these jumps, but nothing would stop her from going ahead.

"Stefanie, if we come through this, I want us to get married." He reached for her hand and held it firmly in his. "I don't want to wait until the war is over."

"Nick, in our eyes we're already married."

"I want to be married before God."

"We'll talk about it," she promised.

Now was the moment for the jump. Tomorrow night at two they were to rendezvous with the escape plane. If they didn't show, the plane would try again the following night. Nick's throat was tight as they prepared for the jump; one never knew when something would go wrong.

Stefanie jumped first. Nick waited the proper few seconds to follow her. The night sky was dark and ominous. Thank God there was not even a sliver of moon, a single star to betray them on their descent.

On the ground they buried their parachutes and prepared to make a long hike. Much later, with some uncertainty, they approached a farmhouse and knocked in the prepared code.

A door opened. "Come inside quickly," an elderly Pole ordered. "The Nazis are growing very nervous. One sign of light and they'll be all over us."

The elderly Pole who was concealing them had known Stefanie's father. A university professor before the Nazis invaded Poland, he was now active in the Polish underground.

"On the farm at least we manage to scrounge enough food to keep us alive," he said wryly. "In Warsaw it is bad."

At dawn they joined their host on the seat of the wagon that was to take them into Warsaw, presumably to sell produce. At the entrance to the city they were stopped. The guards helped themselves to a selection off their cart, then waved them on.

"I can't take you any further than the market," the farmer whispered. "After that God be with you."

Nick and Stefanie had the Cardinal's address and they knew he was expecting a rescue team. With somber faces, heads slightly bent, they walked toward Raisa Seminary.

"We turn here," Stefanie whispered. She smiled at Nick. Imagine what this must mean to him, to rescue a prominent member of his own family.

They knocked lightly at a side door and a woman admitted them, her eyes wary, questioning.

"We are friends of the cardinal come to ask his blessing," Stefanie said, as instructed.

"Come with me." Silently they followed the housekeeper down the hall. The cardinal had no inkling of who was coming to guide him to safety. Nick had considered remaining anonymous, at least until they were aboard the plane and leaving Warsaw behind them, but it was not practical.

"In here." The housekeeper knocked lightly and opened the door.

They walked into a small, simple study. A man in clerical garb stood at the window, his back to the young couple as he drew the drapes tight against the world. Then the tall, erect white-haired man turning to them; the resemblance between Michal and Casimar Raisa was remarkable.

"Cardinal Raisa," Stefanie said softly, "we're here to take you out of Poland."

"I'm not sure I should go. As long as I can be useful here—" His gaze settled on Nick and he frowned oddly.

"You're suspect, sir." Nick found his voice, though his heart was pounding. Yes, he could see it. "Every hour counts. Your usefulness here is over."

"Come sit down. Manya will bring you tea." Casimar sat and gestured them to the sofa opposite him. His eyes never left Nick's face.

All at once Nick's throat went tight. His mouth was dry.

"Forgive me for staring," Casimar said. His eyes moved to a table against the wall. There Nick saw the huge cluster of framed family portraits. "I know it's absurd—" all at once the cardinal's voice was trembling— "but you look a lot like my brother Michal."

"Yes, Uncle Casimar, I'm Nick."

"God has been better to me than I deserve," Casimar said humbly. He rose to his feet as Nick moved to him. "Nicholas. Johanna's son."

"I've waited a long time to meet you," Nick told him. Tears welled in his eyes and were ignored. Casimar stared earnestly at his face as though trying to remember every feature, every pore in his skin. "Mom promised that one day we should meet."

"Nicholas—" Casimar's voice broke as he pulled the young man into a close embrace. "I never dared hope that we would meet."

Over tea Casimar questioned him about the family. He was eager to hear the progress of the war; in Warsaw they were told only lies. Finally Casimar took them into a secret room where they must stay until time to leave for the rendezvous. Stefanie would be a bereaved young widow bringing the cardinal to officiate at the burial of her husband, lying in a coffin in the wagon. Nick, in the coffin, presumably had been beaten to death by the Gestapo.

"The Nazis are used to letting me go to funerals. Outside town we'll find a jeep waiting for us and we'll head for what we hope will be an unguarded segment of the border."

At intervals the housekeeper came into the secret room with trays of food. At last night arrived; then more restless hours passed until they could contrive their escape from the city. Nick thanked God the border was close.

He settled himself in the coffin, stuffy and uncomfortably hot despite the air holes, slightly claustrophobic. Then the wagon was moving. The hooves of the horses seemed shockingly loud in the night-empty streets.

He stiffened at the sentry post. He listened to the voices while his throat tightened in alarm, but then the wagon was moving again; they had passed inspection. He heard the simulated soft weeping of Stefanie as the bereaved widow.

At last the wagon came to a stop. Someone pried at the top of the coffin; the lid lifted; he leapt out.

"The jeep is right under the trees," Casimar told them. "Come."

"We're running ahead of schedule," Stefanie said, frowning. "It's better to delay here a little before we go on." She turned to Nick for confirmation and he nodded.

All at once Nick knew what he must do. "Uncle Casimar, there's something I wish for very much," he said urgently. "Will you marry Stefanie and me?"

Nick reached for Stefanie's hand while the cardinal gazed from Nick to Stefanie. "Now?" he asked. "Here, like this?"

"I want to be married on Polish soil," Nick insisted. "By Casimar Cardinal Raisa."

"You will require a legally accepted marriage in the United States," he cautioned. "The necessary papers—"

"Uncle—Casimar—please, just marry us."

Nick and Stefanie knelt before him on the warm Polish earth and Casimar made them man and wife in the sight of God and the church. He blessed them and prayed for their safety. For one tender moment Nicky held Stefanie in his arms and kissed her; then Casimar leaned forward to kiss the bride and bridegroom.

"Now we must go," he said brusquely. "We must arrive exactly on the moment, in time to meet the plane and with no time to be spotted by the border patrol. I never thought," he added with a touch of humor, "that I would welcome the opportunity to be on Russian soil."

They climbed into the waiting jeep. Nick took the wheel; Casimar directed him toward the Russian border. They drove through open fields in a protective darkness, ever conscious that death might be seconds away.

Casimar knew this route well, Nick discovered, having spirited out so many Polish leaders. "Stop about a hundred yards ahead," Casimar instructed. "The border guard comes through here no more than twice a night. Usually at eleven and again at three."

"We could almost walk across." Nick commented.

"Impossible," Casimar sighed. "The Russians shoot on sight. They fear infiltration by Nazi spies. They recognize an Allied plane if one flies overhead and they see it; we have learned a lot since Germany turned on Russia."

They parked the jeep in a clump of trees and climbed out. Their plane was due in exactly one minute. There was no sight or sound of it; so far, so good. They all scanned the sky and looked at their watches. Stefanie had the best eyes of anyone Nick knew; she spotted it a good five seconds before he could make it out. "Right on time," she remarked.

The tiny biplane made a short landing and stopped almost on its nose. They ran for its door as it started to back and turn for the takeoff. Obviously the pilot wasn't waiting.

Then they heard a car coming fast. It roared up over a bank and flashed its lights on the plane, the jeep, the three refugees. *"Halten! Halten jedermann!"* A warning shot rang out.

"You two get in the plane. Don't wait for me." Casimar bolted for the jeep. At the bottom of the bank the German staff car nosed into a ditch and balked. The driver spun his wheels as his passenger, Leutnant Felzer, swore and tried to get off a shot at Casimar, now screened by the grove he had parked in.

Nick shoved Stefanie at the plane. "Get that damn door open," he shouted at the pilot. He turned and dropped, drawing his service pistol, prepared to give Casimar covering fire.

"Get the hell in the plane, son," Casimar screeched.

"Sorry, Father, no can do." Nick shot a hole in the windshield of the German vehicle. The driver stopped trying to back up and started to shoot at Nick and the plane.

Stefanie stood with one foot on the ground and one foot in the plane to stop the pilot from summarily taking off. "Nick! Nick!"

Casimar had the jeep in gear and was inching between two trees, trying to keep some cover between himself and the enemy. Clear on one side, he roared into a backward U turn and then shot around the grove and straight at the Germans. "Get in the plane," he shouted one last time, and then he crashed head-on into his ancient foes, the Germans.

Nick allowed shock to stop him cold for a bare moment, then was up and diving into the plane; the pilot was on his way out of there with or without his passengers. As the craft jerked, its heavy door slammed on Nick's knee and he shrieked with pain.

Indifferent to everything but the imminent danger of being discovered by enemy aircraft, the pilot wheeled sharply and was in position to take off. The door eased off Nick's leg for a moment and then slammed on it again, harder than the first time.

The pilot gunned the engine in neutral before starting his takeoff. Stefanie, resolutely controlling her feelings, took advantage of the pause to haul Nick's leg on board.

As she swung the door wide to slam it, all three of them looked out at the ruins of the two vehicles in the ditch. Just then they heard a kind of muted roar, and a gout of flame reached into the sky. Stefanie shut the door on Casimar's pyre and turned to Nick.

"There's a bullet hole in your shoulder," he said, and fainted.

"Jesus," the pilot whimpered, and got the hell out of there at last.

Chapter 39

Johanna returned Monday morning from a much-needed weekend at Southampton, which saw the family during these summers of wartime only for brief snatches. Josip dropped Johanna, Melissa and Boleslav at the door on Fifth Avenue and moved on to garage the car.

"There's the postman." Johanna stopped short at the door while Boleslav unlocked it. "I'll wait and see if there's mail." There had been nothing from Nick for long weeks now, and no word of Jason from the War Department, though the family refused to abandon hope.

"A letter from overseas," the genial postman greeted her, "along with the usual."

"Thank you, Pete," Johanna smiled. Pete had been on their route for eighteen years.

She stood before the house and ripped open the envelope. Each time a letter from Nick arrived she seemed to acquire a fresh lease on life.

For a moment her throat tightened in alarm. Her son had been wounded. "Don't worry about me," he wrote.

"I'll be good as new in time, but it'll probably take months, the doctors warn me, before the leg is healed. I expect to be shipped to a hospital in England shortly.

"But I have sad news. I saw Uncle Casimar. It was a wonderful meeting, but he died saving my life."

Johanna clung to the knowledge that her Nicky was safe and probably done with the war. But she lay sleepless for endless nights, mourning for Casimar. The Raisa brothers were all gone. But now, she told herself in an effort to wrest herself clear of futile anguish, there were other Raisas to carry on the family name and tradition—Bernie and Nick and a grandson, Jason—if he wasn't lost somewhere over the South Pacific.

With the arrival of the New Year fresh optimism swept through the country. The war was going badly for the Germans. In the Pacific Allied troops took Luzon in the Philippines. From the hills came a handful of Americans, hidden from the Japanese by friendly natives since the invasion. They were taken to hospitals, checked out and given extensive leave. Early in March Vicky received a personal phone call from the War Department. Jason was alive and well. The family rejoiced.

Johanna worried about Nicky's continued hospitalization in England, though he wrote he would soon be coming home.

"I'm bringing you a very special present, Mom. I think you'll be pleased."

The only present she wanted, Johanna thought wistfully, was her boy in the house again. She hoped he was being honest with her about his recuperation; she fought off nightmare conjectures. No matter what, she vowed, Nicky would have a fine home and love. The years that were left to her would be devoted to his care.

In April President Roosevelt died in Warm Springs, Georgia. People throughout the country were shaken and grieved. How sad, Johanna thought, that he had not lived to see the end of the war. A dozen days after the death of the President the United Nations Conference opened at San Francisco, with delegates from fifty nations in attendance.

Early in May Bernie called to say that Jason was on his way home. He would come first to his grandmother's house, where the family would gather to welcome him. Molly cooked for two days in preparation for the joyous occasion. They knew only that Jason was due to arrive in New York on May seventh.

Johanna arose early and was at her desk by eight, which was normal for her. She took pride in being the first on duty in the offices of America-International. Bernie and Vicky were arriving on a morning train and would go directly to the house. Lucy would cut her afternoon class to be sure she was home by the time Jason arrived. Helen, Tony and the children would come in mid-afternoon.

By shortly past ten, pausing to drink the cup of coffee Marya had brought to her, Johanna decided she could manage to leave by two. Any time now she expected word about Nick's arrival. She felt such happiness.

"Mrs. Raisa!" One of the stenographers burst into her office without even a knock. "Mrs. Raisa, the war is over in Europe. The Germans have surrendered."

"Thank God," Johanna whispered, "thank God."

There was still a war being fought in the Pacific, but in the streets of New York there was uninhibited celebration as word of the German surrender circulated. Johanna closed the offices for the day, though the shipyard would remain open because of the rush of orders. Rather than bring Josip out into the mad traffic Johanna left the office and sought the subway. *The Germans had surrendered!*

Hanging from a strap among a jubilant northbound crowd, Johanna thought about Poland. More than one million Polish-Americans had gone into uniform in this war. The Poles had formed an army in Great Britain and in Russia. Now was the time for Poland to emerge as a democracy.

She remembered the memorial services for Paderewski at St. Patrick's Cathedral in the summer of '41. He had been buried "temporarily" in Arlington Cemetery, his body to be moved to Polish soil when Poland should be a democracy. With the war over that time must be soon.

By the time she arrived home Vicky and Bernie were already there and drinking coffee in the library.

"Mama." Bernie hugged her to him. "Our prayers have been answered. Jason's coming home to us."

"And soon," Vicky put in, "we'll be here again to welcome Nicky."

"We're all here now," Bernie said. "The next time the bell rings it'll be Jason."

At twenty minutes to four the doorbell rang. The library was charged with electricity as Bernie, followed by Vicky, raced to the door. Johanna stood in the hall to watch for the first sight of Jason.

"Mom!" Jason grabbed his mother and kissed her hungrily. "Dad!" He hugged his father and submitted to a kiss.

"Jason, you're so thin," Vicky clucked, "but never mind, you're home now."

"Grandma!" Jason hurried to meet Johanna. "Still the most beautiful grandmother in America."

"Compliments will gain you nothing," she laughed, swaying with Jason in delight. "Welcome home, darling. We knew you'd make it."

"I wasn't always so sure myself," he said wryly. "But it sure as hell is wonderful to be home."

When everybody had properly welcomed Jason, they settled about the library while Bernie opened the champagne and served them.

"Jason, would you like something more substantial than champagne?" Johanna asked. "Molly can fix you up a plate to hold you until dinner."

"Molly's cooking I'm ready for any time," he said exuberantly, and soon a tray appeared.

For a while they listened absorbedly to Jason's accounts of what happened in the intervening years. Then Jason was full of questions—about life at home and especially about Nick. "What exactly happened to his leg, anyway? He said he wasn't shot, but he didn't volunteer any information."

"I don't know either, Jason," Johanna sighed. "He's been very coy about it. All I know is that we expect him home soon and that he's gone through a lot of surgery on his knee. He expects to be off crutches any day. That's what he said in his last letter, over three weeks ago."

The doorbell rang with three sharp blasts.

"Who can that be?" Johanna frowned, hating an intrusion. "I'll get it, Melissa." She hurried off to the door, pulled it open and froze in joy.

"I told you I'd be home soon, Mom." Nick leaned on a cane and clutched his mother with the other arm.

"Nicky, what a wonderful surprise!" Then she noticed he was not alone. "Jason just arrived too. Both of you safe and home. Nicky, how marvelous. But who's this?" Johanna beamed at the young lady.

"You know that present I promised you. Here she is." He reached for the hand of the young woman beside him. "Mom, I couldn't just say it in a letter. I had to tell you in person. This is Stefanie, my wife. Uncle Casimar married us just—just minutes before he died to save us."

"Stefanie." Her hands trembling and face mirroring her happiness, Johanna reached to pull Stefanie to her. "Welcome to the family." A montage of mentions of Stefanie in Nicky's letters flowed together. Here was a bright substantial young woman, and so lovely. "Come inside and meet the family."

"Mom, there's another present." Nicky dropped one arm about his wife and the other about his mother. "Stefanie is pregnant. In five months—or thereabouts—there'll be another Raisa."

"I don't deserve such happiness, but I'm so grateful, my darlings."

"You deserve it, Mom," Nick said with love. "Dad always said you were the finest Raisa of all."

Epilogue

Poles and Polish-Americans alike hoped that with the end of the most terrible war in history Poland would at last become a democracy. Alas, this was not to be. The new Polish government—whose elections were denounced officially by the United States and Great Britain as unfair—was in the hands of the Communists.

The Polish armed forces who had fought so fearlessly with the Allies were now homeless. They refused to go back to Poland while it was controlled by a Communist government. Valiant Polish men and women, ironically, were imprisoned in the Soviet Union.

Nearly one-hundred thousand Polish refugees came to America after World War II, all of them dedicated to the establishment one day of a free and independent Poland. Even today Ignace Jan Paderewski, Polish piano virtuoso, patriot, and one-time prime minister and foreign minister of Poland lies in Arlington Cemetery until Poland is a nation of free people and he can go home again.